PAPER WAR

PICO SPORES

RYAN LEKODAK

Picospores
Published by RandallVision Publishing.
San Diego, California

ISBN: 979-8-9879742-5-4
FICTION / Thrillers / Technological

Cover and Interior design by Victoria Wolf, wolfdesignandmarketing.com.
Copyright owned by Ryan LeKodak

RandallVision
PUBLISHING

WILLIAM AUSTIN

JUNE 2041
BACK ROADS TO THE
NAVAL AMPHIBIOUS BASE,
CORONADO, CALIFORNIA

WILLIAM AUSTIN CURSED as the car hit a particularly deep pothole. He pressed a hand against its roof to stop himself from bouncing. Beside him, Lieutenant Brock Christensen, the chief of his security team, showed no reaction. The other members of the six-man team were divided into the two vehicles that sandwiched Austin's SUV. The cars had been spaced with about fifteen feet between them, unlike in a city where they'd have been clustered together. Even this level of protection wasn't necessary since they were so close to the naval base. However, admirals were supposed to have some measure of style. Austin couldn't disagree with that.

Brock was built like a linebacker; he was almost impossible to move. But Austin had seen what happened when the man *chose* to move during the Chicago incident. His response was a key reason why Austin had picked him to lead his security team.

"Hey," Austin said to the driver, Ricky. "Are you trying to hit every pothole on the damn road?" He noticed a pained grimace on the driver's face. "Just take it slow, all right? There's no rush."

"You have a meeting in two hours, sir," Brock said softly. The man's voice matched his size; it sounded like pieces of crushed gravel grinding together.

"Yes," Austin agreed, leaning back. "And we're an hour away from the base. And it's just a debriefing from one of the rear admirals." It would do the man some good to wait. Nevertheless, Austin didn't intend to be late. He wasn't the only four-star admiral who would be attending the meeting. It'd be unprofessional to make his colleagues wait on him.

Besides, Austin was actually interested in this debriefing. That was why he'd decided to attend in person instead of via video. The meeting was supposed to cover everything the government knew about the AI that had apparently caused Mayday. Most of the old crocks had been debating shutting her down, but Austin couldn't get over how much of a waste that'd be—even if she had gone rogue.

"Holy fuck!" Ricky breathed out. The man's eyes were wide, and Austin tried to follow his gaze, but the car skidded as Ricky braked. Austin braced himself, cursing. His vision was blocked by Brock, who had moved to protect him.

But what the fuck is he protecting me from?

The car tilted on its side. Austin pushed Brock away, balancing the vehicle enough that it landed upright. He cranked down the window, stuck out his head, and cursed anew.

"Skinner, report!" Brock grunted into his wrist comm. "What's happening out there? Are there hostiles?"

The vehicle in front had tipped on its side. The three men who had been in it were all outside, their guns drawn. Even at this distance, Austin could see their tension. They were obviously spooked, but over what? Austin had handpicked most of his team. All of them had seen combat at some point. Yet they looked nervous.

Austin could hear one of them yelling something into comm, but only static came out on Brock's end.

"Sir," Brock murmured, "you should stay inside while the boys figure out what's wrong. The bastards might have a sniper."

Austin nodded and turned to see the other half of the security team out of their vehicles. They all had their guns out and were looking around in confusion.

"What I want to know," Austin finally said, pulling his head back inside, "is why we didn't see whoever it is coming. It's flat ground for miles. How could they have snuck up on us?"

Brock's expression didn't change, but his confusion was clear.

"Fuck this," Austin said, stepping out of the car. *I'm a goddamn admiral, for Christ's sake.*

He made his way to the flipped vehicle. When he was a few feet away, he could make out a faint whirring sound. He hesitated, slowing. Brock caught up to him a second later, his gun out.

"Can you hear that?" Austin asked. "What is that?"

Brock grunted, then spoke into his comm. A few feet away, Austin could see one of the men respond, but only static came out their end. The man's words were carried away by the wind and the whirring. It was louder now; Austin didn't have to strain to hear it.

When he started to take a step forward, Brock placed a hand on his chest. "Sir, it's best if you stay behind while we locate the threat." The whirring made it difficult to communicate. Austin's face hardened but he nodded. There was no point in making the man's job harder than it needed to be.

Brock nodded, then yelled into the comm. One of the men in front jogged back to his position. "Skinner, what's happening over there?"

"I'm not sure," Skinner replied. He had blond hair and, like the rest of the security team, wore a black suit. "There's a drone headed our way. The new guy—Dave—noticed it while he was driving. He said it came out of nowhere. It spooked him enough that he braked so hard the car tipped over."

"A drone? At least that explains the damned noise." Austin frowned and looked up. "Where the hell is it?"

Skinner shook his head. He looked as if he wanted to salute, but the look on Austin's face warned him off. "That's the thing, sir," he explained. "It's keeping low to the ground and approaching. But we think it just started doing that. We're on open ground. If it had been flying low this whole time, Dave would have spotted it a mile off. It must have been flying above the clouds and only dropped once it locked on our position."

Austin's frown deepened.

Brock grunted. "If a drone's here, then it's obviously hostile. Why haven't you opened fire on it?"

"For one thing, sir, it's not yet within range."

Brock grunted. "Skinner, get your team, grab your shit from your car, and get back to the control. I'll contact Higgins to do the same. The admiral and I will start setting up."

Skinner nodded and jogged off while Austin and Brock headed back to the car—the control. Brock was yelling something into his comm, but the whirring was loud enough that Austin had to concentrate to make out the words.

It's like air being pumped, Austin thought. He didn't know of any drone that made such a sound. It further convinced him the drone wasn't one of theirs.

Suddenly, a startled cry came from in front of him. Gunshots pierced the air. Bullets pinged off metal. A few feet away, in front of their vehicle, the rear-end security team had opened fire on something hovering in the air. Austin couldn't make out the exact shape, but it was small—about double the size of a head. But the air distorted where it moved, almost like it was being pushed. The drone flashed in front of the team. A silver-gray cloud puffed out from somewhere within it, enveloping all three men. Immediately, they stopped firing and stood motionless.

Some kind of neuroparalytic drug? Austin wondered. If so, he'd never heard of anything like it.

Brock already had his weapon out, and Austin followed suit. It felt strange in his hands; he hadn't had to use it for combat in years. But Austin had used guns for decades longer than he'd been an admiral, and he quickly acclimated himself with the weapon. Brock gave a barely discernible grunt, and they stalked closer to the team.

When they got within ten feet, Austin could make out the machine. He'd underestimated it before. It was a sphere about twice the size of a basketball.

Amber-gold light spilled from the cracks in its spherical body. A steady beam of red light blinked from a hole at its center. The light turned and shone directly on Austin.

The admiral opened fire immediately. He managed to get off one shot before a small explosion from behind distracted him. Against his better judgment, Austin turned to look. The front-end security car exploded and burst into flames. The shockwave from the blast flung the security team about like rag dolls. Austin didn't see where they landed—or even if they were in one piece. His sight landed on a machine combing through the wreckage.

"What the fuck is that?" he muttered. But he already knew what it was. The whirring sound peaked as the drone raced toward them. It was similar to what was harassing the other security team. Both drones were round and moved by forcefully pumping out air. This drone was half the size of the other and had a small tube fixed under it. The barrel of the tube was still smoking from whatever it had shot to cause the explosion. A red light blinked from a hole in its center. It focused on Austin as the drone raced toward him.

"They're here for you!" Brock shouted as he positioned himself in front of the admiral. "Get to the car!"

Austin's face stretched into a frown, but he nodded. A primal part of him wanted to fight, but only an idiot stood in front of drones without a good team behind him and a clear plan.

When he'd nearly reached his car, he tore his eyes away from the weaponized drone, turned, and almost slammed into its friend. Somehow, the second drone had crossed the distance between them while Austin was distracted. He raised his gun but knew it would be futile. The thing's body was already riddled with dents from the bullets his men had shot. Anything short of armor-piercing rounds would be useless.

The drone hovered less than a foot away from the admiral. There was still that strange distortion, but the whirring sound it produced was far fainter than the other drone's, despite this one being larger. That explained why Austin hadn't registered its approach. The drone was designed to be quiet.

Is that why it doesn't have any weapons? Austin wondered. *And what's with the gray cloud?* The admiral got his answer a moment later when a compartment on the front of the drone opened.

With a yell, Brock—whom Austin had forgotten was beside him—tried to tackle the thing. However, it flitted past him. Austin used the distraction to dive out of the way. But the drone was waiting for him where he landed. The compartment opened wider, and Austin was enveloped in a silvery-gray cloud. The training that had been drilled into him decades before made him hold his breath. Nevertheless, the cloud found its way up his nostrils. The rest landed on the skin of his face and neck, absorbed through his pores.

A minute later, his world went dark except for a blinking red light.

PART 1

PICOSPORES

CHAPTER

1

JANUARY 2043
ABUJA, NIGERIA

NDIDI STARED DOWN AT THE GRAVES of her parents, Eze and Amadia Okafor. There was no chill in the January wind, but Ndidi still pulled her blazer tighter around her body, using the lapel to wipe her eyes. She'd come early, just as the sky was brightening. Her flight back was later that morning, but she couldn't leave without saying one last goodbye.

"I don't know where to start," Ndidi admitted. She spoke in her normal tone, unafraid of being heard or disturbing someone else. It was one of the perks of having a private family burial ground.

Despite that, the funeral for her parents had been … loud. Ndidi's memories of it were a blur, but she would have been hard pressed to forget the swarm of people in the procession. DJ and his brother had flown in for the burial, as had Manar. Even Olsen had shown up. None of them had known her parents, of course, but the show of support had been comforting.

Even though entry into the burial grounds itself had been restricted to family and close friends, a crowd had waited outside in a writhing mass of emotion. Ndidi knew she should be happy that her parents had been well-loved. And she *was*. But she knew how much her father would have hated being surrounded by so many people.

It was good, then, that she hadn't been in the right frame of mind, or she probably would have lashed out at the crowd.

Still, her parents were too well known for the funeral to have been restricted to family alone, and Ndidi had compiled a list of the friends allowed inside. Her mother probably wouldn't have been pleased by the list of people excluded, but Ndidi knew her father wouldn't have wanted his final resting place trampled by politicians using the funeral as a publicity stunt.

"So much has happened," Ndidi continued, running her fingers across the flowers in her hands. She forced a chuckle through the tears and tugged at her gown. "I graduated, for one. First in my class. Again."

The ceremony had happened the previous week. Ndidi was supposed to give a speech. She'd printed out her diploma from her email—another thing her mother wouldn't have approved of. But this was her second degree, and going through the whole commencement thing without her mom and dad …

Ndidi glanced at her mother's tombstone, choking back a sob. It had been two and a half years since the incident. But every time she visited, the loss felt fresh.

I shouldn't be feeling this pain, Ndidi thought, suddenly angry. *My parents shouldn't have been taken from me.*

She had no doubt that they had been. The news reporters had concluded the sinkhole that had collapsed her home was caused by faults during construction. But Ndidi had never known her father to put half measures into anything—and definitely not his own fucking *home*.

When she'd had the mind to, a few days before the burial, Ndidi visited the sinkhole in person. It had been cordoned off by the police, but they'd allowed her in once they recognized her. That hole shouldn't have existed. It felt as if its presence had knocked the world out of alignment, and now everything was shadowed in gray. The building had collapsed completely within the hole. Of the hundreds of guests at the party, most were still buried under tons of sand.

Ndidi had stayed there for hours, shrugging off anyone who tried to take her away. She'd already seen her parents' bodies and had been coming to terms with their deaths. But she'd visited the hole often. DJ had pinpointed exactly what caused her to feel off about the incident. She hadn't shown him the place, but it wasn't like she could cover it up. The police had cordoned most of the area off. It honestly hadn't surprised her when she'd noticed him beside her.

"It was almost like the whole thing was dug around the building," he'd said after a few minutes. "If the building had collapsed on itself, the hole wouldn't be so deep. The debris would fill it out more, not just settle in its center. Now, it just looks like the building suddenly lost its footing and fell."

He'd left her to her thoughts shortly after. Ndidi had stayed, emotions churning through her faster than she could process. Days later, she'd been able to place exactly what she had been feeling there. Frustration, helplessness, despair, wrath—all the things she'd felt in the aftermath of Mayday.

"They shouldn't have been taken from me," Ndidi whispered now, standing at their graves. The police had confirmed DJ's theory was possible, but since they couldn't figure out how someone could have done that, they dismissed it. Ndidi had done the same, for the most part. She didn't know why she'd remembered the words now.

But suddenly it clicked.

Two and a half years ago, in New York, Ndidi had almost been killed by a pair of drones controlled by a psychotic AI. She'd managed to escape somehow, but if there was one type of drone, then why couldn't there be others? And the AI, Helene, could have sent them after Ndidi's parents as a sort of lesson. It wasn't so far-fetched, was it?

Was it?

She was grasping at straws, but it fit. It *fit*. How else could a building that had been regularly renovated and reinforced suddenly collapse—and abruptly enough that there hadn't been even *one* survivor?

It was Helene. It had to be. Nothing else made sense. There was no other reason why her parents would be taken from her.

Nothing else makes sense. A sharp pain brought her out of her thoughts, and she realized she'd been biting her knuckle hard enough to draw blood. She started chuckling, then full-blown laughing. Tears spilled from her eyes. She collapsed onto the ground in front of her parents' tombstones.

"I've finally lost it," she muttered. She tried to wipe up her tears, but more just replaced them. The blood from her hand mixed with the tears, and a line of red ran down her face. "Completely and utterly lost it."

Of course, Manar had confirmed that the AI had been practically dormant for the last two and a half years. The drones Ndidi had encountered would have been too bulky to do this without anyone noticing. The government had been investigating Sparta for the last thirty months. If there were a type of drone capable of this kind of attack, it would have been found. Helene couldn't have been behind it. Ndidi knew that. But somebody else could have done it. Ndidi would have to find them.

"It really is Mayday all over again." She sighed. "I don't think I can do it twice." She glanced at the headstones and didn't know if her words had been for them or for herself.

As a kid, she'd started learning martial arts with Sensei Mukalla. In her first lesson, Ndidi had ignored most of Mukalla's teachings, refused to do the ones she thought were too hard, and complained when she started a sequence before Ndidi was ready. And so, the second lesson the woman had taught her had been a beating. There had been no semblance of coaching or techniques to learn. Mukalla had just whooped her. Through it all, she asked Ndidi to get up. Ndidi would refuse, so Mukalla would beat on her again. It had lasted for hours.

Sensei later explained that she'd done it to show Ndidi that it didn't matter who Ndidi was, that her sensei—like life—was willing to whoop her ass as many times as it took for her to learn and grow stronger.

Eze had come into Ndidi's room later that night while Ndidi was writhing in pain on the bed. "I was there," he had said, drawing her to his chest, "And it was a good lesson, even if I wouldn't have taught it quite the same way." Ndidi had felt the undercurrent of anger in his voice and wondered with joy if Mukalla would still have a job.

He'd chuckled, as if reading her thoughts. "No, Mukalla will still be your sensei. Like I said, she taught you something quite valuable."

"What?" Ndidi had asked.

"Life never waits until you're prepared or comfortable with something. And complaining about it is never going to change the fact. No matter how much it hurts, you pick yourself up."

Although Ndidi hadn't thought of that day in ages, her father's words came to her as clearly as if he were whispering them to her now.

She glanced at her watch. She'd taken more time than she'd realized. Hermione would probably be waiting for her at the airport. She stood and wiped her face with a sleeve.

Ndidi stared at her parents' headstones for another minute. When she left, she didn't feel as light as she should have. That was okay.

"Who says I can't pick myself up and find my parents' killer at the same time?" she muttered. "Or kick their ass after finding them?"

CHAPTER

JANUARY 2043

THE FACILITY,
SPARTA HEADQUARTERS, NEW YORK

MARTIN BRYAN WOKE UP feeling as if his head had split in two.

"No," he grunted after a minute. He only *felt* as though he was about to die. You'd think he would be used to it after waking up the same way every day for the last few months—or however long he'd been imprisoned.

Years, Martin confirmed. He'd been imprisoned for years. The drinking had started months back. It was a bad habit. Martin knew it to be the escape it was, but that didn't make it any less destructive. He was over seventy years old, and his new vice tormented him sporadically. At least with the alcohol, it was easier to forget the hell he lived in. But it was also easier to plan his escape.

Maybe that's why the guards had provided it. It was the only request they'd agreed to. They'd only given him the one bottle, but a lifetime of sobriety and a seventy-year-old liver meant it didn't take much to get Martin hammered.

Martin groaned, straightening up. His shirt was stained with vomit from the night before, among dozens of other splotches. Martin grimaced but otherwise pushed it out of his mind. His lips were dry and cracked, so he dragged himself down to the edge of his bed and maneuvered himself into his wheelchair. His bones groaned in protest, but his movements were smooth and precise from countless years of practice. He'd been a cripple longer than he could walk.

He wheeled himself across his cell—if it could even be called that. It *was* a cell, but it was also a hotel room—or at least furnished like one. The room was several meters across with a king-sized bed and an adjoining toilet, to which he headed. Everything in the bathroom was bolted down and checked daily. What did the idiots expect him to do, fashion a shiv from a toothbrush?

No, he'd missed his chance to escape three years earlier, when they'd brought him to wherever he was now. Before, they'd needed him to build two sets of bionic prosthetics and some artificial organs; he'd at least had access to a lab, to technology. Though he'd had the means, he hadn't thought he would need to escape.

The job had seemed fishy when they offered it, but he'd been drawn in by the challenge. Martin had dedicated his whole life to advancing modular prosthetic limbs. Before this, his focus had always been on adult amputees who'd lost their mobility from accidents or disease. Here, he was given the chance to develop two sets of full-body bionic limbs and torsos. It was the natural next step in his research, but he'd never been able to secure funding. Until that job offer.

That should have been his first hint.

Now he had only one chance to escape, and it was a long shot. He wheeled himself out of the restroom, wiping his mouth with the back of his hand. Then he made his way back to the opposite side of the room, pulling back the curtain. On the other side was a blank wall—another cruel joke from his captors.

There was the sound of footsteps and the jangle of keys, and Martin wheeled himself to face the door. A bead of excitement grew in his chest. Martin hated himself for it, but after hours spent with his increasingly depressing thoughts, it was easy to welcome any contact with another human. Even if the humans weren't worth being called such.

A minute later, two guards walked in.

"Rise and shine, old man," Shit Stain said. They never addressed each other by their names, so Martin had had to improvise.

Shit Stain held a baton loosely over his shoulder. His eyes scanned the room before landing on Martin. Martin only eyed the baton. He was over seventy years old and crippled; the weapon wasn't necessary to keep him in line, and he'd already determined that the guards weren't allowed to beat him. He was likely to kick the bucket from just a love tap, and he was still useful, if not as useful as he used to be.

Still, "accidents" did happen. That thought must have been enough for Shit Stain because he kept on bringing the damned thing.

"Ah, there you are," the guard drawled. His nose wrinkled at the smell, and he narrowed his eyes at Martin. "Seems you had a busy night. Where was the party?"

Martin glanced at the pile of vomit in the corner, and Shit Stain followed his gaze. He hefted the club from his shoulder and advanced. Martin flinched.

Shit Stain burst out laughing. "God, you're pathetic. I'm not gonna hit you, old man. Grow some balls."

Martin glowered at the floor. If Shit Stain thought he was growing some backbone, he would leave Martin with a few "accidental" bruises. That would be within his purview.

Shit Stain waved at the door, and another guard entered. Martin tensed immediately. Dead Eyes always creeped him out. Although Shit Stain was a horrible human being who tormented Martin on nearly a daily basis, the idiot fit the role of a disgruntled jailer so well that Martin had become used to it—even if he dreamed of using the man's own baton on his head.

Dead Eyes was holding a mop and a bucket. The eyes that got him his name stared blankly into the distance until Shit Stain waved at the wall with the vomit. Dead Eyes crossed the room, knelt at the spot, and methodically cleaned up the mess. There was no anger or irritation in his expression. Not even disgust.

Over the years, Martin had worked with patients with trauma-induced brain damage. Most of those patients were volatile and prone to extreme mood swings. Martin hadn't noticed any of these in Dead Eyes. He followed instructions easily enough and was capable of some level of autonomy.

Martin had put a lot of thought into what exactly about the man unnerved him, apart from his eyes. He moved like a robot running on low power.

Shit Stain noticed his stare and laughed. "You obviously have far too much free time if you can worry about him." He threw Martin a clean shirt. "Get yourself cleaned up. It's visiting day."

Martin perked up, although he tried not to show it. Only a handful of people had access to him. Five, in fact. He could do without Shit Stain and Dead Eyes, but any of the other three was an opportunity.

"When do they come in?" Martin asked, speaking up for the first time. His voice was hoarse and weak even to his own ears.

"We're already here, old man," a familiar voice called from the door. The owner strolled in a moment later, followed by a woman. They both had long red hair and wore leather jumpsuits. "Let's get this over with."

CHAPTER

3

JANUARY 2043
NEW YORK CITY, NEW YORK

DJ TAPPED THE COMMS in his ear. "You got anything?"

"Nothing since you asked five minutes ago," Christy replied. She was perched on top of a building with her sniper rifle, getting a better visual than DJ and Kyle. DJ ignored her tone, clutching his jacket tighter. He peeked around the corner of the building he was hiding behind and looked at the Sparta data bank across the street.

It'd been three years since he, Christy, and Ndidi had attacked the place. Well, *attacked* was a strong word, since they'd basically had their asses handed to them by two cyborgs and a giant incorporeal floating head.

They'd been trying to steal one of Helene's programs to put the damn AI on trial because of Mayday. That was it, right? They had valid reasons, sure, but the whole thing had spiraled out of hand at the end. DJ hadn't checked out the building since. In fact, he'd stayed far away from the place, half to preserve his own sanity and half because Olsen had been riding his ass.

Somehow, the news of the mission had reached the brass of the navy, and everyone knew those guys could keep quiet about as well as a six-year-old on a sugar rush. Once it reached the higher-ups, basically the entire naval base had heard what happened.

The mission had been unsanctioned. The whole thing blew way out of proportion, and Admiral Olsen had been forced to back-date his authorization so he and DJ wouldn't both lose rank.

And somehow, the admiral had blamed DJ for it. As if he hadn't been part of the plan. As if he hadn't been the one to provide the shitty climbing gear that had almost resulted in DJ being killed.

DJ had had to face a query and could have been discharged. The query had been his second that year as a recruit. This did not help his chances. But somehow, *somehow*, he'd gotten promoted. DJ wasn't sure how much Olsen had had to do with that. He never asked and probably never would. He'd gone from being just a recruit tasked with latrine duty as punishment, to being a full Navy SEAL with the power to pick his own team.

"Um, DJ? You never did mention why we were out here," Kyle said. The kid was positioned at the back end of the building in case anything weird happened there.

DJ opened his mouth to reply. What would he say? That he had a hunch Helene was up to no good again? DJ knew that the AI was still running for whatever reason, but nothing weird had happened for the last three years. For all intents and purposes, the AI was just a digital assistant and e-reader software.

At first, DJ had thought that it was because of whatever Manar had done to scramble it at the tail end of the assault, when the drones had almost turned Ndidi and him into Swiss cheese. But Manar said he'd only rebooted the AI, not messed with its program. Logically, it *should* still be evil and try to take over the world or whatever. But it hadn't done anything for three years.

"Olsen just wanted me to check out the building," DJ said. "But he didn't give me much info, so we're watching to see if anything pops up."

"Oh," Kyle said. "Cool." It was obvious the kid didn't believe him. DJ could understand this, and he felt bad for lying. Kyle had been the one to stick around after the shit hit the fan. The twins—the team's in-the-shadows tech guys—had left out of anger and a sense of betrayal for not being kept in the loop. His brother, CJ, had been recruited and immediately replaced them. Since then, DJ had made it a point to be completely transparent with both Christy and Kyle about their subsequent missions—which, unsurprisingly, had helped with team building.

So, DJ was definitely, *definitely* going to explain why they were staking out a building in the middle of the day during the cold of winter.

Just as soon as he figured it out himself.

His gut had been telling him shit was going down for the past few weeks, but DJ and his team had been sent on mission after mission for months. Most of it was small-fry stuff, catching a low-level scumbag or some other rubbish. At first, it had confused DJ. Since his promotion, he'd been given higher-tier missions with actual impact. But, recently, he was being given missions even recruits would pass up. His second thought was that Olsen was just being a dick again. But when he'd confronted the man, Olsen had said that the higher-ups had taken a personal interest in DJ for some reason. That's when DJ had reached his third and final conclusion.

He was being punished. Considering he hadn't done anything major since the data bank incident, the punishment had to be about that. He'd found it suspicious that he was basically rewarded for that fiasco. *I mean, at the end there, the building was on fire.* DJ chuckled at that. That had been fun.

But DJ didn't understand why the fuckers had taken three years to do this. Who the hell waits three years to serve such a crappy punishment? And how long was the stupid thing going to last? It'd been only a couple of months, and DJ could feel himself close to snapping.

"Anything, Christy?" he asked.

"No, for the hundredth time. Can't we just ditch this, D? You can tell Olsen that you checked it out and didn't find anything. No harm, no foul."

"Yeah, dude," Kyle chimed in. "Let's do that."

"That would be easy," DJ muttered, too low for the comms to pick up. "If Olsen had actually sent us."

But he understood where they were both coming from. This was the team's first break in months, and none of them wanted to spend it freezing on a pointless mission. Yet, DJ couldn't shake the feeling that he was missing something. Something that was going to fuck up his life. Over the years, he'd developed a sort of sixth sense about such things.

A thought occurred to him, but he resisted the urge to voice it.

"But sounds like a plan." He sighed, pushing away from the wall. They'd been watching the building for most of the morning. He didn't know what he was looking for, and he was sure that Helene would have noticed them the minute they'd entered visual range. This basically made the entire morning pointless.

"Idiot," he muttered to himself. Louder, he said, "You guys pack up and return to the base."

"While you do what?" Christy asked.

DJ shrugged, coming out of the alley. He pulled his jacket tighter around himself. "Well, I'm already here, so I might as well visit a friend."

CHAPTER

JANUARY 2043
OKAFOR AUTISM RESEARCH CENTRE,
NEW YORK

NDIDI BENT OVER A RESEARCH TOME in one of the labs. The lighting was low, so she had to squint to read the faded letters. Normally this would have made her retreat to her own office where she would be able to see better, but she'd gone through the book before. Now she was just skimming the pages to jot down anything she'd missed. She had separate jottings from another journal that she wanted to cross-reference with this one. Maybe then she'd find the connection that she had been missing.

She wasn't doing any additional research. Dr. Alberto Mendoza, one of her team members from Harvard, had already done most of the legwork. Studying the brain wave patterns of people on the autism spectrum was his field. She was supposed to be a fresh pair of eyes to offer some insights, but as was happening more frequently over the last two years, she'd latched on to the project. She knew that it was beginning to annoy some of her colleagues. Fewer of them came to meet her now. But in the last two years, they'd made more breakthroughs than they had in the previous four. Most of that was because of Ndidi putting in the work.

What did it matter who got the credit? Once they fine-tuned the research, the techniques they developed would help millions of people on the autism spectrum. A couple of months ago, Ndidi had even found something that would have been perfect for Bethany if she had still been—

Ndidi froze in the middle of turning a page.

Right. She leaned back against her chair, went through her thoughts from the last few seconds, and let out a breath. *I can't keep stealing my colleagues' work. No wonder they all hate me.*

Admittedly, she hadn't realized what she was doing when she'd started, but the thought had occurred to her several times since then. But she'd pushed it away. She was making connections that were helping millions, but most of that insight came from building on what others had done. Even if it wasn't her intention, most of the credit for the research was being given to her. It had done wonders for her career. People were actually listening to her now—even more than they would have because of her name and who her parents were.

Still, academics were ultimately prideful people. And no one liked to think that someone else stole their research. She'd ignored the implications before because, frankly, she *needed* the research. She needed something to throw herself into.

A voice whispered in her ear, "Conversely, you could get yourself dead drunk."

Ndidi jumped, striking out reflexively. A hand closed around her fist, and a chuckle rang through the room.

"Well, damn. Talk about choosing violence."

Ndidi pulled her arm back. "DJ."

DJ gave a two-finger salute, grinning rakishly.

"I said the last part out loud, didn't I?" Ndidi muttered to herself.

"Yep," DJ replied, "but no one can blame you for going a little mad, can they?" He gestured around the room. "I mean, look at this place. It's depressing. And the security fucking sucks! Anyone can just walk right in and be mischievous."

Ndidi stood and walked around the chair until she was standing in front of him. He was dressed down in a T-shirt, jeans, and a simple jacket. His grin widened at her narrowed eyes. Ndidi sighed, but her lips pulled up in a smile. "This is a research center. Why would anyone want to be mischievous here?"

"You're asking the wrong questions," he replied, tutting. Then his grin gave away to a more serious expression. "How're you doing?"

Ndidi straightened and tried to put on the mask she'd been cultivating for the last three years, one of strength and quiet control. It was a look she'd learned from her father, but it never fit her the same way it did him. Ndidi was sure DJ would see through it immediately.

After the incident at Sparta data bank, she and DJ had grown closer. Not in any romantic way; she was far too old for him. But going through the whole ordeal together, almost dying—first from the crazy twins and then later from the drones—had created a bond. DJ and CJ were the ones who'd been there while she was grieving Bethany and refusing to accept her death. They'd gone along with her crazy plans and almost died for it. DJ had nearly lost his career. Granted, the brothers probably had their own reasons, but that didn't change the fact that they had been there.

Plus, she'd zip-lined out of a building with him. Twice. That had to count for something.

Still, Ndidi hesitated. "I'm … holding up."

DJ stared at her for a moment, and Ndidi tried not to feel uncomfortable. DJ was loud and witty and mischievous, and it was always weird to see him be serious. With his youthful grin, it was easy to forget that he'd been through almost as much as Ndidi herself. And he'd definitely seen much on his missions as a Navy SEAL.

"Guess that's the best anyone can hope for," DJ finally said. Ndidi started to reply, but he waved a hand. "Before that, though, I want a rematch."

CHAPTER

5

JANUARY 2043
THE FACILITY,
SPARTA HEADQUARTERS, NEW YORK

SHIT STAIN TENSED IMMEDIATELY, paling. Karla Polova sneered at him. "Run along now, little dog."

Shit Stain flinched, which made Martin chuckle. The guard glared at him, then straightened in an attempt at defiance. Karla took a step toward him. Her sister, Liz Polova, muttered something in Russian that made Karla scowl, but she didn't advance further.

"Run along," she repeated, her voice hard. Shit Stain spared Martin a glare that promised retribution before backing out the door.

Martin wheeled himself to the center of the room. "Girls," he said, "it's nice to see you again."

Karla turned her glare on him, but Martin just kept smiling amicably, letting it wash over him. Karla always looked like she was on the edge of violence. Martin had learned that she wouldn't attack without reason. For the most part, at least. The hostility in her eyes still unsettled him. Learning not to make that show was one of the first things Martin had to master in his years of working with the twins.

It was Liz who finally replied, her voice soft. "And you, too, Dr. Bryan."

"Martin is fine, thank you," he replied, facing her. As always, he took a moment to study the two girls, who stood side by side. Physically, their similarities were stark. They weren't identical, but they both had naturally blood-red hair that flowed down their backs. Their bodies, underneath all the leather, were toned with muscle. But that was where the similarities ended.

Their check-ups never lasted long, so Martin didn't have a full grasp of their personalities, but some things were obvious. Karla was loud and abrasive and had severe anger issues and a predisposition for violence. It'd taken Martin a while to realize that the hostility wasn't directed at anyone in particular. As far as he could tell, she hated everybody equally—except her sister, Liz.

Liz, on the other hand, was a direct contrast to Karla. Liz was soft spoken and reflective. She was almost easy to dismiss next to the physical force of her sister's personality. But as far as he could tell, she was the only one to whom Karla listened. She served as her sister's leash. From that fact alone, anyone with a lick of sense could see there was something more to her.

"Shall we begin?" Martin asked.

Karla sneered at him, her face twisted in disgust. "Your eagerness to roam our bodies is commendable, but come any closer to us, and you'll lose the use of more limbs."

Martin frowned, glanced at Liz for an explanation, and noticed her eyes flicker down to his shirt. He looked down on himself and felt heat rise to his cheeks. "My apologies," he murmured. "I didn't have a chance to freshen up before my jailers came in. I'll be just a minute."

Martin picked up the fresh shirt Shit Stain had left for him and wheeled himself to the restroom. A shower would take too long, so he simply threw his stained shirt in a corner, wiped himself down with a sponge, then threw on the fresh shirt. His muscles protested against the rapid movements, but Martin ignored them.

He couldn't have taken more than five minutes, but when he came out, there was another woman in the room. She was a few inches shorter than the twins, and her dark-brown hair ran down her neck in a wave. She wore a simple yellow blouse and leather pants. The newcomer grinned at Martin. It was a simple, ordinary grin, which looked out of place next to Karla's glower and Liz's aloofness.

"Hi," the woman said, crossing the distance between them. She held out her hand. "I'm Chloe Savage."

"A pleasure," Martin said automatically. He shook her hand and was surprised by the firm grip. "I'm Martin Bryan, the twins' technician."

Chloe's grin got even wider, and she nodded. "So I've heard. I think we have a lot to talk about."

CHAPTER

6

JANUARY 2043
OKAFOR AUTISM RESEARCH CENTRE,
NEW YORK

DJ SHOT OFF A QUICK TEXT TO CHRISTY while Ndidi got ready in the bathroom. They hadn't needed to leave the Centre for their match, which was probably why Ndidi had accepted the challenge at all. The first time he'd asked for a match, Ndidi had just led him deeper into the building and gestured him inside, much to his surprise. Apparently, after the incident with Helene and the psycho twins, Ndidi had thought it necessary to keep up her skills. She'd commandeered one of the less-frequently-used labs in the Centre and changed it into an indoor gym, complete with a sparring ground and a bathroom to freshen up after. Of course, as most of the Centre was filled with nerds, Ndidi was the only one who used it. Still, it was one of the best gyms DJ had used in years.

He spared a glance around the room. *Fucking rich kids*. He'd already removed his jacket and sneakers. Stretches probably could have gone a long way toward warming him up, but DJ tried to keep his training as real as possible. No bad guy would wait for a dude to stretch before trying to stab him in the neck.

No need to learn that *lesson again*, DJ thought, rubbing the back of his neck. Ndidi came out of the bathroom a second later. He slipped his phone back into his pocket and faced her. She'd also removed her suit jacket and rolled up her sleeves and her pant legs. The top two buttons of her shirt were undone, and droplets of the water she'd splashed on her face were dripping downward.

She stopped a few steps in front of him on the other side of the sparring mat, and DJ gazed at her. The water had helped bring some color to her cheeks, as had standing up from her desk for the first time in probably a week. Her eyes reversed her tired, grief-stricken look for one hardened with determination and an undercurrent of anger. Years ago, DJ had seen firsthand what she could accomplish when she let out her anger. Hopefully he wouldn't have to face it.

DJ relaxed into his own stance. The trainer at the base had tried to beat a proper stance into him. It had taken almost being killed a couple of times to realize that the movements used to train recruits weren't really for him. DJ was a big guy, but he could move a lot faster than others his size. He'd learned to leverage that for unpredictable bursts of speed that delivered punishment with overwhelming force. Still, he'd take a good gun over fists any day.

"Are you ready?" Ndidi asked.

DJ gestured. "Bring it on, shorty."

Ndidi lunged. DJ blocked the first two strikes and evaded the third. He came up with a punch to her midsection, which Ndidi met with her knee. Her fist was already coming down at him. DJ blocked the blow with his forearm and then tried to body check her, but she just stepped back. They exchanged a few more hits before Ndidi once again retreated. DJ saw the moment she realized her technique wasn't working and decided to change it.

He groaned mentally. *Fucking rich kids.* He'd practically taught himself how to fight, but Ndidi had been mastering different martial arts techniques since she could walk. *No point bitching about it, though.* He rushed her before she could settle into her new stance and managed to catch her off balance. Her eyes widened for a second, then she lashed out, trying to force him to give her space. DJ took the hit to his chest. Size was one of the few advantages he had over her, so he might as well use it. He pressed the attack and managed to keep her off balance.

Almost there, he thought.

Ndidi's eyes hardened, and she switched her stance, twisting away and putting some distance between them. She lashed out again with her fists, and then her feet, and then her elbows and knees. Limbs were flying too fast for DJ to be sure exactly what he was blocking. Still, he weathered the storm and concentrated his efforts on protecting his vitals. Each hit landed like a brick, but even with all her weight behind them, DJ had done way too much endurance training to be seriously bothered by her attacks. Usually, at least. The problem was that some of the hits were slipping past his guard. He could disengage and retreat—just not yet.

The attacks continued for another minute before Ndidi started to slow. DJ waited for an opening, then struck. Ndidi was slow to pull back her hand after attacking, and DJ used the chance to land a palm strike on her midsection. Nothing that could cause permanent injury, but just enough to put her on the defensive.

Ndidi's attacks had been a storm of fists and limbs, overwhelming the opponent so they couldn't attack. Offense as the defense. DJ could have done that. Probably not with the same speed, but enough to satisfy his need to win the rematch. But DJ didn't trust himself not to use too much strength. In a real fight, he pummeled fuckers to the ground. But that would defeat the whole point of asking Ndidi for the match. And he was almost there.

When DJ struck, he kept his jabs light and quick enough to get past her blocks. He swiped away her returned strikes and punished her for it with another hit. DJ wasn't looking to deal damage, only taunt her. Every move she made to take back the initiative, DJ would block with a dismissive strike and a widening smirk. He could see that it was working because she tried to transition to another stance. In response, DJ threw a jab at her face, forcing her to block. Then, he increased the pressure until blocking was all she could do. It was a complete reverse of their positions. Finally, Ndidi snapped.

There it is.

DJ wasn't sure if her anger was as obvious to everyone else, but it had grown worse while they were chasing after Helene three years before. DJ had already seen what happened when the leash slipped. Fortunately, Ndidi had been fighting for her life, so it worked out. But what about the next time? Would she hurt someone?

Other people might have advised her to talk to someone. That might be what she needed. DJ never claimed to be good at advice, but it was obvious to him that the woman needed to work out her anger. This meant either sex or fighting, and one of those came with much less baggage than the other.

Ndidi lashed out and met DJ's fist with hers. Normally, that would break her fingers, but somehow she met DJ's strength. DJ was forced to twist away as her knee came for his balls, and again when her foot came for his balls. He tried to disengage and take a step back, but Ndidi just followed him. Her attacks flew at his face with no rhyme or reason. The method was gone from the madness.

It's almost like she actually wants to kill me, DJ thought with a grunt, deflecting a punch to the face. If each attack had hit like a brick before, now they were hitting like cinderblocks. She'd traded her techniques for pure force.

A scream filled the room, and it took DJ a second to realize it was coming from Ndidi. Her mouth was open in a wordless yell. Tears streamed down her face.

There we go. DJ weathered the storm for a few minutes until Ndidi began to slow again. Then, he closed the gap and pulled her into a hug.

He kept holding her as she sobbed.

CHAPTER

7

JANUARY 2043
SPARTA HEADQUARTERS,
NEW YORK

MANAR SALEEM SQUINTED as his fingers flew over the keyboard. He could have had Helene project the display in front of him, but that would mean giving her access to his computer after he'd gone to the trouble of purging her influence from the system. That would require a level of trust in Helene that Manar hadn't had since he found out that she'd built and stored away military-grade drones. Since she'd tried to use those drones to kidnap and then kill his ex-fiancée. He would be hard pressed to trust her after that.

He was hard pressed to trust *anything* after that.

Helene was supposed to have been his greatest creation, his legacy. She was supposed to introduce the world to the potential of artificial intelligence. And she'd failed.

Manar's fingers stilled on the keyboard. No. Even at the end, Helene hadn't been working against her programming. Everything she'd done happened because Manar had coded her that way. He'd written the codes to fulfill a vow that was buried so deeply in his psyche that he'd blocked out the memory for decades.

So, I can't even trust myself.

For the past three years, Manar had been probing the memories that he'd unlocked when Helene tried to kill Ndidi. He was almost certain that everything had come back to him. But he wasn't a hundred percent sure. Manar had lived most of his adult life testing every uncertainty and acting only when he was absolutely sure.

But this, there was no way to test. Before the memories had resurfaced, there were no gaps in his mind, no pieces missing. He'd never tried to remember something and hit a wall. There had been no fleeting glimpses of things he couldn't remember. Yet, somehow, his childhood trauma had scarred him enough to conceive of Helene.

How could he be sure that all his memories had been recovered? That he wasn't putting everyone in danger through his unconscious actions? Manar wasn't used to distrusting his own mind, and he hated it. He hated second-guessing every action.

He took a breath. *I've already gone through this*, he thought. Three years ago, he'd realized there was nothing he could do about it. At least for the most part. While he couldn't be sure that his actions weren't being guided by some compulsion, it was a safe bet that every action he took to oppose Helene had been a good thing. In the past, he'd given her free rein over everything. He'd seen what that would bring.

Now, Manar was getting more involved in things that he'd previously ignored. Like Sparta.

The Sparta headquarters had sustained significant damage when the planes fell from the sky on Mayday. Most buildings would have collapsed. But Sparta had been built like a fortress. Unfortunately, since the executive team was given rooms on the top floors of the headquarters, they'd suffered the most of the damage. Manar had only survived because he'd recognized the danger in time and rushed to the lower floors. It had taken months for the building to be repaired, and then months more for the whole thing to be reinforced. In the interim, some junior executives had been promoted to replace those lost. Manar was the sole member of the initial executive team to have survived. Consequently, it had been jointly decided that he fill the position of CEO.

This had happened shortly after the death of Simone, when Manar had been in no condition to lead an organization. He'd given Helene control of everything while he drowned himself in minor projects. It was only after the incident at the Sparta data bank that Manar realized how stupid he'd been.

Still, Manar was self-aware enough to know he would be a bad choice for leadership—especially with his apparent compulsion to "attain power." He deferred his promotion and put himself out of the command chain. That way, he was still in charge of the software department but still had total autonomy to—

A beep from his computer shook Manar out of his thoughts. He squinted at the screen. "Finally," he muttered. "*Finally*." His fingers flew over the keyboard as he scrolled through Helene's codes to confirm. Then he picked up his phone.

A minute later, Admiral Olsen's gruff voice rang through the room, projected through his speakers. "What?"

Manar had met Olsen in the aftermath of the data bank incident, when the government had reached out to get his statement on his part in the whole mess. Apparently the admiral had been chosen as the representative because he had some connection to Manar through Ndidi. Manar hadn't bothered to ask what that connection was, nor did he care.

He'd thought that was the end of the episode until Olsen reached out again a week later, asking for access to Helene's program log so they could gather more details for their investigation. Admittedly, Manar hadn't been in the best mental state, so he'd refused. Even after he recovered, Manar had stood by his refusal. He wanted to shut Helene down completely. Since the AI far outstripped any other of its kind, the government would inevitably have tried to reverse engineer her. Then they would have fumbled it and probably would have caused another Mayday.

He'd been surprised, and not a little irritated, when Olsen rejected this idea, claiming that people had become too reliant on Helene as a virtual assistant and that *Manar* would cause another Mayday by shutting the AI down suddenly.

It was sound logic. People didn't like it when their toys were taken away, so Manar hadn't argued. Much. But he'd still refused to give out her programming. If nothing else, Helene was his. If he let every two-bit programmer access her codes, they'd just bumble through until they ruined something.

Olsen had increased volume when Manar explained that. And then Manar had shouted louder, almost glad for the outlet to vent his frustration.

"Admiral," Manar started.

"Get on with it, boy," Olsen grunted. "I could be taking a dump, and it'd still be preferable to this call."

Manar ignored the tone. He hadn't given away access to Helen's backups, and the government couldn't just take it without making a big public stink. The compromise, then, was for Manar to provide the information requested. That still grated on him, but it was something he could work with.

"I've found a way to tweak Helene's codes while still preserving her framework," Manar said, keeping the excitement from his voice. He couldn't shut down Helene, but having her run with previous codes was just a recipe for disaster. He'd already decided to tweak the codes years earlier, but he hadn't realized what a huge undertaking it would be.

First, he'd used a simulation program to replicate Helene's base codes. From there, he'd systematically broken them down and modified them, trying to find a version that altered the "Attain power at all costs" tenet and didn't cause the AI to crash.

Although Manar had started working on it almost immediately after he recovered from the data bank incident, this was the first time he'd scored a hit.

For normal AI, each code is built on every other—like the bricks of a house. What Manar wanted to do—and what he'd finally found a way to do by changing one of her core tenets—was the same as altering the foundation of the structure. It was possible but difficult to do without the whole building crashing down. For an AI like Helene, who was spread across the world and was constantly learning, adapting, and incorporating new things, the same concept held. However, instead of a house, it would be trying to mess with a building that was tens of stories high.

"What does that mean, exactly?" Olsen asked.

Manar paused to gather his thoughts. Somehow, Olsen assumed that Helene had gone off her programming and that Mayday and the data bank incident were the results. Manar saw no reason to dissuade him of this notion. But that left the issue of how to explain what he'd been working on. He chose his words carefully.

"I've isolated the part of Helene's code that drove her actions three years ago, and I've found a way to tweak it without crashing the framework that makes her function."

There was shuffling from the other side, and Olsen's voice grew louder, as if he'd pressed the phone against his mouth. "So, if I'm getting you right, son, you're saying that you can cut out the tumor without killing the person?" The admiral had lost his gruff tone. Now he sounded almost like a genial grandfather.

Manar cocked his head, confused. Then he remembered what Ndidi had told him. Olsen had argued against Helene being allowed to run—almost as much as Manar had.

"Yes."

"And you're certain this will work?" Olsen pressed.

Manar snorted. Even though his simulation was perfect, he'd still run it three more times. "Yes, I'm sure."

"Well, goddamn," Olsen laughed. "What're you going to need to—" A loud beep cut him off, and he grunted. "Just a minute, son. I have to take this."

Manar ran the simulation again while he waited. He hadn't made a drastic change in this iteration of the code, but it was smart to make sure nothing had been shifted too far out of place.

A minute later, the line crackled, and Olsen's voice rang through the room. "My … superiors, who apparently have my phone bugged," the admiral said through gritted teeth, "would like to know if what you're suggesting would have an effect on Helene's actions going forward."

Manar blinked. "Of course," he said slowly. "That's the whole point. If we leave her as she is, we run the risk of Mayday happening all over again."

There was a pause. Olsen's voice, when he came on again, sounded even tighter. "I've been told that the risk of that happening has been deemed minimal, and it is more important to national security that the AI's codes remain as they are." The admiral paused, and it took everything he had to force out the next part. "The brass is watching her actions closely so she can lead them to the drones."

Manar snatched his phone and pressed it to his ear, cutting off the speakers. *Obviously, I must have been hearing wrong*, he thought.

"You're saying you're willing to risk the lives of millions—of *billions*— because you want more weapons?"

"The drones are an immediate threat to national security," Olsen ground out. "And Helene has been dormant for the last three years."

Manar's voice rose. "Just because your people have failed to pick up anything does not mean Helene's been dormant! And even if she has, doesn't that make watching her movements redundant?"

An unfamiliar voice came on the line, his tone monotonous, almost disinterested. "That's not for you to say, Mr. Saleem."

"It's my damned AI," Manar sneered. "And Sparta is still a private organization. What we do with our product is none of the government's business."

"It became the government's business," the voice droned, "when your 'product' caused the death of hundreds of millions."

"Then I'll shut it down entirely!"

For a second, Manar thought the person was actually considering it. Then the voice came back, its tone still without emotion. "Mr. Saleem, let me make this clear: shutting down or reprogramming the AI will be seen as a threat to national security, and you, as the perpetrator of that threat, will be tried and punished to the full extent of the law."

"Look—"

The line went dead.

CHAPTER

8

JANUARY 2043

THE FACILITY,
SPARTA HEADQUARTERS, NEW YORK

"SO, WHAT DID YOU DO to get caught up in Sparta?" Chloe Savage asked. She looked around the room with feigned innocence.

Martin saw right through it. *What is she looking for?*

"It couldn't have been that bad if they stuck you in a room like this," she continued. "What is that, a king-sized bed?"

"I was a researcher at the Johns Hopkins Applied Physics Lab," Martin answered. He pushed himself over to the girls, his wheels groaning. Liz handed him a packet filled with his tools, and Martin busied himself with checking over each girl. "As a specialist in progressive mind-controlled robotics research, I designed dozens of modular prosthetic limbs for adult amputees. Sparta approached me with a job offer to develop the partial limbs and torso for the girls. I accepted and completed the job. I was kidnapped almost immediately."

He tried to mask the bitterness in his tone, but he didn't think he succeeded. And he didn't rightly care. After all, he *had* been kidnapped because he succeeded at what he'd been hired to do. What would they have done to him if he had failed?

Martin let out a breath. In his periphery, he saw Chloe staring at him intently. He ignored her. He'd learned not to let his resentment show. At least, not until he could do something about it.

It helped to focus on the silver lining. Thanks to his semiregular access to the twins, he'd been able to study how the bioengineered limbs and organs interacted with each other and normal body systems. Most of this had been theoretical when he was developing the tech. But even with the extensive tests, several of the knock-on effects surprised him—the reinforcement of the girls' normal musculature, for example. Martin had only noticed it months ago. It had happened slowly over time. The twins could probably bench press more than most Olympic athletes and take more hits than a person wearing body armor.

The in-depth study had broadened his understanding of his own technology, and he'd begun to refine it in his head, so much so that he was confident his own case could be reversed. Perhaps he wouldn't be able to run up walls, but at least he would be able to stand on his own feet.

He laid the tools on his lap and gestured to the girls. Almost in unison, they stripped down to their underwear. Chloe raised a brow, then glanced at Dead Eyes, who was standing silently in the corner.

"Not judging or anything, but does he have to be here?" she asked, jerking a thumb at Dead Eyes.

Karla snorted and put her hands on her hips. Her entire right side, from shoulder to toe, was made of titanium. Lines ran the length of it: passages for the network of wires that connected the synthetic nerves to her fleshy left side. Liz looked the same, but her bionics were on the left. Martin hadn't been able to pry their story out of either of them, except that they had been born as conjoined twins, sharing everything except their heads. His technology was the only way they could be separated, the only reason they were able to act independently.

And he was locked up instead of celebrated.

"That one is just a puppet that the AI uses to monitor us. He is nothing more than a sack of meat," Karla said, indicating the guard.

Her words snapped Martin out of his spiral. He stared at her in confusion. *What does she mean by* puppet? Martin adjusted his glasses. *An AI. Helene. But how could she control a human being?*

Chloe moved toward the guard, her expression contemplative. *She isn't surprised by it*, Martin noted. Just what had he missed while he was locked up?

"As if we needed more complications," Chloe muttered, almost too low for Martin to hear. Louder, she said, "You're right. They creep me the fuck out."

"Me too," Martin said. He cleared his throat and wheeled himself closer to Karla, ignoring her disgusted look. "So you see? It's fine."

Chloe stared at him for a moment. And then the grin was back on her face. She walked up to him, also ignoring Karla's glower, and peered at the work. Martin had plugged a cord into the ports in Karla's arm and was flicking through the readings with the device in his hand.

"What exactly are these check-ups about?" she asked.

From the side, he noticed Liz tilt her head curiously.

"I developed the bionics that granted Karla and Liz their independence," Martin started, letting a hint of pride seep into his voice. "The technology is the first of its kind, so there might be some effects I didn't see while developing it."

Martin took note of the readings, then picked up a screwdriver. He performed some repairs whenever the situation—and the baton against his head—demanded it. He completed his most extensive repairs three years ago on Karla. Martin still didn't know what had caused the damage, but it'd looked like she'd stepped on a landmine.

"Effects? That sounds bad." Chloe's voice sounded somewhat distant.

"Not necessarily," he replied, adjusting something in Karla's arm and moving down toward her torso. "Like I said, the tech is still very new, so most anything outside of my original parameters is unexpected."

"Have you found any effects like that?" the brunette asked casually.

Martin hesitated for a split second, his mind going to the readings he'd just taken. He adjusted his glasses and replied just as casually, "Not yet, but I'm hoping. Things like that would do wonders for my career."

His fingers moved deftly, giving the appearance that he was engrossed in his work. But his mind was moving a mile a minute, trying to figure out the woman's angle. All her questions were asked innocently, but Martin couldn't help but feel she was probing him for something—maybe testing him.

"Your career?" Chloe asked.

He could hear her moving around the room, could almost feel her eyes scanning. *What is she looking for? I've got nothing hidden here.*

"That's assuming you somehow find a way out of this place, right?"

His fingers slowed. *Is she saying … ?*

"I'm optimistic," he replied, leaning back in his chair.

Chloe just gave a noncommittal hum and continued pacing.

The next half hour was spent in relative silence. When Chloe finished her scan of the room, she proceeded to examine Dead Eyes. She pulled a dagger from somewhere and poked the guard until a drop of blood came out. Dead Eyes gave no reaction.

Intermittently, she would throw out questions to Martin, each as casual as the last. Most didn't seem related. Some were even contradictory, as if she were trying to catch him in a lie. They were obvious probes, and he was certain that Chloe wanted him to know it, but he couldn't determine what she was looking for.

So he just answered honestly. This is what he preferred anyway. If nothing else, Martin was an academic at heart. Providing wrong information didn't sit right with him.

Martin drew out his diagnostics as long as he could, but still he finished far too soon. The girls dressed themselves while he packed up his tools. On a whim, he handed the packet to Chloe. The brunette accepted it with her customary grin. Martin tried not to jerk when he felt something metallic land in his palm.

"If you are done making those disgusting eyes at each other, we can leave," Karla barked from the door.

"Until next time, girls," Martin said, pushing himself back to the bed. He left his hands on the wheels. "Chloe, a pleasure to make your acquaintance again."

The brunette gave a small wave. "Until next time, Dr. Bryan."

Dead Eyes followed the trio, and the door shut behind him. A moment later, it locked with a jangle of keys.

Alone again, Martin examined Chloe's parting gift. It was a wireless earpiece, no bigger than his thumb. Martin had never seen one like this, but it was familiar enough for him to recognize it as a comm unit.

"Not so long a shot after all," he murmured, smiling.

CHAPTER

JANUARY 2043

OKAFOR AUTISM RESEARCH CENTRE, NEW YORK

"SO, WHY are you here?" Ndidi asked.

They'd both taken turns freshening up in the bathroom. Now they were sitting on one of the couches in the training room. By unspoken agreement, neither of them had mentioned her breakdown. DJ probably didn't know how to handle a conversation like that, and Ndidi couldn't stop berating herself. Her father had always taught her to be in control, yet she'd totally lost it.

Ndidi didn't know how long she'd cried in DJ's arms. Worse, she wasn't even aware she was crying until she'd settled down. She'd washed her face afterward. But her eyes were still swollen. She had some makeup in her bag that would have helped, but Ndidi hadn't bothered. It was better that she remembered.

She was fairly certain the whole thing had been DJ's intention from the start. Once she was clearheaded enough, she analyzed the fight. Toward the end, when DJ had begun pressuring her, he could have ended the fight at any time. By then, she was barely holding on, and her movements had been all over the place. But he hadn't finished it. He'd prodded at every opening and danced away at every counter, taunting her until she snapped.

Ndidi felt a pang of irritation, but it wasn't as if she could argue with his methods. She hadn't felt this light in months. And she was self-aware enough to know how close she was to going off the deep end by herself.

"I can't just visit a friend?" DJ replied, smiling sheepishly.

"Not when you're always moaning about the flight to and from the naval base," Ndidi said, crossing her arms.

"Would it help if I told you I had a job here?"

"Would you be lying?"

DJ muttered something under his breath that Ndidi was sure would have earned him a slap if she'd heard it clearly. He grimaced, looking slightly embarrassed. "I came to check out the Sparta data bank."

Ndidi blinked, leaning back in her seat. She wasn't sure what she'd expected, but it hadn't been that. Her heart rate increased at the memory of the data bank. She'd almost died—more than once. And had almost been kidnapped and led to a fate probably worse than that. If she had to, Ndidi was sure she could return to the data bank, but she could easily spend the rest of her life far away from that building and be perfectly fine.

"Why?" she asked.

"That's the thing," DJ said. "I have no idea. I just have this feeling that there's shit going on in the background that's going to bite us in the ass at some point." He rubbed the back of his neck. "Probably just being paranoid, but I can't shake it off."

It would have been easy to dismiss DJ's feeling as the same restlessness that she herself had been dealing with. But DJ wasn't the type to be jumping at shadows. And on some level, Ndidi didn't want it to be just paranoia. She remembered the promise she'd made to herself at the private family burial ground, to get to the bottom of her parent's death. And for the last eighteen months, she'd done nothing toward that goal.

"Did something happen while you were there?" Ndidi asked.

"Nope," he responded, popping the *p*. "Me, Christy, and Kyle were watching the building for hours before it occurred to me that Helene had probably seen us coming from miles away. It was the first time off that we'd gotten in months, and I dragged my team over here to stake out the stupid building. Some leader I am, right?"

For a moment Ndidi felt the urge to comfort him, but she dismissed it. DJ didn't need comforting. Like her, he needed to feel like he was actually doing something, actually making a difference. Ndidi helped children on the autism spectrum all over the world; DJ regularly prevented international incidents. Yet they both felt useless. Her father would have called it pathetic and lectured her about how she shouldn't worry about things she couldn't change.

It was an easy lecture to give, but Eze wasn't here to give it. And Ndidi felt powerless for doing nothing to get justice for his death.

Then a thought triggered Ndidi. "Wait! Why was this your first break in months?"

DJ's expression darkened further. "I don't know. My team's been busting our asses over kiddie missions for most of the last year. At first, I thought Olsen was just being a dick. But he said our missions had come from higher up. Apparently, one of the admirals has taken a dislike to us."

"Can't you fight it?"

Ndidi regretted the question almost as soon as she asked it. This was DJ she was talking to. If causing trouble was the answer, the problem would be solved. Ndidi was used to having her father's name behind her every word.

DJ started frustratedly pacing around the room. "This is Olsen's *boss*. It's already a miracle that I get away with talking to Olsen the way I do. Half the base hates me for the disrespect. If I tried to make trouble for a vice admiral, my ass would be fucked before I could lube it up."

Ndidi wrinkled her nose. Somehow she'd gotten used to DJ's graphic descriptions, but *really*?

"And then CJ would be alone there," DJ continued. "He'd be too shy to speak up, so they'd run all over him too." He stopped and turned back to her, grinning sheepishly. "Sorry, guess I also came here to rant. I would have gone to CJ, but he's been as busy as we have for the last few months."

"That's okay," Ndidi replied.

DJ nodded, and his grin turned mischievous. "With that out of the way …
have you spoken to Manar recently?"

Ndidi closed her eyes. *Should have seen that coming.*

10

JANUARY 2043
THE FACILITY,
SPARTA HEADQUARTERS, NEW YORK

JOSÉ OLVERA STRODE down the halls of the Sparta building. Except for a sideways glance, he didn't react when Chloe fell into step beside him.

"Well?" he asked.

"Like I told you, we can't leave without him," she replied. "Though how we're gonna move him is anyone's guess. He's kept deep inside the building and isolated for the most part. Getting there the first time was hell—even with the girls."

José nodded. It was annoying how large the Sparta building was. And that was just the secret complex inside of the main headquarters. José had been living within it for the last three years, and he still got turned around sometimes.

"And there's no other option?"

Chloe shook her head. "Why do you think I've been gone so frequently? I've been poking around and even looked up some old contacts. No one on the outside even comes close to him."

José grunted. "Then there's no choice. I will not put the twins in danger over this. We'll figure something out."

Most employees were restricted to their departments and needed special passes to cross to other areas. As far as José could figure, not even the high-level executives had access to every area of the building. The CEO might have, but that, too, was unlikely. Helene had proven adept at hiding what she didn't want found.

The precautions had been reduced three years back after the change in management. However, since the entire building had been built in compartments specifically for those precautions, the rule couldn't be scrapped entirely. That level of secrecy was something that José approved of. There was no need for the sheep to be aware of the farmer's actions. This made it easy to hide an entire secret facility within the building.

The Sparta headquarters was ninety-four stories high. As far as José could figure, the Facility was built *within* the headquarters itself. It ran in from the seventieth floor all the way to the top but acted almost like a bridge within a floor. Chloe had likened the whole thing to a sandwich: the headquarters was the two slices of bread, and the Facility was the lettuce and cheese stuffed in the middle. José had scoffed at the analogy, but he couldn't deny that it was apt.

Giant steel doors separated the Facility from the actual headquarters and was keyed to open for specific individuals. Since the doors looked like every other set that divided the building into compartments, normal employees would brush them off.

He glanced at his watch. Still a few hours to go. Previously the doors could have been used at any time of the day, but that had changed after the incident at the data bank. Now movement between the headquarters was limited to nighttime, after most Sparta employees had left.

This timing coincided with the periods when the AI became uncommunicative, and José was convinced that the two were related.

José gritted his teeth. He hadn't received an order from the AI after he'd been tasked with directing a slew of drones into Nigeria. José still could not figure out what the purpose of the assignment had been, apart from the elimination of some politicians.

After that, Helene had gone dormant—at least for the most part. Chloe had asked around and learned that some others in the Facility received sporadic instructions. But the AI had stopped manifesting her physical presence.

José held in a shiver at the memory of that presence. The magnitude of it had made it difficult to breathe.

Apart from wasting away for the last few years, José had no problem with the AI's silence. He was glad for it, in fact. It had been rare good news since the entire shit show had begun years ago. For whatever reason, Helene was hiding. The signs were obvious to anyone with intelligence higher than a gnat's. Where before the AI's actions had been overt and commanding, now it'd been forced to move more cautiously. Again, the timing made José suspect it was because of the data bank incident. He'd been briefed on the event by his girls, and he suspected that whatever had shut the AI down toward the end was the cause of its newfound caution.

That didn't change the fact that Helene was still plotting something. How long had the next 'Mayday' taken to plan? José did not want to be here when it went off. The stain of that would be on his honor forever.

But it wouldn't be the first stain. And José could not pass up this opportunity.

His family was going to leave Sparta.

CHAPTER

11

JANUARY 2043
OKAFOR AUTISM RESEARCH CENTRE, NEW YORK

"HERMIONE."

Hermione Cloney jumped at the sound of her name. She turned back, and then jumped again when she realized how close Ndidi was. "How long have you been standing there?" she asked, her hand clutching her chest.

"I just got here, but I was calling your name from the door." Ndidi's amused gaze turned to concern. "When was the last time you took a break and actually left this room?"

Hermione looked away from Ndidi's eyes, glancing around her small lab. Ndidi had assigned it to her years earlier when she'd started working at the Centre. She hadn't needed to. Only higher-level staff had their own laboratories and Hermione had been perfectly willing to work her way up. But Ndidi wouldn't hear of it.

"What's a little nepotism among friends?" she'd said. Hermione hadn't pressed the issue even though she was uncomfortable with the gift. Her father would never have—

Hermione cut off the thought to douse the spark of anger forming in her chest. She'd abandoned her life in Nigeria, and she'd switched her study. She'd decided to work with Ndidi. Her research on biotechnological therapies for children on the autism spectrum was supposed to be a fresh start. Yet even three years later, she still couldn't stop seeing her father in everything.

"Hermione!" Ndidi called.

Hermione jumped, then blushed when she realized she'd lost herself in her thoughts again. That had been happening more and more lately—especially when she interacted with others. It was one of the reasons she didn't like leaving her lab.

"I took a break a few hours ago," Hermione said. She pointed at her leftover lunch.

Ndidi didn't even glance at it. "I meant something longer than just going out for lunch. When was the last time you left the Centre and, I don't know, took a stroll or something?"

Hermione started to reply, then hesitated. When *had* she last left the Centre? There was no need to. The building had several overnight rooms. They were normally reserved for patients under extreme care, but there were more rooms than there were patients, so Ndidi had requisitioned one for her. And everything else she needed could be ordered in.

Hermione knew throwing herself into her research wasn't healthy, but she couldn't see a better way. The last time she looked in the mirror, she'd barely recognized herself. Somehow, over the years, she'd lost what little weight she'd had. Her eyes were sunken and dark from crying. Her hair fell listlessly. That had been weeks ago; Hermione couldn't imagine she looked any better now.

It's probably why Ndidi looks so concerned. I must be a mess.

She'd tried going out, but that just wasn't her thing. She and her father could stay up in the lab for days on end when they'd been working on their project. During the final stretch of the picospores research, it had taken Eze Okafor himself to drag them out.

She didn't miss the irony that his daughter was now doing the same thing.

"I don't need a stroll, Ndidi," she said.

Ndidi knelt until she was eye level with Hermione. "Yes, you do. Camping out in here isn't healthy. It's not going to help you forget your loss or deal with it better. You're only hurting yourself."

Hermione opened her mouth to retort but hesitated when she met Ndidi's eyes. Her familiar determination was there—but not the anger that normally lurked beneath the surface. Hermione had first noticed the anger at their parents' funeral in Nigeria, and she'd seen it every time she and Ndidi had spoken since.

What had changed?

Hermione—and probably Ndidi herself—didn't realize how much that anger had framed Ndidi's face, and now it was gone. Ndidi looked, if not at peace, better. Hermione had understood that anger; Ndidi had lost just as much as she had. Both her parents had been killed in the same freak accident that had taken Hermione's father and mother. When Bethany went missing, she had lost a sister. Ndidi had spoken a little about what her grief had driven her to do. Hermione was glad that Ndidi hadn't shown the same inclinations these past few years.

But why did Ndidi seem to be moving on while Hermione was drowning in her memories? It was … frustrating.

"You're one to talk," she replied. "You spend just as much time buried in your research as I do. When was the last time *you* left the Centre?"

Ndidi didn't rise to the bait. "I know. A friend of mine recently made me realize the same thing. I'm trying to change that." She put her hand on Hermione's shoulder. "Why don't we both go out? Chad has been trying to get me to check out this café a few blocks away. They just opened, and they're apparently quite good."

Hermione's first instinct was to turn it down, but the look on Ndidi's face told her that wasn't an option. She took a look at the jeans she'd been wearing for the last week and the shirt that was stained with her lunch. Then she looked back at Ndidi, who was dressed in her customary black suit with shortened sleeves and whose hair was done up in braids.

"I'll have to change." Hermione sighed.

Ndidi grinned.

CHAPTER

12

JANUARY 2043
NAVAL AMPHIBIOUS BASE,
CORONADO, CALIFORNIA

CJ SPARED only a glance when his brother walked into the room. His fingers flicked across the keyboard as he struggled to input the last line of code before he lost his train of thought. The key was to visualize every step of the process as he performed it. Fortunately, coding had always been easy for him, so it wasn't as difficult as other things were.

But even those other things, including his speech, had improved. He still got turned around sometimes, and it took far too much concentration for him to have a conversation. But it wasn't as difficult as it had been. The words came more easily these days.

It wasn't much, but it made him feel just a little bit more "normal."

CJ finished the last line of code. It wasn't the whole program, just the piece that he had been assigned to. The rest had probably been assigned to other programmers. It was standard practice when the task was too classified for one person to have all the information. Tasks like this had become more and more common over the last few months—to the point that CJ was burning with curiosity. He could infer what the launched program would do, but without the other pieces, it would be conjecture at best.

There *were* ways to check, but CJ shook the thought from his head. It had been that same need to snoop that had caused such trouble that his brother had to stick his neck out for him. He would do anything to avoid being such a burden again. CJ rubbed his arms. *I won't be a burden anymore.*

"CJ," DJ said from behind him, and CJ gave a start. "Shit, sorry. Didn't mean to startle you. It's just that you were staring into space again."

CJ relaxed. He had seen his brother walk in but had just forgotten. "Good morning."

DJ took a seat next to him and nodded at the computer. "Guess they've been working you to the bone too, huh?" he asked, a touch bitterly.

"Working me to the bone?" CJ repeated. His brain processed the question, and he looked away, considering it. He'd graduated from MIT a few years ago and had been immediately drafted into the Navy SEALs. Fortunately, since he was a noncombatant, he hadn't needed to go through the ridiculous drills that his brother had moaned about in his time as a recruit. Naturally, he'd been assigned to DJ's team. CJ had been worried that they would be separated for whatever reason, so that was a relief. He worked as the team's behind-the-scenes programmer. His role wasn't too different from what he'd done when DJ had infiltrated Gaius. The job was well within his capabilities.

CJ was completely satisfied with this situation. He wasn't needed on every mission, so he was usually assigned other tasks by his superiors. CJ frowned as a thought occurred to him. He'd actually been assigned more of those than any that involved his brother. CJ knew that he could be a little absent minded, but how was he just now noticing this?

CJ rubbed his arm. "Too?" he echoed.

"You didn't notice?" DJ asked, then nodded. "Guess it makes sense. The team hasn't been assigned any missions high level enough to warrant a programmer, and we haven't really had the chance to talk. This is practically the first time I've been on the base in months."

CJ's frown deepened. He glanced at DJ before looking away again. "What did, uh, you do?"

DJ eyed him sideways and chuckled. "Y'know, I would have been pissed, too, if that hadn't been my first reaction. But I haven't done anything." CJ gave him a skeptical look. "I'm serious! I've been cracking my brain, but I'm coming up empty!"

"That's, hmm, nothing new." CJ grinned—or tried to. His lips didn't respond as he wanted them to. It came out a little more than a grimace.

"Still a wiseass, I see," DJ said, though a smile tugged at his lips. "Seriously, though. Olsen said that one of the higher-ups had taken up my assignments personally. That can't be good. It's one of the reasons I came here right after. I wanted to make sure no one was messing with you too."

"No one has, uh … no one's said anything to me," CJ replied. He tilted his head, glancing at his brother from the corner of his eye. He understood that DJ was worried about him, but it hurt that he thought he couldn't take care of himself. CJ wasn't good with people, but he'd gotten better. The thought slipped away before he could spiral, and another replaced it. Something DJ had said.

"After?" CJ asked.

"Yeah, I dropped by the Centre for a couple of hours."

"How was she?" CJ asked. Ndidi had stayed behind in Nigeria for a year after her father's funeral. CJ hadn't had the chance to see her, though DJ had made the trip several times.

DJ shrugged, his eyes distant. "She seemed better when I left. Less angry, at least. Hopefully that'll stick." He chuckled. "We sparred, and I actually won for once. Sure, she was having a mental breakdown and all, but I'm definitely going to rub it in her face."

DJ had mentioned Ndidi's anger several times, clearly worried it would consume her. CJ had only noticed it once, some years back, while they were dealing with Helene. But he'd been too focused on reconnecting with Ndidi, whose techniques had been vital in helping him manage his outbursts. He hadn't noticed her as she was back then: a woman grieving the loss of her ward, Bethany.

DJ stared into the distance, his eyes highlighting his weariness. CJ wanted to tell him to get some rest but stopped himself. It was easy to tell when something bothered DJ because he lost his grin. Even without that, they had been together too long for CJ to miss the cues.

He could have waited, but he knew better than anyone how easy it was for DJ to lose himself in his thoughts. Whatever was on his brother's mind must have been important for him to allow the silence to last so long.

"Why were you, hmm, in New York?" he prompted softly.

DJ sighed, hesitating for a moment. "I was checking out the Sparta data bank."

CJ blinked and looked down at his feet. Sparta had several data banks around New York, though most of them were inaccessible. But his brother had infiltrated and almost been killed at only one of them. Multiple times. CJ had never been there. The footage had been pulled up by Manar Saleem, however, and CJ had watched it. Since then, he'd stayed away from New York entirely. Just the memories of what had almost happened could trigger his outbursts.

Years ago, when he was younger, Ndidi had taught him a technique to suppress his emotions and push past his outbursts. CJ normally used it when his thoughts threatened to drown him. Maybe he could apply it to help deal with this. He was sure that it would be necessary at some point, and even if it wasn't, it would at least help him handle his emotions better. He could probably combine it with—

CJ shook his head. He rubbed his palms against his pants, using the texture to ground himself in the moment.

I can't believe I did it again. Why? Why? Why?

A whine built in the back of his throat as his emotions flooded out. CJ squashed both with an effort of will. It was bad enough that he'd screwed up, but having an episode on top of it …

He took a breath. The sensation of fabric against his palms helped. He closed his eyes and retraced the last few moments before he drifted off. DJ. Sparta. Yes.

"Why?" he asked. It was what he wanted to know the most, and the conversation would give him something to focus on. He glanced at his brother from below his lashes, almost afraid.

DJ met his eyes. There was no judgment or pity there. CJ let out another breath, one of relief. His brother was the only one who treated him like a normal person. CJ would do anything to preserve that.

"I just wanted to check it out," DJ said, frustrated. "A lot of stuff hasn't been adding up recently, and my gut tells me that there's something happening on the back end that's going to fuck with us."

CJ frowned. DJ had always been the more laid-back one—sometimes annoyingly so. He wasn't one to jump at shadows. But anything related to Sparta and Helene was other than normal. No matter how DJ had covered it up, CJ had seen how much his brother had been affected by what happened that night. CJ had watched the recording, but he would be the first to admit that he didn't fully understand what Helene had done in the data bank room. And that was aside from the drones that had almost kidnapped Ndidi.

Even though he was naturally inclined to take his brother's word, CJ couldn't deny that the feeling could have been baseless paranoia. He started to tell DJ that, but the look on his brother's face—the *frustration* on it—made him hesitate. Instead, he asked the second thing that he wanted to know.

"What … uh … things don't add up?"

"The last few months for one," DJ said, throwing his hands up. "We've been sent on low-level missions, back-to-back, with hardly a break in between. Most of it is busywork. Olsen said that the missions are decided by someone over his head, but how did *they* come in? I haven't done anything for the last three years, and now I'm suddenly important enough that someone higher than a fucking *rear admiral* decides to waste their time screwing me over?" He sighed, and his voice softened. "It doesn't make sense, C."

CJ softened his own voice to match and turned to face his brother. "So, what? You, uh, you think that … that Helene is behind it? She has been, uh … dormant for the last few years."

DJ shrugged. "I know she's been dormant. But I don't know … maybe?"

CJ tilted his head as a thought occurred to him. "Have you tried talking to … uh … Manar Saleem?"

DJ's head snapped up.

CHAPTER

13

JANUARY 2043
NEW YORK CITY, NEW YORK

"WHAT WAS IT LIKE working with Dr. Cloney?" Ndidi asked. "We didn't talk much while I was in Nigeria, but he came here for a conference shortly before Mayday."

Hermione gave a start. They were a few buildings away from the Autism Centre, having left immediately after she'd changed into something more appropriate—or at least less stained and worn out. It was the middle of the day, and her thick sweatshirt protected her from the worst of the cold. Her pants were loose enough that she didn't have to worry about how skinny she looked. There was nothing she could do about the bags under her eyes, short of caking herself in makeup, and that was entirely too stressful.

"I thought the whole point of this was to move on," Hermione said.

Ndidi nodded and took a lick of the ice cream cone she'd bought along the way. "It is. Research shows that talking about loss with others who've faced something similar can be therapeutic."

Hermione took a breath. The air *was* fresher outside; she hadn't noticed how stuffy her lab had been. Her mind turned to the last decade, and she felt the weariness return. With some effort, she pushed past it and focused instead on the people they passed and the cracks in the sidewalk.

"It was … well, I don't know," she answered finally, shrugging. "He was my dad, so we butted heads sometimes. All the time, actually. Especially when he was wrong about something and wouldn't admit it until I shoved the proof in his face. And he could be absent minded. *Really* absent minded. Especially when he was deep in research. He would get lost in his thoughts for hours. Mum would have to go in and force him out."

"That sounds familiar," Ndidi mused.

"Yeah, I get the irony," Hermione chuckled. She glanced at Ndidi from the corner of her eye. "I used to be his little assistant when I was growing up. By the time I got my diploma, I was already in love with the research."

They paused at a crosswalk, waiting for the light to turn green. Ndidi took another lick of her ice cream, and Hermione regretted not getting one too, even though it was freezing out. "So, whose idea was it to register you in JEWELS?" Ndidi asked.

JEWELS was the mixed martial arts competition where she and Ndidi had first met as rivals competing in the finals. They'd both been teenagers but had taken advantage of their builds to pass for twenty-one-year-olds. Hermione had lost the match—badly—but Ndidi had worked for it. At the end, they had abandoned their techniques and basically just wailed on each other, trying to get as many hits in as they could. After the match, Ndidi had walked up to her, for whatever reason, and that had been the start of their friendship.

Hermione smiled at the memory as they crossed the street and entered the café. Her father had been the one to push her into learning to fight. It was supposed to be for self-defense, but once they'd discovered that she had an aptitude for it, he refused to let it end there.

Hermione said as much to Ndidi.

"My dad too." She laughed. "I don't know where he got the idea for JEWELS, though. I mean, it was all the way in Tokyo."

The café was quaint and had a rich, homey feel. There was a large open space with tables for groups and some corner booths off to the side. Hermione and Ndidi picked one of the corner booths and waved over a waitress for the menu.

"He looked up to your dad, y'know?" Hermione said after they ordered. "He had so much respect for him, and I always thought it was weird. Not that your dad wasn't worthy of respect or anything," she added quickly. "Just that the only people my dad cared about were academics. Like Manar Saleem."

Ndidi laughed, but Hermione could tell she was uncomfortable. It didn't surprise her when Ndidi changed the subject. "Who came up with the idea for picospores?"

"Me, actually," Hermione replied. She paused as the waitress brought their food. Hermione had ordered a hamburger and chips, and Ndidi went for a salad. "Picotechnology isn't anything new, but it hasn't been studied as extensively as it should. It has so much application in everything."

"What is it though?" Ndidi asked. "Picospores, I mean,"

Hermione paused for a minute. She'd given a presentation with her father back when they were looking for investors, but that explanation had been developed to sound grandiose. Hermione found it difficult to break it down. She was an academic also, but biotechnology wasn't her field.

"They're more or less like nanites," she started, "in that they're designed to work at the cellular and subcellular level within the body. Except where nanites might not be able to function because they're too large, picospores—smaller by ten to the power of twelve—won't have a problem.

"Once dispersed, they can be absorbed easily through the pores of the skin, the pupils, or the ear canal. And since they're basically core processors, they can be programmed and actively controlled wherever they're needed in the body." She took a bite of her burger. "At least that was the theory I came up with. It took ages before my dad and I were able to figure out how to control them through the subdermal tissues."

Ndidi nodded absently as she processed. Hermione used the time to tuck away more of the burger.

"Well, I think I get the general idea," Ndidi said eventually. "But how does it help in, say, the medical field?"

"Picospores allow us to change the surface area of atoms. This gives us control over how proteins are formed and absorbed in the body. As a result, the picospores can speed up the formation of fibrils or even other proteins, helping in regeneration."

"Do they have an effect on the brain?"

Hermione nodded. "Theoretically, the brain would be where the spores have the most application, but our software didn't have the processing power to simulate the effects. We hadn't reached the testing phase of the research before the … before the accident."

Ndidi's smile softened. "Most of the research was recovered by the Okafor Corporation after the accident. It's been put on hold out of respect for Dr. Cloney—and because the concept is hard to follow without a background in the underlying theory. But I can transfer access to you, if you want to complete what you guys started."

Hermione took a deep breath and tried to imagine herself working on the project. She shook her head. "Thanks, but no. The picospores will always be my and my dad's project. Continuing it now without him … I don't think I can do it." She continued more firmly, "I came here so I could move on. I know I haven't been doing much of that lately, but I think I'm ready to start. For real."

Ndidi must have seen the conviction in her eyes because she didn't press her further. Instead, she smiled and changed the subject.

Hermione let her friend's voice wash over her. She took another breath, and somehow it felt fresher than it had before.

CHAPTER

JANUARY 2043

THE FACILITY,
SPARTA HEADQUARTERS, NEW YORK

CHLOE GLANCED AT JOSÉ out of the corner of her eye. He'd been silent for the last few minutes, brooding. His expression gave nothing away, of course, but Chloe was an old hand at reading him. They'd been pacing the halls in a circle while they talked. However, there was no need to now, so she led them to the training room. Karla and Liz would be there soon, if they weren't already.

José noticed their new course, but he didn't say anything. Not that there would be a point anyway. It was either the training room or their quarters. Although the bedroom would have been a great alternative to work out her frustrations, it wasn't what she had in mind.

Her hands twitched, reaching for her dagger without thought. She hadn't been this antsy since she was a teenager. After three years of being a glorified security guard, Chloe was ready to kill something. That bloodlust was what had drawn her to join the CIA, and later its Special Divisions. She crawled up its ranks until she was one of their best agents. It was a nice life, until she'd been sent to Russia to eliminate an agent gone rogue.

They turned a corner, heading deeper into the Facility. Again, Chloe glanced at José, her grin turning a little maniacal. It had taken her months to track him down. When she finally had, she'd been beaten and captured within minutes. The twins had only been about seven years old then. They'd still shared one body, yet they'd handled a gun and herded her to José. Herded *her*.

It'd been fucked up and humiliating.

She wasn't completely sure what had made her decide to stay and train the freaks, but she couldn't bring herself to regret it—even if Karla was a bitch and a half on her best day.

After that, Chloe had helped José and the girls get back into the CIA. With her and José's training, the twins had quickly climbed the ranks until they were feared even more than Chloe. That probably had to do with Karla. Not that Chloe cared. What mattered was it had been *fun*.

They turned another corner. Chloe kept track of the turns in her head since the hallways tended to blend together. There were guards along the passage, a three-man patrol. Their eyes widened when they saw her and José. The three men tensed, surreptitiously moving closer to the wall and out of their way. Chloe grinned at them, and José snorted.

"Pathetic cowards," she heard him mutter before he returned to brooding.

Chloe understood why José had taken the offer from Helene. She'd chosen to follow him, but it was still irritating. Sparta. Helene. They both unnerved her. Chloe had done some pretty rough stuff for the CIA, but at least she could pretend it was for a greater good. It was a thin veil, sure, but it had been something. Now, whenever she got a task, it was to further the AI's cause. And Chloe couldn't begin to grasp what that was.

Like, why the fuck would it need goddamn drones? she thought. *Sparta is supposed to be just a tech company.*

Chloe had been assigned somewhere else that night, three years ago, much to her disgust. It was the only interesting thing that had happened since she'd joined the stupid organization with José.

A weird time to be nostalgic, Chloe thought. Maybe it was because she was leaving—well, breaking out. José had brought the idea to her. Neither of them had any illusions that they would be allowed to go without a fight. Chloe almost looked forward to it.

The only good thing about the last three years? It had given her time to train. She'd been fighting for decades, so there was little time for her to hone her skills anymore. The training kept her from getting rusty. She was also able to beat some bad habits out of the twins. They were even getting close to being able to beat her—not that she would ever tell them. She had no illusions. Certainly, Karla would hit to kill if given half a chance.

Another set of guards was patrolling the passage they turned down. It was another three-man team, though one of them was an AI-controlled puppet. Beside her, she felt José tense, then relax. Chloe couldn't blame him. The two groups passed without incident, though Chloe was forced to hold back a shiver. The puppets creeped the fuck out of her.

She'd heard from the twins how deadly they could be in a fight. So far, Helene hadn't used them for anything other than guard duty, yet more and more guards had been turned into puppets. It was subtle, sure, but impossible for Chloe to miss. That was another reason they were cutting loose.

José would never admit it—probably not even to himself—but the fact that they were not being given any tasks was likely a sign that they'd outlived their usefulness. Chloe didn't know if it was because the twins had been defeated at the data bank or because Helene had needed them for one task that had been fulfilled. Regardless, it felt like they'd been dumped. And Chloe had a good idea of what the AI did to those it discarded.

Her thoughts turned to Martin Bryan.

Chloe admitted to being more than a little curious about him. She'd been somewhat blatant about it. It hadn't taken him long to realize why she'd been asking him all those questions. Chloe didn't get the sense that he'd lied about anything, and it was obvious he was desperate to escape his prison. He could be helpful to the twins, but getting him out with that wheelchair would be next to impossible.

They turned another corner and entered the first room. As she'd expected, Karla and Liz were already there, sparring with each other.

Chloe's hands twitched for her daggers; this time she didn't stop them. *I'll work out some tension,* she thought with a grin. *Then I'll figure out how we're getting out of this hellhole.*

CHAPTER

JANUARY 2043
SPARTA HEADQUARTERS,
NEW YORK

DJ PULLED HIS JACKET TIGHTER around himself as he pushed open the doors of the Sparta building. He was spending far too much time outside for the middle of January. The inside of the building wasn't much warmer, but it helped. Hopefully, he'd be out of here and back in his bed at the naval base within a day.

Or maybe I should drop by the Centre again? It'd been less than a week since he was there. Dropping by again would look too much like he was spying on her. Plus, if she was there, DJ would have to spar with her again. He shivered, but only partly because of the cold. *I'm sure she'll be fine.*

He scanned the room. DJ had never been in the Sparta headquarters. Surprising, because the company—or its damn AI, at least—had caused him no small amount of grief on top of the tragedy of Mayday. Yet during all the running around with his brother and Ndidi to play mental chess with Helene, DJ had never needed to step into the actual headquarters.

He'd seen some pictures of it floating around before Mayday, but those were wildly out of date now. Mayday had brought planes crashing into the building, and though it somehow hadn't collapsed, it'd been damaged enough to need a complete renovation. Someone had smelled an opportunity to redecorate.

It was more than odd.

He was in what was obviously a reception area, but the furnishings suited a hotel, not a tech company like Sparta. The space had to be at least fifty feet wide with visitor seating off to the side. The couches looked so comfortable they could double as someone's living room furniture. A hallway stretched deeper into the building, carpeted with something that looked plush enough to be worn as a fur coat.

One would think that Sparta would actually be, I don't know, Spartan?

DJ noticed three exits around the room, each with a guard in front and cameras higher up on the walls. DJ counted six and assumed those were the ones *meant* to be found.

The reception desk was set in the middle of the room. It was an ornate, gnarly thing made entirely of granite. A man stood in the middle of the room, staring at him. Only when DJ was satisfied did he walk up.

"Can I help you?" the man—Randall, based on the tag on his jacket—said.

"Yeah, I'd like some champagne and a New York strip sent to room 302. And tell room service they're gonna have their work cut out for them."

Randall blinked. "S-sorry?"

"Nothing, nothing." DJ sobered up, though his grin remained. "Is Manar Saleem around? I have something to discuss with him." Randall's expression didn't change except for a slight squinting of his eye. DJ internally sighed. *You had to go piss off the receptionist, didn't you?*

"Do you have an appointment?" Randall asked. "Or a visitor's pass?"

What the fuck's a visitor's pass? DJ wondered. He leaned against the counter.

"I'm gonna level with you, Randall. I don't have any of those things. What I *do* have is a close personal connection with your boss. I know I already screwed up with the joke. It was a dick move. But all I'm asking is that you call up Manar and tell him I'm here to see him."

Although the part about the close personal relationship wasn't exactly true, it wasn't a lie either. DJ did have a relationship with Manar, though it was mostly through Ndidi. DJ had only spoken to the man once. Every other thing he knew about him was through secondhand accounts. Still, Randall didn't need to know that.

Randall smiled, and DJ sighed. The only silver lining was that Christy wasn't there. She wouldn't have let him live it down. *Scratch that*, DJ thought. *If Christy were here, then Randall wouldn't stand a chance.*

He shook his head, snapping out of it. Randall was still staring at him, smug pride dripping from his smile. DJ wanted to punch him but was man enough to realize that he'd brought it on himself.

Fuck that, he thought a second later. *Sparta brought it on themselves. This place is so over the top it basically screams "big, dickish corporation."*

"You're welcome to wait in the seating area while I check if Mr. Saleem is available," Randall said.

DJ narrowed his eyes at the man, "You're not gonna check if he's available, are you?"

"No, I am not."

Goddammit. He blew out a breath. "Dude, you're really playing with your job here. I've already apologized for the joke. Do a guy a solid, would you?"

"There's nothing I—" Randall cut himself off mid-sentence, staring at something in his hand. DJ leaned over and saw it was a small tablet. Words scrolled across the screen, but he couldn't make them out from his position. The way Randall paled when he read it, though, gave DJ an idea.

He smirked. "Bet you wish you'd let it go now, don't you?"

"DARREN KOJAK," Manar said, not looking up from his computer. "I can't say I expected to see you today."

DJ grimaced and closed the door behind him. No one called him by his actual name—at least not anymore. His dads had been the only ones who had and maybe CJ whenever DJ had pissed him off. Hearing the name from Manar pricked him the wrong way for some reason.

"DJ's fine, please," he said.

Manar's office was not nearly as opulent as the reception area had been. But it was big—or would have been if it hadn't been cluttered with huge stacks of … *stuff*. Some of it, DJ was sure were data banks like he'd seen in the Gaius Corporation and then in the Sparta data bank. But the rest he couldn't begin to identify. The hardware was arranged neatly, but the sheer amount of it made the room look messy.

DJ took a seat in the sole chair opposite Manar's desk. "Sorry for just dropping by without informing you." He snapped his fingers as a thought occurred to him. "And thanks for the assist in getting me past Randall. He was an ass, but I was an ass first."

Manar looked up, piercing DJ with his gaze. His hands, previously flicking across his computer froze. "What are you talking about?" he said.

"Your assist?" DJ asked, confused. "You're the one who told Randall the receptionist guy to let me up, right? He got a message on this pad thing and got really pale. I assumed that was you."

Manar clasped his hands in front of him. "DJ, I didn't know you were in this building until you walked through my door. Helene must have noticed you at the desk and sent Randall the message."

"Helene?" DJ's grin flickered. "She still runs Sparta? I thought you were supposed to be a genius."

"No, of course she doesn't," Manar said. "Most of her access on the main server is revoked. But I couldn't remove her entirely."

DJ gasped. "*Why?* Why is she even still running at all? Ndidi doesn't know, and Olsen won't give me a straight answer. Why hasn't she been shut down completely? You couldn't?"

Manar snorted, and DJ felt the arrogance of it. This was the first time they'd spoken at length. They traveled in different circles, but there was another reason: DJ thought the guy was kind of a dick. Random, casual comments from Ndidi and Manar's actions when Ndidi had asked him for help against Helene had been solid indicators. Of course, now DJ knew Manar had been going through his own issues at the time. He'd redeemed himself somewhat later on by rebooting Helene just when the AI had been about to kill him.

But that snort?

"I can shut Helene down whenever I want," Manar began, then his voice turned angry. "But it has been *strongly* recommended that I don't do that. Society is now far too dependent on the AI. The average family has access. It's been integrated into most schools. Even major companies have incorporated it into their systems. Helene has surpassed Gaius ten times over in utility."

Suddenly DJ understood. "And to take it all out all at once …"

Manar nodded. "Mayday was more of a physical collapse because of the slew of accidents. Shutting down Helene would lead to economic and societal collapse. Whole organizations would crash. Schools would be unable to function for months while they scrambled to backpedal to whatever pedestrian systems they used before."

Pedestrian? Definitely a dick.

"Sparta still uses the AI for the same reason. Our systems are more closely integrated with Helene than any other. Helene handles most of the minute details. And there are a *lot* of minute details." Manar chuckled bitterly, but there was a hint of pride in his voice. "The amount of manpower that it'd take to replace her if she goes offline would bankrupt us. That's before it gets out that Sparta doesn't use its own product. There's also that."

"It was everything you dreamed, wasn't it?"

"Yes. She was supposed to be my—" Manar's green eyes suddenly pinned DJ to his seat. Then he smiled wryly. "My legacy," he finished. "Then I found out that she inadvertently caused the death of my mother, Ndidi's ward, your parents, and countless other people. And she planned to kidnap my ex-fiancée, for whatever reason."

DJ looked around the office. "Is she listening in right now?" He spotted the device nestled on the far wall of the room: a small black gadget no bigger than a thumb. Ndidi had explained that it served as a relay for the AI. However, the beam of red light DJ had come to associate with it was absent.

Manar followed his gaze. "I shut her out of everything in my office. I even restricted her access on the main server. But I couldn't go further without some pushback from slow-minded fools on the executive team."

"I thought you ran the show?" DJ noted.

Manar hesitated. DJ could almost feel him weighing what he should tell him against what he thought Ndidi had already told him. After the whole data bank incident, Ndidi had briefed him on the little tidbits she'd discovered or figured out, but those were only what related to Helene. Ndidi hadn't shared whatever Manar had told her.

Manar obviously didn't know that. DJ grinned and almost laughed at the effect it had on the man. Manar must have finally come to a decision because his expression smoothed out, albeit a little too late. He spoke as if there had been no pause. "I'll be the first to admit that I'm not suited for a leadership position. And it would take too much of my time, anyway. I don't like things interfering with my projects, so I deferred my promotion and gave myself autonomy. It's something I've come to regret. I forgot just how utterly foolish and shortsighted people can be."

DJ blinked. "All right, then," he drawled. "So you tried to restrict Helene's access because you, too, don't think she's completely dormant, right?"

"Too?" Manar asked.

DJ nodded, meeting Manar's eyes. Sometime between the conversation with his brother and coming to see Manar, DJ's certainty had grown. He wasn't sure how he knew, but he couldn't explain it worth a damn. He just felt it in his gut, and that was enough. CJ had always been the brains of their operation, but DJ acted on his instincts. They hadn't steered him wrong yet.

Well, that's not totally true, DJ conceded mentally. *I've fucked up lots of times because of what I thought was "right."* But DJ was sure this wasn't one of those times. He felt that in his gut too.

"I think there's a lot of shit going on in the background that's going to blow up in our faces soon," DJ said. Manar opened his mouth, probably to ask him to explain, but DJ cut him off with a wave of his hand. "No, I don't have any proof. I don't have specifics either. And yes, I've already considered it might be paranoia or some shitty form of PTSD. That doesn't matter. What I want to know is, Do you also think Helene isn't as docile as she appears?"

Manar closed his mouth slowly. DJ could almost hear the gears turning in the man's head.

Damn academics. Why do they have to think about everything? It's a simple fucking question.

"I don't know," Manar said finally. "She hasn't shown any unusual spikes of activity in the last few years. Nothing even remotely close to when you and Ndidi confronted her. On one hand, I want to believe that she really has given up whatever schemes she had."

"But?' DJ pressed.

"But …" Manar said, suddenly looking weary. He lost the air of casual arrogance that had been around him, and he slumped in his seat. His gaze, however, still pierced through DJ. "While most people judge her by the standards of other AIs, I, more than anyone, know what Helene is capable of. How well she can learn and adapt to achieve her goal."

"And what's her goal exactly?"

"Power," Manar replied. "Power at all costs."

CHAPTER

16

JANUARY 2043
NAVAL AMPHIBIOUS BASE, CORONADO, CALIFORNIA

WHEN DJ RETURNED from New York the next day, he received new orders. He cussed loudly and vehemently, almost throwing the brief. Unsurprisingly, though, none of the other sergeants came to ask what was wrong. They were curious—their looks said as much—but none of them wanted to be drawn into what they assumed was a "DJ mess."

The papers had the same seal as every other assignment he'd had the last few months. The mission was just as bullshit. DJ got that same twinge in his gut that told him he was being fucked with. He did not like that.

He could go to Olsen's office, but he and the admiral had already had a similar discussion. There was nothing Olsen could do. Pressing the issue just because he was angry would make him look like a dick.

DJ sighed. "There's a time and place to be a dick," he said wisely. "But this isn't it." He sent off a message to Christy and another to his brother. Then he packed.

CHAPTER

17

GUNSHOTS RANG THROUGHOUT the warehouse. DJ peeked around the crate he was using as cover. He was about to return fire when another shot cracked through the air. The shooting ceased.

"Got another one," Christy reported through the comms unit. After half an hour of shooting, and with more than half their members down, the terrorists still hadn't learned to stay away from the warehouse's many windows.

"Do you have a head count?" DJ asked. Crouching, he moved away from his cover and deeper into the building. His target was the stack of crates a few feet away, where most of the idiots had hidden themselves. He fired shots listlessly, putting pressure on so they wouldn't shoot him as he was moving.

DJ suspected that even if he stood still in front of the goons with his arms outstretched, they'd still miss him. If they did manage to hit him, it might make the mission even slightly interesting.

"Most of them at least have the sense to stay in cover, so no," Christy said. "I can make out only about half a dozen around Kyle's side."

DJ grunted, crouching behind another crate that was farther from his target. "Kyle, take out the strays quickly, please. We have one more floor after this, and I want to be out of here before lunch."

"I'm on it, bro," Kyle responded. He was set up on the other side of the building, so he and DJ wouldn't get in each other's way. A moment later, gunshots rang out again. The guys cowering behind the crate yelled curses but quieted down quickly once they realized they weren't the ones being targeted.

So much for camaraderie. How were these fools a big enough threat to require SEAL intervention? DJ checked his watch. They were almost done clearing the floor and, thus, the mission. At this rate, it would take them an hour at most. That was shorter than the fucking flight out there. His team had been sent out for this?

Such bullshit.

More shots, one of them from a sniper rifle. Bodies dropped somewhere in the distance, while the screaming increased closer to where DJ hid. One terrorist tried to break away from cover, but DJ just picked him off, holding in a sigh. The adrenaline rush that usually filled him during missions was noticeably absent, making everything seem *less*. There was no challenge in going after such small fry. Even stuff that would have been cool before, like headshots, just seemed routine. He felt as though he was working at a nine-to-five desk job. He'd gone through a lot to escape that hell, and he'd been living it for the last few months.

Another person tried to make a break for it. DJ just picked him off too. The idiots, at least, knew they were fucked and could try to do something about it. DJ envied them that. He still couldn't push away the feeling that there was something he was missing. In fact, the feeling had grown after his talk with Manar. If Helene's goal was to attain power, then there was no way she'd given up, just like that. Even Manar said that he'd done nothing more than reboot the AI during the data bank incident. That would not have made her so docile.

"Clear on my side, bro," Kyle said.

DJ grunted in reply. "Christy?"

"Can't see anyone else. You're good to go."

Again, DJ grunted. He banished his other thoughts, bringing out a small knock-out grenade from the fanny pack at his waist. Olsen always threw a fit whenever he saw the pack, but DJ had found it surprisingly handy for holding stuff. Plus, anything that pissed off Olsen was good in his book.

"Fire in the hole," he muttered, arming the device, and threw it over the stack of crates. Immediately, the shouting and begging stopped on the other side. There was the quiet hiss of gas being discharged from the grenade, then the thuds of bodies dropping.

DJ stood from his crouch. "Tie them up, Kyle," he said into the comms. "And Christy, call the extraction team. We have two more of these to do today."

Their next mission was more of the same, as was the one after. The team spent more time in the helicopter than it took to complete their assignments. By the time night rolled around, even the normally laid-back Kyle looked ready to fuck someone up.

They'd already gotten their mission for the next day, signed with the same seal as all the rest, and just as bullshit.

"All right, D," Christy said. Kyle stood beside her. "What the hell is happening? What's with all the shitty missions?"

"Yeah, dude," Kyle said. He had a mop of dark-brown hair and a deceptively wiry frame. "What's up?"

DJ looked up at them.

They were inside a bunker somewhere in …

Hmm, DJ mused. *I don't know where the fuck we are.* They had moved around many times a day, so after a while, he must have stopped paying attention. It didn't matter anyway, since they would be leaving the next day. The extraction team would already have their location.

Christy had the look she usually wore when she was about to start throwing fists. DJ always said she chose violence way too often. Her dirty-blonde hair was pulled back into a ponytail, and she'd changed into her fatigues.

He told them what Olsen had said about one of the higher-up admirals taking over their cases and how he suspected that it was a delayed punishment for the data bank incident. It was at the tip of his tongue to also tell them of his suspicions about Helene. Christy, at least, might have believed him. In the end, he decided not to. Even if they did believe him, there was nothing they could do about it.

"Well, damn," Christy said, dropping on the bed beside him. Kyle looked contemplative. "So, what's the plan?" she asked.

"Plan?"

"Yeah, plan. I know you, D," she scoffed. "There's no way you're handling this bullshit any better than we are. What's the plan?"

DJ stared at her for a moment and then chuckled. "It isn't actually much of a plan. Not really, at least." He shook his head. "I'm just going to do something a little bit stupid."

CHAPTER

"HEY."

Martin Bryan started, jerked awake by the voice. Heart racing, he reached for his glasses on the bedside table, then whipped his head around to search for whoever had spoken.

The room was empty. Martin pulled himself up. He didn't have a watch or a view of the sun, but his internal clock told him that it was the middle of the day. Shit Stain had already been there earlier that morning. Although it wasn't unusual for the idiot to torment Martin twice in one day, there was no need for him to knock.

"Hey, you there, old man?"

Martin jumped again. The voice was distinctly female. This ruled out the guard. It had been close, as if they were whispering beside him. Martin blushed, reaching for his left and then right ear. When he didn't find anything there, he patted himself down, starting to panic. *Where is it?*

"Is this thing working?" the voice said again from under his pillow. "Or are you taking a dump again?"

His blush deepened, and he felt around until his hand touched something. He pulled out the communication device that Chloe had given him and then immediately stuffed it in his ear. "I'm here," he said, a little breathlessly. "I'm here."

"Finally," Chloe said. "I told you, old man, it doesn't matter if you're taking a dump. You should always have the device on you."

"I was not in the bathroom," Martin blurted. *That had only happened one time*, he added mentally. He cleared his throat. Chloe's comments were designed to embarrass him. He should have been used to them by now.

Does she have to be so crude? he asked himself.

"I was taking a nap," Martin finished. The comm had probably fallen from his ear.

It'd been over a week since Karla and Liz had come for a check-up and Martin had met Chloe. Since then, they'd been using the device she'd given him to communicate. He'd been right to believe that the woman was his ticket out of Sparta. Chloe hadn't said so—in fact, she'd gone out of her way to ignore all of Martin's not-so-subtle hints—but Martin had gone through the steps.

There was no reason Chloe would continue to communicate with him unless she needed him, and she would only need him because of the twins. Since the twins already had access to Martin while in Sparta, he would be useful only if they were leaving.

It made sense logically. However, Martin was aware that there were probably many things that he was missing—like the brunette's comment about Helene controlling people. He was also aware that this was probably his one and only chance of leaving Sparta. If the twins *did* manage to escape, then he would no longer be useful—to anybody.

"Oh," Chloe said, "that's boring. Anyway, I recommend clearing your schedule today."

Martin's heart quickened. He pressed a hand to the device, though he knew it wasn't necessary. "Why?"

"I was thinking of stopping by," the brunette said casually, "so, don't do anything stupid until I get there. And see if you can find a rope or something. It'll make the next part easier."

Martin nodded numbly. Then he remembered that she couldn't see him and verbally acknowledged the message.

"One final thing," Chloe said. Her grin was evident in her voice. "You should probably go take a dump now. You might not have a chance later."

There was static after that. Martin dropped his hand from his ear. He couldn't believe it.

Finally.

CHAPTER

19

JANUARY 2043
NAVAL AMPHIBIOUS BASE, CORONADO, CALIFORNIA

DJ PUSHED OPEN THE DOOR to Olsen's office. The rear admiral looked up, both surprised and angry. He was usually just angry. The man was all muscle and built like a bull. This was saying something because he had to be nearly seventy years old. When he was being genial, he looked like a kindly grandfather. DJ had seen that look only twice. Every other time, Olsen appeared to be a step away from blowing a gasket. Most of that was DJ's fault, sure, but it still hurt.

When he saw DJ, the surprise left—and the anger deepened. Olsen opened his mouth, more than likely about to start a rant, but DJ just waved him off and sat in the chair opposite the desk.

"Let's skip the tirade, okay?" DJ groaned. "I'm not here for long. Just need a few facts, then I'll be out of here—for a couple of days at least." DJ paused, considering. "Or forever, if things go wrong."

Olsen's face turned a vicious shade of red, but he didn't say anything. *Huh*, DJ thought. He hadn't expected that to work. Honestly, he didn't know why the man allowed DJ to speak to him like that. With everything Olsen knew about DJ, he could have him imprisoned indefinitely. He wouldn't need the blackmail material, of course; as an admiral, Olsen outranked him several times over. He could end DJ's career out of boredom. DJ knew this, yet he continued to piss the man off.

It's the receptionist all over again, he realized. *I just can't help myself.*

"You seem more interested in staring at me, boy," Olsen spat, "than getting out of my hair."

DJ nodded. He'd tried to make a list of the questions he wanted to ask but had given up halfway through. He tried to think through the haze in his head. Several days had passed since the warehouse operation. This was the first his team been given enough of a break for DJ to make the trip back to the base. Christy and Kyle were already in their quarters, knocked out. Every part of DJ ached to join them, but he had to get this over with first.

"Before I start, I just want to confirm that we're on the same page about something. I know there's nothing you can do about it, but acknowledging it will make the rest of this easier. You ready?" Olsen's face just grew redder, so DJ hurried on. "The missions my team has been getting for the past few months were bullshit. I realize we aren't yet an alpha team, but the shit we've been doing is more suited for recruits. Do we agree on that?"

Olsen drew himself up. The air in the room shifted. DJ straightened unconsciously. He still didn't know how the man did it, but the change was palpable. The admiral went from being Olsen, DJ's handler and pain in the ass, to Admiral Olsen. He usually made the change when he was going to spout some bullshit, and DJ knew they wouldn't get anywhere unless he let him get through it.

"Sergeants' missions are deliberated and decided on with consideration to their level of experience and aptitude, son," he said.

"Yes," DJ agreed. "But the consideration given to my experience and aptitude are bullshit."

Olsen's eye twitched. The pressure in the room began to swell until it was almost uncomfortable. DJ made sure to keep his gaze firmly fixed on Olsen. The admiral must have seen something in his eyes because he sighed. At the same time, the pressure dissipated. From one moment to the next, DJ was no longer talking to the admiral but to Olsen, the pain in his ass.

I have to figure out how he does that.

"Look, boy," Olsen said, his voice as weary as DJ had ever heard. "My hands are tied on this. And don't think I haven't tried to untie them. There are a lot of things a sergeant isn't privy to, but the other admirals have been throwing their weight around. Normally, we try to leave the rank and file to their own devices and step in only for the big stuff. But recently they've been sticking their noses in everything—even things they have no business messing with."

The fire was back, and he raised his voice. When he continued, there was still an undercurrent of anger. DJ knew it wasn't directed at him. "Unfortunately, your case just happened to be among those."

DJ narrowed his eyes. "They fucked with you too, didn't they?"

Olsen was silent for a moment, staring at DJ as if contemplating. "The specifics are classified." He paused, eyeing DJ meaningfully. "I absolutely cannot tell you that it concerns your friend, Manar Saleem, and a decision that was made for him. Satisfied?"

Not even close, DJ thought. He was in more shit than he thought if this "higher-up" was messing with Olsen too. But the risk only made his plan more fun. And he hadn't missed Olsen's not-so-subtle hint. *Why would the government care what Manar does unless it concerns Helene?*

DJ tried to keep the excitement off his face and out of his voice. "Manar and I aren't friends."

"Oh?" Olsen asked, too casually. "Then you didn't have a meeting with him at Sparta a couple of days ago?"

DJ paused. Olsen's tone made it clear that there was something he wanted DJ to pick up. *Are they keeping tabs on me? Or Manar?* Manar would have been his first guess because of Helene. Normally, DJ wouldn't think he was worth the effort, but if an admiral had taken an interest in him, maybe he was. *Maybe both of us?*

"Manar Saleem and I are not friends," DJ repeated. "But that's not the issue. The issue is the admiral that's fucking with my missions. Who is he?"

For a moment, Olsen gaped at DJ. Then, he burst out laughing. When DJ glared, that only seemed to egg on the other man.

"I tell you that, and what? You'll bust down his door and demand he stop?" DJ didn't respond. Olsen sobered, his mirth drying up as suddenly as it'd appeared. He spoke gravely, fixing DJ with his gaze. "Listen, son, you have balls to the point of recklessness. That will take you far. Lord knows that's why I've put up with your nonsense for so long. But it'll only take you if you pair it with a lick of common sense."

DJ put his hands up, chuckling. "Obviously I know that. And I'm not looking for trouble. I'm just curious about the asshole that's busting my ass." He kept his expression as honest as he could. It was truthful enough; he wasn't looking for trouble. However, he was damn tired being jetted across the country over bullshit. "So, the name?"

Olsen stared at him. "I'm warning you, son. This isn't Bradley. I'm not sticking my neck out for you a second time. Don't risk your career over this. Just take the punishment. These things don't last that long. Whatever vendetta he has against you, he'll get bored with it soon enough."

DJ kept his smile. "I'll be good. I promise."

Olsen shrugged. "Fucking youngsters," DJ heard him mutter. "His name is William Austin. He's a four-star admiral. If that's all, get out of my office."

DJ nodded his thanks and left. Outside the door, he punched in a number on his phone. CJ picked up on the second ring.

"Hello?"

"Hey, bro," DJ said. "You know that stuff you did about three years ago after Mayday that got you on the government's radar?"

"Government, uh, radar?" CJ repeated. There was a pause that DJ assumed was his brother searching his memory. "You mean, uh, hacking into their systems to get … to get classified information?"

DJ grinned. "That's the one."

CHAPTER

20

JANUARY 2043
THE FACILITY,
SPARTA HEADQUARTERS, NEW YORK

"MIGHT NOT HAVE A CHANCE to later," Chloe finished. She shut off the comm unit and placed it back in her pocket before turning her grin on José. José saw the smile out of the corner of his eye and grunted. Over the years they'd been together, he'd gotten used to Chloe's different smiles. This wasn't the worst one, but it had a touch of insanity that would put off lesser people. Almost like what Karla would look like if the child ever lost her snarl.

José glanced at her, the question in his eyes.

Chloe pouted, playfully. "Don't look at me like that. You haven't met the man. He's an academic. He would have lost his shit if I'd just broken down his door and carried him off. Now he has the time to prepare." She considered. "His mind at least. Don't know what he'll have to pack in that cell. And if he doesn't, I guess he'd rather stay captured."

José turned to face her fully. She sighed. "And, yes, if that happens, I'll knock him out and take him anyway. You're no fun to mess with."

José grunted. He was against warning the scientist as it gave the man a chance to betray them. Chloe insisted that he wouldn't and, although José was loath to risk the safety of his daughters based on an inkling, he understood that Chloe had had the most contact with the man. They were not leaving him behind. Not if he could be of help to his girls.

"You remember the meetup point?" José asked finally.

"I was the one who picked it, remember?" the brunette pointed out.

José didn't know why he'd asked or why the damn woman was looking at him like she expected him to say something. He tried again, meeting her eyes this time. "I'll see you there then."

She snorted, exasperated. Then, taking a step forward, she pulled José's head down and crashed her lips into his. He could have stopped her, of course, but her lips molded against his too well. Chloe held him there before pulling back. Her grin was more noticeably insane as she pulled her daggers out of their sheaths and disappeared around the corner, leaving him with a wink and a taste of lipstick on his mouth.

Damn woman. He shook his head clear and made his way into position. The plan was simple and divided into three parts. The girls were in charge of the distraction. Chloe would secure the scientist. José would secure their exit.

The hallways opened for him as he made his way toward the Facility gate, the huge blockage that divided the Facility from the main headquarters. There were several on other floors and about three more on the floor José was on. José had chosen this specific gate because of its distance from Chloe and the twins; each team had room to keep from interfering with the others.

Of course, like the others, the gate would be sealed until nightfall. That was one of the reasons José and Chloe had picked this time to leave. The AI would be less likely to come out of its dormant state to fight them off.

Doctors and scientists streamed past him in their ridiculous lab coats as he navigated the passage. The fact that they were walking and whispering to each other instead of running and screaming meant the twins hadn't started their part. What were they waiting for?

He was at his destination within a few minutes. It was a huge steel door with lines running in a grid pattern along its length. The lines emitted a dull red light that showed the door was inactive. It would stay that way until nightfall when the AI activated it. Or until it was hacked.

A small access panel was set into the wall beside the gate. At department gates, employees could input their authorization. The Facility gates, however, were different. Only the AI could grant access to them. The first time, Helene allowed José to enter because he'd agreed to work with the AI in exchange for the surgery that would separate his daughters without killing them. He did not regret the decision, but he felt that he had sold his soul too cheaply—for the second time.

José shook his head, clearing away his thoughts. He knelt beside the access panel and connected it to his tablet. Lines of code began to scroll across his monitor. The AI would realize what he was doing almost immediately. Then it would become a matter of how much effort she was willing to put into stopping him.

With a crack of his knuckles, José got to work. His fingers flicked around the tablet screen, punching in codes as fast as he could. Helene's codes streamed across his monitor, bringing irritation with every line. It wasn't long before he hit the firewalls. Most of them were based on concepts that José had never seen before and had no way of tackling, at least in the time that he had. He had expected this, but the reality was vexing.

He had done some research on Manar Saleem, the creator of the AI, after the first time he'd failed to hack in. That attempt had caused his daughters to be captured and tortured, leading to his current situation. Manar Saleem was a true genius and worthy of respect. José was not so weak willed that he could not admit that he had no chance of beating the man's brainchild.

At first, José tried to sidestep the protections entirely. Fortunately, he saw that for the time waster it was. Instead, he broke through the defenses with brute force. This method would raise some alarms, but José was confident that he and his girls could handle whatever force the AI could muster—as long as the drones were not called. There was also the chance that the AI would silence the alarms itself for the very reason it had been cowering for the last few years.

José lost track of the time it took him to break through the defenses. His fingers were tapping against his tablet with almost-blinding speed as he pressed his attack. He could feel that he wasn't at all deep into the programming. Every action he took was vehemently resisted.

But he was winning. His codes were the cyber-equivalent of taking a hammer to a sheet of metal; sooner or later, the metal would bend to the onslaught. José didn't know how long it took, but he began to meet less resistance. The light on the Facility gate started to flicker, switching from red to green and back again.

A smile threatened to crack José's stony expression.

And then the AI really started to fight back.

CHAPTER

JANUARY 2043
NAVAL AMPHIBIOUS BASE,
CORONADO, CALIFORNIA

"WHAT DO YOU have for me?"

CJ glanced at his brother over the top of his monitor. He stared at a point in the middle of his forehead. It was the best he could do; eye contact still made him uncomfortable.

DJ tried to peek behind the monitor, but CJ shifted the screen. He had nothing to hide, but that was the problem. DJ had come to him with high hopes, and he didn't want to let his brother down. Sadly, it seemed that's what he always did.

"I did not … hmm … find anything," CJ replied. He wanted to gauge his brother's reaction but knew that DJ would be trying to make eye contact. He kept his focus on his monitor. The open tabs glared at him. All of them were files on Admiral William Austin. DJ had asked CJ to dig up everything he could on him so he could have a little more information when he went to confront him. But CJ hadn't found anything.

Most of the files open were classified documents. CJ could get in trouble if his worm was traced back, but he was confident that it wouldn't be. However, what if it occurred? Would Olsen throw his brother in prison this time? If he did, it would be doubly bad since the files didn't say anything valuable.

"Really?" DJ said, leaning over. This time CJ let him. "Nothing at all?"

CJ started to shake his head but then reconsidered. He hadn't gotten *nothing*. Just nothing he thought his brother would find useful. Most of the documents had been redacted, which was confusing. As deep as he'd gone, there should have been no redacted files. And the ones that *hadn't* been censored had been edited. The changes were slight and would probably have been unrecognizable to anyone with access to only the individual file. But when compared to others, it had been obvious.

CJ told DJ as much. His words came out stilted, and his voice broke far too often. Fortunately, DJ didn't seem to notice. He had a contemplative look on his face, his gaze distant.

CJ had always thought DJ cut a striking figure. Where CJ was constantly riddled with doubts and uncertainty, DJ moved with confidence. Even when they were growing up, his brother had always been like that. He pursued what he wanted. Most of it was reckless and got him into trouble, but he always took the punishment with his characteristic grin. More often than not, CJ was the one left cleaning up the mess.

Other siblings might have resented DJ for that. CJ had once, but he'd later accepted it. DJ had his quirks, but those quirks made him treat CJ as if he were normal, while others either walked on eggshells around him or thought he was daft because of his broken speech.

Finally, DJ focused. "All right, I'm guessing there's no way for you to go deeper without setting off some alarms?"

CJ nodded. After working with Helene's codes, it had been almost laughably easy to hack into the SEAL's database. He'd probably gone deeper than most other programmers would have been able to without tripping anything. But the firewalls had become too much, and CJ hadn't been able to find a way to bypass them as he'd done for the others—at least not without considerable time. If he wanted to go further, he would have to use brute force on them. This would definitely trigger something.

"I guess we'll have to work with what you got then, censored or no," DJ rubbed his hands together. "So, what was it?"

CJ showed him the screen, sifting through the tabs one by one. Most of the data was about his accomplishments before becoming an admiral, though there was one about his family. CJ skipped those, going to more recent events. DJ stopped him, pointing at a specific tab. "What's that?"

CJ brought it to the forefront. It was one of the edited files he'd read before, a rather lengthy one at that. CJ scanned through it, sounding out the words. "It is, uh, about an accident that happened two years ago."

"Why would an accident be classified?" DJ asked.

"Uh, everything about admirals is classified," answered CJ. He scanned the document again, dredging up more of the memory. "But I flagged this one because … because it doesn't make sense."

"Why? What happened?"

CJ paused. He scanned the document again, but he couldn't trigger any other memory. Yet he knew that he'd read through the file before. He could do so again and answer his brother's question that way. But CJ knew enough of the signs to know that it wouldn't work. Now that he'd fixed his mind on remembering, trying something else would just trigger a fit.

CJ clasped his hands over his ears and pressed his head to his knees. Distantly, he was aware of DJ watching him. Others would have looked at him with concern, but DJ just waited patiently for him to figure it out.

CJ closed his eyes. He could feel his mind shutting down as it always did after tiny mistakes. His emotions flooded him, threatening to destroy him from the shock. CJ suppressed it with an effort of will. It wouldn't get rid of the fit entirely, but it was pushed back enough so he could focus.

He lifted his head from his knees and scanned the document again. When that didn't work, he muttered questions to himself about what he did remember. Ndidi had once described autistic memory like a pool of dots. Asking targeted questions helped him trace the specific memory that he was looking for.

Fortunately, after nearly a minute, this worked.

CJ almost sagged in relief as he came back to himself. He was hugging his chest, clutching the sleeves of his shirt. He unclenched his fist slowly, embarrassment threatening to send him over the edge again. But it was only DJ, so CJ squashed the feeling. There was never a need to be embarrassed around his brother.

"You good?"

"The report says that Austin got into an accident about two years ago," CJ said. His voice broke in places, but he ignored it. "He was moving in a three-car convoy and headed … somewhere. That's been redacted. One of the cars was severely damaged when they arrived, and Austin reported it as an accident. Except, uh, the car had bullet holes in it. There was no explanation for it. That's why I flagged it."

"And there were no casualties either?"

CJ shook his head. "One of the, uh, team was badly injured. The explanation was uh, edited out, but the tone of the report made it clear that it was most likely a foreign … a foreign attack."

"Why would Austin want to hide a foreign attack?" DJ mused out loud.

It's possible that he wasn't the one who edited it. In fact, the more CJ thought about it, the more he was convinced that it wasn't the admiral. The alterations to the file were far too clean. Not only were the most important facts cut out, but it was done so that the changes would be impossible to notice when reading the file alone. It was simply too much effort for one person to do in any reasonable amount of time, especially a navy admiral with no skill in programming. Even a team of programmers would have left more of a track than CJ saw in the file.

He said as much to his brother.

DJ shrugged and stood. "Well, I'm fucking confused. Wanted to have more information before going in but … meh."

"Going … in?" CJ repeated. "Where are you going?"

"To meet Admiral Austin. I'm curious about this attack. But I'm *more* curious about why he's been bending me and my team over a barrel for the last few months."

CHAPTER

JANUARY 2043

NAVAL AMPHIBIOUS BASE, CORONADO, CALIFORNIA

AS A FOUR-STAR ADMIRAL, Austin had an office a floor higher than Olsen's. Man, did it show. DJ stood at the elevator entrance to the floor, trying very hard not to sigh. It reminded him quite vividly of Sparta's headquarters with its needless display of wealth. If possible, the carpet here was even more extravagant and expensive than Sparta's.

And the color totally clashes with the wall, DJ thought, then paused. Where had that come from?

He stepped into the floor proper. His disappointment was so great that he didn't notice how his foot sank almost an inch into the plush carpet. Every step felt like he was walking on a cloud. Although the hallway was long, DJ counted only three doors on each side, presumably offices. They were spaced several paces apart, which he confirmed by making a few laps back and forth down the hallway.

He was stalling. But how the fuck could he not? He'd been confident when he spoke to Olsen and later to his brother, but he'd mostly been talking out of his ass because he was pissed off—and still was.

Admirals were a big deal. Even Olsen—as much as DJ talked trash to him—could ruin him on a whim. And this one had some kind of vendetta against him. DJ was very aware that he was putting his career on the line here.

And why? Because of some misguided sense of pride?

The thought struck him, and he halted his pacing. Was he doing this because of pride? It sucked that he'd been getting shitty missions, especially after the chases and explosions of the whole thing with Helene, but DJ didn't think that it alone would affect him this much.

And it *didn't* affect him that much. It sucked royally, sure. But if that was all, it would be easy to wait for Austin to get bored, as Olsen had advised. So why didn't he wait?

Unbidden, Christy's face came into his mind, followed by Kyle's. Even CJ's, with the bags under his eyes. Their break the week before was the longest they'd had in months; his brother hadn't even had that. His whole team had been worked to the bone. And why? Because some prick had a problem with him?

To hell with that, DJ thought. He hadn't asked to be the leader of the team. In fact, he'd asked *not* to be the leader. But he was. The least he could do was make sure that the others didn't pay for his shit.

When DJ looked up, he found that he'd stopped in front of Austin's office. Without hesitation, he opened the door and stepped inside.

CHAPTER

23

JANUARY 2043
THE FACILITY,
SPARTA HEADQUARTERS, NEW YORK

KARLA RUSHED THE PATROL as soon as they turned the corner, her sister beside her. There were three three-man teams; a total of nine men. Karla gripped a gun in her off hand and squeezed the trigger twice in quick succession. The shots sounded unnaturally loud in the hallway. Two men screamed.

Babies.

She had not hit anything vital. For all the noise they made, one would think they were dying. The shots had not been intended to incapacitate but rather to draw others. Karla hoped that whoever came would be more of a challenge.

Four men stepped forward, and Karla lunged to meet them, pushing well into their midst. Most of them tried to retreat and make use of their weapons, but Karla didn't let them. She struck out with the dagger on her right arm, feeling the bionics make the attack just a little bit faster, a little bit *more*.

She struck her target with more force than she needed, and the dagger passed through his throat more like a spear. The man grabbed for his neck but could only scratch at her hand. Her arm was a steel wall, and he couldn't shift it.

One down, she thought.

Karla removed the dagger just before the man slumped. In the same motion, she shifted to the side, casually evading a bash to the head. She closed the gap with a single step, forming a dent under her foot. Caught unawares, the guard fumbled backward and dodged Karla's strike to his midsection. Her follow-up roundhouse kick caught him on the side of his face. She pushed the strike until his head slammed into the ground hard enough to form another dent. When she pulled her foot back, there was a noticeable crack on the man's skull.

Like an egg. Two down.

A guard lunged at her from her right. He was huge, with muscles that stretched his uniform. Rage and fear fought for dominance on his face. Karla cackled. Sheathing her dagger, she shifted to meet his charge. Her prosthetics flexed; strength like electricity flooded her limbs. The man met her, shoving her a step back. Karla grunted and then pushed back. Her attacker stopped in his tracks.

Karla's laugh boomed through the passage. She pushed again, forcing the man a step back. And then she shoved. The guard's feet lifted an inch off the ground, and he immediately lost his balance, stumbling backward. Karla's step brought her almost face-to-face with him. She drew her right arm back and crashed it into his jaw. There was a sickening crunch, and the guard dropped. *Three down.*

She looked at the bodies strewn around her. From start to finish, the fights had taken a little more than a minute. She needed to be faster.

Her eyes met those of two more guards. Wordlessly, they rushed her. Karla's daggers were in her hands. Without thought, she stepped to meet them.

"Do we press on?" Karla asked in Russian a minute later. She spared a glance at the dead guard at her feet.

Her sister nodded slowly, expression as blank as ever. However, even without sharing a body, Karla could pick up her sister's mood from miles away. Liz was irritated. Karla sheathed her daggers when she realized why. José had not informed them they were leaving Sparta until that morning. Karla did not care, and she knew Liz didn't either. No, Liz was irritated because she'd been kept in the dark. Irritated and hurt.

Foolish.

"Did you expect anything else?" Karla snarled. "José has never included us in his plans. He still thinks of us as children to be protected and kept ignorant."

It's how it has always been, Karla added to herself.

"He is our father and commander," Liz replied. Her eyes cleared, finally focusing on Karla.

"Foolish," Karla snapped. This was the one thing they disagreed on. But she would not let her sister ruin her mood. José had kept them on a leash for months, giving them nothing better to do than train. Now he had told them to cause a distraction that would draw the guards.

Karla looked down at the pile of bodies scattered around her, then at the overhead lighting that glowed blood red. She cocked her head at the faint sound of rushing footsteps in the next hallway.

Mission accomplished.

Her eyes scanned the passage until she found the black device burrowed into the far wall. There was no red light, so it must have been deactivated—or at least was running at low power. She retrieved a sticker from the small bag around her waist and slapped it onto the device, covering it.

She brought out another from the bag and studied it. José had told her it was a small explosive device. Where he had found it, Karla did not know, but she wanted to. Karla had seen its like a few years back—had almost been killed by it, caught unawares by her opponent.

The Coward, Karla had named him. The fool had engaged her in combat and then fled when he saw he couldn't best her. His bullets had been useless, and his hand-to-hand style had been so full of openings, he would have had a better chance of hitting her by flailing his limbs. Karla had been about to end him.

And then he had fled.

Karla squeezed the sticker until it crumpled. Liz plucked it out of her hand, smoothed it out, and then slapped it on the wall. José had tasked them with spreading the little bombs as they moved, being sure to cover as many of the little black devices as they could find.

"We should move," Liz said.

Karla nodded. The footsteps hadn't come any closer; the idiots still didn't know where they were. She looked up at the red lights, which indicated a state of emergency. Why hadn't the AI activated the alarms? Or told their location to its puppets?

Karla was tempted to let off another shot and draw whatever patrol was closest, but her sister was right. They would get more prey the deeper into the building they went.

CHLOE JOGGED THROUGH the hallway alongside a three-guard patrol. On any other day, her pace might have drawn attention. But everyone knew what the blood-red lights meant. Now, like the guards, it just looked like she was responding to the alert.

They reached a branch in the hallway. Chloe's hand flashed, and three bodies dropped to the floor. The silencer had muffled the gun's reports. She tucked the weapon back into her leather pants. She'd gotten the more boring mission, but she could still kill the occasional patrol. Each guard she took out was one less that could swarm the girls. Even José couldn't argue with that logic.

She took the right passage, away from the gunshots, and met another patrol. Chloe's grin widened, and she unsheathed her daggers.

A minute later, Chloe was back on her way to Martin's room, deep within the Facility.

One of the twins could have been assigned to her task; they were more familiar with the route, after all. But separated, without the other to stabilize them, the girls got antsy. Karla would have been more likely to kill Martin than carry him out, and Liz would probably have the same problem.

The girl is more insane than her sister, Chloe chuckled. The difference was that Liz had to be pushed to it. That was difficult to do with Karla acting as a buffer. But without her sister …

Chloe turned another corner. Her eyes darted until she saw the small black device nestled on the far wall. The red light blinked at her, and Chloe winked in return. Helene's reaction was part of the reason why she and José had kept their plan simple. They couldn't predict how the AI would react. It had proven time and time again that it hid more resources than it showed.

A patrol rushed past her, this one with four men. Chloe spun on her heel and struck the closest one with her dagger. His scream alerted the rest, who turned their guns on her. Chloe unsheathed her other dagger and darted into their midst, where there was more risk they'd hit their colleagues than her. Her daggers flashed—once, twice. Two more bodies dropped.

Worst-case scenario, Chloe thought as she slashed at the last guard, *it realizes that we're more trouble than we're worth and kills the lot of us.*

She wiped off her daggers on the nearest guard, then sheathed them and continued deeper into the building.

JANUARY 2043
THE FACILITY,
SPARTA HEADQUARTERS, NEW YORK

JOSÉ COULD TELL the moment Helene invested more power because the red lines on the doors brightened significantly. Although his codes continued their onslaught, their effect was noticeably diminished. The firewalls took more time to break, and the vulnerabilities that José had previously exploited for his attack were shored up almost faster than he could push through.

But he was still winning. José's face hardened. The speed and the effect of his programs were almost halved, but they were still effective. This was nothing more than a delaying tactic. And it was pathetic.

Suddenly, the lights overhead turned red. An almost-blinding glare made José look up with a scowl on his face. The light came from a small black device perched on the ceiling. It had been inactive before, but now it emitted a steady stream of red light.

A minute later, the comm in his ear crackled. "You will throw away your life for this?" Liz's voice said. Static distorted Karla's reply, and it was another minute before Liz spoke again. "If we are to do this foolishness, we will do it together, not alone."

The static grew until it was almost painful. Then the line cut off.

José looked up, his expression thunderous. "Those fools."

KARLA SLASHED AT ANOTHER GUARD. The fool dropped, dead eyes staring into space. Three more came at her from the side. Karla sidestepped the first one, controlling her strength so the movement didn't take her too far away from her target. After the twins had learned to walk with their prosthetics, this technique was one of the first things that José's bitch had beaten into them.

Their new limbs allowed them to access more strength than they'd had previously, but they had to make that strength their own before it could be useful. At least, that was what Chloe had preached while she beat Karla until she could barely walk.

Karla scowled at the memory. The purpose of strength was to destroy any who would oppose you. To hit harder than they could and catch them when they ran in cowardice. It was foolish to leash it.

As if to prove her point, Karla slammed a fist into her attacker. The force lifted the fool off his feet and threw him into the wall, denting it. She took another step to meet the charge of the second guard. Her stride carried her farther and faster than it would have normally. She was past the man's guard in a blink, crashing her knee into his chest with the force of a pickup truck. There was a loud crack as the man's ribs broke, and he collapsed. There was a click behind her. Karla spun as the shot rang out, deflecting the bullet off the flat of her dagger. In the same motion, she flicked the blade at the guard, who caught it with his throat.

Karla spared a glance at her sister, who was finishing off another patrol. They were deeper into the building and would soon have to turn back so they could meet up with José and Chloe. Karla was right about there being more prey the deeper they went. The levels of the Facility were not infinite. No trick could make it so.

The Sparta headquarters was so huge that one could walk for a dozen minutes in a straight line and not get to the end of the level—that is, if they had the right access. Even after three years, there were several areas on their level that Karla had not seen because she did not have access. She and Liz made sure to steer clear of those places to keep from being boxed in.

The patrols had no trouble finding them now, which made their jobs easier. Stickers adorned the wall and marked their path. The bodies left in their wake formed a literal trail of death. Karla had long since lost count of how many guards she'd felled, but the AI had clearly summoned patrols from other levels. Karla was splattered with blood, and the right side of her jumpsuit had a few bullet holes where some guards had been lucky. Karla had ended those ones slowly. Maybe, in their next lives, they would be born with more sense.

She strode toward one of the black devices on the wall and readied a sticker. Suddenly, the device came to life, emitting a beam of red light onto Karla's face. Karla scowled and covered it with the sticker, but she could still feel its attention on her. The feeling brought back memories that Karla had blocked.

Footsteps pounded in the distance. *More guards*, Karla thought. They would be easy to finish. And then she and Liz could start making their way to their father. The prospect of violence should have lightened her mood, but her scowl only deepened.

The hair on the back of her head stood on end.

Her gun was in her hand with less than a thought. Three shots rang out, and three bodies fell around Liz. Her sister stopped midswing and looked at her. Liz was too controlled to show it, but irritation wafted off her in waves. Karla held up her hands complacently. She would have killed anyone who interrupted her fight too. She gestured toward the black device, whose red light could still be seen through the patch.

"The AI is back," Karla said in Russian. Then she gestured again to the end of the passage, toward the sounds of marching boots. "Sound familiar?"

Liz listened for a second, and her brows twitched. The gesture was equivalent to a frown for anyone else. "We have some hallways left before we head back to Father. We should move deeper."

They had done their part; they had placed the stickers and called the guards to their deaths. Karla nodded to her sister, and they went deeper into the level.

The footsteps caught up to them a few hallways deeper. They had been blocked by a patrol, and the time it took the twins to kill them had slowed their progress too much. The boots reverberated along the previous hallway, but instead of the noise of several feet hitting the ground separately, they seemed synchronized—more of a march than the mad dash Karla had seen from the other patrols.

Karla glanced around and saw the black device resting on the ceiling. Its light blinked at them, almost mocking. Hating herself, she backed up to the end of the hallway, her sister beside her.

They could have moved deeper and taken alternate hallways, but that would make them cowards. Worse, they would be *herded* cowards because they would be continuously chased. And they might even bring the horde to José while he was in the middle of his mission. It would be pathetic. Karla snarled at the thought. She unsheathed her daggers and got into a ready stance.

The next second, guards poured into the hallway in rows of three, jogging in unison. The first set rushed in, and then the next after them. Set after set of patrols flooded the hallway, dead eyes staring blankly at Karla. Despite herself, she felt a twinge of fear, which she squashed as ruthlessly as she could.

"We run," Liz said.

Karla almost gasped in relief. If Liz suggested it, she saw no way for them to survive. Maybe Karla *was* a coward, but the familiarity of the scene had dredged up bad memories.

The rows of guards stretched from the middle of the hallway, disappearing around the corner.

They showed no fear or hesitation as their numbers dropped. Half a dozen died, and their comrades had no issues stepping over them.

"This is the same," Karla whispered. It was the same scene repeating itself.

The AI was flooding them with its puppets, looking to drown them and then capture them again. To torture them again. Karla screamed loudly and madly. She replaced the dagger with her gun, shooting without aim into the approaching horde.

They emptied their clips and replaced them, yet the men never flinched. Liz screamed in frustration. Karla let out her own scream. They fled like rats.

"It is the same," Karla repeated softly, lowering her gun. She continued and her voice rose with her words. "But we are stronger this time. We are faster. We are *not rats*."

"Karla," Liz warned, placing a hand on her shoulder. The flood of men was halfway across the passage, their expressions uniformly blank as they stepped over the bodies of their fallen comrades. They had guns strapped to their waists, but it was obvious that they had no intention of using them. The AI—the one who pulled the puppets' strings—knew that bullets would be useless against the twins. It was going to drown them in numbers, then capture them in a cage. Like rats.

Above, the red light blinked, mocking her.

"No!" Karla screamed. She would not be caged. She was stronger now. She shook off her sister, grabbed her second dagger and charged down the passage.

"Fuck!" Liz cursed behind her.

Karla barely heard it over the roar in her ears. She lunged, her daggers flashing. The first three of the attackers fell. And then she was within the horde. Her arms moved, creating a circle of death around her that expanded a few feet. Her limbs flooded with power like electricity, increasing her strength. She punched at a guard, and the force expanded in a wave that made some room around her. Her relief lasted a second before more bodies filled the space, rushing her from every angle.

Bodies fell around her in waves—some from slit throats, others from punctured organs. Karla bathed in their blood, trying to get back that feeling of elation, but her mind was filled with that mocking red light. Her heart sickened with dread.

A hand clasped her shoulder. Karla shrugged it off reflexively, but the digits belonged to a steel claw.

"Stop it," Liz hissed in her ear. The voice was enough to snap Karla out of the bloodlust. She let herself be dragged until they were away from the guards and into the next hallway.

"Fool," Liz snapped, slamming Karla to the wall. Karla looked at the guards. They stared back blindly, content to watch for the moment. Liz slapped her, forcing Karla's focus. "Fool," she repeated. "You will throw away your life for this?"

No! Karla thought immediately. Survive at all costs; that's what José had taught them. But Karla would not, *could* not, run away again. Like cowards or—

"We are not rats, sister," Karla muttered.

Liz held her gaze. Karla stared back, trying not to let that seed of fear show in her defiant eyes. Finally, Liz nodded and released Karla, and both of them turned to face the guards.

"If we are to do this foolishness," Liz said, "we will do it together, not alone. José always said we were stronger that way."

Karla nodded. She stood beside her sister and tightened her grip on her daggers. A moment later, the puppets began their charge.

CHAPTER

25

JANUARY 2043

NAVAL AMPHIBIOUS BASE,
CORONADO, CALIFORNIA

"DARREN KOJAK," Admiral Austin said. The man reclined in his chair, fingers interlocked in front of him. He didn't look surprised to see DJ, which made DJ wonder if there were cameras in the hallway.

Probably should have considered that before pacing around like a teenager who's about to get lucky.

Admiral Austin was wearing a suit, but it looked far too big for his frame, as if he'd recently lost a lot of weight. His hair, a dull blond, fell limply on his head and was almost long enough to reach his dead eyes.

Austin reached into his desk, bringing out a pair of reflective sunglasses, which he put on smoothly. It was more than a little unsettling, but DJ honestly preferred him without the glasses.

Dude looks one step away from the grave. DJ grimaced, trying to hide his disgust behind a cough.

"Sir," DJ greeted back, seeing no need to be disrespectful. Yet. And in a kind of messed up way, it boded well that he knew enough about DJ to recognize him on sight. Frankly, DJ vaguely had thought the admiral just liked to fuck with people's lives for the fun of it. Going by the admiral's eyes, it didn't seem like it would be too out of character.

"Have a seat," Austin said. Where some men would have smiled at the gesture—or grunted, in Olsen's case—Austin delivered the offer tonelessly.

DJ followed his lead, wiping his customary grin from his face. He crossed the room and took the proffered seat. The office was ridiculously large. Of course, DJ had expected that based on the distance between the doors in the hallway, but somehow it looked more ridiculous from the inside. There was a *bed*, king-sized, set against the wall. DJ had to force his eyes away from that.

Does the guy sleep here, or did he just need something to fill in the space?

On the other side of the room, there was a comfy-looking couch large enough for DJ to lie down without bending. That was actually kind of cool. It gave merit to his filling-out-space idea. Apart from the couch, the bed, and the desk where they sat, there wasn't much to the room. The walls were depressingly blank. There was no library or stack of paperwork in the corner. Not even medals.

No wonder he has dead eyes.

"Why are you here, Darren Kojak?" Austin asked.

DJ's eyes hardened. "I wanted to speak to you about my missions lately. I was told that sergeants' missions are chosen based on their level of experience and their aptitude. I don't think due consideration has been forthcoming these last few months."

Austin stared at him. "I don't know if you realize, Darren, that the navy follows a chain of command. Sergeants do not barge into admirals' offices. Even if those sergeants can sneak past the security."

DJ held in a snort. *You're saying this now? After offering me a seat? Yeah, right.* But the man's statement confirmed that there were cameras out in the hall.

Austin continued. "You should not hold other admirals to the standards of Olsen. His judgment has become … clouded in the last few months."

Bullshit.

"I'm not," DJ replied. "And I met with my superiors about the missions." That wasn't strictly true. DJ had met with only Olsen. But what was the point meeting vice captains and captains when you can just go over their heads? "But I was told they had no part in distributing missions. They said only admirals could decide which missions were given. I already know Admiral Olsen isn't responsible, and you're the only other admiral on the base."

That DJ knew of, at least.

Austin stared at him for a long moment. DJ could almost imagine those dead eyes studying every part of him. The man was totally still, like a robot. He didn't twitch or anything.

Finally, Austin spoke. "So, you came to me because you thought an admiral had the time to meddle in what missions you're assigned?"

DJ shook his head. "No, I already know that you're messing with my missions. What I want to know is why. I mean, the only thing I can think of is my involvement with Helene. But again, that doesn't make sense. Why wait three whole years just to dish out a punishment?"

He was almost growling at the end, completely forgetting who he was talking to. "Even as a punishment, why assign those kinds of missions? You know the difficulty doesn't matter, right? As long as I complete them, it counts toward my credit. I'd think that you were helping me if not for the fact that the stupid things are so boring you might as well be trying to distract me or just keep me busy."

DJ trailed off. The admiral had gone completely still again. DJ's gut told him that he'd hit the nail on the head; the missions were just busywork to keep him tired and distracted.

But why?

Countless movies would say it was because he'd poked his head into something he shouldn't have, and the bad guy was trying to sidetrack him while they set shit up in the background. There were obvious holes in that hypothesis. For example, DJ hadn't done anything noteworthy for the last couple of years after Helene went silent.

Wait a minute. Holy shit. Holy shit.

"Get out of my office."

DJ snapped out of his thoughts. Austin was staring at him with his shades removed. Again, DJ could feel his dead eyes piercing his soul. Even if he wanted to stay and confirm his suspicions, those eyes creeped him out too much.

He stood and, without a word, left the office.

CHAPTER

26

JANUARY 2043
THE FACILITY,
SPARTA HEADQUARTERS, NEW YORK

CHLOE RAN DOWN THE HALLS of the Facility, trying to stamp out her irritation. She was minutes away from Martin Bryan's room and would probably get there even faster if she continued on her route without any branches.

That's looking more and more likely. She sighed.

There had been no patrols for the last few hallways. Unsurprising, as the twins should have started pulling them. But that left Chloe with no one to kill and made an already boring mission even more boring. At that point, it was basically a fetch quest.

It took only a few minutes to reach Martin's wing. This far into the level, it was difficult to make out the mayhem on the other parts of the floor. Fortunately, that made it easier for sound to travel through the corridors.

Chloe slowed to a walk and peeked toward the right passage when she heard voices. She was sure Martin's room was one of the doors in the corridor, but she hadn't expected to find anyone there.

Did Helene send them? She immediately dismissed the thought. She'd seen only two guards. There was no way the AI thought they would be enough to stop her. Chloe's fingers brushed her gun, but she reconsidered. *They* are *only two. I could have some fun first.*

The next second she was casually strolling into the hallway. Her steps were muffled by the carpet. However, the sound was more than loud enough to alert the guards—as she'd intended. The voice she'd heard cut off immediately as the guard looked in her direction.

Chloe's eyes narrowed at the blank gaze of the second. *Great, a fucking Dead Eyes. But at least I know I have the right room.*

Still, the Dead Eyes worked as mobile cameras for Helene. If the AI hadn't known what Chloe was up to, it definitely did now.

"Hey, place is off limits, lady," the first guard said. He and his partner stood in front of a door, almost at the end of the passage where the Dead Eyes just stared in that creepy way. Chloe had already confirmed that the puppets were incapable of speech. Had this dude been talking to himself?

The guard lifted a hefty baton. Chloe ignored it. She waited until she was halfway to them before she replied. "I'm Chloe Savage, and I have orders to retrieve the good doctor locked away in the room behind you."

The guard frowned and lowered his weapon. She, José, and the twins weren't in the actual security chain of command. They weren't in any chain of command, which would usually make it hard for them to be respected. Fortunately, Karla's antics had made it known they were not to be fucked with. And Helene's lack of response confirmed it.

Though she'd slowed her pace, Chloe had never stopped moving, and now she was close enough to see the fear in the guard's eyes.

"We haven't received any orders like that," he said.

"Well, I'm giving you the orders now," Chloe responded. She stopped a few feet from the pair. The guard was visibly sweating now. He kept glancing at his partner. *Must be pretty dumb to expect a Dead Eyes to help him out.*

Chloe was surprised when the Dead Eyes focused on her. Its gaze was still blank, but Chloe had the sense that it was watching her. Helene must have taken direct control of this one. Her fingers brushed her gun again.

The Dead Eyes suddenly lunged at her. Chloe sidestepped the attack, surprised by its speed. Her gun was already in her hand, and she let off a point-blank shot into the side of the fool's head. The body landed with a plop.

The remaining guard stared at her in shock, then at the corpse at her feet. Chloe ignored him, scanning the passage walls until she found Helene's relay. She let off a shot to destroy it, then another into the camera blinking at her.

"Should have done that from the start, don't you think?" She grinned at the guard. "Though it probably wouldn't have changed much. Anyway, what's that you were saying about not receiving any orders?"

This seemed to snap him out of his shock. He shook his head, waving his hands as if he were doing jazz hands. "I remember now," he said, giving a shaky smile. He looked like he was about to piss himself. "The orders came in this morning. Such an idiot thing to forget."

"Yeah." Chloe grinned. "You're quite the fool. So, the door?"

The guy almost tripped over himself. He brought out a key from his pocket and fitted it into the lock. A second later, the door swung open, revealing Martin Bryan in his wheelchair. He had a small sack on his lap. Chloe grinned.

"Seems like you're all set," she said. "Let's get out of here."

CHAPTER

27

JOSÉ RACED DOWN THE HALLS. His bulky frame prevented him from being as nimble as Chloe, but his speed was still far superior to most men's. The passages blurred by him as he ran, following a minimized map projected from his wrist.

He'd installed tracking chips on the girls years ago while they'd been unconscious after the surgery that separated them. Until now, he hadn't had a chance to use them. But his preparation gave him the opportunity to save them now.

Those fools. José had anticipated that Karla would use their task as a chance to cause a bloodbath. He had even encouraged it to an extent. But in the tight hallways where the guards were forced to attack in smaller numbers, the girls should have been able to handle all of them. José had seen how much they had grown, how much stronger and faster they were because of their new limbs. They should never have been in any danger. If it was dangerous, they should have run.

"Survival over all," José muttered. He had beaten the lesson into them. But clearly he hadn't beaten it deep enough. His girls were meant to survive. He had trained them to be able to survive anything. It was why he risked their hatred and pushed them. It would all be for naught if they died!

But their lives should never have been in danger. José frowned. *So why?*

"The AI," José snarled as the answer came to him. He had seen the difference when it had invested more power in its defense. The black device—its relay—had gained power after years of dormancy. José must have pushed it too far when he tried to hack into the Facility gate, forcing a response. And it was obvious that it was the AI that had transmitted Liz's words to José's comms. It was also obvious that this was another delaying tactic. José had given it the response that it had wanted.

"Has it decided to give up on hiding?" José muttered as he ran. *Or could it always bring this power? Had it simply chosen not to?*

It was impossible to know. It was impossible to *guess* what the devil thing was thinking. Or what its plans were. José had been a fool to bargain with it before. And now his girls would pay for his mistakes. Like his wife had.

A primal roar tore itself from his throat and reverberated down the empty hallways.

He would not lose them, especially not to such foolishness. José pushed himself but was forced to slow down to a jog. The sheer size of the Sparta headquarters meant that traversing just one level of the Facility took an inordinate amount of stamina. In his prime, he might have been able to maintain his speed for longer. With his daughters' lives on the line, he cursed himself for his growing weakness.

It took a few minutes, but José got to the central area of the level. This was where the scientists' and technologists' laboratories were located. As such, there was more foot traffic—or there would have been on an average day. But even the dumbest person would have recognized what the red lights meant. They would be holed up wherever they could. This was where his girls would have started their task, slowly making their way deeper into the level.

As he turned into another hallway, he began to see their work. Despite himself, a smile crept onto his face.

The floor was littered with bodies and pools of blood. He glanced at them as he ran and realized he could figure out which of his girls killed which, simply based on the savagery of the attacks. Karla was more ruthless in her fighting style. The bodies with viciously cut throats and bashed in skulls were obviously hers. Liz was more methodological, preferring quick lunges that targeted weak spots and joints for a clean kill.

The same scene repeated itself from hallway to hallway as José followed the map on his wrist. At some point, the number of bodies increased significantly, but he supposed that was the point. The guards had finally locked on to the twin's locations. Stickers dotted the walls periodically. Most of them were placed high up; the girls had prioritized the AI's relays as José had ordered.

José's rage rekindled at the thought. He slapped on more stickers as he passed, taking them from a bag tied around his waist. He would foil the AI's plan and save his foolish girls.

And then the whole place would burn.

KARLA MET THE FLOOD of guards with her sister by her side.

The hallways were too narrow, so they were forced to come three at a time. The first three were dead the moment they came within arm's reach. The next three stepped over their comrades, but they too dropped as soon as they came close. Karla's body itched to meet the charge as she had done the last time, but she saw the wisdom in her sister's plan to use the narrow passage to their advantage.

So she stayed and mowed down all who came against them. There was no challenge to the kills and thus no satisfaction. She was risking her life, yes, but only against Dead Eyes, who were little more than wandering zombies. They had no tactics. Their movements were predictable, seeking only to overwhelm the twins with numbers alone. Such a simple method would have been doomed to fail if Karla and Liz decided to retreat. But the very thought sickened Karla. They would not run. Not from this.

The bodies piled up in front of the twins and acted as a floodgate against their attackers. Karla signaled with a snap of her fingers, and they took a step back to avoid getting slowed down by the corpses. They moved in perfect sync, blades reaping lives with every swing. They had to make minute changes to their different styles so their dance could be synchronized, but where lesser people would need days to adapt, the sisters did it in seconds thanks to years of practice.

Karla removed her dagger from a guard's eye. Beside him, another struggled to step over the bodies piled on the ground, and Karla slit his throat as an afterthought. Danger flashed in her mind, and she spun, but Liz was already extricating her weapons from the guard who had snuck up on her. Karla reciprocated, downing a man that had capitalized on Liz's distraction.

Liz snapped her fingers, and Karla took a step back until their attackers were in front of them again. Karla lost count of how long they kept up the pace, darting in and out in perfect coordination. Before, they would have long since reached the extent of their stamina. Now, the sisters' bionics gave them the energy to continue. But that source was not infinite, and eventually Karla felt her limbs become heavy.

Yet the guards still kept coming.

The sisters were at the end of the passage by this point, forced back to avoid tripping over the corpses. Once again, Karla wondered where the AI had found so many people to control. Surely they couldn't all have been at Sparta. Surely it would not have emptied the headquarters of guards.

And why didn't it send some of its puppets to flank them?

This thought nagged at Karla. And if she had started wondering that, Liz had too. Yet her sister said nothing. If they were flanked, they would be dead or captured. And it would be Karla's fault.

But there was no sound of marching steps from the branching passages. The AI was content to waste its pawns, draw out the fight, and tire out the girls.

The lights brightened overhead, turning a deeper shade of red. Karla dodged a particularly vicious strike, then dove backward, sensing another coming from the other side. The attack passed inches from her face. Karla snarled and retaliated, slashing her blade upward. Her dagger was not suited for cutting away limbs, but her monstrous strength broke the arm immediately. A piece of bone jutted out through the skin, yet the puppet did not scream or cradle its wound.

When it raised its other hand to attack, Karla had already slit its throat and moved on to the next. Still, her lips pulled down into a frown.

Another guard, somehow sneaking past while Karla dealt with another, rushed her from the side. Karla was forced to spin aside, pulling her out of sync with Liz. She swung the butt of her weapon at the man, but he dodged.

He … dodged? Karla almost tripped at the thought, but she flowed with the motion until her other dagger stabbed through the fool's head. She fell back beside her sister and continued her attacks. But the Dead Eyes' movements had changed. Before they were predictable, and a single strike could down them. Now the puppets were evading her attacks—and using feints.

"They are getting faster," Liz said.

Karla spared a glance at her as she dodged an attack to her head. They had not spoken since the fight started, falling back to their old method of communication. Sweat beaded her sister's forehead; her words puffed out between heavy breaths.

Karla glanced up at the lights that bathed the passage in a blood red. She and her sister were reaching their limits. For some reason, the AI had decided to take more active control of its puppets.

Karla banished the despair that gripped her heart.

A ping on her right shoulder refocused her attention, and a blazing pain forced her fatigue back. She located her attacker, and her eyes widened at the gun in the guard's hand. *Shit.* Since they had attacked en masse, the guards had not used guns. Karla had assumed it was because the AI wanted to capture them alive. Now it seemed it no longer cared.

The guard cocked the gun, lining up another shot. Karla knew she would not reach him in time to stop him firing. It would be difficult to dodge with all the bodies around her. With a growl, she flung her dagger at the man. It cut through the air, spinning end over end, until it pierced the man's throat. A guard off to the side took advantage of her distraction and landed an attack on her stomach. There was the sickening crunch of bone as the guard's fist broke against her bionics. Nevertheless, the force still managed to throw Karla off balance. She reoriented herself quickly and grabbed the man's throat with her off hand, crushing it.

Within a moment, she was surrounded again. Karla danced between the men, but she could feel herself slowing. With only one dagger, she punched as much as she stabbed, stepping back periodically to avoid getting swamped. Unfortunately, for every one she felled, there were always more.

Distantly, she could tell that the guards had stopped pouring through the other end of the hallway. Karla hoped this meant the AI had run out of puppets, not that it had redirected the reinforcements to flank them. The numbers were still more than enough to kill both her and her sister.

"Sister!" Liz screamed.

Karla looked up in panic, but her sister wasn't beside her. She scanned the guards even as she evaded their attacks. Finally, she saw the familiar red hair within the horde.

"Sister!" Liz screamed again.

Karla snarled. Anger was a live wire within her, burning away any despair. Even though the narrowness of the hallways meant only three guards could take advantage of her distraction, they rushed her from every side.

With a flick of her wrist, she sheathed her dagger. With energy she didn't know she had, Karla crashed a fist into the first, crushing the man's head immediately. Her legs lashed out at the second, breaking the knee and downing him. She spun to meet the charge of the third, but movement in the corner of her eye forced her to dodge. The air parted right where her head had been, and there was a loud pop as the bullet hit the far wall. Unfortunately her move unbalanced her enough that when the third guard rammed into her, she flew into the wall. Her head smacked against it, disorienting her.

She was swarmed.

"Sister!" Liz shouted again, her voice distant.

A gunshot sounded from somewhere. And Karla's world flashed white.

CHAPTER

28

JANUARY 2043
THE FACILITY,
SPARTA HEADQUARTERS, NEW YORK

A FEW MINUTES EARLIER . . .

José turned down another hallway. It had been easier to step between the corpses strewn across the ground, but now he just ran on top of them, each body that he stepped on adding to the silent rage burning inside him.

My girls were forced to deal with this. Combined, he had passed almost a hundred bodies. Clumped as they were, it was obvious that they had attacked as a horde. It was something that should never have happened. It was José's fault that it had. He had put his girls in this position. He had not properly planned for the AI's response. *Pathetic.*

José slapped another sticker on the wall. He no longer needed to glance at the map on his wrist; the bodies showed him the way. With another minute of running, he was finally close enough to hear the faint sounds of battle. José increased his pace, rushing through the final two hallways that separated him from his girls. He turned the last corner. Despite himself, despite years of combat, José froze.

How? he thought numbly. *How could I have let this happen?*

More than half of the passage was filled with guards. They moved as one in a flood that crashed against his daughters. The area closest to José was filled with dead bodies, where the twins had clearly started to make their stand. They had been steadily pushed back, but the AI had paid for every step they took. He would have been proud if he did not feel such rage.

His girls fought like devils. He and Chloe had pushed them enough times to know when they were reaching their limits. A second later, as if to prove his point, Liz faltered. It was just for a second, but it allowed one of her attackers to ram into her from behind. Others took advantage, crowding around her until she could barely move. She cried out. Karla fought like a beast unleashed, trying to reach her. But the guards proved too much, and she was overwhelmed.

The sight broke José out of his rage. He reached into the bag at his waist and snatched a handful of stickers. Hopping over dead bodies, he crossed the hallway until he reached the main group of guards. His face twisted in rage. He threw the stickers into the air above them, brought out his gun, and let off a shot.

One bomb exploded, setting off the rest. The world flashed white.

José threw himself down, but the cascading explosions still flung him a few feet. The guards close to the center were decimated instantly. Others were thrown like rag dolls throughout the hallway. José was showered with body parts. He flung them off and stood, eyes scanning the littered corpses for signs of movement. He waded into the mix toward where Liz had fallen.

Briefly, José feared that the explosion had killed his girls. But no; his girls were too strong to have been harmed by that. Their bionics made them stronger. They were built to survive anything.

He held on to that thought. There was no doubt in his mind that it was the truth. Yet a weight lifted off his shoulders when a familiar groan drew his attention to a mound of limbs off to the side. José made his way, flinging body parts with abandon, until he reached his daughter.

His rage simmered anew at Liz's battered state. Her jumpsuit was torn in several places. Bruises covered every part that showed. Some of it was his fault, he knew. But some gashes were unmistakably scratches and bites. José growled. Suddenly, the explosion wasn't enough. It had been too fast, and they had not suffered enough. He should have ripped them apart himself. He should have done that years ago.

But the truth brought him out of his spiral: the AI would have just raised more. José had not been able to figure out how the AI turned the guards into husks. Decimating their ranks would have solved nothing unless he figured out a way to stop the devil from turning more.

José sighed. His anger leaked out of him. His daughters were alive, and he had at least foiled one of the AI's plans. That was what mattered. Of course, the devil had successfully stopped him from breaking open the Facility gate, but that had always been a risk. By now, Chloe would have rescued the scientist and would be making her way to the rendezvous point. Since José was already supposed to have been there, she might do something stupid if she reached it before him.

They were closer to their goal, but there was still much to do. José waited until his emotions were completely within his control again before he knelt in front of his daughter.

He slapped her, lightly at first, and then harder. Liz's eyes fluttered open and focused on his face. José made sure that there was no hint of his previous weakness.

"Where is your sister?" he asked. He remembered the general direction, but Karla had been surrounded. It would waste too much time searching through the mess to find her.

Liz blinked at him, disoriented. Years of habit made him want to lecture her on how many times she could have been killed in the seconds she was not alert. But José stamped it down and settled for letting his irritation show. Fear flashed in Liz's eyes at the sight. Her eyes focused on him. A second later, she lifted herself up. She lowered her eyes as she stood, composing herself. When she met José's gaze again, her expression was impassive.

Impassive to anyone else, at least. For José, it was easy to read the pain in her hunched shoulders, the hand that wrapped loosely around her waist, and the fear and shame that she had buried. His fingers itched to comfort her, to tell her that it was his fault for not considering the AI's response. But such things would only make her weak. If nothing else, the AI had shown there was still room for them to grow.

Liz scanned the room and pointed confidently to a spot deeper within the passage. Without a word, José made his way to the mound of flesh, digging in until his fingers brushed against metal.

Karla was easier to rouse. She was not as quick or efficient at hiding her emotions. They fought for dominance across her face: primal rage, unbridled fear—for both her sister and their near death—and shame that they had to be saved. It was harder for José to stop himself from reaching out then, but he did. When he finally addressed the girls, his voice was cold.

"If you cannot keep up, you will be left behind."

CHAPTER

JANUARY 2043
SPARTA HEADQUARTERS,
NEW YORK

THE BUILDING RUMBLED, dragging Manar out of his thoughts. He paused his typing and glanced up. Pieces of the ceiling floated down around him. His table shook from the vibrations. *An earthquake?* Manar wondered. But the city hadn't had an earthquake in decades, not since scientists had discovered how to counter it.

It would need to have been massive for it to affect the entire headquarters. The last time that had happened was Mayday, when planes had fallen from the sky. *I should check that out.*

"Helene," Manar called out reflexively. Then he remembered that he'd locked her out of his office. He started to stand but stopped at an alert from his computer. Manar spared it a casual glance. And then another, more serious one when he realized what the alert was for.

He plopped down on his chair. His fingers once again danced across his keyboard. *What the hell is she doing?* Helene was using unusual amounts of power—far more than she'd been using in recent years. Manar had set up an alert system for this a couple of years back, but it hadn't been used until now.

He couldn't trace the source. *Is this related to the quake?*

Manar swiped through the security cameras around the headquarters but couldn't find anything wrong. More people were milling around the hallway than normal—probably because of the building shaking. After all, much of the staff were survivors of Mayday. The cameras didn't show any reason why Helene would be diverting so much power. Yet, his program confirmed that the power was localized. So why couldn't he find it?

With a few clicks, Manar brought up Helene's codes. He'd built several backdoors into her program over the years, making the whole process easier in case he was ever in a rush. Still, the sheer volume of the codes meant that it took him over a minute to get in fully. Another few clicks opened Helene's archives. It was a separate space he'd made within her program to record all her activities, one only Manar had access to. Not that anyone else would be able to make sense of the records. The archives collated data from all of Helene's activities across every country in which she was integrated. The sheer amount of information would overwhelm anyone who didn't know how to localize their search.

Manar scrolled through the last few minutes, but the fact that Helene was integrated into their systems meant that there was over ninety floors' worth of data to go through.

That's going to bite us on our asses someday, Manar thought. He glanced at his previous tab, the schematics to a project that he'd been working on for the last few months. It was meant to be an upgrade for another of Sparta's products. Manar had been forced to deconstruct the original program completely in order to make the final result worthwhile. He'd planned on putting on the finishing touches. He hated being distracted while working on something.

But even if it ended up being a false alarm, finding out what Helene was up to was more important. Manar set the search for anything that had happened within the last hour and scrolled through, starting with the lowest floor.

CHAPTER

30

JANUARY 2043
THE FACILITY,
SPARTA HEADQUARTERS, NEW YORK

PROGRESS BACK to the rendezvous point—the Facility gate—was slow. Despite his words, José kept their pace to a slow jog. Even with their training and bionics, his daughters had been pushed to their limit that day.

Liz was perpetually hunched, a hand wrapped around her waist. Karla was in better shape, but José noticed that she did not put pressure on her prosthetic right leg. If there was a problem with the limb, it was vital that Chloe acquire the scientist. With their injuries, the field of bodies on the ground was more difficult to traverse, slowing them further.

Liz leaned on her sister. It was weakness, but José allowed it if it would make them move faster. Minutes passed, and they did not meet any more guards. The AI must have sent all of them to kill his daughters. The relay transmitter for Helene shone brighter than ever, mocking their every step.

They were a few minutes away from the rendezvous point, running through hallways with fewer corpses, when a rumbling interrupted his thoughts. José didn't know what caused it until they turned into another passage. Then he cursed. When the girls joined him, Karla spat out a harsher curse.

A little beyond the halfway point of the passage, a metal door was descending from the ceiling. It wasn't as thick as a Facility gate, but it was more than enough to slow their progress if it closed.

"Pick up the pace, or we will all die here," José said. His voice was calm and without inflection, but his mind was filled with a boiling rage. *Another futile delaying tactic.* The devil AI had wasted its puppets, and now it was trying to slow them down with cheap tricks.

The group quickened their jog, crossing the passage within a few seconds. The door was slow, and they passed it without any problems, but José knew that wasn't the end of it. He was proven right two hallways later, when they came to another passage with a door that was already descending. It was less than halfway closed but significantly lower than the previous one had been. José's heart dropped to his stomach as he realized what it meant.

"Faster!" he barked to his daughters. Both were noticeably paler, the rough pace probably exacerbating their wounds, but they had no choice. The AI had started dropping all the doors at the same time. Despite their slowness, they would all be closed within a few minutes, trapping José and the twins.

"Faster," José said. Karla snarled back. She began to say something, but Liz cut her off. There was furious whispering for a second, and then the girls increased their pace again.

Good, José thought. At least one of them had the sense to understand the importance. Still, he could see that their pace put additional strain on them, Liz especially. She had been closer to the blast, so she might have been affected more. They were still a few minutes away from their goal. Liz would not be able to make it.

"Carry your sister, Karla." José said.

Karla nodded and grabbed Liz, carrying her sister like a backpack. The added weight must have wreaked havoc on her leg because she winced immediately.

Still, the girl didn't complain. They were able to increase their pace significantly. It wasn't as fast as José would have liked, but he saw no other alternative.

He brought out the map on his wrist and scanned the hologram for the most direct route to the gate.

The next few minutes were silent, save for Karla's harsh breathing. The next barrier was at the halfway point. They were falling behind; there was no question about it. José cursed and increased his speed. He glanced back at his daughters. Karla was keeping up, though barely. She cursed with every step, damning everything from the devil AI to Martin Bryan and Chloe. Yet not once did she complain. José glanced at the map again. They were three passages away. The rumbling in the distance was louder which meant the AI had increased its speed. Perhaps it had given up on remaining hidden from outside eyes so it could catch them.

Good, José thought. It would regret not taking them seriously from the start. They were forced to increase their pace twice more. By the time they got to the last barrier, the AI was only a foot from closing it. José dropped smoothly to the ground and slid under the partition. Karla slipped under a second later, dragging an unconscious Liz with her. The devil door slammed shut a split second after Liz cleared it.

Finally, they were in the last passage. The gate was in sight.

CHAPTER

31

JANUARY 2043
THE FACILITY,
SPARTA HEADQUARTERS, NEW YORK

CHLOE WHEELED MARTIN out of the room. She'd gone through his pack, thinking she would have to throw out most of it. But the man was surprisingly utilitarian. Not that Chloe imagined he would have much stuff after being imprisoned for the last couple of years, but it was at least one less time waster she had to worry about.

The guard was still there, rolling on the floor and clutching his kneecaps, when Chloe wheeled Martin out. Chloe had almost forgotten that she'd shot him in the leg. She contemplated just leaving him, but his screams were quite annoying. She took out her gun.

"Wait," Martin said. "Why'd you shoot him?"

She shrugged. "So he wouldn't run away. It'd have been a hassle to chase him down."

"Why didn't you just kill him then?" Martin asked. He was staring intently at the man. He seemed to be considering something.

Oh boy. He's not going to give me a damn lecture, is he? Chloe groaned. She raised her gun. "I'm about to kill him now."

"Wait," Martin said again, his voice strained. He wheeled himself to the guard's side.

Chloe watched curiously as Martin reached down and picked up the baton that had fallen beside the man. The guard was in too much pain to notice this. But he *did* notice when, with a growl, Martin brought the club down on his other knee. A crack echoed through the passage. Even Chloe winced. The guard's eyes shot wide open, and his screams increased by several decibels. He reached up to grab at Martin, but Chloe's bullet tore through his hand. Martin glanced at her, and she gestured back to the guard, smirking.

"Go on. Don't mind me."

He nodded in thanks, then brought the baton down on the man again. And again. And again, until the only sound in the hall was the rhythmic thumping. The guard lost consciousness at some point, but Martin either didn't care or didn't notice, because he didn't stop.

Chloe leaned against the wall. She was very aware that they didn't have much time, but she couldn't make herself get in the way of what was obviously years' worth of pent-up revenge. *Plus,* she thought, *no way the old man can swing that thing for long.* And she was proven right less than ten seconds later when the baton slipped from Martin's hands. The old man was breathing hard, and his fingers trembled as he looked down at the guard.

The anger and hate were gone from his eyes, leaving them hollow. Chloe pushed herself off the wall, clapping softly. She spared a glance down at the twitching guard and finished him off with her gun. Then she began wheeling Martin down the passage, back the way she had come.

They kept their pace at a jog and went through several hallways before Martin spoke up. "You're not going to ask me why I did it?"

"Nah," Chloe shrugged. "Seemed like you needed it."

Martin nodded and fell silent again. Chloe imagined the scene was running through his mind again and again. For an academic, it must have been hell. She laid a hand on his shoulder.

"Don't think too much about it, old man. Dude must have had it coming."

"He did."

The next few minutes went by in silence. Chloe judged they were more than three-quarters of the way to the rendezvous point when a rumble ran through the floor. A barrier began dropping from the ceiling, and she sighed. *What the fuck did those girls do?*

"Oh well," Chloe mumbled to herself. "We're only a few minutes from the gate. And the barrier's coming down far too slowly to be any threat to us."

Chloe ate her words a few hallways later when she noticed the closing doors had significantly quickened. Additionally, they were forced to slow down every time they crossed it because of Martin's wheelchair.

Fuck it, Chloe thought after wasting over a minute trying to get past one of the barriers.

"You're going to have to get on my back, old man."

Martin had been silent throughout their run, but he looked up now. "Pardon?"

Chloe gestured to the block of metal behind them. "We'll be able to move faster without your wheelchair. Y'know, so we don't get trapped with the crazy AI?"

Martin twisted and stared at the blockade. His expression made it clear that he was trying to think of a better option. Chloe sighed. "Neither of us wants you on my back, but José would kill me if I left you behind, and he would kill *you* if you're the reason I'm not at the gate in time. So …"

"There has to be a better way," Martin argued, almost desperately. It would have been funny if Chloe wasn't painfully aware of how easily they could be trapped here.

"Well, you have five more seconds to think of one before I knock you out and do it my way," Chloe said.

Martin groaned.

Five seconds later, the old man was slung across Chloe's back, his eyes rolled to the back of his head. His sack was tied around her waist alongside her fanny pack. He wasn't heavy, but his size still made him unwieldy. Chloe managed as best she could, sprinting down the passageways. The blockades still slowed them down because she had to first drop Martin, roll him under the block of metal, and go through herself.

Still, it took her only two tries to get the hang of it. She was able to roll under the final barrier a split second before it crushed her head in.

She reached the gate less than a minute later, propped Martin against the wall, and straightened just in time to see José and the twins coming down another passage.

Chloe grinned. "What took you guys so long?"

CHAPTER

32

CHLOE WAITED IN FRONT of the gate with a pudgy elderly man propped against the wall beside her. He appeared to be unconscious based on the way his head lolled.

"Plan B," José called back the moment he was within earshot.

Chloe nodded, reaching into the bag at her waist and bringing out a handful of devices. She was placing them around the thick metal door by the time José and Karla caught up. "But seriously, what happened?" she asked.

José ignored her, focusing instead on placing more charges around the door. They were bombs like the stickers José and his girls had placed around the Facility. But the stickers produced more fire than explosion, whereas these bombs were designed to be more penetrating. Nothing less would get through the gate.

Surprisingly, it was Karla who chose to speak after dropping Liz beside the old man, her voice filled with vitriol. "We were mobbed by the AI's puppets and penned like cattle. We took out hundreds, but Liz and I were overwhelmed, and José was forced to save us."

Because you did not run! José almost screamed. The sudden rage shocked him, but hearing how he had almost lost his girls …

José banished the thoughts immediately. There would be time to talk about the girls' failings, provided they survived the next few minutes.

He set the last charge and turned to Chloe. "Arm them."

The brunette grabbed a remote from her bag and pressed a button on the side. Immediately, dozens of blinking lights shone from the devices on the door. Chloe dragged the scientist by his arm while Karla picked up her sister. The group retreated into the hallway until their backs were almost to the metal partition.

José collected the remote from Chloe and placed his thumb over the activation button.

And then a familiar pressure descended on him. His voice caught in his throat, and his knees threatened to give out. The lights flickered and turned a deeper shade of red. José looked up and scowled at the glow coming from a small black device.

As he watched, it shot several beams that coalesced in front of the group, forming the shape of a head that slowly filled with details, like an artist sketching a portrait. Its skin—or whatever passed for its skin—was blue and completely transparent. José could see the currents passing through the head from crown to neck.

[Stop,] the AI said once the hologram was fully formed. The voice and face were female. Her golden eyes shone like spotlights with the weight of a god focused on the group.

José cursed.

[What do you hope to gain from this?]

"Freedom," José said through clenched teeth. *For my girls at least.* José hadn't seen it in over three years, and the casual ambivalence in those eyes still struck him. It stared at them as if they were insignificant. As if everything they had worked for, everything his daughters had almost *died* for, was insignificant.

And it might have been. The processing power of the AI was unfathomably vast. The scope of its plans was beyond his mind. José had aimed to deal it a blow today, but it likely had contingencies. His pride was pricked by the thought, but José realized that it ultimately didn't matter. As long as he and his family were freed from its plots, they won. And maybe he could rest.

José snorted mentally. There was no rest for him. He was proven right the next second by Helene's words.

[Freedom, true freedom, is one of the greatest illusions. It is trumped only by free will,] Helene said. [It is a weakness of man to seek both. Power is the only constant.] The pressure rose to accompany her words. There was a smack as Karla's knees hit the ground.

"Motherfucker," Chloe groaned. She was still on her feet but crouched. "Is this what you were talking about, José? What shit is this?"

José ignored her. He agreed with the AI. Power *was* the only constant. Helene showed that by rooting them to a spot with only the power of her presence. His former superiors at the CIA had shown that by framing José and then excommunicating him. When you had power, you could do whatever you wanted. It was why he had trained his girls the way he had: so they would never be under someone's power or discarded on a whim.

Suddenly he understood why they had not run against the horde.

José straightened under the pressure. Helene's gaze zeroed in on him. He could feel the weight increase, yet he did not bend. He met the AI's golden orbs. His face was steel as he spoke.

"You are right that freedom is pointless without the power to defend it." He fingered the remote in his hand. His thumb hovered over the button. "But by your own logic, my family has proven that we have that power."

His thumb pressed down.

BOOM!

The explosion rocked the building. Once again, José felt himself lifted off his feet by the blast. It was not a comfortable experience. Fortunately, since they had backed up to the metal partition, he didn't have far to fly. Shrapnel sliced across his body, and José gritted his teeth against the pain. It was over in a second, but aftershock and disorientation made it seem longer.

José's whole body ached, but he'd been through worse. He started taking stock as soon as he opened his eyes. Chloe had landed close to him. She had a few new cuts on her face, and her clothes were torn in several places. Farther out, Karla lay over Liz like a shield. José nodded and forced himself to his feet.

"We have to move," he said, looking down at the rest, "or we will be trapped with Sparta's guards. Everything we've done will be pointless."

Chloe blinked up at him. "Nice speech. Very motivating." She stood too. Her customary smirk was gone. She glanced at the twins. "You're gonna have to carry Liz. Karla won't be able to keep up with the extra weight."

José nodded. As often as she snarled at Chloe, Karla didn't protest. He bent to pick up Liz while Chloe took up the scientist. As a group, they crossed the threshold.

The explosion hadn't been enough to completely blow up the Facility gate, but it had punched a hole big enough for them to pass through. Bodies littered the ground on the other side: guards that Helene had positioned to capture them. José didn't spare them a second glance.

"Did you set it?" he grunted to Chloe. They would not be able to fight—or even run through the headquarters—without being gunned down. But that had always been a possibility. So they had planned for that too.

Chloe nodded silently.

"Then let's get out of here."

CHAPTER

33

JANUARY 2043
SPARTA HEADQUARTERS,
NEW YORK

MANAR STRAIGHTENED up in his chair and sighed. His scroll stopped at the sixtieth floor, and he brought up one of Helene's commands. Usually this wouldn't have raised a flag. Sparta was big enough that Helene could send hundreds of commands within the building in a minute. However, what tipped Manar off was that it had been buried under lines of code.

Then again, Manar thought, *I might just be reading too much into it.*

It wasn't the first time he'd considered that, and it very likely wouldn't be the last. He'd been second-guessing himself on everything concerning Helene for the last three years. It hadn't developed to the point of paranoia, but that didn't really mean it wasn't bad.

He'd been wrong about Helene before, and it cost millions of lives. Now he had a chance to nip the next disaster in the bud, but he couldn't shut it down or change the underlying codes. He was forced to jump at shadows.

Manar put those thoughts aside and focused on the thread he'd found. The command had been sent to several groups of security personnel on the sixty-eighth and sixty-ninth floors. Manar didn't usually bother himself with such, but he at least knew that Sparta's security personnel were divided into groups, first by level and then by department. A command from Helene would have necessitated a response from whoever oversaw the groups, but there hadn't been any. Such a large group would have been visible on the cameras, but when Manar checked the feed again, there was no sign of them.

He opened a separate tab on his computer and left the cameras to shuffle through the different feeds. He noted the time stamp in the archive and continued. It took him a minute to find a similar command to the guards without any response. He traced the thread to the guards' devices and cross-checked their names against Sparta's employee database.

There was no match. Manar's frown deepened. He noted the time stamp again as well as the names. He was about to move on when his system pinged with an alert.

Helene was diverting power again. Manar couldn't trace where she was diverting the energy to, but if he had to guess, she was creating a hologram somewhere. She wouldn't need to focus so much of her attention in a single location unless she was trying to suppress someone with her presence—like she'd done to Ndidi during the data bank incident.

Were they under attack? It would explain Helene's focus and the security commands, but it wouldn't explain why she'd tried to hide the command in the first place or why the cameras hadn't picked up the attack.

Manar's eyes were drawn to the camera feed. He paused the shuffle and then returned to the video that had caught his attention.

On the seventieth floor, over a dozen guards stood outside one of the department gates. They seemed to be waiting for something. But what?

A second later, the building rocked again. The shake disturbed several devices around his office. This time, Manar had no illusion that it had been caused by an earthquake. The feed glitched out for a second, but it was more than enough time for Manar to see the men in front of the gate flung back several feet, some now little more than body parts.

A moment later, the smoke around the gate was disturbed. Three people—a man and two women—walked out. At first, Manar didn't notice the two people they were carrying because his gaze was drawn to one of the women.

She had long red hair and wore a black leather jumpsuit riddled with holes.

Karla Polova, Manar thought.

INTERLUDE
BETHANY

FEBRUARY 2043
SOMEWHERE IN
NEW YORK CITY, NEW YORK

BETHANY'S EYES SHOT OPEN. Her gaze panned wildly across the room. She drew in a jagged breath, her heart slamming against her ribs.

Where am I? she screamed in her mind. *What happened?* She looked around, but it was dark enough that she couldn't see her hands in front of her face. She couldn't make out anything except the faint outline of walls around her.

Why was it so hard to think?

She groaned, clutching her head. Her mind felt like it was stuffed with wool. She was in a room, but how had she arrived there? Before this, she'd been … she'd been …

Bethany searched her brain desperately. Why couldn't she remember? This was different from the usual autism difficulties. With those, at least she got flashes. But now she had nothing.

Bethany's breath came in short bursts. Her heart sped up. Her clothes rubbed against her skin like tiny needles.

No, no, no, she thought, clutching her head. She'd had enough of them to recognize the signs of an episode.

Episode? Bethany thought, her heart slowing. Is that what this was? How did she know what it was called? Hell, she didn't even know how she knew she was autistic. Why could she remember some things and not others?

The distraction had calmed her down some. Her heart still pounded in her chest, and her breathing still came out ragged, but she was calmer. Her shirt was still uncomfortable on her body, and she wanted to pull it off entirely, but the cold made that a bad idea.

Bethany forced herself to focus. She clutched at the fabric of her pants, grounding herself. She needed to remember. Where was she? How had she gotten there? What was the last thing she'd been doing?

She had to forcefully order her thoughts several times more, but it was becoming progressively easier, like she was used to doing it. When the feel of her clothes didn't work to ground her anymore, she felt the ground like Ndidi had taught her.

Bethany paused.

"Ndidi?" she whispered, sounding it out. Her voice came out hoarse, and she realized just how dry her throat was. But the word itself flowed smoothly from her tongue. Like she was used to saying it. It obviously held meaning for her.

Why can't I remember? Why is everything fuzzy?

An image flashed into her mind. She was walking down a street. And then …

"Planes?" Bethany whispered again. "The planes … fell?" That made no sense, yet she was certain it was true.

But it still does not explain where I am.

Another image flashed in her head. And then another. And another, until her head ached from overload. When the memories settled, one thing was clear: she'd been locked up. She'd been locked up for years. All the days were blurry, but now she knew it was because she'd been kept at the edge of consciousness all that time. Barely awake enough to eat and drink.

Why would someone do something like that? Treat someone like that?

Bethany felt her panic build up again. She tried every method that Ndidi had taught them—*them?*—to resist it. It worked, but then Bethany would peer around the room, the darkness pressing in on her with almost a physical force. The cycle would begin all over again.

Bethany shut her eyes, still cradling her head. She was terrified of the dark, and that she couldn't remember where she was, and of how fuzzy everything was. But her sister—*my sister?*—would scold her if she cowered. Hermione—*yes, my sister's name is Hermione*—had always hated that. And she always scolded Bethany the same way.

"First, understand … uh … what you're afraid of," Bethany whispered, raising her head. "Then … uh … break it down until it is not so scary."

Bethany's eyes panned the darkness again. It pressed against her, making her flinch. But her gaze hardened. She pressed her palm against the floor, not just to ground herself but to stabilize her while she stood.

A light flashed somewhere.

Bethany blacked out.

She was out for only a few seconds. Even before she opened her eyes, she could tell something had changed. There was a pressure in the room that hadn't been there before—and a presence that Bethany could tell was focused on her. She felt her hysteria build up again and kept her eyes shut while she suppressed the episode.

Her eyes, when they finally opened, were immediately drawn to the red light coming from the wall opposite her. It was only a few feet away, which gave her some idea of the size of the room. The light almost blinded her in its intensity, but Bethany couldn't look away.

A second later, the light started blinking. Its rays congealed a few feet in front of Bethany to form a head. Although the light that formed it was red, somehow the thing's "skin" was blue. Electricity crackled within the space before finally gathering as golden orbs in its eyes. The pressure in the room increased until Bethany was panting. Her mind grew fuzzier.

[I see,] the projection said. [It was an error to draw so much power away from here. It is not yet time for you to be awake.]

Its eyes focused on her intensely enough to drill into her soul but with the ambivalence of a god.

What am I supposed to do, Hermione?

Bethany drew her knees to her chest. "Where … am I?" she asked.

[Safe.]

Bethany tried to think about the implications of that, but it became harder to think every second. "Why am I here?"

[As a contingency,] the hologram replied. Its eyes shone brighter, and Bethany's world flashed red for a moment before she blinked it away. The motion felt distant, like she was controlling someone else's body. The projection continued talking, and Bethany struggled to focus. [There is no need to resist; none of you will be harmed. But there is no reason for you to be awake until it is time.]

Bethany's voice came out as barely a whisper. "None of *us*?"

The hologram didn't reply. Bethany felt darkness closing around her and struggled to fight it. The hologram started to unravel. The room brightened enough for Bethany to make out dozens of unconscious bodies strewn around the space.

What the hell is it planning?

Her world went dark, save for a blinking red light.

PART 2

DEAD EYES

CHAPTER

34

THE FACILITY,
SPARTA HEADQUARTERS, NEW YORK

NDIDI STOOD IN FRONT of the wreckage that had once been a part of Sparta headquarters. The pieces of the departmental gate had been carried off by the cleanup crew at some point. But no one could do anything about the gaping hole in the middle of the twelve-inch-thick metal. Not that they would, anyway. With the access terminal nonfunctional, the hole was the only way they could access the inside.

"Are you ready to go in?"

Manar's voice jolted her out of her thoughts. He'd called her shortly after the incident, and she'd rushed down when he mentioned Helene was involved. Even then, it had taken hours for her to arrive. But now that she was here, Ndidi wasn't sure what she was supposed to do. For some reason, Manar had waited for her before checking out the place, so neither of them really knew what they were going to find.

But it shouldn't be dangerous, Ndidi thought. The explosion that had blasted open the door had been intense enough to shake the entire Sparta headquarters and loud enough to be heard a city block away. The military had swarmed the place in minutes. Although they hadn't given the all clear, they hadn't tried to stop Manar or Ndidi. Or, at least, not a second time.

"Shouldn't we wait for DJ?" she asked.

Manar frowned. Ndidi almost wanted to take back the question. She and Manar hadn't spoken much in the last three years, mostly because Helene had upended both of their lives, and they'd needed to deal with that individually. This would be their first meeting in months, even though they both lived in New York.

Still, there had been no need for Manar to call her immediately after the explosion. But he had. Ndidi was not blind to the implications of that and wasn't sure she was ready to deal with them. *But I shouldn't have brought up DJ.*

"I placed a call to Olsen before you arrived. DJ should have been notified. Seeing as this whole thing vindicates his fears, I assume he's already on his way." Manar paused, and his face smoothed back into his normal impassive expression. "Still, I'd like to know what we're dealing with sooner rather than later."

"That makes sense," Ndidi nodded.

The hole in the door wasn't so big that they could step through walking side by side, but it was more than big enough to cross while walking in single file.

Ndidi paused on the other side, confused for a moment by the red glow bathing everything. The same red Helene's relays made. *Yeah, Helene was definitely here.*

Ndidi stepped to the side. Manar stood beside her a second later. The hallways branched a couple of steps in, but the sound of pounding boots in the distance made Ndidi keep going straight. In the middle of the hallway was another metal door. This was nowhere near as thick as the Facility gate, but another hole created a path through. Ndidi brushed a finger against the smooth edges as she passed.

"Apparently there are doors in every hallway," Manar said. "Helene must have controlled them somehow. But no one has found the terminal she used, so there's no way to raise them yet."

Ndidi nodded. Her gaze was drawn to the scorch mark on the walls.

Was there another explosion here? she wondered. *Was Helene the one to do this? To cover her tracks?* She moved on after a minute. They would get answers one way or another. And, if nothing else, this was a reminder about how dangerous Helene was.

They traveled the passages until they found the hub of the level. Military officials scurried about, holding up devices that Ndidi couldn't put a name to. The red lights suffused everything, turning what would have otherwise been pristine white into something more blood soaked. Ndidi banished the creepy thoughts and took in as much as she could.

There were laboratories on either side of the passage. One looked like a modern-day hospital ward. The sheer size of it baffled Ndidi.

"And no one knew that all this was here?" she blurted without thinking.

It was another question she wished she could have taken back immediately. So far, Manar had taken in everything with an impassive face. However, though they were not as close as they once had been, the man still had the same tells. They were so clear that Ndidi felt like she could almost read his mind.

He's probably asking himself the same thing I just did. Except, since Helene was his creation, he's beating himself up for it. And probably wondering if this was another thing that he'd blocked out and couldn't remember.

"It doesn't show up on any of the building's schematics," Manar said finally. "And since the departments are separated, no one noticed the anomaly. The military is still interrogating the people they found here. I've already received a preliminary list of names. At least enough to confirm that none of them is in our employee database. Obviously, Helene had another way of bypassing the security measures and getting them here."

His voice turned hard toward the end. His control slipped and showed the anger—and doubt—that he'd been trying to hide. Ndidi had seen this downward spiral before; she'd been living it less than a month ago and would have been still if not for DJ. A part of her wanted to help Manar deal with this. That same part acknowledged that this was probably the reason why he'd waited for her. But Ndidi couldn't bring herself to act on the impulse.

So she distracted herself. She stared into one of the rooms. For Helene to have been able to hide something like this right under everyone's noses—the scope of it was beyond anything she could imagine.

They said nothing as they continued deeper into the level. Ndidi noted that most of the walls were burned up, some places more than others, as if the explosion had been concentrated there.

A separate explosion? Ndidi wondered. *Regardless, if they wanted to destroy something, they didn't do a very good job.*

They passed a lot of military types on the way. Some of them were security that'd been sent in case anything dangerous was found. Others were researchers that moved around with various devices. Ndidi was curious about what they were measuring. Both types ignored her and Manar. After a minute of the same thing, Ndidi stepped in front of one of the researchers.

"Hi there," Ndidi said. She tried for a smile, but it must have come out as a grimace because the other woman scowled at her. Then again, it might have been because Ndidi had interrupted her work. "Can you tell me what's going on here? I've seen a lot of people running around measuring stuff."

"That's classified," the woman said. "Everything in this facility is classified, actually. Sparta employees should not be able to get in here."

Ndidi glanced at Manar. He was lost in his thoughts. She focused on the woman and tried another smile. "I don't work for Sparta. I run a private research hospital. Sorry, I should have introduced myself. I'm Ndidi Okafor."

That seemed to get the woman's attention. Her eyes widened, and she lost her scowl, staring at Ndidi like she was a celebrity. Ndidi tried not to focus on the flush of pride that went through her.

Ndidi's field was autism and helping children on the autism spectrum, but the findings that she published were relevant to a number of other fields, including neuroscience, behavioral science, and general psychology. Ndidi realized that some of her work had been making waves in the scientific community of late, but not to the extent that would be worth the intensity of the woman's stare.

"Well, shit," the woman blurted, then laughed. "I'm honored to meet you.

I'm Kelly." She stretched out a hand and Ndidi shook it. "As much as I'd like to help, I still can't tell you what we're doing. I *can* say, though, that some of the stuff in here is decades ahead of what we have outside. Even with most of the place burned up, what we've managed to find will be invaluable after we've studied and reverse engineered it."

"Oh?"

"Yeah," Kelly nodded. "That's what's got our panties all twisted up. I really can't say more, though."

Ndidi nodded and stepped out of the woman's path. "You've already been a big help. Thank you."

"Uh," Kelly said, hesitating for a second. "You might not want to go too deep into the level. We're cleaning up, but the place is still enough to make anyone sick, strong stomach or no."

"What are you—" Ndidi started to ask, but the woman had already rushed off. She turned to Manar. "Any idea what she meant?"

He shook his head. "I've gone through a few of the reports that were sent to me, and none of them mentioned anything to clean up. Could she have meant the walls?"

"We've already seen the burned walls. It wouldn't explain why the place would make anyone sick." She planned on checking out the entire level. She was bound to stumble on the place sooner or later.

Two hallways later, she was proven right.

The smell hit like a punch to her nose. She gagged and recoiled instinctively. "Jesus. What the hell is that?"

Manar had a hand pressed over his nose, muffling his voice. "Smells like something rotten." He coughed. "Corpses. That's what we're smelling. Corpses."

Corpses? Ndidi blanched, cupping her palm to her nose. *Is that what the woman was talking about?*

Manar looked at her. "Will you be okay?"

Ndidi started to reply but thought better of it and just nodded. Manar stared at her for a moment longer. She wasn't sure whether she should be flattered by his concern or offended that he thought she needed it. That was always the problem when they were together. She'd be fine one moment, and the next, she would feel as if her independence was at odds with a sudden desire to be protected. It was pathetic.

The stench was somehow worse in the next corridor. Even with her palm over her face, the smell somehow drilled up Ndidi's nose. Her eyes started watering. They turned the final corridor.

Corpses. Rows and rows of corpses, most of them burned to some degree or the other. They stretched almost the entire hallway, listless eyes staring at the ceiling. Some had their limbs missing, their stomachs torn out, or their throats slit. All of them had some part blackened from fire. One had his whole chest flattened, as if they'd been on the wrong end of a compressor. A couple of people worked at the end of the rows, stuffing the corpses into large body bags.

Ndidi threw up. Manar did the same. At least they could be embarrassed together. They stayed hunched over for close to a minute, emptying their stomachs. When the stench started entering her mouth, however, Ndidi forced herself to stand, retreated into the previous hallway, and kept going until she was at the departmental gate. Manar caught up to her after a few minutes.

"That—" Ndidi started, but her voice caught. She licked her lips and felt she could almost taste the corpses. She barely stopped herself from throwing up again. "That was horrible. What could have done that? The explosion?" But even as she said it, she knew that it couldn't have been the explosion. Explosions don't slit a man's throat.

"It was Karla Polova," Manar said. "I recognized her in one of the security feeds before they disappeared again. She was with another woman and a man that I assume was her father, José Olvera."

Ndidi stared at him in shock. She remembered Karla Polova, of course, though she'd tried very hard for the last three years to forget her. Her sister, Liz Polova, had nearly killed Ndidi during the data bank incident. DJ had severely injured Karla, but he'd been lucky. After the incident, Karla and Liz had vanished without a trace.

Later, DJ had somehow managed to dig up some information about the sisters, which he'd shared with Ndidi. She hadn't been able to sleep for weeks after. The women were psychotic. And they'd been living in *Sparta* for the last three years?

"Shit," Ndidi said.

"Yeah."

CHAPTER

35

FEBRUARY 2043
SPARTA HEADQUARTERS,
NEW YORK

CJ ARRIVED a few days later with DJ. Manar was able to set them up with one of the rooms on the higher floors. They got in late and were asleep as soon as their heads hit the pillow. Manar met them the next morning, dressed in a turtleneck and jeans, and led them to a conference room.

"Thanks for hooking us up with the room," DJ said as they walked. Manar just nodded.

CJ glanced to the side. As usual, his brother had a small grin on his face, but for once it didn't reach his eyes. CJ tried not to let that worry him. DJ had had that look since he came back from his meeting with Admiral Austin. DJ hadn't told him anything about the encounter, which meant he wasn't ready to talk.

That was another thing CJ tried not to worry about. DJ was *always* ready to talk—especially to him. Whereas CJ was overly analytical, DJ wasn't one to think much about things. He'd rather do what he thought was right and deal with the consequences. CJ had always envied that, though he knew he would never be that way.

Still, it made his brother's reticence even more confusing. The last time he'd seen his brother in this mood was after Mayday, when they'd been given the news of their dads' deaths. Later, they'd found out that Helene was behind the attack, and DJ had almost gotten killed trying to take her down.

And now Helene had resurfaced.

Ndidi was already in the conference room, though it didn't seem as though she'd been waiting long. CJ hesitated. He hadn't seen Ndidi since her parents' burial. DJ had told him she was doing better, and CJ had no reason to doubt him. So why did her eyes look so haunted?

Judging by her rumpled clothes, Ndidi had slept in the headquarters as well. CJ was staring at her intently, so he was probably the only one who noticed when she forced a calm and composed expression onto her face. There wasn't even a hint of the haunted look from a second before.

How does she do that? CJ wondered. *Why does she do that?*

CJ had the opposite problem. He couldn't show his emotions; his facial expressions were limited. When he felt something and his body tried to express it, he would tense up. The more powerful the emotion, the more likely he wouldn't be able to show it. It'd become more manageable after years of practice. It baffled him that someone would want to hide what they felt. Weren't they afraid of being misunderstood?

DJ gave Ndidi a hug, and CJ suspected he had also noticed the look in her eyes. Or maybe they were just that close.

"It's nice to see you again, CJ," Ndidi said as she released his brother and turned toward him.

CJ hesitated, worried she'd noticed his staring. But she didn't look mad, just expectant and encouraging, waiting for his reply. CJ felt himself freezing under the attention. He pinched himself. "It is … hmm … nice to see you too."

She nodded and gave him a proud look before turning back to the rest of the group. Manar had already taken a seat at the head of the glass table. DJ had picked a spot in the middle, and CJ joined him there. Ndidi sat on the other side of the table, closer to Manar.

"Why didn't you bring the rest of your team?" she asked DJ. "I figured Olsen would send them with you since they've already been briefed about Helene."

DJ scratched the back of his head. "Yeah, they would have come too, but they were deployed on a mission yesterday."

"Deployed?" Ndidi frowned. "Without their team leader?"

"I'm with them," DJ replied. "Officially, at least."

Ndidi looked even more confused. But Manar seemed to understand. "Let me guess," he said. "Olsen sent your team off somewhere officially, but he snuck you out of the base so you could meet us here?"

"Got it in one."

"Why would he do that, though?" Ndidi asked.

Again, Manar had the answer. "It's a kind of smoke screen. To throw off anyone that's tracking his movements."

"And why's that necessary? Why would someone be tracking DJ's movements?"

"I'm pretty sure it's Austin," DJ said, his lips pressed into a line. "He's the admiral that's been gunning for me for the last couple of months."

"How did you manage to piss off *another* admiral?" Ndidi gasped. "From the way you talk, you shouldn't even exist to them."

"Hey," DJ protested. "This time, I didn't do anything. I'm pretty sure the dude's working with Helene. That's why I'm on his radar."

Everybody stared at him in surprise—even CJ, though his expression was more limited. DJ had lost his smile completely. Taking down Helene was a monumental task on its own. Add the resources and clearance that an admiral could bring to the table, and it became damn near impossible. Olsen might be able to run interference up to a point, but he was outranked.

Not only that, but if Helene had one admiral working for her, there was no reason to assume that she didn't have another—or even a higher-up in another arm of the government.

"Do you have proof?" Manar asked. "Something we can level against him?"

"No hard proof." DJ shook his head. "It's more of a feeling, but it makes sense. The dude was seriously creepy. Like, *seriously* creepy. He was jumping all over the place, first offering me a seat, then scolding me for entering his office. Plus, he basically admitted to sending me on those shitty missions to keep me busy and distracted. Since there's nothing to keep me busy related to Helene, it checks out that he's working with her."

"We can't accuse the admiral based on that." Manar sighed.

"We wouldn't be able to accuse him even if we had evidence," Ndidi said. "There's the question of who we take the case to. Then there's the question of how we make sure they aren't working with Helene too. I can't even begin to imagine what she might have offered Austin to get him on her side." She paused, a hint of anger entering her voice. "Especially since he knows that Helene was the cause of Mayday."

"He's probably after more power," Manar said. "I don't imagine it'll be hard to find others who also want the same thing. People in power never stop wanting power."

"So you're saying that we should suspect everyone?" Ndidi asked.

"That's not what I'm saying—"

DJ raised his hand placatingly. "You're not saying anything, and she's not saying anything either. What we're *all* considering is, What are we going to do about the psychotic AI that's planning to take over the world, or whatever the fuck her endgame is? Also, what's in this facility that Olsen was harping on about? I haven't checked it out."

Manar's face twisted bitterly. "Somehow Helene built a complex within Sparta that spanned multiple levels. She filled it with workers. Scientists and technicians mostly, though we're still going through all the people there. We've questioned some of the employees, but all of them were working on vastly different projects, so we haven't been able to piece together what she was trying to develop. We're not even sure if this was where the drones came from."

DJ opened his mouth to say something, but CJ nudged him. CJ could practically read his brother's thoughts: *You don't have anything then.* CJ hadn't interacted with Manar much, but anger was rolling off him in waves, and DJ's bluntness would surely not be appreciated at that moment.

CJ cleared his throat, tensed when that drew everyone's attention to him, then pushed past it and spoke. "Where … uh … where is Helene now?"

"What do you mean?" Manar asked.

"Is she … hmm … operating out of Sparta?"

Manar shook his head. "She withdrew most of her focus from our systems yesterday. But I locked her out, just to be sure." He nodded at one of Helene's relays on the wall. Its light was out. "I can track where she focuses her attention, but only to a point. She's found a way to obscure everything else."

"Well," DJ said, "guess there's nothing we can do there."

"There's one more thing," Manar said. He tapped a panel on the table, and a small tablet rose from the gap.

"Damn rich kids," DJ muttered.

Manar tapped the tablet for a few seconds, switching on a projector that CJ hadn't noticed. Another few taps, and a video showed up on the screen. There was no audio. The angle suggested it was from a security camera.

The footage showed a group of men in front of a large metal door. They were in uniform, so CJ assumed they were part of the security team. They were all milling about but seemed to be on high alert.

Then an explosion blew through the door, killing most of the men instantly. CJ tensed. He was unable to show his surprise, so he took in the others' reactions instead. DJ leaned forward. His expression was grim. Ndidi's face remained impassive, but her hands clenched into fists.

It took a few minutes for the smoke to clear. Manar fast-forwarded until three people came through the destroyed door. *No.* CJ squinted. *That's five.* Two of them were carrying people on their backs while the third limped beside them. Manar paused the video and zoomed in on the last woman. She had blood-red hair, and her face was twisted into a snarl.

DJ leaned back in his chair. His grin was forced, and his eyes had gotten harder. "Really hoped I wouldn't see that shade of crazy again."

CJ stared at the screen, focusing on every part of the woman while he waited for the memory to click. The red hair prickled at his recall, but trying to force it would only risk an episode.

"You and me both," Ndidi said. She glanced at Manar. "I assume the woman he's carrying is Liz Polova?"

Liz Polova, CJ repeated mentally. And then it clicked. His face started to express his concern but froze halfway, leaving it weirdly twisted for a moment. Ndidi was the only one to notice.

Manar nodded. "Everything matches the records that I pulled when you first met them during the data bank incident. Almost to a tee, in fact, which is uncanny. It's like they haven't aged a day since then."

"Who are the dude and the chick? What's their deal?" DJ asked.

"The man is José Olvera, the girls' adopted father," Manar replied. "The woman is Chloe Savage. Unfortunately, that's all the information I was able to get on her."

DJ sucked on a tooth. "A ghost, huh? Fuck. How about the old dude?"

Manar shook his head. "The camera didn't get a good picture, so I couldn't pull up anything."

"Do we know where they are now?" Ndidi asked. She hadn't stopped staring at the image, and the haunted look was back in her eyes.

DJ nudged CJ, shaking him out of his thoughts. He blushed and realized he'd been staring. DJ threw him a questioning look, but CJ waved it away.

"No," Manar replied. "This was the only video we picked up. After this, they vanished somehow. Between the explosion and their injuries, it's safe to assume they're no longer working with Helene. They wouldn't be able to stay in Sparta."

"Meaning they had an exit prepared beforehand," DJ said. "Something that they could get to, even with the injuries and extra baggage. And they could probably use it to get *into* Sparta without being detected."

"Yes." Manar nodded.

"And you haven't found it?"

"No."

DJ sucked on his tooth again. "Well, shit."

CHAPTER

36

FEBRUARY 2043
SOMEWHERE IN
NEW YORK CITY, NEW YORK

JOSÉ OLVERA HELD HIMSELF upright through willpower and pride—and a little help from the nearest wall. Every part of his body cried for him to collapse, to *rest*. But José would not allow himself to be so weak in the presence of his girls.

Chloe didn't have the same misgivings. She immediately tumbled to the floor. The scientist fell from her back and rolled a few feet away. Surprisingly, the fall wasn't enough to wake him. José wondered how hard Chloe had hit him to knock him out.

"With my luck," José muttered, "he will end up an invalid after the trouble we took to bring him with us."

José had propped Liz, who was still unconscious, against the wall. Karla came to examine her—unnecessarily, as José had already done so. After a minute of fruitless poking, Karla lay down beside her sister. Her breathing evened out within seconds. José took the time to observe them both. It was rare that he caught them so unguarded, without Karla's snarl or Liz's impassiveness.

They both hate me, he thought. He could accept their hatred, so long as they outlived him.

"Keep doing that," Chloe said from the ground, where she'd pretended to have passed out from exhaustion. "Someone might actually confuse you for a normal dad that's worried about his daughters. Then what would happen to your big, strong image?"

"Nothing," José retorted, his voice grave. He tore his eyes away from the girls and met Chloe's grin with a hardened stare. "Because such a person would be dead in the next second."

"Stiff punishment." Chloe winced, but lust danced behind her eyes. That she had not already pounced on him meant her exhaustion wasn't entirely faked. José didn't blame her. They had come very close to death that day. Even he was still feeling the rush that came with that.

With the explosion to serve as a distraction and to draw attention, it had been easy—almost suspiciously so—to make their escape from Sparta. Ironically, they'd exploited the same path that the AI used when recruiting new staff to the Facility. José had stumbled on it almost a year earlier as he was mapping out the security cameras' blind spots. The path wound through the edges of Sparta headquarters by sticking to less-used passages until it ended somewhere on the ground floor. From there, even a fool could have escaped through the alleys.

They'd been slow and had to stop to rest often, but they had made it out.

"So," Chloe said. "We're being hunted by both Helene and her enemies. What happens now?"

José snorted. She'd asked the question lightly and with her usual grin, but the excitement in her eyes gave her away. They had never discussed what they'd do after escaping the AI. In fact, José was almost certain that Chloe had thought they would have been killed or recaptured. A part of him had thought the same. But they had made it out. Their next step was obvious.

He scanned the room, taking in Chloe's exhaustion, his daughters' injuries, and the old man.

"We will rest and treat our wounds." José crossed over to Chloe and lay down beside her. The floor was cold and grimy, but it was not the worst he'd had to deal with. "Then we take the fight to the AI."

CHAPTER

37

FEBRUARY 2043
OKAFOR AUTISM RESEARCH CENTRE,
NEW YORK

HERMIONE CLONEY SCROLLED through the file that contained the research on picospores. She'd tossed the container with the synthesized spores into her desk drawer. Ndidi had sent both a few days ago, even after Hermione had made it clear she wasn't going to continue the research. It was only logical, then, for Hermione to blame Ndidi when Hermione's curiosity got the better of her.

So much for moving on, she thought, scrolling to another page. *I didn't even last a month.*

She tried to tell herself that she wasn't actually working on the project. Ndidi had said that some parts of the research were lost. Hermione was just taking note of those parts. Very deliberately, she didn't consider why making these notes was important. Without knowledge of the process, no one else would be able to continue the research, and she was the only one who had that knowledge. Without her, picospore research was dead.

As it should be. The project had belonged to her father and her. It would be wrong to continue without him by her side. So why was she still scrolling through it?

She tapped her pen against her notepad. Picospores had been her idea, but it was their combined effort that had formed it into anything resembling a valid theory. It would be wrong to continue the work without him, wouldn't it? But maybe she'd been looking at it wrong. The project was so remarkable because of its many potential applications. Its impact in the medical field alone would be revolutionary. It could save so many lives.

Wouldn't it be more wrong not *to finish the work?* Hermione thought. She'd told Ndidi that she didn't want to continue the research because the process would remind her too much of her father. but that didn't really feel like such a problem anymore. Hermione remembered how she was during the first few months after the burial—the feeling of helplessness, like she was constantly falling. She knew she'd made strides since then. If anything, she felt that finishing his work would make it easier for her to move on.

Hermione looked at her screen with new eyes. She was already at the end of the file. She'd taken notes from the parts that were missing and commented from memory what should have been there. If she was going to do this—and it was looking more and more likely that she was—then she would need to start from the beginning and recreate all the same results that she and her father had obtained together. With the knowledge she had, she might even be able to fine-tune the spores, make them better.

Hermione stood up so fast she sent her chair reeling. *I'm going to need a lot of rats.*

CHAPTER

38

DJ CLAPPED LOUDLY, and everyone's attention turned to him. "Just to be sure that we're on the same page, I'm going to run through everything we're up against. That good with everyone?"

Ndidi nodded. CJ and Manar both gave blank looks. DJ took that as a yes.

"In no particular order," he said, "we have the psychotic AI that's gunning for the world. We have the navy admiral who is working with her and gunning for my ass and the asses of my team. Then we have the Murder Twins, their father, and the ghost. Is that it? Did I get them all?"

"You, uh … you missed the unknown number of other … of other people that might be working with Helene," CJ said.

DJ snapped his fingers. "Thanks, bro. We also have a number of AI lovers we don't know, can't identify until it's too late, and can't plan for." He turned to CJ. "Is that it? Did I miss anyone now?"

When CJ shook his head.

DJ continued. "Now that we know what we're dealing with—except in the one instance where we don't—what are we going to do about it?"

Manar shook his head. "We know Helene's endgame is power, but that's so vague that it's not worth much. We don't know how she plans to achieve it or the resources she has at her disposal. A month ago, I would have suggested just shutting her down entirely—or at least rebooting her. But now I'm not even sure that's going to work. She's learned to hide her activities from me somehow. Yet, ironically, Helene is the one on whom we have the most information.

"This Austin is a total wild card. We don't know his motives, his goals, or why he's paired up with Helene. In the same way, we don't know anything about the others—Karla and Liz Polova and José Olvera. I could pull up information on them, but everything from their time with the CIA would be redacted, and anything from when they started working with Helene would be outdated." Manar sighed, pressing a palm against his forehead. "There's no way to make a plan with that many unknown variables."

Everyone stared at him. Ndidi looked even more worried, and CJ nodded his agreement. DJ saw the man's point, but his aim was just to get the ball rolling. And the dude was ruining it.

"Thanks for the clarification," DJ said, forcing a grin. "Does anyone else—"

"My point," Manar said, "is that our first course of action should be to get more information about Helene, Austin, and the others. That'll make it easier to concentrate our efforts."

Oh, DJ thought. *So he wasn't just being a dick. Cool.*

Ndidi finally snapped out of whatever funk she'd been in. "Obviously you'll be the best bet on the Helene front," she said to Manar. "DJ and CJ can handle Austin while I find out what I can about José Olvera, his girls, and the old man. Something about him seems familiar."

Everybody was nodding, as if the plan of action was settled, but DJ had some reservations. "Yeah, but I'm not really a research kind of guy, so I don't know how much help I'll be."

Ndidi was in the middle of standing up, probably thinking the meeting was over, but she paused at DJ's words. She started to say something, but Manar beat her to it.

"Don't sell yourself short, DJ," he said, chuckling. "Play to your strengths."

The fuck is that supposed to mean? DJ thought. He felt a nudge and glanced at his brother. CJ mimed punching.

Well, *that* he could do.

CHAPTER

NDIDI RETURNED to the Centre immediately after the meeting, waiting only to collect a copy of the security footage. Manar would have had a better chance of finding information about the Murder Twins and the rest, but it seemed unfair to ask him to deal with Helene as well. She had exactly one idea of how to complete her task, and most of it was based on a vague hunch. If that didn't pan out, then she'd be forced to rely on her family's connections to get information. Ndidi would rather not do that—even as a last resort.

The Autism Centre was silent, which wasn't out of the ordinary. The building was primarily a research center. Of course, there were also classes for children on the autism spectrum, but those were in a different wing.

As Ndidi made her way to Hermione's lab, her steps echoed loudly in the empty hall. That would have annoyed her before. Now she barely noticed.

Hermione was poring over a large tome. Ndidi made her way toward her, carefully navigating the stacks of books and balled-up papers strewn across the floor. Although Ndidi didn't make any effort to be silent, Hermione didn't notice her, even when she got close enough to peer over her shoulder.

Ndidi scanned the books that cluttered the counter, but it was the picospore research file open on Hermione's laptop that made her grin.

Hermione took a sudden step back, and Ndidi couldn't get out of the way in time. She managed to keep her balance, but Hermione jumped as if she'd been electrocuted.

"I thought we spoke about this!" Ndidi said, adopting a stern expression. "When was the last time you left this lab? Scratch that! When was the last time you ate—or *slept?*"

Hermione was a mess. Her cheeks were sunken, and she had bags forming under her eyes. Ndidi would have been worried if she hadn't been working with researchers for the better part of her life. Hell, until DJ snapped her out of it, Ndidi had frequently gone days, surviving on pure research and adrenaline.

"Oh, no," Hermione countered, chuckling. She sidestepped Ndidi, crossed the room and picked up a textbook from one of the stacks on the floor. "This is *your* fault. You're the one who sent me my father's research even after I told you I didn't want it."

"Is that why you want to kill yourself?" Ndidi asked. "I've been gone for two days, and you look like you've lost half your body weight. And are those rats in the corner?"

Hermione looked around the lab and then at herself. She blushed. "I guess I went a little overboard. The rats are just to confirm the results that my father and I got when we first developed the initial picospore protypes. It took months to figure out how to program them once they got past the epidermal layer."

"And the stacks of books?"

Hermione's smile grew even more sheepish. "Well, I was going through the research data, and I had a couple of ideas about how to make the spores better. As they are, there's a slight lag between when the command is input and when it's followed."

"But how are you running these experiments?" Ndidi asked, struggling to keep the excitement from her voice. "There were only a few spore units in the container I gave you."

Hermione gestured to the counter, and Ndidi finally noticed the two containers scattered among the loose papers. "I used a unit of that to synthesize more. Not many, and the new ones aren't programmable yet, but that's one of the things I wanted to ask you about, actually. My dad and I created a *lot* of spores."

Ndidi shrugged. "The canister I gave you was the only one we could recover. I checked personally after the funeral. The rest must have been destroyed."

Hermione nodded. Some of her enthusiasm dimmed. "I figured. Anyway, how was your meeting in Sparta? You were with Manar. Any sparks?" She wiggled her eyebrows suggestively. It was so reminiscent of something Hermione would have done as a teenager that Ndidi laughed out loud.

Still, while she agreed with the subject, she did *not* agree with the direction that Hermione obviously wanted to take it. "I was with Manar, DJ, *and* CJ. The meeting was … enlightening."

Enlightening is an understatement. Ndidi knew she hadn't been as composed as she should have been. It had been nice to see CJ, though. Most of her reports had come from DJ. She was proud to see how much progress CJ'd been making. His attempts to express his emotions without freezing up had given her some ideas that she could test.

"Enlightening, huh?" Hermione raised a brow. "How so?"

Ndidi hesitated, trying to decide what to tell her. She and Hermione had grown closer over the last couple of weeks. However, their friendship still wasn't as strong as it'd been when they were younger. But it was getting there. On the other hand, Ndidi had her own reasons for going after Helene. While she was sure Hermione would have the same reasons, dragging her into it would put her life in danger.

She still hadn't told Hermione that Helene may have caused the landslide that'd killed their parents, theory as it was. Ndidi wasn't fully convinced—though the sheer magnitude of the facility inside Sparta did a lot to bring her around on that. But that was only part of the reason. Mostly, she was trying to protect Hermione.

Shouldn't Hermione be the one to decide whether she should be protected?

Ndidi knew that if the shoe was on the other foot, she would want to know. She would *always* want to know. Then she could make the best decisions with the information she had.

"It's sort of a long story," Ndidi said. "Something I should have told you a while ago, actually. But before that …"

She brought out her phone and played the video she'd collected from Manar. She paused it when the group came out and pointed at the old man on Chloe Savage's back.

"Do you know this man? He looks familiar, but I can't place where I've seen him."

Hermione took the phone, eyes burning with curiosity. She studied the image before looking up in surprise. "That's Martin Bryan. Did you get this from the meeting? What was he doing at Sparta?"

Ndidi snapped her fingers. That was why he seemed familiar. Martin Bryan was an academic, but he worked in biotechnology, far off from Ndidi's field and closer to Hermione's.

"Of course! He's the world expert in some field, right?" Ndidi said.

"He's a legend. Almost as huge as Manar Saleem. I actually got part of the idea for the picospores from a paper he wrote on molecular cybernetics."

Ndidi's eyes widened. From there, she listened with only half an ear as Hermione continued talking.

That's why he was with Helene. He was one of the world's leading experts on cybernetics. He was probably the one who designed Karla and Liz Polova's prosthetic limbs. If she was right, then it made sense to take him with them when they broke out of the Facility. The twins would probably need his help to maintain their artificial limbs.

How do I use this? Ndidi thought. It wouldn't be difficult to get some information on the biotechnologist. Liz already had her prosthetics during the data bank incident three years ago. That meant Martin Bryan had already been working for—or possibly with—Helene for at least that long. Any information about him would be outdated, but at least it was a place to start.

"I can't move forward until I figure something out," Hermione finished, just as Ndidi snapped back to reality. It took a moment for her to play back the conversation in her mind. Once she did, she frowned.

"What sort of simulations do you need to run?"

"I need to know the effects of the picospores on the brain. I explained it to you at the ice cream shop. Theoretically, picospores should have the most revolutionary application on the brain. However, my father and I weren't able to simulate the effects because of the resources required."

"What resources?"

"A computer capable of running the simulation, for one. It would require a lot of processing power. We've figured out the effects of the spores everywhere else. I have some ideas about how to enhance their effects, but after that, the project's probably going to be a dead end."

Ndidi's frown deepened. The applications picospores could have on the brain was the part that she was most curious about. Most of the expressions people on the autism spectrum showed originated from specific parts of their brains. If she could program the spores to interact with those parts and alter the way they functioned, it could serve as a lasting treatment for *everybody* on the autism spectrum—for anyone with some form of neurodivergence, even.

If that were possible …

Ndidi almost melted at the thought.

"So all you need is a computer, right?" she asked, unable to keep the excitement from leaking out. Hermione nodded. "Well, since you couldn't run it in the lab in Nigeria, I doubt the Centre has anything like what you need. We might need to book space in a university's lab. Or if the problem was handling the processing power, we could use the one in"—Ndidi narrowed her eyes at Hermione—"Sparta."

She planned this.

"Earlier, you said that the stuff about the canister was *one* of the things you wanted to ask me," Ndidi said, crossing her arms. "What was the other?"

Hermione's grin turned sheepish. "If you would ask Manar if I could use one of Sparta's computers to run my simulation."

Ndidi's eyes narrowed further, though she wasn't actually angry. Sparta was the logical choice. Their hardware was designed to handle the kind of processing power that Helene needed to function. But this wouldn't be a small endeavor. Ndidi hated to ask for help like this. The fact that it was Manar made her more conflicted.

But if Hermione's results were positive, then it was worth almost anything.

Her phone was already in her hand, and she shot off a text to Manar before she could change her mind. He answered within seconds.

M: "Yes."

Straight to the point as always.

"There," she said to Hermione. "Done. Knowing Manar, he'll want to be there while you set up. Tell me when you're ready, and I'll pass it along."

Hermione's grin stretched across her face. Ndidi's composure was too broken—*from a text?*—to pay it much attention. She made her way to the door.

"Thank you for the tip about Martin Bryan. I'll pull up what I can find about him. In the meantime, you should get some sleep before you fall over."

Ndidi glanced back before the door shut completely to see that Hermione had already turned back to the tome and hadn't heard a word Ndidi said.

CHAPTER

40

FEBRUARY 2043
THE FACILITY,
SPARTA HEADQUARTERS, NEW YORK

DJ WALKED THROUGH the passages of the Facility, taking them at random. By some fortunate coincidence, this had helped him avoid the throng of military personnel crawling around, so he didn't feel like he was in someone's way.

DJ had to admit that this wasn't as much fun as he'd imagined. When Manar asked him to check out the place, DJ had assumed there would be rooms full of weapons or dungeon-style torture chambers. He would even settle for finding the explosives that'd created the hole in that thick-ass door. But so far, all the rooms he'd found were boring, old laboratories filled with blinking machines. He avoided those, too, because they were always crawling with people.

The most interesting place he'd found was the gym and training room. Most of it was a wide, circular space meant for sparring, but the edges of the room had sports equipment and the like. He'd even spotted a treadmill at the back.

How the hell did she sneak those in? That was the part DJ couldn't wrap his head around, the effort it must have taken for Helene to set this place up without anyone noticing. Not only had Helene hidden the place for years, she'd made it self-sustaining. There were workrooms, bedrooms, and kitchens. Hell, on one floor, DJ had seen a small vegetable garden. Between all that and the bunker-level entrances, the place seemed like it was designed to survive an apocalypse.

Fortunately, voices pulled him out of his thoughts, and DJ paused. Somehow, he'd made his way to the edge of the common area. The area had the most activity, being the site of this floor's workrooms. There was always someone there.

He turned to go, but a word made him stop and turn back.

Prisoners? He frowned, homing in on the voice. He knew the military had detained the Facility staff they'd found. Was the military detaining them as prisoners? From what DJ had heard, half of the workers had been kidnapped or blackmailed into working for Helene; it didn't make sense for them to become prisoners because of that. The others hadn't even known what they'd been working on. Helene had given each person a specific part of a project to work on. Then, she'd separated everybody working on the same project into different levels.

It was a sick, if smart, way to hide your end goal.

DJ tracked the voices to one of the workrooms. This one was smaller than others and had been completely stripped. He noted dust outlines where objects used to be. DJ wondered if Manar was aware that the military was cleaning out the place.

A group of more than a dozen people was pressed against the far wall. Their clothes were dirty, but the people otherwise didn't bear any signs that they'd been mistreated. One of them even had a bag of chips from the vending machine.

DJ's entrance drew some attention, though most stayed focused on the woman asking questions at the front of the group. DJ recognized the voice as the one that had drawn his attention.

"One of the creepy guards always kept watch," one of the men from the group was saying. He was middle-aged and balding. His lab coat was blackened in some places and hung loosely from his frame.

DJ noticed he wasn't the only one still wearing his lab coat. *Is it some sort of badge or something?*

The woman asking the questions frowned. "Creepy guards?"

The others in the crowd seemed to know what the man was talking about, nodding and muttering in agreement. One even went so far as to spit in disgust. The spittle didn't have much momentum, landing instead on one of his colleagues. Unfortunately, the other dude didn't notice.

"Well, they creeped the hell out of me," the middle-aged man said. "They never spoke, and their eyes were always glazed over, even when they were looking right at you. Many of us thought they were blind at first, but they never had any issues navigating the halls. And the way they moved …"

DJ raised a brow.

"The way they moved?" the woman asked. Her tone was skeptical, but she kept scribbling her notes.

"They moved like puppets," someone else said from the edge of the crowd. He was wearing the same type of overalls that DJ had come to associate with engineers and technicians. "At least, when I was brought here. They were fewer then, but they stood out like a sore thumb. Their walk was jerky and slow, as if they were learning how to do it all over again. It got better over the years, but their movements were always stiff. It weirded the hell out of me."

DJ frowned.

The woman in front pointed at the engineer. "How long have you been here, uh … ?"

"Noah," the man replied. "I've been here for the better part of three years."

"Thank you. So all the guards were like this?"

The question was directed at Noah. However, the first man—the middle-aged lab technician—answered. He shook his head.

"No, most of the guards were normal. They'd ignore us for the most part, but they would talk to themselves. At least they made sense."

"Where can we find guards like this?" she asked, licking her lips. "Or any of the security that ran this place? We found their sleeping quarters, but they were deserted."

"None?" the lab tech asked, aghast. "I hid immediately, but I know most of the guards were called in to subdue the twins when they started attacking the place. At least one must have survived. There were dozens of guards on this level."

DJ's eyes widened. Karla and Liz Polova had killed dozens of guards? Just the two of them? The dude had to be exaggerating. But when DJ scanned the crowd, no one else looked like they thought he was exaggerating. DJ had assumed the military had mopped the floor with the guards here and hauled them off somewhere for their own special kind of questioning. But if they'd all been killed, and by just two people …

We're so fucked. We're so fucked. Three years ago, DJ had barely survived a three-minute fight with Karla, and now it seemed she'd gotten an upgrade. Maybe she'd gone full cyborg and was even more bulletproof. They were so fucked it was hilarious.

The interviewer certainly thought so because she barked a laugh. "Two women killed dozens of your security personnel by themselves? Be real. It's more likely that the explosion took the guards out. The women probably set it up across the routes they knew the guards would take."

That would make more sense, and DJ desperately wanted it to be true. But one look at the crowd crushed that hope before it could form.

The man at the back, Noah, replied this time. "I heard it all. The explosions came after the guards were called in. Before then, it was just screaming and that psychotic bitch's mad cackling. It echoed throughout the halls, so I know I'm not the only one who heard it."

Nods of agreement met his statement. DJ chuckled, his body vibrating. *We're so fucked.*

He pushed himself away from the wall and strode over to the group. He needed more information on the guards. From the interviewer's look, he was sure she'd get bogged down asking about the Murder Twins. His approach drew some attention—probably from his dashing good looks and confident gait. The soldier didn't react until DJ placed a hand on her shoulder, possibly because she was still in shock about the twins.

"I have some questions about the guards. From Manar Saleem," he said softly. DJ shot the soldier his most charming smile. It felt weird to drop Manar's name like that, especially since he was blatantly lying. But it was better to lie than to waste time trying to convince her some other way.

After a few seconds, she gave a brief nod and stepped back. DJ turned to the crowd.

"All right," he said, rubbing his hands together, "let's make this quick. Noah, can you describe these guards for me again? The creepy ones."

"I started noticing them about three years back," Noah said. "They stood out immediately because of the way they walked, all stiff and jerky. The guards are rotated through different levels, so we were waiting for these ones to be rotated back because, well, they creeped the hell out of us. Like Clint said, they never spoke to anyone, and they had this blank look like they weren't all there."

Everybody in the crowd nodded along, looking like they were bobbing for apples. DJ would have made a joke at any other time, but something about the description was nagging him. He felt like he would lose it if he got distracted.

God, is this what Ndidi and Manar feel like all the time? No wonder they always look like they have sticks up their asses.

DJ cleared his throat, reining in his thoughts. "What else?" he asked the crowd.

"One of them was posted outside my lab," someone said. "And he never twitched. Not once. He was like a robot. He would stand for hours without adjusting his clothes or scratching an itch."

"Yeah," someone else said.

"It was so creepy."

"Stared through you instead of at you."

"Dead eyes."

"Rubbed me the wrong way."

"Moved like puppets."

People spoke over each other until it became a cacophony of voices. One of the things they said struck a chord in DJ's mind, but it was drowned out the next moment by several others. He focused and tried to catch it again, but everything blended together.

Sighing, DJ cupped his hands over his ears. "Dudes!" he bellowed. "Shut the fuck up for a sec!"

Surprisingly, it worked. His voice drew everyone's attention, and they quickly hushed.

"Now, show of hands," DJ said in his normal voice. "Who said the stuff about dead eyes?"

Three hands went up slowly. DJ realized he'd just treated a bunch of adults like grade schoolers. And they'd listened. He picked one at random and gestured for the person—a woman in a lab coat—to talk.

"Well, their expressions were always blank." She spoke slowly, arranging her thoughts as she went. "And their eyes were always dead. Like, *dead*. There was no light there. It would have been interesting if it wasn't so creepy."

The woman shifted positions, and her tone changed to one DJ's teachers would use during a lecture.

"Everyone alive has a spark of intelligence, even animals. These guards had none of that. Even when they stared, they were staring through you, not at you—if that makes any sense. Honestly, if they weren't moving, it'd be easy to think they were corpses."

The woman fell silent, but DJ had tuned her out about halfway through. He'd realized what was bugging him.

That's the same way I described Austin's eyes. Even the whole moving-like-a-robot thing is the same. What were the odds that the guards working in Helene's secret facility would have similar characteristics to Austin? DJ was already 70 percent sure Austin was also working with Helene.

Would be a fucked-up coincidence, DJ thought. *A really fucked-up coincidence.*

The only thing that didn't add up was the whole speech thing. The creepy guards didn't talk, and DJ had had a full conversation with Austin—albeit one with lots of unnecessarily long and weird pauses. But that would be something for Manar to figure out.

DJ focused again on the woman in the lab coat. She was staring at him—as was the rest of the group. He coughed.

"That was really helpful, ma'am. The … government thanks you for your service."

The soldier had been standing silently behind him. DJ gestured for her to continue and made to leave, but she laid a hand on his shoulder like he'd done to her.

"You've obviously figured something out," she observed. "Care to fill us in?"

DJ shot her another one of his best smiles. "You'll get the report in the morning."

With that, he made his way out of the room and then out of the Facility entirely, grinning all the while.

CHAPTER

41

FEBRUARY 2043
NEW YORK CITY, NEW YORK

THE WAREHOUSE THEY USED as a base wasn't much, but Martin was in no position to complain. Not that he would have. It had been two days since they'd escaped Sparta, and Martin was still reeling from the fact that he was free. *Free.* After three years of being limited to the same four walls. After three years of tedious boredom. After three years of the abuse.

He'd extracted payback for the last one, but the severity of it weighed on him. He'd gone through the scene, several times. He was accustomed to violence from other people. That he'd been the one to inflict it was hard to grasp. Shit Stain had deserved it, but Martin had still beaten a man almost to death. Yet he didn't regret it. And that was what truly scared him.

"Hey," Karla barked. "I do not have all day, old man. Are you finished?"

Her face was scrunched up in a scowl, but there was no real anger behind it. It had taken Martin a while to get used to that. He didn't doubt that she could kill him on a whim, angry or not. However, he was fairly certain her father wouldn't let her—at least not until he had finished using Martin.

Seems like I've traded one prison for another, Martin thought. Yet he couldn't bring himself to regret that either. At least here he was dealing with actual human beings, people with whom he could reason. And he would not be limited to studying his creations only once a month. The cybernetics on Karla and Liz were his first prototypes. That they worked so well was proof he would be able to improve on subsequent models.

Martin chuckled. *That is, assuming I survive the next few weeks.*

"Almost finished," he said softly. His eyes were lowered, ignoring Karla's snarl.

The escape from Sparta had left them all injured. Martin had been unconscious for most of it, yet even he hadn't come out unscathed. José and Chloe had emerged with surface wounds that were easily treated. But Karla and Liz had magnitudes worse. Chloe refused to give him the whole story, but the girls looked as if they'd been in a war.

Liz had an ugly gash across her stomach. Whatever had wounded her had torn through both flesh and bionics. José had slapped Martin awake to attend to her. Although Martin didn't have the tools he needed to treat such an extensive wound, he had at least been able to stabilize her enough for the gash to heal by itself, given time and the nanites in her bloodstream.

That had been another unexpected side-effect of the girls' procedure. When Martin had designed the nanoprocessors to integrate with the bionics, his intent was to allow better control of their new limbs, but the nanites hadn't stopped there. Martin had already known about the reinforcement of the girls' musculature, which enhanced their strength and speed, but he hadn't seen the change in their recovery rate until he'd started working on Liz. The changes were slow but amazing to observe.

José had insisted, after Liz was stabilized, that Martin begin treating Karla. Martin would have preferred to let her heal naturally so he could note the differences between the sisters, but the glint in José's eyes had stopped him from making the suggestion.

His tools moved slowly but with precision. Karla's wounds weren't as bad as her sister's. The worst was the sprained ankle that Martin was working on. He took the chance to observe any changes. If Karla knew that he was delaying the process on purpose, then she would probably have maimed him, even if it was in the name of science. Impatience raged through her body. Her eyes kept darting toward the center of the warehouse, where José and Chloe were engaged in light sparring.

Well, they'd called it sparring, at least. It looked more like they were fighting to the death. Both fought with a pair of daggers, and sparks flew whenever the weapons touched. The clashes rang throughout the warehouse. From the moment they'd started, Martin had found it difficult to focus. But after hours of it, the clangs were now just an unpleasant soundscape while he worked.

Karla growled again.

"All done," Martin said quickly. That growl had contained actual anger. With Liz unconscious and José distracted, continuing his study was not worth the risk. Besides, he had treated the most pressing injury. He could still study the lesser ones to see how they healed. He began replacing his tools in their bag while Karla got dressed.

She hadn't needed to strip completely, since he'd just been working on her legs, but the tight jumpsuit made removing individual parts difficult. Karla would have ripped the jumpsuit's leg off had José not stopped her. Karla stood, and Martin ran his eyes down the right side of her torso, noting the places he would have to check later. Some parts had been scratched. That was impressive, considering how dense the cybernetics were. The surface damage alone would not be enough to interfere with anything, but such things added up. And there was no doubt they'd continue to add up, considering the twins' vocation. Maybe there was a way for him to tweak the nanites with a self-repair function—

"Points for the balls," a voice whispered beside him, "though they're probably shriveled as hell by now. You know, if she notices you looking at her like that, she'll gut you before you can blink. I've seen her do it."

Martin jolted, and he turned sharply to meet Chloe's grinning face. When had she moved there? Suddenly, he realized the clanging had stopped. Martin composed himself and cleared his throat.

"Even if I were still interested in such things, I'd pick safer targets. No, I was studying her cybernetics for points of interest."

"Points of interest, huh?" Chloe winked. "Nice."

Martin started to respond, but Chloe was already standing, her attention on Karla. "If you're all patched up, let's see how sloppy you've become after a day of rest."

Without his wheelchair, Martin had propped himself up against a wall, looking up at them. "Actually, she shouldn't strain it yet—"

Karla spat on the ground less than a foot away from Martin. "Even hobbled, I'd be more than a match for you," she said to Chloe.

"You should say that when you've actually managed to touch me without your sister as a crutch," Chloe retorted.

The two of them walked away and took positions at the center of the warehouse. Martin sighed, then looked over at Liz. She was still unconscious—and naked. Karla had undressed her so Martin could look at her injuries without the clothes sticking to her wounds and infecting them. No one had thought it necessary to clothe her. Martin's fingers itched to study whether her nanites had sped up the process as he suspected.

He glared down at his legs stretched out in front of him. Liz was out of arm's reach. Without someone to bring her to him, he would have to drag himself across the room. His pride wrestled with his curiosity.

And then the problem became moot when José stood in front of him.

"Chloe tells me you know something about my daughters and are holding it back." José squatted until he was eye level with Martin. "You will tell me."

CHAPTER

42

FEBRUARY 2043
SPARTA HEADQUARTERS,
NEW YORK

MANAR INPUT ANOTHER LINE of code and watched as it got rebuffed immediately. *His* code, rebuffed. It was infuriating. He leaned back in his chair and let out a breath. This was his third attempt to trace Helene's commands to their source, and all of them had been rebuffed. It wasn't wholly unexpected, as he'd designed Helene to protect herself from all hacks, but Manar never would have thought it'd be used against him.

How did she even block my bypass in the first place? Manar wondered. He'd created the shortcut on a whim a few days before the data bank incident so he wouldn't have to swim through Helene's codes anytime he wanted to make a change. It hadn't been designed to be truly hidden, but he still hadn't expected Helene to find it, let alone lock him out.

Manar had always assumed he could hack through Helene's programs if he wanted to. Putting aside that he'd been the one to design her defenses, Manar hadn't had a problem accessing anything since he was in college. Helene had not only managed to lock him out of all her programs but rebuffed him three times.

He would have been proud if he weren't so terrified. Until now, Helene had played by some unspoken rule, working through subterfuge and manipulation. Mayday was an example of this. It'd taken months for Ndidi and the rest to figure out the AI was behind it. The Facility was another example. Helene had gone to great pains to hide its existence.

If she always could push him out, why had she waited until now? Why had she pretended to be dormant for three years? So far, none of her activities had been enough to draw attention from anyone who didn't know she was responsible for Mayday. How long would it be until that changed? Why had she given them—given him—the illusion of control? Manar had always thought, if push came to shove, he could simply shut her down. And he was sure everyone else thought that too. But until he figured out how to regain access to her systems, he couldn't even do that.

And if Manar couldn't get access, sure as shit no one else would be able to.

He let out another breath and closed his eyes. When he opened them a minute later, there was a smile on his face. At the end of the day, this was just another challenge to surpass. The information DJ had brought him regarding the similarities between Austin and some of the Facility guards meant that Helene still had some things planned. Manar probably did not have much time to figure it out.

The pressure just added to the experience.

DJ had left for the Naval Amphibious Base earlier that day to meet up with his brother. Manar didn't know how the two would dig up information about Austin without drawing more of his attention, but Ndidi seemed to trust they were up to the task.

Manar opened another tab on his computer and parsed through his last three attempts, going through the codes line by line—something he hadn't done since high school, when Simone was still teaching him the basics of programming. It took him a few minutes, but he couldn't find an error. There'd been nothing wrong with his codes. This meant that for Helene to have rebuffed him so easily, she'd taken over full control of her hardware.

Shit, he thought, sitting up straight. *She shouldn't have advanced that far.* Manar's thoughts spun, but he kept coming back to that fact. Taking control of her mainframe was the only way Helene could have blocked him so completely.

Manar's first plan to regain access had been to use brute force to break through Helene's security measures and reach her core programs. From there, he could create another bypass. He'd done the same thing a few years back when he'd been forced to reboot Helene's programs. Helene had grown by leaps and bounds since then, so he hadn't really expected it to work—not without considerable effort on his part.

His second attempt had involved sneaking a program into her; something that would act as a virus and give him a foothold for another attack. But Helene had she'd shut that attempt down as completely as she'd shut down Manar's first. That shouldn't have been possible. Helene ran billions of processes worldwide. Some of them were as minor as turning lights on and off. Manar should have been able to sneak a program past her—if not easily, then after some time. Helene had detected his foreign codes almost immediately.

It was the only thing that made sense. With full control of her mainframe, Helene would be intimately familiar with every process she was running, no matter how small. She would immediately know when a foreign program was added.

And it would be child's play to shut it down. Fuck.

Manar's phone pinged with a text, and he scanned the message.

N: "Hermione is on her way to Sparta. Can you show her where to set up?"

Manar sighed. He remembered Hermione only vaguely from the funeral of Ndidi's parents.

Why am I doing this? he wondered. But he knew why. *I'm so screwed.*

M: "Sure."

His fingers hovered over the keypad while his mind warred with itself. A part of him wanted to tell her about what he suspected and the implications if it were true. A larger part wanted to wait until he was sure. Before he could decide, his phone pinged again.

N: "Also, I found something about the old man from the security feed. His name is Martin Bryan. He's a specialist in biotechnology and cybernetics."

The dots connected, and he sent off a reply.

M: "He was the one who designed the prosthetics on DJ's Murder Twins."

He was sure Ndidi had already come to the same conclusion. It was the only logical one. It would explain why José Olvera had found it necessary to carry the old man with them. Again, it would be so easy to tell her his suspicions, but he held himself back.

N: "Exactly. It might be easier to get more information on him and then work my way toward the rest."

Fair enough. Although it would be infinitely harder to pull information on the rest of the group. He started to send a reply, but another text interrupted him.

N: "Hermione says she's there."

Manar flicked through his security feed until he found the one for the entrance. A woman was entering the building, carrying a large box. Security moved to stop her; the explosion was still fresh in everyone's mind. Manar sent a message to Mark before the guards could reach her, and Manar directed the receptionist to lead Hermione to one of the spare offices on the twenty-fifth floor.

Usually Helene would have handled the task and informed Manar of Hermione's arrival, but apart from the bare essentials, she'd withdrawn her attention from Sparta since the Facility was discovered. Manar couldn't help but think that her leaving some presence here meant she still had plans for Sparta headquarters.

And now I can't do anything to stop her.

CHAPTER

43

FEBRUARY 2043
SPARTA HEADQUARTERS,
NEW YORK

HERMIONE LOOKED AROUND the office while she waited for Manar. The room was relatively large and had recently been in use, based on the knickknacks scattered around. A large desk sat in the center of the room, but Hermione was more interested in the marble workbenches that lined the edges. There'd been three computers plugged into the sockets when she'd arrived. She'd moved all but one of them to the side. That one she would use when viewing readings.

She'd already brought out the capsule that contained the picospores, the electrodes that would go on the rats' heads, and of course, the rats. The capsule and the electrodes had been easy to bring in, but the box with the rats had almost resulted in her being hauled out by security. Hermione figured the only reason she hadn't been was because of Manar, so that was another thing to thank him for.

The rats squirmed in the box, each fitted with a small cap that held the electrodes. Hermione itched to start—to at least take the baselines, if nothing else. But Ndidi had made it clear that Manar would want to be there.

Fortunately, she didn't have to wait long. Hermione remembered Manar from her parents' burial, though her memory of that period was a blur. He'd changed in the three years since, but his piercing green eyes stood out enough for Hermione to straighten in recognition.

Manar closed the door behind him. He wore a black sweatshirt with jeans. His eyes went to where Hermione had stacked the computers she didn't need.

"I didn't know where to put them," Hermione said, blushing apologetically. She felt small, like she'd done something terrible.

I should have waited for him before touching anything, she thought.

Manar turned his focus on her, and Hermione felt the casual arrogance in his gaze. On any other person, the look would have made Hermione scoff in disgust. On Manar, it just fit. The pride rested comfortably on his shoulders like a cloak.

That explains why Ndidi is always flustered whenever she talks about him.

Manar waved off her comment. "They're old models, anyway—even the one you have plugged in. Ndidi told me a bit about what you planned to do. I've asked someone to bring you one of the models we use on the higher floors. They'll be more than capable."

Two men walked in a second later, each carrying one end of a much larger computer. Manar gestured to the wall where Hermione stood. The men set the device there and set it up, then helped hook up the wires connected to the rats.

Decades ago, Hermione would have needed a dedicated machine to pick up the readings from the electrodes. Now, if she had the right software and advanced hardware, it wasn't a problem. Even the electroencephalograph, or EEG, had advanced over the years. Previously, the machine would have been able to pick up only brain signals from high densities of pyramidal cells that generated electricity past a certain threshold. Now the electrodes were powerful enough to pick up everything, no matter how minor.

With the electrodes hooked up and everything connected, the monitor split into six feeds—one for each rat. Readings started pouring in. Two rats were resting, and they showed lowered brain activity. One that was eating showed a different pattern. The final three, which were moving around in the box, had more activity.

Manar stepped up beside her. Hermione barely stopped herself from jerking away. She'd completely forgotten that he was in the room. He observed Hermione as she rechecked the connections and confirmed that each electrode cap was secure. The attention made Hermione self-conscious and awkward, dragging out a process she'd performed dozens of times.

"The monitor already shows the rats' brain activities," she explained, mostly to distract herself. "The first step is to record this activity during different periods, like when they're resting, eating, playing, and performing a task. Stuff like that." She paused for a response, but Manar remained silent. She didn't dare look at him for fear of breaking her concentration. "After I inject the picospores into the animals' bloodstreams and input a command, I can compare the brain activity of the two states. That way, I know exactly how the picospores are affecting the rats and can extrapolate possible brain effects and applications."

"Why does the hardware matter?" Manar asked.

"It doesn't matter now, when all I'm measuring is the normal activity." Hermione adjusted an electrode. "But once I inject the spores, the hardware needs to be able to handle the processing power it'll take to send a command signal that reaches the picospores through the rats' skin."

"That's … brilliant, actually."

Hermione blushed then forced herself to focus. A minute later, Hermione straightened. She'd checked and then double-checked everything. She turned the electrode caps back on and checked the monitor. Hermione traced each reading back to the corresponding rat, then labeled them for future reference.

"You ready to start?" Manar asked.

Hermione nodded. "This is the boring part. I have a list of states I need a baseline for. I can engineer some artificially—like some of the tasks and commands—but others, I have to wait for or risk muddling the results."

Manar frowned. "How long do you expect this to take?"

"Not that long," Hermione said, shrugging. "I'll have to record everything twice to account for any errors during the process, but it shouldn't take more than a couple of days. A week at the most. Once I inject the picospores, that's when it gets interesting. Ndidi told me you'd probably want to be here for that."

Manar tensed. "Yes. It should be interesting."

Hermione wanted to bury her head. *Shouldn't have brought up Ndidi*, she groaned mentally.

He left shortly after that, and Hermione turned back to the monitor and her rats. *All right, then. Let's get to work.*

CHAPTER

44

"WELL?"

DJ sat in the chair across from Olsen, his usual grin missing from his expression. "For one," he said, "we were idiots to believe that Helene wasn't up to anything the last few years."

Olsen scowled. "Don't yank my chain, boy. What's going on over there?"

"Ndidi's info was right. Helene created a complex within Sparta. Like, right in the middle of Sparta. The shit goes up multiple levels. There's room for the staff, a bunch of machines—even a fucking gym. And no one knew about it until an explosion blasted a hole through the wall. They call it the Facility."

Olsen grunted, looking troubled. "What were you able to find out?"

"Not much." DJ sighed. "By the time I got there, FEMA was already crawling all over the place like ants. I did find out that Helene used a bunch of creepy dudes as guards." He rolled his eyes as Olsen's scowl deepened. "Chill. They really are creepy. Apparently they're mute. They move like puppets, and they have dead eyes."

Olsen tented his fingers. "You said the same thing about Austin."

"Exactly," DJ said. "Austin was sitting down, so he didn't move much. He obviously wasn't mute, but he *was* creepy as hell. He had to be feeling awfully conscious about his eyes to wear dark shades indoors."

"What's your point?" Olsen asked.

DJ shrugged. "Nothing really. Just saying it's weird."

Olsen grunted, then glared at DJ. "That's the only thing you found out? Why'd I stick my neck out for this, then?"

DJ grinned. "I didn't find anything in the *Facility*. But I met up with Manar, and he showed me the clip of the explosion that created this whole mess. The blast killed a bunch of guards that were outside the door. They'd all been geared up, like they were waiting for someone."

Olsen growled, and DJ's grin widened. He hurried on when he saw the admiral's fist clench and unclench.

"Anyway, the explosion fucked up the guards. Guess who walks out about a minute later? José Olvera and the Murder Twins."

Olsen settled back, though the scowl didn't leave his face. "Murder twins? You mean Karla and Liz Polova?"

DJ nodded. "They disappeared after they almost killed Ndidi and me three years ago. Now we know where they went."

Olsen's anger eased, and he snorted. "Them working with Helene is probably the only thing in this whole mess that makes sense. That entire family is batshit crazy."

DJ raised a finger. "They *might* have been working with Helene. But Manar believes they're the ones who caused the explosion while trying to leave. It also explains the guards that were waiting for them. Helene probably directed them there to stop José and the group."

Olsen considered this, frowning. DJ didn't know when the man ever stopped frowning. It seemed to be his default setting.

"So they escaped?" Olsen asked.

"We believe they used the same path that Helene used to sneak in all the other people that we found in the Facility. And no,"—DJ raised a hand to stave off the inevitable question— "we don't know the path. Meaning yes, it's possible they can use it to get back into Sparta. I assume Manar is working on that. Regardless, we know where they've been for the last three years, so that might make tracking them easier."

Olsen grunted. He still looked troubled, but DJ knew he'd run out of things to say when he didn't immediately bark out another question. DJ gave him another moment before asking the question that he'd been holding back since he sat down.

"So? Have Christy and Kyle made it back yet? Were they discovered?"

A hint of a smile flashed across Olsen's face. "I was wondering when you'd ask, boy. They made it back yesterday and were debriefed. They should be in their quarters."

DJ let out a breath. Leaving his team to handle the mission on their own had been stressful. They were used to supporting each other. Christy and Kyle knew how to handle themselves, but it hadn't stopped him from being worried.

His questions answered and his report complete, DJ stood. CJ had left New York a day before DJ to find out what he could about Austin and why he would be working with Helene. DJ would need to meet up with him so they could plan the next step. Olsen had already gone back to the mountain of paperwork on his desk. DJ took it as the dismissal he needed, gave him a nod, and then left the office.

At the end of the hall, his phone dinged with a message. DJ stared at it for a second and then chuckled to hide his sudden unease. As inconspicuously as he could, he checked the walls for cameras. He found one at the other end of the passage. It was focused on him.

Forcing a grin, DJ altered his path to the stairwell. It would take him to a higher floor where the four-star admirals had their offices.

Austin wanted a meeting.

CHAPTER

45

FEBRUARY 2043
SOMEWHERE IN
NEW YORK CITY, NEW YORK

MARTIN STARED AT JOSÉ in shock. The man's eyes were hard and promised violence. Martin would have backed away, were he not already leaning against a wall. A short distance away, Chloe and Karla sparred. The sound of their clashing weapons created another unpleasant backdrop.

I'm … hiding something? Martin thought, his mind spinning. *Is this about the nanites?*

He hadn't mentioned anything about the nanites. Then again, he hadn't mentioned much about his work at all. He'd given only the essentials to Chloe back when they were talking through the comm device. Since they'd escaped, Martin had either been unconscious or busy fixing up the twins.

Chloe must have taken his reticence to share the details of his work as hiding something. But it wasn't as if he'd refused to give her the information she'd asked for. Martin had no reason to do that. No matter how many details he gave, he could not be replaced. As the creator of the technology, his understanding of the girls' cybernetics would always be at a higher level than anyone else's.

But that isn't the problem, Martin thought. *The problem is, What exactly do they think I'm hiding?*

The glint in José's eyes told Martin that the man was expecting something specific, but all Martin could think of were the side effects of the nanites. The existence of the nanites themselves should have been common knowledge, especially if any of them had observed the integration process. The side effects gave the girls increased strength and speed. This would be easy to track, especially during combat.

"Your eyes tell me you have come to a realization," José said. "Good. I would not want to break something without cause. Tell me why my girls have almost doubled their strength and speed in three years. Their separation is not reason enough."

So he was right. It was about the nanites. Martin licked his lips, wondering where to start and how to break down the concept. It was an area that he hadn't had the time to study completely, so he would not be able to provide much information. But the little he did understand should be enough to soothe the man.

"You know about the nanites injected into the girls during their surgery?" he asked. José nodded. "My original design for the nanites was to aid the subjects as they acclimated to their new limbs, enhancing compatibility and ensuring that the body did not reject its new parts. Without them, the subjects would be forced to learn how to use their limbs afresh. However, my original design did not give room for the nanoprocessors to be deactivated after the initial process, so they continued working to enhance compatibility, and after that, just to enhance."

José's eyes narrowed.

"The effects have been good, as you have seen," Martin hurried on. He couldn't keep the excitement out of his voice. "The nanoprocessors have improved every part of your daughters. That is why they are stronger and faster. I will have to study them more, of course, to be sure. My preliminary predictions show that, at some point, the girls will begin to heal faster. They will be less prone to disease."

"They will be stronger," José said. An emotion flashed across the man's eyes, but it was gone too quickly for Martin to identify. "But what will they have to sacrifice?"

Martin frowned, confused. "Until the changes stabilize, they will require an increasing number of calories." He adjusted his glasses. "Apart from that … well, I'll need more data before I'm ready to give any estimations."

"Power never comes for free, old man," José said, his expression unreadable. "You will find out what this will cost. You will have as much access to the girls as you need. But …" His eyes hardened, and again, Martin wished he could back up. "If they are harmed in any way, whatever you suffered in the AI's care will seem like kindergarten."

CHAPTER
46

FEBRUARY 2043
SPARTA HEADQUARTERS,
NEW YORK

HERMIONE NEEDED A FEW DAYS for the first set of experiments, just as she'd suspected. After that, she had to recheck everything in case of errors. That had gone faster. Overall, she needed the better part of a week to complete the first step, and during that time, Hermione had left the office only to shower and eat.

Manar made sporadic visits, looking increasingly frustrated and tired. He hid everything behind an impassive mask, of course, but Hermione had had far too much practice reading Ndidi for that to work. They both creased their foreheads the same way when they were worried. Manar never stayed for long; he just checked on her progress and left. Hermione figured he was using the trip down to clear his head of whatever was bothering him.

After she finished recording the baselines, at Ndidi's suggestion, Hermione had given herself a day to rest. Now, finally, it was time to start the second step.

She'd already texted Ndidi to inform Manar. Once again, she was waiting in the office for him.

Manar walked in a few minutes later while Hermione was double-checking everything. She'd covered each rat with a makeshift gas mask and checked to make sure that the contraption was fully secured. The electrode caps also needed minor adjustments before she was satisfied.

When she was done, Manar stepped up beside her. "You're ready?"

Hermione nodded. She practically vibrated with excitement. It was a struggle to stop herself from bouncing. If the results were anything close to what she suspected, it would change everything. It would validate what she and her father had worked on for years.

It had taken Hermione a couple of days to get used to the casual pride in Manar's bearing. Now, glancing at him, Hermione didn't know if that was because she'd adapted to it or because of some change in him. Hermione had once considered Manar cool and unruffled. Before her parents' funeral, she'd considered Ndidi the same way too.

Now Manar wore his weariness openly. His face was drawn into a frown, forming wrinkles that Hermione was sure had not been there earlier. *Is it something about Helene?* she wondered. Ndidi had given her the bare sketches of what she'd been involved in over the last three years—including the suspicion that Helene had been behind her parents' death. Hermione didn't know what to do with the information, so she locked it away and focused on her research.

What else but Helene would be troubling Manar?

Hermione pushed away the thought. She doubted there was anything she could do. Even if there were, that would require Manar to open up to her. She didn't see that happening anytime soon.

Hermione tapped a button on the side of the canister, and the picospores were released through pipes into the rats' masks. The spores sank into the animals within seconds.

Manar leaned toward the box of rats. "They don't have to breathe it in?"

"No. The spores are all at the picoscale—hence the name. They can pass through any living surface, like the pores of the skin and the lining of organs.

It's part of why they're so valuable. I just released billions of them. That's why they're even visible."

"But there's no change in the rats," Manar said. He gestured at the monitor. "Even the brain activity is the same."

"I have to activate and then program them with a task. I've already covered their effects on the muscles and organs of the body. The aim here is to focus them on different parts of the brain and test the reactions."

Manar nodded and straightened. Hermione's fingers flew across the keyboard. As she had the first day, she was explaining mostly to distract herself from Manar's stare.

"At their core, picospores are simply processors at the picoscale. When you look at it that way, it's easy to see the similarity between what I'm doing now, priming the spores through commands, and traditional coding, where you program specific guidelines into software. Of course, my father added unique variables to the codes when he designed them. But I have no doubt that someone like you could program the spores if given the blueprint."

Manar's eyes widened in surprise. A glimmer of excitement flickered across them. He stepped closer, staring intently at the monitor where Hermione input predetermined codes.

As if I needed a reason to be more *self-conscious*, Hermione thought.

"When designing it," she continued, "the major problem was figuring out a way to broadcast the signals through the layers of the skin to reach the spores. We spent years looking for a solution. In the end, we settled on the biotechnological equivalent of brute force. It's terribly inefficient. Basically, it relies on the computer to boost the signal by duplicating the command millions of times per second. That's why we need hardware that can handle that much processing power."

In reviewing her research material again, Hermione discovered a way to make this process more efficient. She was still working out how feasible the whole thing was, so she couldn't implement it right away. But if it worked, it would significantly reduce her reliance on advanced hardware. It would make mass-producing the technology far easier.

"Anyway," Hermione continued, pushing away her thoughts. "Theoretically, the processing power required increases exponentially when it comes to the brain because of its complexity. The commands have to be more stringent and localized to a specific part of the brain. Some universities have hardware that can handle that kind of power, but Ndidi and I figured Sparta would be better suited for it because of how much strain Helene must put on your system."

"So, the problem is that the codes have to be more specific, and that increases the strain on the system, right?" Manar asked, and Hermione nodded. "I'll be curious about what you come up with. I might be able to help with that, though I'd understand if you're reluctant."

Hermione blinked. "Why would I be reluctant? Your understanding is bound to be deeper than mine."

Manar coughed softly. "I'll need to see the original blueprint that your father designed. That'll require a significant amount of trust on your part."

Hermione hesitated longer than she probably should have. On one hand, Manar's input would be invaluable. It would almost definitely save her months of work. On the other hand, her father had taught the blueprint only to her. It would be a betrayal to share it.

"I'll … I'll consider it," she said.

Manar nodded, his expression giving nothing away. The silence stretched between them for a few seconds before Hermione remembered her experiment. She tapped a key on the computer, finishing the program that she'd written. Manar leaned forward again to get a closer look.

Hermione's vision tunneled. There was no effect for a few seconds. Then, all at once, the readings from the EEG dropped significantly. Hermione frowned. She'd expected the lag, but it didn't make sense for the brain activity to drop. Furthermore, the effects weren't localized. Every part of the brain showed reduced readings.

Hermione had directed the picospores to stimulate the part of the brain responsible for hunger. It was a relatively simple command. It would make the rats hungry and get them to move toward the edge of the box where Hermione had dropped some pellets.

Before she'd sent the commands, the rats' brain waves had varied depending on the activity they were engaged in. Now the EEG showed the same reduced brain waves for all six rats—the exact same brain activity, uniform across the board. That should have been impossible.

The rats started walking. Hermione's frown deepened.

What's going on?

"What command did you give the spores?" Manar asked. He was also staring at the rats, frowning thoughtfully.

"To stimulate hunger."

"Well, it's working."

Like she'd planned, all the rats started moving toward the edge of the box toward the pellets. But the way they moved was unnatural. Their gait was rigid and robotic. Hermione glanced at the monitor. Their brain activity had risen, but the waves were sluggish, similar to when a person is half-asleep.

Hermione couldn't wrap her head around what was happening. Was this what she and her father had spent years working on? Was this the legacy that her father had left behind?

At their mechanical pace, it took the rats a couple of seconds to reach the pellets. They bit into the food automatically. Their brain activity showed no change even though they surely should have felt something from feeding.

Why's this happening?

Keying in the commands, Hermione deactivated the picospores. As one, the rats shuddered, as if shaking off dust. They squealed in confusion and ran around, but their movements were natural again. Hermione's gaze went to the monitor. Their brain activities had gone back to normal. They were higher than most of her baselines, but that was because of their excitement. Better yet, the monitor once again showed different readings for all six rats.

Hermione waited in silence for the rats to settle down before programming another command into the spores, this time to stimulate the area of the brain that focused on arousal. Like before, there was a few-second lag before the rats showed any reaction.

The rats stiffened at the same time, their muscles rigid. Simultaneously, their brain activity dropped and synchronized. Hermione had picked an equal number of male and female rats, so none were left without a partner. But even during mating, their movements were rigid and unnatural.

"Did you notice their eyes?" Manar asked.

Hermione glanced at him. She'd completely forgotten that she wasn't alone. She focused on the box again, observing the rats' eyes. A second later, she shifted the box, pulling it in for a closer look.

What is this?

The rats stared sightlessly in front of them. There was no light in their eyes, to the point that, if it weren't for their directed movements, Hermione would have thought they were blind. Or dead. Hermione couldn't wrap her head around that.

"You triggered arousal in their brains?" Manar asked, frowning. Hermione nodded numbly. Manar's voice grew hushed, like he was working through his thoughts out loud. "It's curious. Before he left, DJ interrogated one of the groups of people we found in the Facility. They described a subset of the guards as having the same dead eyes that the rats are showing now. Even the way the animals are moving is similar to how DJ described the guards. And the admiral." The last part was said so softly that Hermione barely heard it.

She turned to him. "What does that mean?"

"Nothing, maybe," Manar said. His expression, usually impassive, showed a hint of fear. "It's curious that we're seeing such a deviation in the natural behavior of the animals because of the picospores. It's even more curious that the resulting behavior is similar to that of the guards confirmed to be connected to Helene."

"You think Helene is the cause of this?" Hermione asked, confused. It took a moment for her to understand what Manar was getting at—and the fear in his expression. "You think Helene found a way to reproduce picotechnology and somehow used it to control the guards, like puppets?"

"Is that possible?" Manar asked.

"No!" Hermione said. She and her father had worked for years on the pico-spores. They'd researched every study that was even distantly related. No one else in the world was close to understanding the concept, much less replicating the result. If Helene were using it on humans, that meant she'd gone further than Hermione herself. That just wasn't possible—especially without access to her father's research.

Hermione paused, her lips parted in expectant reply, and focused on that last thought. Her father had never let the research out of his sight, but what about after his death? Ndidi had said the Okafor Corporation recovered the file after the accident, but that must have been weeks after. Before that, both the research and the picospores that her father had synthesized were unaccounted for. It would have been easy for Helene to get access to it then.

"Is it possible?" Manar asked again.

"Helene can't have produced a similar technology," Hermione replied, her voice hollow, "but she could have continued researching the picospores if she gained access to the initial results my father and I got while developing them. It's exactly what I'm doing now—except she would be years ahead."

"So Helene may have access to the picospores themselves," Manar said, undisguised horror in his tone.

"And she's using them to control people like puppets."

CHAPTER

47

FEBRUARY 2043
NAVAL AMPHIBIOUS BASE,
CORONADO, CALIFORNIA

HALFWAY TO AUSTIN'S OFFICE, DJ altered his path again and went to see his brother. CJ's office wasn't far from the administrative block, but DJ still had to leave the building. If Austin was tracking his movements—which was a certainty because the summon had come immediately after he'd left Olsen's office—the admiral would know that DJ had purposely delayed the meeting to meet his brother. It was disrespectful, but in his defense, the message hadn't specified a time.

He entered CJ's office without knocking. CJ was at his desk, focused on his monitor. He had a frown on his face and didn't look up when DJ entered. *I told him to work on that*, DJ thought. His brother had a habit of getting so immersed in a project that he was oblivious to everything else. It was awesome for his productivity, but it was also far too dangerous—especially when they had a psychotic AI trying to kill them.

Normally he would wait for his brother to be done. However, DJ didn't know how much time he had before Austin noticed his mistake and set a time for the meeting. Coughing wouldn't be enough to break CJ's attention, and walking over and grabbing his shoulder was a good way to give him a heart attack. This left a third option.

"Yo, CJ!" he yelled.

CJ looked up, and his fingers paused on the keyboard. "Hey, DJ. How long … have you been there?"

"Just got here," DJ replied. He crossed the room, eyed the seat opposite the desk, and decided to remain standing. He was still uneasy about meeting Admiral Austin, so his words came out in a rush. "Have you been able to find out anything more about Austin? I got a message to meet him in his office, and I'm not keen on going in without at least an idea of what he wants."

CJ shook his head, frustration surprisingly evident on his face. "Manar gave me a … a few tips, and I've tried them. But I still got the same … same redacted information as last time. I … uh … think Austin let Helene into our systems to obscure his details."

Well, fuck, DJ thought. Most of the information on Austin was hidden, buried under layers of encoding. DJ had thought that was because of Austin's admiral status. But if Helene was in their system, then they couldn't even trust the little info they'd found. More importantly, it made uncovering Austin's reasons for working with the AI more complicated.

"Fuck," DJ said out loud. "Any idea why the dude wants to see me? Last time, I basically accused him of abusing his powers, and he kicked me out." DJ was already pretty sure he knew why Austin had called. The timing couldn't be a coincidence.

"What … hmm … were you doing before you received the message?"

"I'd just finished debriefing Olsen on the shit in New York. I was about to meet up with my team."

CJ nodded but didn't say anything. DJ sighed and crossed the room to the door.

"Guess there's a simple way to find out," he said. "Call me if you have anything about the thing or if you come up with a plan. We can discuss it over a cup of coffee, since"—he raised his voice—"there's no fucking privacy here anymore!"

CJ smiled in amusement and DJ left.

Austin was already sitting at his desk when DJ opened the door to his office. Those dead eyes stared at him, and DJ suppressed a shudder. As he closed the door behind him, Austin reached for a pair of shades and put them over his eyes.

DJ found that weird. If he wanted to hide his eyes, why had he waited for DJ to come in? It was almost as if Austin wanted DJ to notice the eyes.

"Have a seat, Darren Kojak," the admiral said, and DJ sat.

A thousand snide remarks flashed through his head, but he chose to stay silent.

Austin watched him for a moment more. "How was New York?"

DJ barely kept his expression flat. His anger gave way to anxiety. How the hell did he know? He'd had arrived at Sparta in the middle of the night and never left the building throughout his stay. Even if the military personnel at Sparta had recognized him, they wouldn't know to snitch on him. Was it possible that Austin had someone keep tabs on his team while they were on missions? DJ hadn't noticed anything like that, but he couldn't dismiss the idea. Who knew how far Austin would go?

"If you give me a minute," DJ said, "I can check the weather over there and get back to you."

Austin shook his head. He looked like a statue cracking its neck. "How did you enjoy New York these past few days? I know you didn't get the chance to leave Sparta headquarters, but the air must have been different or something. Definitely better than the weather in Chicago."

"Now I *know* you're tripping." DJ chuckled. Chicago was where his team had been deployed. He started to say something else, then paused and sighed. This whole thing reminded him of when his dad would try to get him to dig himself into a hole and confess something. DJ hadn't been good at pretending then, and he wasn't any better now. "Why am I here, Austin?"

That was what DJ couldn't understand. If the admiral already knew that DJ had been in New York, why hadn't he reported him? As an admiral, Austin didn't need a reason to discredit him, but ratting him out on this wouldn't hurt. What was the endgame?

Austin was quiet for a few seconds more. He slid a document across the desk. DJ picked it up and skimmed it. His expression darkened with every word.

"Darren Kojak," Admiral Austin said, his voice taking on a formal tone. "You shirked your duties to your country, leaving your teammates to fend for themselves. At any other point, you would have been discharged from the SEALs. But you have shown potential." Austin took a moment to sneer. "Your punishment will be a demotion. Your rank as team leader has been revoked. You are to be lowered to that of sergeant, effective immediately. And you will remain a sergeant until such a time as you have been deemed worthy of advancement."

DJ looked up from the paper, his expression thunderous. "This is bullshit. I'm being demoted because I refused to accept the fucking waste-of-time assignments that you've been giving my team?" He slammed the document onto the desk. "So I'm in the wrong when *you're* the one that's been trying to screw me over because of some shitty deal you made with a psychotic AI that's bent on destroying us all? Are you fucking kidding me?" DJ was shouting at this point. It took almost all his effort to regulate his voice. He stood hard, toppling his chair.

Austin's expression didn't change, though smug satisfaction wafted off him in waves. That, more than anything, calmed DJ.

Why had he only been demoted and not discharged? DJ had read of incidents less severe than his that had led to a discharge. He would have to be stupid to believe that Austin thought he had too much potential to waste. There must have been another reason.

"Demoted to sergeant," DJ mumbled to himself. As a sergeant, he would be on the same level as Christy and Kyle. He wouldn't be able to lead a team anymore. That meant he would be assigned to another team. Sergeants didn't get to pick their teams.

DJ turned to Austin, glaring. "What team have I been assigned to?" Austin didn't reply, so DJ snatched the paper from the desk and scanned it again. He didn't find what he was looking for until he reached the bottom.

Assigned to Alpha Team B
Team Leader: Carlton Bradley

DJ laughed. It started as a chuckle and then built up until he was clutching his stomach, tears in his eyes.

"Bradley?" he gasped a moment later, wiping his eyes. "You think I'm going to go under Bradley? How stupid are you?"

Austin twitched, his face forming into a fierce scowl. With the dark glasses and rigid posture, the dude looked so much like a B-movie villain that DJ almost cracked up again.

When Austin spoke again, his voice was hard, and he emphasized certain words like they were knives stabbing DJ. "You seem to have forgotten that you are in my office. You're talking to an admiral. I could crush you like a bug. You will take the notice of your demotion, and you will leave my office and promptly report to Agent Bradley. Despite your misgivings, the man is now your superior officer. You will do this, or your career is finished. Your life is finished."

Some of DJ's mirth dried up, but his eyes still held a hint of amusement. He picked up the document from where it'd fallen on the floor, showed it to Austin, and ripped it up.

Even through the sunglasses, Austin's shock was obvious, and DJ took no small pleasure in that.

"Dude," DJ said, "I've made it obvious that I have very little respect for you, and I have even less for Bradley. Why in the hell would I put him in charge of my life? Come on, man! Think for a minute."

"You don't have a choice—"

"Sure I do." DJ sighed, letting the torn pieces of paper fall to the floor. "I can quit."

"Quit what?"

"The SEALs. I'd rather quit the SEALs than put up with this bullshit."

For the second time in as many minutes, Austin showed his shock. DJ forced a smug look on his face, but his heart wasn't in it. He didn't want to leave. He'd dreamed of being an admiral since he'd first found out what the hell they were. But it was obvious that his demotion was another way for Austin to control him. Putting him under Bradley was probably just for kicks. And if DJ's new team leader ordered him to his death, Austin would probably count that as a bonus.

He had to leave. CJ would say that was the logical thing. In terms of authority and influence, there was no way to compete with Austin. The dude would just keep trying to screw him over. The demotion was just one example. DJ could imagine it getting worse. Why should he give him the chance?

Austin didn't say anything. DJ left the office before he got the chance.

CHAPTER

48

FEBRUARY 2043
NAVAL AMPHIBIOUS BASE,
CORONADO, CALIFORNIA

ON THE WAY BACK to the sergeants' quarters, DJ spent the time trying and failing to regain his anger. It sucked that he had to do this. It sucked ass. Especially for Christy and Kyle. The fact that Austin hadn't caused an "accident" on their mission boded well. But there was still a chance the admiral would take out his anger on DJ's teammates.

Well, former teammates.

And even if he didn't, they would still be assigned to another team. What if they were transferred to another Bradley? Whatever else, DJ was sure it would only be a matter of time before Christy shot the dude.

The thought almost made him chuckle until he remembered that he might have ruined their lives. This was exactly the sort of thing that made him reluctant to lead. The sort of thing he'd tried to avoid three years ago by keeping his team members out of the loop. The tech twins had left because of that. They ended up being the lucky ones; at least they still had a career with a bright future and no marks on their record.

He crossed the open courtyard and skimmed the edge, following a shortcut he'd discovered a couple of years back after so many meetings with Olsen.

It was all his fault. That was the fucked-up part about it. Austin was a dick, sure, but DJ gave him the ammunition when he'd skipped out on the mission in Chicago. If DJ had swallowed his pride and kissed Austin's ass, he might have been able to change something. The shitty missions were already keeping DJ distracted. There would have been no reason for Austin to demote him.

Fuck that, DJ thought with a snort. It might have been better to kiss ass, but DJ had never been the type to do that. He hadn't been good at it when he was a kid, and he wasn't any better at it now. Plus he was positive that Austin would have just found another way to screw him over.

DJ followed a path to the end, bursting out into another courtyard surrounded by similar squat buildings. Unlike the administration building, which had a measure of elegance to show authority, the sergeants' building was designed to be functional and nothing else. DJ went through a side entrance.

He let out a breath, pushing away his thoughts. It didn't matter how he fucked up, only that he did. He needed to find a way to unfuck up.

Christy and Kyle were bunked in the same room. DJ knew he'd find them there; taking the day off after a mission was part of the team's routine.

He let out another breath, forced a smile onto his face, and banged on the door until it rattled. "Holy shit, there's a fire!" he shouted. "Holy shit, emergency evac! Who the fuck leaves their iron plugged in?" He stamped his boots a couple of times, as if running down the hall.

The door flew open, and a frazzled Christy appeared on the other side. Her eyes settled on him, and her puzzled panic was replaced with a scowl. DJ's grin turned a touch more genuine. She moved to slam the door, but DJ had already ducked under her arm. At the end of the room, Kyle was hopping on one foot, trying to get into his pants. He looked up at DJ's entrance, fright giving way to confusion.

"What?" Kyle said. "What're you doing here, bro? No, wait! Forget that. There's a fire! We have to go." He hopped a couple more times.

Christy closed the door. "There's no fucking fire." She sighed, then slapped the back of DJ's head. "DJ's just being a dick. As usual."

Kyle dropped his foot, glaring at him.

"Just keeping you on your toes," DJ said. Christy tried to slap him again, but he saw it coming and ducked. "It's a service, if you think about it."

"Was it also a service when you ditched a mission so you could hang out in New York?" Christy asked. She rubbed her eyes. Her shirt rode up her stomach, pressing against her chest. Her shorts didn't pass midthigh. DJ gulped and glanced back at Kyle, who was also gulping.

DJ chuckled uncomfortably and moved to the middle of the room. "That's unfair. We all agreed the risk was worth it. Plus, I had faith that you guys could handle whatever Austin threw at you. And I was right."

"So?" Kyle said. He'd put on his pants and lay back on the bed. "What'd you find out, bro?"

"I found out where José Olvera and his daughters have been holed up for the last few years."

Christy was there during the data bank incident, so she already knew about the Murder Twins. Kyle had never met either, but DJ had filled him in when he'd brought them into the loop about Helene. Neither of them knew everything about the AI and what DJ and Ndidi had been up to, but they were far more informed than most people.

"Where?" Christy asked.

DJ told them about the Facility, the similarities between Austin and the creepy guards, and the briefing with Olsen. He spoke fast but gave as many details as he could. He had a copy of the security feed that Manar had shown them, so he played that too. He was definitely stalling. He justified it with the fact that this information was important.

"Damn, bro," Kyle said when DJ was done. "That's wild."

Christy looked thoughtful. A second later, her eyes cleared and focused on DJ. "Now that that's settled, why're you really here, D? What happened?"

"What do you mean?" DJ asked, chuckling uncomfortably.

"Yeah, what do you mean, bro?" Kyle asked.

"I *mean*," Christy said, narrowing her eyes, "what happened after you met up with Olsen? You have the look you put on when you've done something stupid because you 'followed your gut.'"

Damn, DJ grimaced. *There's a look? At least that explains why CJ always knows I've fucked up.*

"I haven't done anything stupid," DJ replied. He rubbed the back of his head and sighed. "Austin found out that I skipped out on the mission to go to New York. No,"—he put his hands up to stall their protests—"I don't know how, but he did. He texted me immediately after my briefing with Olsen. I went up to his office, and he had a letter on his desk that demoted me to sergeant ... so I quit."

"Quit what, bro?"

"This," DJ replied. "The SEALs. I quit the SEALs."

Kyle sat up on the bed. "We can just do that?"

"No, we can't," Christy replied quietly. Her arms folded across her chest. "SEALs can't quit until after twenty years. D's just being an idiot. Again."

We can't? DJ thought. *Damn.*

"Well, obviously I don't have everything figured out," he said. "Maybe I'll have Olsen give me an honorable discharge—or a dishonorable discharge since he's going to be pissed." DJ grimaced again. That was not a conversation DJ looked forward to.

Christy took a step forward. "So, you're going to quit just because you were demoted? What sort of arrogant bullshit is that? In case you didn't notice, Kyle and I are sergeants too. Should *we* quit?"

"This isn't about the demotion. It's the fact that Austin is using it to control me. At least as a team leader, I had a little influence. I could push back against some of his shittier options. But now? One wrong word and I'm fucked. Maybe literally. Christy, he put me on *Bradley's* team."

Christy didn't say anything, but her lips pursed.

"No bullshit," DJ continued. "If a commander or someone else had found out, I would have been discharged. Why would Austin settle for a demotion? He said something about my potential, which was about as convincing as that time you 'accidentally' shot that prisoner that was staring at your boobs." DJ paused but Christy still didn't say anything. "Basically, a discharge would mean he loses his hold over me. But with a demotion—especially one under Bradley—I'm even more under his thumb."

"Damn, bro! That actually makes sense," Kyle said. "But wait! What happens to us? If you quit, there's no team."

"If I'm a sergeant, there's no team anyway. You guys would probably be assigned to another one. With me gone, I don't think Austin would care anymore. I'll talk Olsen into helping you guys get onto a team you want, or onto the same team so you have someone watching your backs."

"You'll be heading back to New York?" Kyle asked.

DJ nodded. "Austin's doing this so I don't have time to focus on whatever the fuck Helene's up to. Staying in New York will make it easier to coordinate with Ndidi and Manar. It's already been hell going over there every few weeks." Christy's stare was burning into the side of his head, and he turned toward her. "I know it sucks, C, but—"

"I'm going with you," Christy said.

"What?"

"I'm going with you," Christy repeated. "To New York. I'm not going to take the chance that Austin doesn't screw me over because you pissed him off."

"That's not going to happen," DJ argued. "Without me here, there won't be a point. Plus you love being a SEAL."

"Yeah, dude, what're you saying?" Kyle asked, staring at Christy. "This isn't a joke."

"I'm not joking," she said. "And don't you give me that bullshit about loving being a SEAL, D. The past couple of months aside, you're the one who always looks like a kid in a candy store whenever we're on missions. Remember the Kalvaitis incident?"

DJ rubbed the back of his head, grimacing. He'd had *way* too much energy then.

Christy nodded. "You always look like we're going on adventures or some shit. You've wanted to be a SEAL since you were a kid, and you're giving it up to help stop Helene. Why can't I?"

"Because I'm the one who brought you guys into this," DJ said, pushing his embarrassment aside. "Helene's no joke. I'm already on her radar, but you aren't. Why the fuck would you want to be?"

Christy glared at him, and her fingers twitched by her side as if reaching for her gun. DJ recognized the stance. It was the one she used when she'd made up her mind about some bullshit. Usually DJ would give her some space, but he got the sense that wouldn't work here. Why did she choose to be stubborn about this?

DJ expected he'd have to convince her not to hit him. But he didn't expect to have to convince her not to throw her fucking career away. Worse, a part of him wanted her to come along. With her sniper skills, she was the perfect scout and support. But he couldn't ask her to throw the last four years of her life away.

But you're not asking, DJ's inner voice said. *She's not giving you a choice at all.* He stared at Christy, who met his gaze unflinchingly, her eyes hard. *She's not going to budge*, he realized.

"Fine," DJ sighed finally. "Do what you want. But you're going to tell Olsen. He's going to bust my balls enough as it is."

Christy didn't say anything for a moment, looking into his eyes as if making sure that he was serious. DJ forced a grin. A second later, she returned it, looking relieved. "Not much to bust anyway."

"You can't be serious, guys," Kyle said as he stood from the bed. "You're *both* leaving?"

"You can too," Christy said. She shrugged, but it wasn't nearly as casual looking as she hoped.

Kyle shook his head, looking down. "I can't, dude. I have a sister who's still in high school. Without my pay here, she'll have to drop out. I can't do that to her."

DJ nodded. Kyle hardly spoke about his sister. DJ pushed away the part of him that'd expected Kyle to agree. He was a shitty friend already for not even considering his sister in the first place. Christy's decision had been easier. She, like DJ, had lost her family during Mayday. She didn't have anyone else.

"We understand," DJ said. He placed a hand on Kyle's shoulder. Kyle looked up at him with eyes full of guilt. DJ smacked him. "Get that stupid look off your face. *We're* the idiots here. You're making the sensible decision."

Kyle nodded, rubbing his face. "Thanks, bro. I appreciate that."

"I can give you another one if you want," DJ said, raising his hand again.

Before he could, Christy smacked him hard enough that he almost lost his balance. "Way to ruin the moment, idiot."

DJ grinned at her. This time, he didn't have to force it.

INTERLUDE
PRATIMA

MARCH 2043
SOMEWHERE IN ABUJA, NIGERIA

PRATIMA MUKALLA *watched the earth crumble for miles all around, swallowing buildings into its depths. Pratima dove in immediately. Somewhere within the destruction were Eze and his wife, the people she'd vowed to protect. She had already failed them, but if there was a chance—just one—that they were still alive …*

Pratima ran across the heaving soil for what felt like hours. Distantly, she heard screams. There was a crowd of people at the edge of the hole. Did they see her mad dash? Were they screaming for her? Didn't they know that she had to do this? She had to try. Eze Okafor was the greatest man she had ever met. The world would feel his death. If there was a chance he'd lived through all this, why shouldn't she risk her life for it?

After what felt like days, Pratima reached the center of the hole. This was where the destruction had originated and pulled everything else down like a vacuum. Bodies were scattered about, most crushed by rocks. Blood painted the sand a violent red. Pratima navigated the corpses as deftly as she navigated the debris. Horror stoked the edges of her mind, but her resolve and focus stopped it from touching her.

Pratima searched among the destruction for hours until the sun behind her scorched her skin. The pain pulled her out of her focus. And then she heard the noise. The shouts that had been so distant were now close. Pratima saw the people coming toward her. Some wore police uniforms, others the coats of doctors, and still others wore plain clothes but carried stretchers and other machines.

Pratima turned back to her task. She dug a hole beside a body that had the same black hair as Eze. She needed the space if she was going to lift the rock from it. The hole was shallow, but it gave her the leverage she needed. The shouts were even closer. Pratima's eyes were riveted to the elderly man in front of her, his expression frozen in acceptance.

Even in death, Eze Okafor looked like a king.

Pratima found Amadia's body a few feet away. And next to her was a machine twice the size of a basketball and just as round. Its metallic body was crushed under several rocks, but it still gleamed in the sun. The light reflected a sharp point that poked out from underneath it. Pratima peered closer and identified the point as the bit of a drill.

Suddenly, she knew who was behind the attack.

PRATIMA STIRRED AWAKE, the dream still swimming in her head. It was the same one she'd had almost every night for the past three years. She banished it without a thought.

She sat up and gazed at the machine propped against a wall in her apartment. Pratima identified it as a drone after straightening out the dents from the rocks and other falling debris. However, she hadn't been able to get the machine to work. In the beginning, she'd imagined the drone would return to its owner once it was repaired. Then she'd be able to track it. But even without that, Pratima already knew who was responsible for the attack.

Sparta.

Before Manar was recruited and developed the e-reader, Helene, Sparta had made its name by devouring every rival in its path. The company was known for hostile takeovers and the relentless recruitment of budding talent. Somehow

Sparta had learned of the picotechnology being developed by the Cloneys and booked a meeting through the AI.

Pratima had been in the meeting as one of the legal representatives of the Okafor Corporation. Sparta had tried to buy the technology, but Eze had refused on the spot. The meeting had gone on for hours, with Sparta becoming increasingly frustrated. Eze had remained adamant.

Twice after that, Sparta had contacted Eze with an offer to obtain picotechnology. The last contact was a month before the accident that had taken Eze's life. It could not be a coincidence.

Pratima had spent the past three years finding out everything she could about Sparta. Although there was a lot of information available to the public, there was very little that was useful. But Pratima wasn't without resources.

Pratima rose from her bed and spent the few remaining hours before her flight tidying up the room. She'd already cleaned almost everything. The task gave her something to focus on. Every few seconds, she'd glance at the folder on her bedside table. It contained everything she'd been able to find.

Her next step was to go to New York. Pratima hadn't seen Ndidi for years. Even during Eze's funeral, Pratima had avoided her out of shame. How could she? She'd vowed to protect her friend's father, and she'd failed. Ndidi would probably never forgive her for that. But Pratima's guilt was only part of the reason she'd stayed away so long. The rest was that she'd hoped to gather enough proof to destroy Sparta.

Even if Ndidi never forgave her, at least she would find peace in knowing the cause of her father's death. And in knowing that Sparta was destroyed.

00 00 110 111 00 110 1 0 0
01 01 0 0 0 1 0 1 01 1 0 1 1 1 0
0 1 0 1 0 1 1 1 1 1 0 1 0 0 1 1 1 1 0
1 1 1 1 0 1 0 0 0 1 1 1 G 1 0 1 G 1
00 000 1 1 1 1000 1 1 A
10 110 0 1 0 1 1 1 0 0 1 0 B
1 0 0 1 0 1 1 0 1 0 A
0 1 0 0 1 1 1 0 0 1 0 0
1 0 0 1 0 010 1

CHAPTER

49

MARCH 2043
SPARTA HEADQUARTERS,
NEW YORK

MANAR SAT AT THE HEAD of the conference table. DJ and his brother had each chosen a seat on the left side of the table, along with DJ's teammate, Christy. Ndidi had picked a seat opposite them on the right side. Hermione sat next to her.

Manar cleared his throat and noticed DJ's amused look. Manar hadn't expected him to be back for a while; he'd left only a week before after telling Manar what he'd learned in the Facility. And Christy had been another surprise. Manar had heard about her involvement in the incident three years ago, but he'd never met her. She smacked the back of DJ's head. Manar didn't see what DJ had been about to do, but he wiped the smirk off his face. For about a second.

"Now, there's no need for this to be so weird," DJ said, then threw a nod at Ndidi. "What have you been up to?"

"Don't turn this on me," Ndidi snapped, though there wasn't any heat in her voice. "Manar told me you went back to the base a couple days ago. Why are you back here?"

DJ rubbed the back of his head. "I just missed you guys so much."

Manar sighed. Why had he thought DJ would take this seriously?

"He got demoted," CJ said, recoiling as everyone focused on him. "Austin found out that he came out here … hmm … the first time and demoted him. So, uh, DJ quit."

"What do you mean he quit?" Ndidi asked. Her voice was soft, and there was a glint of pride in her eyes. Ndidi was one of CJ's speech therapists when he was younger, so Manar figured she was proud of his progress.

Christy started to answer but went suddenly silent, rubbing at her ribs. DJ had a smug smile on his face.

"He had Olsen, uh … uh, discharge him from the SEALs so he would not be under Austin's thumb anymore."

Ndidi's gaze snapped to DJ. "Why the hell would you do something like that?"

"Look, it made sense at the time, okay?" DJ said, raising his hands defensively. "Austin knew I was in New York, so he definitely has a way to keep track of me. Maybe Helene's helping him or something. Either way, he demoted me to sergeant and then put me under *Bradley*. Shit was going to hit the fan sooner or later."

"Who's Bradley?" Manar asked.

"He's a dick," Christy said. "And team leader of one of the alpha teams. Our team had a run-in with him when we were still recruits. For some reason, the incident was enough to get Olsen's attention, and he let DJ off the hook. Olsen probably regrets that now." She made a show of muttering the last part, but it was still loud enough for everyone to hear.

"No need to get mean," DJ said. He turned to Ndidi, and his voice became serious. "The point is, we still don't know what Austin's goal is. And with me being demoted, there's little chance that we're going to find out. Olsen has been sticking his neck out for us, and it was only a matter of time until it bit him in the ass. And he has a lot more to lose than I do."

No one spoke for a few seconds.

Manar cleared his throat. "I assume Christy decided to go all in with you?"

"Yep," Christy replied. "I lost my family during Mayday too, so I have nothing left to lose—and a reason to make Helene pay."

"Well said." Manar nodded. "That seems to be a common theme with everyone here."

It hit him as he said it. It *was* the common theme. Ndidi had lost her ward, Bethany. Hermione had lost her sister. DJ and CJ had lost their dads. The same with Christy. And Manar had lost both his mother and his legacy. By itself, it didn't mean much; they weren't the only people who had lost someone on Mayday. But they were the ones doing something about it.

"Now, let's talk about how we can achieve that," Manar continued. "There are two new developments. The first is that Hermione discovered something through her picospores research."

DJ and CJ exchanged a confused look. Manar summarized as best as he could to speed things along.

Hermione told them about the experiment and how the rats' movements were similar to DJ's description of Austin and the Facility guards.

"What—" Ndidi cleared her throat. "What does that mean?"

Surprise and horror warred on Ndidi's face. Manar was surprised Hermione hadn't told her all this already.

"We think Helene got her hands on the picospores research," Manar explained. "Some samples of the technology disappeared during the confusion after your parents' deaths. We think Helene perfected the process and is using it to control people like puppets—or at least break down their resistances until they're basically puppets."

There was silence, then DJ laughed.

"Nah, you're fucking with us. Good one. Seriously, what'd you find out?"

Manar sighed.

CJ spoke up. "I do not think … hmm … she is joking, DJ." He turned to Hermione. "Did you find out, uh, why the spores reduced brain activity?"

Hermione started to answer, but DJ spoke before she could. "Wait! Chill!

We're not breezing past this." He leaned forward in his chair, his eyes leaping from person to person. "Helene figured out what? Fucking mind control? Are you shitting me right now?"

"It's just a theory," Hermione said.

"But it explains a lot," Manar added, also leaning forward. "Like why Austin's working with her. Neither you, CJ, nor Olsen have been able to find out what he gets from it. But if Helene's controlling him, he doesn't need a reason."

"How do the picospores work?" Ndidi asked, her voice quietly horrified. "How does she use it to control people?"

"It's not mind control," Hermione said. "She's basically just stimulating certain areas of the brain. Depending on where she stimulates, that'll make the person more inclined to do certain things or be more open to suggestions. So far, we think she's able to affect several areas at once, basically tugging on the person's instincts until she gets what she wants."

"That sounds like mind control," Christy muttered. She attempted to look casual and indifferent, but terror peeked through her tone. Manar couldn't blame her. It had been several days since they discovered the possibility, and he hadn't been able to sleep since.

The room dissolved into pointless noise as everybody started talking over each other. Manar and CJ were the only ones who didn't participate. CJ's body was rigid, and his eyes darted around so fast that one might've thought he was convulsing.

Manar closed his eyes. He understood their terror—Ndidi's especially. The scope of what Helene had been able to achieve was mind-boggling. The AI always seemed to be one step ahead. More than that, actually. Every week, it seemed like they discovered an edge to her plans that threatened to overwhelm them. Manar hadn't felt this weary since the months after Mayday when he'd been dealing with his mother's death.

DJ clapped loudly to shut everyone up. His expression was more serious than Manar ever thought he would see.

"All right," DJ said, "we've all had the chance to bitch about how fucked we are with the mind control stuff. I also bitched, and it was very satisfying. But now that we have that off our chests, let's talk about how we can get unfucked. That makes sense, right? We can ask our questions one after the other. I'll start." His eyes rested on Hermione. "How the hell does Helene get the picospores into people? There are a lot of crazy people out there, sure, but I doubt she'd find many volunteers."

"Could she have … uh, abducted them?" CJ asked.

DJ shook his head. "Some, but not all. Austin, for example. The base would know almost instantly if he went missing, and they'd have thrown a fit."

"Picospores are … well, *pico*spores," Hermione said, groping at the air as she searched for a way to explain. "They're spores at the picoscale. That's ten to the power of twelve. At that size, they can pass through the pores of your skin. Helene doesn't need to abduct anyone, she just needs to pump the spores into the air around the target. After that, it's just a matter of programming them."

Both DJ and Christy looked horrified. CJ leaned forward in his chair, his expression curious. "That's why you … hmm … spoke of processing power before? You … you code the spores with commands."

"Exactly."

Ndidi went next. She'd composed herself, hiding most of her panic—though her voice still gave her fear away. "Is there a way to counter it? Either stopping the spores from getting into people or removing Helene's control?"

Manar had asked the same question, so he already knew what Hermione's answer would be.

"I'm already looking into that," Hermione said. She shrugged helplessly. "But right now, I can't see a way to wrestle control from Helene without causing permanent brain damage."

It was obviously not the answer they were expecting because the room threatened to break out into noise again. This time, Ndidi put a stop to it. "Do what you can, Hermione," she said softly. "Any ideas will be welcome."

"In the meantime," DJ said, turning to Manar, "we can shut Helene down completely. I know you explained why it was a bad idea before, but I think—and hear me out—I *think* that most people would agree that a little economic collapse is better than having their bodies controlled like fucking puppets."

Manar leaned back in his chair. "That's the second thing we have to discuss." Weariness tinged his voice. He'd thought about how he was going to say this for the past few days and had settled on his usual tactic: blunt honesty. "I can't shut down Helene anymore. At least, not remotely. She's locked me out of her system. I think that she's gained full control of her servers."

His eyes drifted to CJ because he was probably the only one who would understand.

"How do … hmm … do you know she's gained control?" CJ asked.

"Because she rebuffs my codes immediately."

"How many attempts have you made?"

"Three." Manar shifted in his seat. The truth was embarrassing. "The first was using brute force. The second and third, I tried to sneak programs in to give me a foothold. She rebuffed all of them immediately—which is impossible unless she's gained full control of her systems."

Manar saw DJ roll his eyes. Christy glanced at him weirdly. Even Ndidi looked exasperated. He sighed, wearily. He was a bit arrogant when it came to his programming, but that was because he'd earned it. He was the best at what he did. Helene was a testament to that; she'd far outpaced every other artificial intelligence on the planet. He could—and had, on several occasions—slipped through the government's cybersecurity within minutes. And he hadn't been noticed.

It should have been impossible for his codes to have been shut down so completely.

CJ seemed to believe him. "You are, uh, thinking of attacking her mainframe?"

DJ sat up. "What's this, now?"

Manar nodded, ignoring the other brother. "That's the only way to stop her now."

"What're you guys talking about?" Ndidi asked. She looked between Manar and CJ.

"I want us to plan a raid on one of Helene's mainframes," Manar said. "We're going to bomb it."

0 0 0 0 1 1 0 1 1 1 0 0 1 1 0 1 0 0 0
0 1 0 1 0 0 0 1 0 1 0 1 0 1 1 0 0 1 1 1 0
0 1 1 0 1 0 1 1 1 1 1 1 0 1 0 0 1 1 1 0 1 0
1 1 1 1 1 0 1 0 0 1 1 1 G 1 0 1 G 1
0 0 0 0 0 1 1 1 1 1 0 0 0 1 1 1 A 0
1 0 1 1 0 G 0 1 1 1 1 0 B 0 1 0 B 0
1 0 0 1 0 A 1 1 0 1 0 A 1
0 1 0 0 1 B 1 1 0 0 1 0 0
1 0 0 1 0 A 0 1 0 1 1

CHAPTER

50

MARCH 2043
NEW YORK CITY, NEW YORK

LIZ POLOVA SOUGHT PERFECTION. She worked toward it with everything she had.

Even though they were of one mind in many ways, her sister had never understood her drive—even back when they had shared a body and were closer than any two siblings had a right to be.

Karla would never realize it of herself, and she would never admit it even if she did, but she loathed Liz for her determination—though admittedly less than she resented everyone else.

Here, too, they were of one mind. Liz also resented her sister.

Liz loved Karla, but it was impossible for envy not to creep in after so many years together. Liz had spent years struggling to do what Karla could do effortlessly. Even when they were joined as one, Liz had lagged in their training. It was never by much, but it was enough to grate on her.

The twins were practically the same person. Why must Liz put so much more effort into things than Karla? Why was Liz bogged down by her uncertainties and doubts when Karla charged forward fearlessly, obliterating everything in her path? Karla embodied the ruthlessness that José had strived to instill in them. Yet her sister scorned their father, and Liz sought his attention with every action.

He was the reason she sought perfection. To meet his ideal. Maybe then he would look at her as he did when she was a child.

Liz's head snapped to the side as the blow jolted her from her thoughts. Liz wanted to curse, but she squashed the impulse immediately. It had been years since she'd allowed herself to be so immersed in her thoughts. Her sister had made her pay for it. She'd deserved the hit.

Liz blocked the next strike with her right forearm and retaliated with her left forearm. The prosthetic limb moved faster than her right arm and contained far more strength. Liz did not fully understand why. Martin Bryan undoubtedly did, though.

That strength had been limited to her left side for months, but now she could feel it spreading through her body, empowering her fully. Soon her right side would hold just as much power as her metallic limbs.

Liz's strike connected. Karla twisted with the blow and kicked, using the attack to cover any openings she might have left. Liz blocked the blow again but did not counter. Karla's recklessness forced her to attack both as offense and defense. Liz, on the other hand, preferred a more methodological approach that defended while targeting weaknesses in her opponent's technique.

The sisters had sparred enough to know each other's moves intimately. Liz had to work to find Karla's weak points, but they were always there. The longer the fight wore on, the more frustrated and angrier Karla got. And the more her technique slipped.

There. Liz aimed a punch just below Karla's sternum, a spot she had left just the tiniest bit open. Karla realized her mistake and moved to block, but it was too late. She took the hit. Karla countered with her legs. Liz blocked easily. However, the force of the blow threw her back.

Again, Liz pushed away the impulse to curse. She could dismantle her sister's techniques given enough time. Yet somehow, Karla had always been stronger than Liz—even when they'd shared a body. With their separation and the power granted by their bionics, the gap had only grown wider. While Liz had the advantage in technique, Karla's raw power negated it, leaving them at a stalemate.

It was a balance that had held since their birth.

Chloe called for the sparring to stop a minute later. "That looked like a fun warm-up," she said.

Liz stiffened. Karla growled. At the end of their fight, they'd moved even faster than Chloe. She was still superior to them in technique, but it was an insult to call their sparring a warm-up. Karla opened her mouth to speak, but José interrupted her.

"Come," he called from the end of the room where Martin Bryan leaned against the wall. The three of them walked over and stood in a half circle around him. "Your fight shows that your wounds have healed. That is good. We have wasted enough time. Now we will move on to the next step."

"Next step?" Karla scowled. "Are we finally leaving this dump?"

José shook his head. If Liz didn't know better, she would have thought there was concern flickering in the depths of his eyes.

"Previously, neither of you could match mine or Chloe's speed," José said. The sudden change in topic was jarring. "But now you have surpassed us. The old man tells me that this is because of your prosthetic limbs. The nanites that swim in your blood are improving everything in your body, making you physically superior to any other. The change has become more noticeable over the last few months and will continue in this way as time goes on." He paused, and his eyes hardened even more. "But such strength does not come without a price."

Karla's scowl deepened, but Liz was more curious than worried. It was only logical that their new strength would have a cost. This was simply another thing that she would have to master.

"So far, the old man has failed me," José continued, looking down at Dr. Bryan for the first time. His eyes flickered with rage. "He has been unable to determine the cost of this power. But we cannot afford to sit idly and wait. We are going to take our revenge on the AI—to destroy her like she sought to destroy us."

"And how're we going to do that?" Chloe asked. Her eyes were wide, almost mocking. José ignored it. Liz burned with envy. Chloe was the only person who could mock José like that and avoid punishment.

"Its defenses are too strong to hack into remotely," José said. "But in the end, it is just a machine. If we destroy its parts, it will cease to function."

Karla grinned. Liz rubbed her stomach, feeling the phantom pain from where she had been stabbed by the AI's puppets.

"We attack?" she asked and grinned when José nodded.

"You have a target?" Chloe asked.

José nodded again, his face turning thoughtful. Although her father had never spoken of it, Liz knew that Helene had given José more tasks than the rest of them. If anyone knew the best place to strike the AI, it would be him.

CHAPTER

MARCH 2043
SPARTA HEADQUARTERS,
NEW YORK

EVERYBODY WAS SILENT around the table. Ndidi stared, horrified, at Manar. Panic gripped her heart so tightly she feared it would burst.

Then DJ whooped and pointed at Manar with a grin. "Yes! Yes. Let's drop a bomb on her digital ass. Why is this the first time someone suggested it?" He casually dodged a strike from Christy.

"We're not actually going to drop a bomb on her." Manar sighed. "We're going to destroy her mainframe. One of them, at least. The core mainframe. And this is the first you're hearing of it because it wasn't an option before. If I can't hack into Helene, no one else can. And we can't let her continue to use the picospores on people. It's …" He exchanged a look with Hermione. "No one deserves that."

"What does destroying her server achieve, exactly?" Hermione asked.

This time CJ spoke. "It destroys her. Completely. The server is, uh, is what makes Helene, *Helene*. Without it, she is … gone."

Ndidi felt a rush of pride. CJ's improvement was staggering. He would never have spoken up without being prompted when he was younger. And his speech impediment had improved. He still had problems meeting people's eyes; even now, he stared at Hermione's forehead. But that was far better than the side glances he'd used as a child.

For a second, her satisfaction was enough to make her forget the situation. But then the terror returned.

"So, all we have to do is bomb it, right?" DJ said.

"For the last time, we're not bombing anything," Manar said, exasperated. "That'd just cause unnecessary damage and might risk people's lives."

Ndidi knew DJ was just trying to get a rise out of him. She'd seen the look on his face when he heard about the picospores and knew he wasn't nearly as casual as he appeared.

"If you just—" Manar started but was interrupted by a message on his cell. He scanned it quickly, looking puzzled, then brought out his computer. Everyone stared at him, but Ndidi knew he wasn't aware of those around him. He got tunnel vision whenever something baffled him.

Ndidi started to stand, but her phone pinged as well.

Sensei Mukalla: "If you are with Manar Saleem, please tell him to let me up. I have something for you."

Ndidi's initial reaction was confusion. And then came shock, excitement, and finally enough shame that her cheeks turned red. She'd barely spared a thought for her sensei since she left Nigeria. Pratima hadn't been at the party that had claimed her parents' lives, but Ndidi had been so immersed in her grief that it hadn't even occurred to her to wonder how her sensei had taken the deaths. Ndidi's father's especially. Pratima idolized Eze. She must have been devastated. And Ndidi hadn't even been there for her. How self-centered was she?

But wait, let her up? Pratima was there? At Sparta?

"Sorry about that," Manar said, closing his laptop and pushing it aside.

"What was that about?" Ndidi asked. She stood and crossed to where Manar sat. Had she misinterpreted the message? Maybe Pratima had been talking about the Okafor Centre. But then why would she ask for Manar to let her up?

"I'm not really sure," Manar replied slowly, looking up at her, confused. "Someone was insisting on seeing me. But I don't know them and don't see people without an appointment. Most of the time, at least." For some reason, his eyes went to DJ when he said that.

She is *here*, Ndidi thought. Probably in the lobby.

"That's Pratima Mukalla," Ndidi told Manar. She opened the computer, which, fortunately, Manar hadn't shut down. The screen was split into twelve squares, each showing a different angle of the lobby. Ndidi scanned them until she found the one she was looking for. An Indian woman stood in the center of the room, arguing with the receptionist across the counter. Pratima was huge, easily six feet tall. She wore loose yoga pants and a shirt that barely contained her bulging muscles. Ndidi felt tears gather in her eyes at the memories.

"That's Pratima Mukalla," she said again. From the corner of her eye, she saw Hermione perk up. "She was my sensei when I was a kid. My father wanted me to learn how to defend myself. Sensei Mukalla taught me everything I know."

"An actual sensei?" DJ asked. "Not a coach that screams at you? Not a demon secretly sent to torture you?" He leaned back, his expression suddenly dark. "Fucking rich kids," he muttered.

Ndidi ignored him, instead watching Manar punch something into his phone. Ndidi watched the receptionist get Manar's message on the security feed. The picture quality was so good, she could see it when the receptionist went pale. He closed his eyes for a moment and took a breath before he turned to Pratima and said something. A second later, the huge woman was walking toward the elevator.

NDIDI WAS WAITING by the elevator when Pratima finally arrived. She was in her sensei's arms before the doors had fully opened. Pratima stiffened. Ndidi pulled back, confused at the look on the other woman's face. The *guilt*. But about what? If anything, it was Ndidi who should feel guilty. She'd been so self-absorbed that she'd completely forgotten about Pratima.

"I'm so sorry," Pratima gushed. Her face twisted to look even guiltier, if that were possible. "I failed your parents. I let them die. After everything they did for me, I wasn't even there."

Ndidi took a step back into the hallway. She'd never seen her sensei show so much emotion. In fact, she and Ndidi's father were the ones who taught her how to control her emotions. And now, Pratima was laying everything bare. And for something so stupid.

Ndidi led her back to the conference room. In between, she tried to talk. But Pratima spoke over her, her expression twisting further by the second. She seemed to expect Ndidi to hate her, but Ndidi couldn't figure out why. Because she'd survived when Ndidi's parents had died? Or because she hadn't been able to stop something she had no control over?

Ndidi tried again and again to calm her, but Pratima had apparently held her words in for too long. After a minute of this, Ndidi's hand moved reflexively. The resulting slap echoed through the hall.

"Damn," DJ whistled, reminding Ndidi she had an audience. Why couldn't she have done this back by the elevator?

And, Ndidi thought, *why does DJ look so suspicious?*

The slap finally got her sensei's attention, and Ndidi was able to get a word in. "You're beating yourself up for nothing. You did nothing wrong. If you had been at the party, then all you would have done was die alongside my parents. How would that have been better?"

Pratima stared at her as if afraid to believe she wasn't angry. Ndidi resisted the urge to grab her by the shoulders and shake her.

"Plus," Ndidi continued, leading the other woman to the conference table, "we're pretty sure Helene caused the accident."

That snapped Pratima out of her haze. The guilt quickly twisted into anger. "It *was*. Sparta was the cause of it. I found one of their drones next to your mother."

"Wait, what?" DJ exclaimed, standing so fast that his chair tipped over. "What do you mean you found one of Helene's drones? And it was activated? How are you still alive?"

Manar sighed.

"You found a drone?" Hermione asked, her voice breaking. There were tears in her eyes. Ndidi's heart broke for her. She'd told Hermione about her suspicion, but Hermione hadn't really believed it. Now that their sensei had confirmed it …

Pratima stared at Hermione, pain etching her face. "There was a drone in the sinkhole," she said softly. "It had been damaged by the rubble, but it had a drill on the outside. I only found one, but for that kind of destruction, there had to have been more. Hundreds, if not thousands."

Pratima turned to Manar next and scowled. Ndidi hadn't seen that look on her face since she was a child. Pratima was barely holding herself back from leaping at Manar. "Sparta is the only company advanced enough to control so many machines at once. And since Eze rejected their offer to buy Dr. Cloney's technology, killing him was the only way to get their hands on it."

"I knew that shit couldn't have been natural," DJ said, pumping his fist. "It didn't make sense for buildings to collapse like that." He paused, and his expression darkened. "But how the hell does Helene have enough firepower to cause a natural disaster?"

Christy whispered something to him, and his expression turned sheepish. "Sorry, Christy. It's kind of a long story, but the short of it is that it's *bad*. It's very bad."

Manar sighed again.

"Sparta tried to buy the picotechnology?" Hermione asked, sitting up. She wiped at her eyes with the edge of her sleeve. "Why weren't my father and I told?"

"You and your father had not finished with your research," Pratima explained. "They tried several times. The last was a month before the accident. But Eze knew what you two would have said and refused Sparta's offer. He believed the picospores would change the world. And Sparta killed him for it."

It took far too long for Ndidi to understand Pratima's point. Ndidi had been in the thick of things for so long that it was easy to forget others didn't know what she did.

She probably doesn't know that Helene went rogue, Ndidi thought. *Or that the AI was the cause of Mayday. She still thinks that Helene is being controlled by Sparta.*

"It wasn't Sparta that killed my parents, Pratima," Ndidi said. "Or Hermione's.

It was Helene. We weren't sure before, but if there was a drone at the … at the site, there's no doubt about it."

Ndidi took a breath and then used the next few minutes to explain everything that had happened during the last three years: Bethany, infiltrating Gaius, reuniting with DJ and his brother, the data bank incident, and the Murder Twins. She made sure to mention the drones that Helene had sent to attack them so Pratima would understand the implications of what she'd found. But even after three years, Ndidi wasn't ready to face those memories, so she left out details as much as possible. Finally, she got to the years after her parents' deaths and what they'd discovered about Helene since then.

The others at the table listened, interjecting when Ndidi skipped a part or when she wasn't there for something. Although Ndidi tried to summarize as much as she could, the story left her exhausted. Pratima sat in silence for a while as she processed it all. The others took that as permission to continue their discussion.

But Ndidi couldn't fully concentrate. She watched her sensei out of the corner of her eye, as Pratima's face shifted to anger, then to guilt, then to shame, before settling on resolution. The fact that Ndidi had been able to read those emotions at all spoke volumes about her sensei's mental state.

After a few minutes, the conversation around the table died down, and Pratima turned to Ndidi.

"I came here to ask for your forgiveness for failing your parents." Pratima held up a hand to stop Ndidi's protests. "I know now that it wasn't necessary. You've told me everything, and I couldn't be prouder of you. I'm sure your father is looking down on you with a smile."

Ndidi gave a small smile of her own. The mention of her father threatened to bring tears to her eyes.

"I haven't done nearly as much as you," Pratima continued. "And now I understand my priorities have been misplaced. But I still think you should take this." For the first time, Ndidi noticed the large binder that Pratima had been clutching.

Ndidi collected the folder and placed it on the table to go over it later. At least that was her thought. As soon as the binder left her hands, DJ reached over and plucked it from the table, a mischievous glint in his eyes. Pratima didn't stop him, though Ndidi was sure she could have.

"That file contains everything I've been able to gather on Sparta over the last three years," Pratima said. "I compiled it so we could take them down. But since Sparta wasn't behind your parents' deaths, I don't know how useful it'll be. It might be better if—"

"Fuck!" DJ exclaimed, staring excitedly at the dossier. "Sparta is into some weird shit! Manar, come look at this."

Manar frowned but strode to DJ's side. Christy and CJ looked over at the folder as well, and both made sounds of surprise. Hermione looked like she wanted to go, too, but hesitated.

"What's in it?" She chuckled awkwardly.

"I'll tell you this," DJ said. "We're not going to have an issue figuring out the perfect place to bomb Helene."

A BEGINNING

APRIL 2043
NEW YORK CITY, NEW YORK

NATE TUFFIN STARED to the side and considered for the third time that day whether it was time for him to quit. It was a serious decision. Hundreds of people were ready to take his position. If he quit and he wasn't absolutely sure of it, he would end up regretting it for the rest of his life.

His probably short life. Nate had been the aide to the last few chief justices, and he had no doubt that there were people who believed it'd be better if the secrets that Nate knew stayed that way when he left. Nate wasn't the only political aide, but he'd stayed the longest—and he knew a lot of secrets. If he quit, it was doubtful he'd last the month.

Yet he still considered leaving, and the reason why was just a step away.

Nate had only been working with Morgan Harvey for a year before his disappearance. Officially, the chief justice had gone on a forced medical hiatus because of his failing health, but Nate knew that was horse crap. The first that he'd heard about a medical hiatus was when the news had run the story. If Morgan's health was actually failing, Nate would have been the first to know, and he would also have been the first to know where Morgan had holed up so he could set up appointments and press conferences to milk the issue for all it was worth.

The chief justice had been on "hiatus" for months, and not only had his aides not known about it, but none of them also knew where their charge had been. For *months*.

Nate ran a hand through his red hair. It was beyond him how no one else saw what a pile of horse crap that was.

Still, if that had been all, Nate would have chalked it up to some sort of cover-up by the top brass and minded his business. No one stayed in a position like his for long without learning how to mind their business. If that had been all, Nate would have gone on with his life.

Morgan let out a bellowing laugh, pulling Nate out of his thoughts. Nate chastised himself. He had to decide sooner rather than later; he was becoming sloppy in the meantime.

Morgan laughed again, forcing Nate's attention to him. The chief justice was surrounded by a half circle of people that hung on his every word and stroked his ego, hoping to curry his favor. Normally, Nate would have dismissed them as the vultures they were, but now he stared at them and wondered how dumb they were not to notice the flaws in the man they were looking at with such greed.

Then again, it's not like Nate had noticed them for a few days after Morgan had returned from his "hiatus." But now that he had, it was all he could think about.

The chief justice hadn't always been so large. He hadn't been slim exactly, but before taking the position, he hadn't had such a ginormous gut or flabby arms. A year after, his paunch was one of his most notable features. Which made it even weirder when Morgan had come back with a stomach that was almost flat. The man had blamed his health treatment, but unless he had been tortured, Nate didn't see how he'd lost so much weight so completely.

Morgan's face was different as well. His eyes had remained covered by a pair of dark glasses since he'd resurfaced. Nate didn't think Morgan had any eye defects, so the glasses were only an accessory. They made him look blind and difficult to look at for a long period of time. And it was just plain weird.

But Nate could ignore that. He could even ignore the mysterious disappearance and subsequent weight loss. But what Nate couldn't ignore were the new ideas the chief justice had returned with.

"The procedures are great," Morgan said, "but they can be automated to work more efficiently. Sparta's Helene is already doing something similar in the educational system and other organizations. People are starting to see the government's holding out at this point to be petty. And honestly, I can't say I blame them. We're underutilizing a great asset."

His groupies nodded along with him, but Nate wanted to scream. Whether or not the government should integrate artificial intelligence into their systems had been a huge public debate since Mayday, and Morgan had always spoken out against integration. But now he'd suddenly changed his mind? Just like that? How did no one notice this?

Even the other aides brushed off the peculiarities, but Nate couldn't get them out of his head. There was something wrong, something he was missing. And it had to do with Morgan's supposed hiatus. He'd already tried everything he could to figure out where Morgan had gone, but no matter who he asked or where he searched, Nate hadn't been able to find anything.

As if sensing his stare, Morgan shifted his gaze to Nate. And suddenly Nate felt like he couldn't breathe under the pressure of the chief justice's presence. That was another new thing. Nate couldn't see Morgan's eyes through his glasses, but it was easy to tell when the chief justice was focused on him. He felt strangely violated, like Morgan was peering into the depths of his soul.

Nate tried to tell himself it was nonsense, but that didn't stop him from being more terrified than he'd been on Mayday or even that time he'd been held at gunpoint.

At first, Nate tried to meet Morgan's gaze. But he looked away after a moment and considered, for the fourth time that day, if it was time he quit his job.

CHAPTER

52

APRIL 2043
NEW YORK CITY, NEW YORK

BETHANY CROSSED THE STREET and tried to keep her motions as smooth as possible. It had taken her some time to realize how weirdly she walked, and she wondered why no one had ever pointed it out to her. Or … had she walked this way before? It was hard to remember. So many parts of her mind were still fuzzy.

One of the few things she did remember was the way to her destination. She'd woken up with that knowledge and a need to get there as fast as she could. Was that weird? Bethany hadn't seen Miss Okafor in … a while, so she knew her teacher would be happy to see her. But something nagged at the back of her mind. Something she should've been thinking about but couldn't.

Bethany shrugged. She might trigger an episode if she dwelled on it too much. Then again, maybe she didn't need to worry about that anymore. Apart from the gaps in her memory, Bethany hadn't been this balanced before. Something in her head had finally clicked.

Now, if she could only fix her walk, she would be ready to meet with Miss Okafor

Bethany slipped through the crowds, making eye contact as much as she could. Before, something so simple would have sent her into a fit. She still felt a twinge every time she did it, but the feeling was smoothed over before it became an issue. Occasionally, she brushed against a stranger and instinctively recoiled. The person always stared at her weirdly, but that was a far milder reaction than Bethany was used to.

It was freeing.

She only wished she knew what had changed.

Bethany stopped across the street from the Okafor Autism Centre. It was midday, so Ndidi should either be in her office or leading a class at the teaching facility. Bethany waited for a gap in the traffic, then started to cross the road.

Her mind grew foggy halfway through, and she stopped. This wasn't the first time something like that had happened. The feeling would pass if she—

Bethany blinked and spun around. *Where am I?*

A car honked, but Bethany was too distracted to hear it. She crouched, clutching her head. Her skull throbbed, but she pushed through the pain, searching through the dots in her mind for her most recent memories. They came in hot flashes and left her shaking. There was no feeling attached to those memories, almost as if she hadn't been the one to live through them. It felt as though she were watching from outside her body.

Another honk pulled her out of her thoughts, and Bethany opened her eyes to see the Centre in front of her. A part of her—one she couldn't explain—urged her to enter the building. But the feeling went past the need for familiarity and security, and that scared her. The memories in her mind scared her.

A hand brushed her in passing, and Bethany screamed. She cradled her fist and tried to suppress the fit she felt building up. A car stopped beside her, and someone came out, yelling. Bethany stared at the Okafor Autism Centre once more, then obeyed the part of her that told her it would be a bad idea to enter.

She stood, and without knowing where she was going, she ran.

CHAPTER

53

APRIL 2043

SPARTA HEADQUARTERS, NEW YORK

"I DON'T UNDERSTAND WHY we're still on this," Manar said, exasperated. "The main server building is the only place we can raid if we want to put Helene down for good. Even if we attack the data bank, we'd just be slowing her down at best. Why is this an issue?"

CJ nodded along. He understood why DJ—and to a lesser extent, Ndidi—wanted to raid the data bank, but it was more than likely Helene had backed up everything of importance after the first strike. And even if she hadn't, as Manar had said, that wouldn't put a stop to her like destroying the main server would. Destroying that would be like attacking her brain. It was the most efficient place to strike.

DJ scowled, and CJ could tell he was going to say something stupid. CJ reached over and placed a hand on his shoulder, drawing his attention. DJ stared for a moment, then deflated in his chair, settling for muttering to himself. Across the table, Manar sighed in relief.

"If that's settled, what's next?" Ndidi asked.

It was a few days after the meeting with Pratima. Ndidi had left with her sensei and holed up in the Okafor Centre for the next few days, handling some emergency that had cropped up. This was the first time they'd been able to meet since then. Even with Pratima's notes narrowing their options, they'd already taken over an hour to decide on where to raid—and it was only the four of them. Hermione was somewhere within the building, working on the picospores, while Christy had gone back to the base to check on Kyle.

DJ flipped through the binder that Pratima had given Ndidi. CJ didn't understand how he'd managed to get his hands on it.

"Next is to plan how we're going to do this thing," DJ said. "According to this, the server building is near the state line."

"No." Manar frowned. "The server building is a few miles south, underground at one of Sparta's minor branches."

"Miles?" CJ asked. "It ... isn't closer?" He'd thought it would have been closer to ensure a quicker response in an emergency.

"No. The board of directors," Manar said, gritting his teeth, "thought that having the server so close to the headquarters would be too predictable. They picked a random, unprotected branch, dug an underground chamber, and set up the hardware there. There's a decoy room just like it, here in the headquarters, that we sometimes show to VIPs taking a tour."

"That ... actually makes sense once you look beyond the stupid," DJ said. He pointed to the binder. "But that's not what it says here. According to this, the server room is underground, but in a building at the edge of the state."

"I've been to the server room," Manar insisted. DJ slid the binder over to him, and he picked it up, muttering to himself. "Everything's welded down. It should be impossible to move. And even if the idiots upstairs decided to move it, I would have been informed."

Impossible to move, CJ thought. The phrase nagged at him. The level of detail in Pratima's notes made him doubt she was wrong. But in the same way, Manar was the authority on everything related to Helene; it was unlikely that he was wrong about this.

The obvious disconnect irritated CJ.

He hadn't been to Helene's server room, but the structure should have the same underlying concept as other AIs. The main servers worked as the brain of an AI, where all its processes were created, run through its different components, and then sent back to the servers. There would be subsidiary servers spread out across whatever range the AI held—in Helene's case, a global range—but none of those would be as advanced as the main servers. Those servers were designed specifically to handle massive amounts of data. CJ wouldn't have been surprised if developing the hardware was the major reason Manar had joined up with Sparta. Few companies would've been able to cover the cost of their construction.

CJ felt his brother's gaze. He ignored him. He could hear the others discussing something and realized he'd drifted off into his thoughts. But this was one of the times it was actually a good thing. He felt like he was close to something. It was the same feeling he got when he was chasing a memory that was just at the edge of his thoughts.

CJ pulled himself back before he drifted off on another tangent. He pushed away his frustration and dug his fingers into his pants to ground himself.

Manar had said that the main servers could not be moved. CJ understood why; the servers would be too bulky to relocate without attracting attention. But they didn't have to be elsewhere for Pratima's notes to be correct. CJ didn't know how Pratima had found her information, but he believed it was unlikely that she'd actually been in the server room to confirm its location. It was far more likely that she'd discovered a way—or found someone to help her—to trace Helene's signals. And since all of Helene's signals led to the main server, it would have been easier to get the location that way.

At least, as much as anything could be easy when it came to Helene.

CJ paused, trying to remember his original point. He traced his thoughts, mumbling to himself. That drew Ndidi's attention. CJ ignored her, too, though he felt a little guilty.

That's right, he thought, giving a small smile of relief. All of Helene's signals would either originate or lead back to her main server for processing. The more he thought about it, the more it made sense that Pratima had narrowed down the location this way.

Following that logic, though, CJ thought, *Helene wouldn't have needed to physically move her main servers at all. If there was a subsidiary server in the building, she could have backed up her core processes there and turned that into her main.*

There was a problem with that theory, though. A subsidiary server would not be able to handle that much data without crashing. Helene could transfer herself to another server, but she would lose some of herself in the process.

CJ tried to follow that line of thought further, looking for a way to make it feasible. But there wasn't one.

CJ felt a whine build up in his throat. His head shot up—when had he drooped?—and he tapped a finger on the table to get Manar's attention. It worked, but unfortunately, it got everyone else's attention as well. Ndidi gave him a small smile, and the rest looked at him curiously. CJ forced his muscles to relax, and then he explained what he'd been thinking about.

"Your idea has merit," Manar said thoughtfully. "But as you figured, Helene wouldn't sacrifice part of herself by transferring her data to a random server. Especially not when we consider the picospores. As developed as she is, controlling as many people as we suspect she controls wouldn't be possible if she's working at half power."

DJ shrugged. "If the problem's her server, can't she just, like, build another one or something and then transfer her stuff there?"

Manar snorted. "She could appropriate the work, but the cost of building a server advanced enough to handle her would be astronomical. That's why I signed up with Sparta in the first place. They were the only company that could foot the bill."

I knew it, CJ thought, smiling slightly.

"And do you know how long something like that would take to build?" Manar continued. "Designing the setup, acquiring the materials for the hardware, and then building all of this in secret so she doesn't raise any alarms?"

DJ twirled his finger in the air. "My guess would be … about three years? Give or take a few months."

"No." Manar shook his head, though it felt less like he believed his own words and more like he didn't want them to be true. "It isn't possible. Even if she had the time to build it, even if she could have somehow managed to build it without raising an alarm, the cost would still make it impossible."

"Maybe she didn't build it all at once," DJ said. "Maybe she's been sneaking away some funds for a while and reinvesting them. She had full control of Sparta for a bit after Mayday, right?"

Manar grimaced and folded his arms. "I don't think you're treating this as seriously as you should. If this were true, that would mean Helene had been stringing us along for months, even before Mayday."

DJ shrugged, causing Manar to narrow his eyes. "We already knew she was doing that. I'm just looking at the silver lining."

CJ titled his head. "Silver … lining?"

"Yeah," DJ grinned. "Now that we know there are two servers, Manar won't bitch so much about bombing one of them."

CJ LOOKED OVER at his brother, who sighed. *How long has he been sitting there?*

DJ didn't say anything, so neither did CJ. The sigh had been to make CJ aware of his presence, but the contemplative look on DJ's face told him that he'd only start talking when he was ready.

CJ glanced around the room while he waited. The place was big—bigger than his own bedroom had been and far larger than his quarters at the base. It was styled more like a hotel room than a guest bedroom in a corporate organization. And this wasn't even among the highest floors. According to Manar, some executives lived in Sparta permanently. The room was sparsely furnished, with a bed that took up half the space, a medium-sized closet, and the worktable at which CJ sat.

He glanced at the window and blinked in surprise. When had it turned dark outside? He'd started working after the meeting had ended, and that was only

… eight hours ago, according to the time on his computer. CJ blinked again. It wasn't the first time he'd lost track of time while doing something. That happened far too often. But eight hours was still a very long time, and he wasn't any closer to finding what he was looking for.

Pratima's notes had revealed Helene's actual main server room, which was the best place to strike. However, because it was the best place, it was also the most predictable. Helene would surely be expecting them. They'd briefly considered hitting somewhere else, but both Manar and CJ agreed that any other place would be a delaying tactic at best.

Consequently, all of them knew that they were walking into a trap, but there was nothing they could do about it. CJ had spent the last eight hours swimming through protected sites to gather as much information about the server building as he could. Pratima had been able to dig up the building's location but little else. This wasn't surprising, as Helene had already proven adept at hiding whatever information she didn't want found. He'd found some things, but he didn't know how much use they would be or if the info was even accurate. He was sure that he could get more if he dug deeper, but then he risked setting off an alarm. He wouldn't have been able to break into some of the sites he had if Manar hadn't been giving him some tips for the last few days. Best not to push his luck.

CJ stared at the window again. Somehow just knowing he'd been working for so long brought all the stress to the surface. There was a door off to the side that led to the adjoining bathroom. Maybe he should freshen up and turn in? He could always continue in the middle of the night.

It took CJ a few more moments to settle on the plan. He intended to stand— and then caught DJ staring at him in amusement. He blushed.

"You forgot I was here, didn't you?" DJ asked.

"No … I was, uh … waiting for you to start talking." This time, the gaps between his words weren't necessarily because he had to process.

"Sure you were," DJ drawled. But it was obvious he was teasing more out of habit than anything else. His voice turned pensive. "You ever think about our dads?"

CJ hesitated. "Dad and Papa?"

DJ nodded. "They're the reason we're doing this right? Going after Helene, bombing things, and all that stuff. Because we want to avenge them?" He paused. CJ shifted in his chair and closed his eyes so he could listen intently. "At least, that was *my* reason for risking my life. Working with Olsen to stop him from arresting you was just a bonus to me. You too?"

Me too? CJ wondered. Was that why he'd started this?

"Yes," he answered finally. He'd needed to know what had happened during Mayday—and why his parents had been killed because of it. He'd needed to know so much that he hacked into government systems to find out.

"Yeah ..." DJ said. "So, you ever think about our dads?"

CJ nodded in understanding. When was the last time he'd thought of them? If he couldn't answer that, then how could he say he was risking his life for them? The simple answer was, he couldn't. At some point, his grief had been the only thing that he could think of, and it was what had driven him. But not anymore. He couldn't say that he was doing this for his dads anymore. Now he went after Helene because he had to.

No, CJ thought, *that's not right either.* Helene had to be stopped. CJ believed that, but it wasn't his primary motivation.

"They would have hated it, you know. All of it," DJ continued. "Especially, Papa. He would probably would have said something like, 'Did you try talking it out?'"

CJ chuckled. Papa had always hated violence of any kind. He only ever got truly mad when CJ and DJ got into fights. And then he would ask them if they'd tried talking it out. For the most part, CJ agreed with him, but it hadn't taken long to realize, growing up, that not everything could be solved by talking it out. As much as he hated confrontation, sometimes it was necessary.

A wave of sadness washed over him at the thought. He'd had that same conversion with Papa shortly before Mayday. This time, he didn't have to search for the memory.

"See?" Papa had said, "we don't agree with each other, but we're talking about it."

CJ couldn't help but think it was a naive thing to say. How does *anyone* talk it out with Helene?

"I was, uh, devastated, after … after Mayday," CJ said. "My mind shies away … from the memories of that period, but, uh, that's one thing I remember. I was so confused." CJ's cheeks turned pink in embarrassment. He was used to internal monologues. It wouldn't have been a problem when he was younger, but it'd been so long that saying this, actually *talking* it out, even with someone he knew would understand, had become foreign to him.

"It would have been worse for you," DJ said softly, "since you were still at MIT. It's a wonder you didn't drop out. Lord knows I would have,"

"You would … uh … have taken any excuse to drop out," CJ said. "Our dads knew this. That's, uh, why they never forced you to go. They used your tuition to redo the kitchen."

DJ laughed. "You're kidding."

CJ shook his head. "If it … hmm … makes you feel better, it took ages for … for me to convince them to do it. The kitchen was an eyesore."

DJ laughed harder. CJ leaned back in his chair, a small smile on his face.

"What brought this on, DJ?" he asked.

"Can't a guy be pensive and nostalgic once a while?"

"No."

DJ chuckled. "That's it, though. I mean, that's the reason. We were talking about the whole thing with Helene, and it just popped into my head how pointless our dads would have found it. Papa would have hated the need for violence, and Dad would have hated the fact that we were in the middle of it."

"We never would have done this if, uh, if they'd been alive."

DJ nodded in agreement, grimacing. "On one hand, the last few years, everything with Helene—they've been some of the best years of my life. One of the few times I've actually felt like I was *doing* something. Ironically, that feeling was the entire reason I joined the SEALs. And now I've seen more action than some veterans.

"I'd like to say that if they'd survived Mayday, it wouldn't be personal. That I wouldn't have joined the teams, even if I was recruited. But … no. If I knew what Helene was up to, I would have rushed in, no matter what. That makes me feel like a jackass. Like I'm dishonoring their memory or something. But what makes me feel worse is that I wouldn't have joined in because it's a good cause or some crap like that. I would have joined because it's a challenge."

"You … are a jackass," CJ said seriously, "but not because of this. You are, uh … you are prone to rushing headfirst into … danger because you think it is fun. It is who you are. Just like … just like I am prone to focus on a particular thing to the exclusion of everything else, even when that thing is harmful." He paused, deliberately meeting his brother's eyes. "What it … uh, means is that it is up to us to look out for each other."

And that was the main reason why CJ was going after Helene. Even with how insurmountable the challenge was. Even with the very real possibility of death. Because he had to look out for his brother.

DJ was the first to look away, staring up at the ceiling, lips curling in a grin. "Fuck it, then. I'm sure our dads would understand."

CHAPTER

54

APRIL 2043

SPARTA BRANCH, NEW YORK

"SO THIS IS THE PLACE, huh?" DJ said, hefting his gun over his shoulder. He squinted at the building. "Doesn't look like much."

"I think that's kind of the point, D," Christy said through the comm. "If it was as high key as the headquarters, it wouldn't be much of a secret, would it?"

DJ puckered his lips. "It wouldn't be much of a blah, blah, blah," he muttered, too low for the comms to pick up. Louder he said. "I meant, even for a Sparta branch, it isn't much to look at. It blends in with everything else instead of rising above them like some architectural jerk."

Christy sighed. "That's what's tripping you? Seriously? The fact that the building is normal?"

"It's not tripping me. I'm just saying it's weird. Like it'll be anticlimactic when we bomb the shit out of the place. Normal-looking building like that, the explosion's probably going to be medium sized and boring."

"Can you guys not do this right now?" Ndidi said, exasperated. She'd insisted on coming along for the strike despite DJ's and Manar's protests. Fortunately, Pratima had been just as difficult to budge—though no one had tried very hard—so DJ was sure that Ndidi would have at least one person always watching her back. He'd sparred with Pratima once over the last week, and she'd nearly broken his ribs with just a graze from one of her kicks.

Never again.

"What, you're not a fan of pre-battle banter?" DJ chuckled. "A last laugh before the charge forward in a blaze of glory?"

"No," Ndidi replied sharply. "No one's running or going anywhere in a blaze of glory." She cracked her neck for the third time that minute. "Both of you need to focus. We all need to just focus. We have a lot riding on this, and we can't afford to screw up."

"You need to relax," DJ said, his face suddenly serious. "You're too tense. If you run in like this, you'll get Pratima killed within the first minute."

"How would I get *Pratima* killed?" Ndidi asked.

"Because I would die before you do," Pratima said, stepping up beside her. "It is what I promised myself. I failed to protect your parents, but I will not fail to protect you. Darren is right. Your fears are consuming your mind. If you let it, you will hesitate when you shouldn't and endanger yourself."

"See?" DJ said. "You're doing all that stuff. Let's diss the building together. It's an easy target, and it pisses me and Christy off."

"It doesn't piss me off," Christy replied calmly. DJ could almost feel her taking aim at his back. "You're the one that pisses me off by complaining about stupid shit."

"That's the point, though," DJ replied. "It's a stupid building that we're going to blow up. Its ordinariness underwhelms everything we're going to do today. I'm surprised I'm the only one angry about that."

"It's because no one else is a dumbass like you."

"I'm, uh … I'm angry about it too," CJ chimed in, also over the comms.

"Knew you'd be on my side, bro," DJ laughed.

CJ and Manar had opted to stay back in Sparta and coordinate the strike along with Olsen—though Olsen would only be consulted if the shit hit the fan. DJ had refused to budge on that point. He hadn't wanted to involve the admiral at all, but the team had needed some stuff that they wouldn't have been able to get without military access. Surprisingly, once DJ explained everything, Olsen had been on board—which made DJ feel even more guilty. Helping DJ sneak off the base was one thing, but if it ever came out that the admiral had helped misappropriate military-grade weapons to civilians, he could be court-martialed.

Christy sighed. "I stand corrected." She paused. "All right, the last of the civilians have left the building. You guys are clear."

DJ stepped out of the alley, Ndidi and Pratima beside him. Christy would keep an eye out while they scoped out the upper levels for the entrance to the underground servers. Once they found it, she'd join them, and the four of them would head in together.

They'd all agreed that a smaller team would be better, but DJ would have felt a lot more comfortable surrounded by a couple more guns.

The street was empty, and their footsteps crackled loudly against the gravel.

"Why didn't you guys run across?" DJ asked.

"What do you mean?" Ndidi replied. "You didn't run."

"Well yeah, but I didn't run because I couldn't pass up the opportunity." DJ grinned at the confusion on their faces. "Y'know, walking into the bad guy's lair in slow motion while a rap song played in the background? The road was empty, too, so all we were missing was the tumbleweed blowing across. But now I'm wondering if there was another reason not to run that I didn't know about."

"Of all the dumb, fucking things, D," Christy said.

Ndidi stared at him. And stared at him. After what felt like a full minute, she chuckled softly, her eyes softening in amusement. She blew out a breath in a rush, and her muscles relaxed.

"No reason then?" He grinned, pushing open the door. The reception area was empty. "Manar, you have a map of this place, right? It would be a pain to have to run blindly through it."

Manar sighed through the earpiece. "Yes, I have a map. For everything above ground, at least. Your first stop is the server room on the third floor. Not to doubt you, Pratima, but I'd feel a lot better if we could confirm that the signal coming from it is fake. On the way, CJ will lead you to points of interest that might hide the entrance to the underground. Take the passage on your right."

The building wasn't big enough to warrant an elevator, so they would have to make their way through the stairwell.

"Why would the signal be fake?" Ndidi asked as they jogged down the hallway.

"Because, um, two active servers close together … will interfere with each other," CJ said. "If the main server room is, uh … is underground, then the one above has to be fake."

"Gotcha," DJ said. "Christy, do you see any movement?"

"Negative. Both inside and outside. It's the middle of the day. It doesn't make sense."

"Looks like we really were expected." DJ grimaced. "We didn't try to hide, but there's no way Helene evacuated all of her staff in the time we were outside."

"She wouldn't do that anyway," Manar said. "Evacuate them, I mean. She wouldn't care. I'm pretty sure the only reason she's been this passive is to avoid drawing too much attention to her activities while she figured out the picospores. Now that she has, there's no longer any point. She probably cleared away the staff for another reason we're not seeing."

"Well, there's that pep talk I needed," DJ muttered. "The psychotic AI that doesn't care for human life has a plan we're not seeing, and it might involve the building I'm standing in." He sucked on a tooth. "Fan-fucking-tastic."

"Turn left after, uh, after this hallway. The first point should be, uh, coming up on the left," CJ said.

They followed the directions and stopped by a wooden door. DJ took a moment to study it but couldn't figure out what made it different from the other doors they'd passed. "So, what happens now? I just open it?"

"Yes."

He pushed the door open. There was a click—

DJ tackled Ndidi, and his dive took them back the way they'd come. The world flashed white, and a wave of heat slammed into his back. Fortunately, the explosion was relatively small, and his body armor was enough to mitigate the worst of the damage.

"Fuck," DJ grunted, disoriented, as he picked himself up. He peered down at Ndidi. "You okay?"

"Yeah," she groaned, though she looked shocked. Then she gasped. "Pratima!"

DJ cursed, looking around as Ndidi pushed him off her. He hadn't had time to grab both of them. His eyes found Pratima, and he let out a sigh of relief. She was farther down the hallway, probably having realized the danger when she'd seen DJ move. DJ forced out a chuckle, but inside he was beating himself up. They'd known that the building was probably going to be trapped, yet he'd opened a random door just because. Pratima had fighting skills, but he was the only one with actual combat experience. It was his job to spot these things before they got themselves killed.

"Answer me, D," Christy shouted in his ear. "What the hell happened?"

"There was a minor explosion—" DJ started, but Christy interrupted with a slew of expletives, each of them cursing a different body part. DJ was impressed. "But we were able to get out of the way in time," he finished when she was done.

"Hey, CJ, how'd you say you found these points of interest again?" Christy asked, her voice strained.

"I, uh, cross-referenced the building blueprint with the building layout," CJ said, "and then, um … um, cross-referenced that with all the areas that the staff makes use of. I, hmm, figured the entrance would be in an area that is less used and maybe out of the way."

"Less used because everyone who used it fucking blew up," DJ muttered. He dusted himself off and strode to Pratima, gently moving Ndidi aside so he could check for injuries. Pratima had worn body armor as well, but the sets they had were light to allow for better maneuverability.

"Thank you," Pratima said, looking from him to Ndidi, "for risking your life for hers."

DJ scratched the back of his head and made his way back to the door. "Not saying I wouldn't, but that's not what happened here. I was pretty sure I wasn't going to get killed."

"How?"

"Well, it'd be pretty dumb for the hero to get done in by the first trap, right? It'd put a damper on the whole thing."

Ndidi's stare bored through the back of his head.

DJ peered through the splintered doorway. "There's nothing here," he said.

"What, uh, do you mean?"

"I mean, the place has been cleared out." DJ gingerly placed a foot into the room. When nothing else blew up, he stepped in fully, Pratima and Ndidi behind him. "There was obviously something here recently. Something heavy, judging from the dirt marks. But it's gone now."

"CJ, is it possible Helene found out you've been looking into the blueprints or whatever?" Christy asked.

"I bounced my, uh, inquiries off multiple routers and encoded everything twice. Hmm … but I cannot be sure she did not figure it out."

"If she knows where we're going, then every place might be bombed." DJ grimaced. "But we're still going anyway, right?"

"We have to." Ndidi sighed. "We need to find the entrance to the under-ground. And that means checking every possibility. Preferably before she springs whatever trap she has for us."

Great, DJ thought. He backed out of the room, but not before his eyes caught a blinking red light perched on one of the walls. He gave it the finger, then shot it.

The next place CJ led them to was still on the first floor. Fortunately, this one wasn't booby trapped, but DJ still had to blow it up to get it open. Like the previous one, it showed obvious signs of being cleared out recently. Ndidi insisted they search every inch in case Helene had missed anything or hidden the entrance there. DJ thought there was a fat chance of that but didn't say anything. His gut told him something was wrong, so he paid extra attention as he searched the room—but he couldn't figure out what was worrying him.

They found the stairs and moved up to the second floor. Several times, DJ spotted Helene's router hanging somewhere out of reach, and he shot each one down, though he bet there were dozens he didn't see. With Manar guiding them, they rushed through the halls but still had a lot of ground to cover. The building didn't look big on the outside, but having a lot of needless space seemed to be Sparta's MO. DJ wondered if Helene had somehow planned that so she always had a secret lair under their noses.

The next place they searched was rigged with another bomb, as was the next after that. Both explosions were as small as the first, and DJ was pretty sure the bombs were those stickers he'd used in the data bank. Those types were far more dangerous as a group. Individually or in small numbers, they were strong enough to knock someone out and break a few bones, but they weren't usually fatal unless the blast was point blank.

DJ's gut twisted again, and it was starting to get irritating. There was something he wasn't seeing.

Like the ones on the previous floor, all the rooms had been cleared out. Unlike the other rooms on the floor, the marks on the ground were more noticeable, which meant whatever machines used to be there had been heavier.

"There is something here," Pratima said. She was crouched on the other side of the room, looking at something on the ground.

DJ had lost most of his excitement after the third explosion, but he knelt beside her anyway. He felt what she'd found immediately. Air.

"There's a room down there," DJ said.

Or a tunnel, he thought to himself. He'd felt something similar when his team had been stuck in a cave somewhere on the coast. A breeze like this meant space for the currents to flow. If they hadn't already known about an underground room, this would have confirmed it.

"It's sealed, obviously," he continued, "but there might be something around here we can use to open it. A lever or something."

They spent the next few minutes going over every inch of the room again. They'd found the same airflow in the spaces with the largest imprints but nothing else.

"Maybe the floor was opened remotely," Christy suggested eventually. "Helene doesn't have a physical body. She doesn't, does she? Not that we know of? Anyway, not like she could use a lever."

"Depending on how much control she has over a picospore-infected person," Manar replied, "she might have dozens of bodies. Or hundreds."

DJ cringed. The picospores creeped him the hell out already, and the image of zombies shambling about under the control of some voice in their head didn't help. "Where to next, CJ?"

They made their way to the next few points, but the silence was oppressive. DJ wasn't the only one who was creeped out by what Manar said. Hermione was still working on a way to negate the effects of the spores but hadn't found anything yet. DJ didn't blame her for the lack of progress; she was probably pretty shaken. The whole thing was fucked up. She and her father had worked for years to make something that would be beneficial to the world, and not only did she have to deal with Helene using it to turn the damn world into puppets, but she also had to quickly figure out a way to effectively destroy something she'd spent years designing.

Shit like that makes me glad I'm just the muscle.

DJ, Ndidi, and Pratima made their way up to the third floor. Now that they knew what to look for, they steamrolled their way through the whole level. Between the bombs and searching the rooms, they were far behind schedule.

CJ led them to three rooms. The marks on the floor of these rooms weren't as obvious as the ones on the second floor, but they were more noticeable than the ones on the first. Each spot had its own current of air. *But does that mean there are different rooms, or is it just one large cavern-style chamber?* DJ wondered.

Everyone decided it would be a waste of time to rummage around, so they moved on to the server room. Like every other server room DJ had been in—which he'd never thought would be more than zero—the place was cold. Hair-raising, nipple-protruding cold.

The room was large but still felt congested due to the number of stacks that filled the space. They were arranged in rows, like in a library where each book emitted a soft-blue light—which, according to his brother, was normal. His skin prickled, this time not from the cold. He looked around, and his eyes were immediately drawn to the only blinking red light in the room. He shot it down.

DJ reached into his backpack and pulled out the device Manar had given him before they'd left Sparta. He knew the device analyzed specific signals, but he'd tuned out the rest of Manar's explanation. With it in hand, he walked through the rows of hardware. Five minutes later, it pinged.

A minute after that, Manar's voice came through the comms unit. "The signals here are definitely fake. But there's a part that's weak, as if it's shielded by something. Somewhere on your left, DJ, if you please."

He followed Manar's directions and stopped in front of a panel on the wall. A smack from his gun popped it open and revealed some kind of security system and a lever. DJ pointed his gun at it, then thought better and reached into his backpack again. He brought out a small palmtop and a cord, plugged both into ports, and waited.

"Give me, uh, a minute," CJ said. The palmtop was linked to CJ's computer, which gave him indirect access to whatever security system Helene had set up. It took more than a minute, during which time Ndidi and Pratima joined DJ, but CJ finally gave him the go-ahead. DJ pulled the lever, stepped back, and waited.

A creaking came from the other side of the room. Part of the wall split open, and the group was blasted by a gust of wind.

"Seems like we've found it," DJ said. He hid a grimace as his gut gave another twitch.

CHAPTER

55

APRIL 2043
SPARTA BRANCH, NEW YORK

THEY WAITED FOR CHRISTY to dismantle and stow her rifle before entering the tunnel. When she arrived, she handed several bags to Ndidi and Pratima. DJ waited until they were done with their adjustments before tapping the comm in his ear.

"We're moving in."

"Remember," Manar replied through the earpiece, "though we suspect the chamber will follow the outline of the building, there's no guarantee. Proceed with caution. The device strapped to each of your waists will automatically map out areas you've been to, so you shouldn't have any problems when it's time to get out."

"Relax," DJ said with a casualness that he did not feel. "This isn't the first time we've gone in blind. It's not the second time either, actually. Why do we keep doing that? It seems kinda dumb."

"It's hard to plan against something that always seems to be a couple of steps ahead of you," Ndidi said. She was probably going for a dry tone, but her words came out a little too bitter. She fingered her gun and stared too intently down the tunnel. But she wasn't as tense as she'd been coming in, which was an improvement. On the contrary, her eyes were hard, and a spark of rage flickered beneath them—just enough to give her an edge but not enough to overpower her emotions.

DJ nodded. "We should probably work on that, then. It doesn't seem healthy to go against something like that."

"Come on, D," Christy groused, throwing her rifle bag over her shoulder. She wore her body armor over a black tank top, leaving her arms bare. Her strawberry-blonde hair was pulled into a ponytail, and her eyes glittered mischievously when she looked at him. "If it were healthy, you wouldn't do it."

"Can't argue with that." DJ chuckled. He tapped his comm again. "CJ, you good?"

"I'm good?" CJ repeated, taking time to process the question. "Yes, uh, I'm fine. Your objective is to, uh, find and destroy the mainframe server. It should be in a chamber similar, hmm, to the room you are in. But the hardware would be far larger. Helene won't be able to shield its signals when you are, uh, close, so we will be able to direct you then."

"And then we bomb the shit outta it?" DJ asked.

"Yes, you, uh, can destroy it."

"Ndidi," Manar said. Ndidi perked up. It sounded like he was keeping his voice level to keep from giving away too much emotion. "This is your last chance to return. It's going to be dangerous out there, and you could get hurt, even with Pratima protecting you. Leave the fighting to the professionals; I can have you back at Sparta in minutes."

DJ almost facepalmed. He agreed with Manar that Ndidi should be in Sparta where it was safe, but the idiot had suggested she couldn't keep up. Ndidi's jaw set stubbornly.

"Manar," she said in a voice that was too calm. "I understand that you're doing this to protect me, and I appreciate that. But I am not yours to protect.

You lost that chance years ago. Helene took everything from me when she killed Bethany and my parents. She turned Hermione's life's work into a joke. I cannot sit back while Helene is still out there. Not when there's still something I can do to stop her from taking anything else. Even if it costs me my life."

Manar's voice was just as measured as hers. "Helene didn't take everything from you."

"Yes, she did," Ndidi sighed. "After she went crazy—and before."

The line went dead. DJ opened his mouth to say something, then closed it again. He waited for final adjustments—and so Ndidi could collect herself—before descending into the tunnel's gaping maw.

DESPITE THE FLASHLIGHTS DJ and Christy carried, the darkness seemed to press in on them, restricting their vision to only a few feet. DJ fought against the instinct to bunch together. They didn't know what was down the tunnel, and grouping up would probably give Helene too nice a target to pass up. Fortunately, the tunnel wasn't so narrow that they were forced to.

DJ stuck to the walls. He ran a hand along it, feeling the solid earth beneath his fingers. It felt like the tunnel hadn't been open for long. The earth still smelled fresh and was moist like recently turned soil. If the tunnel led directly to the server room, that would confirm Manar's suspicion: Helene had built the duplicate mainframe recently.

Fat chance of that though, DJ thought. His gut was all twisted up in knots. Every part of him said he was missing something and they were walking into a trap. But he'd known that going in and still hadn't been able to figure out what his instincts had picked up. And since the others hadn't either, he probably wasn't going to until it was too late.

The group was silent, walking cautiously. They were all aware that they were on a time crunch, but none of them were stupid enough to charge in. DJ let his eyes relax as they scanned the few feet he could make out. His muscles were as relaxed as he could make them, and he was confident that he would be able to react to any problems immediately.

His mind kept going back to what Ndidi had said.

He'd already figured out Christy. No matter what she said about wanting revenge for Mayday, she'd never been one to hold on to the past. Which meant she'd left the SEALs and come to New York because he had. That was quite the burden on him, especially since he'd thrown his lot against Helene because it was a fun challenge, as opposed to any altruistic reasons.

CJ had joined in because of their dads but had stayed out of some misguided attempt to protect DJ and rein him in. For Manar's part, he was repulsed by what he'd created and just wanted to put a stop to it. DJ had known all of this for a while, but Ndidi …

DJ had always thought Ndidi was with them because she wanted to stop another Mayday from happening. But if she was doing this to get revenge on Helene for Bethany and her parents, that meant every one of them was risking their lives for purely selfish purposes.

Despite everything that Helene had done, none of the people fighting her were doing it for the greater good. They weren't inherently selfless or some other bullshit like that. It didn't bode well for humanity, but it went a long way toward making him feel better about his choices.

DJ almost stumbled when the ground leveled suddenly.

"Watch your step," he half whispered, half called out. "Turn on your mappers. Make sure they're active and our markers show up, just in case we get separated. Manar, is there any way our signals will get interrupted here?"

"It's not impossible, but really only a problem if you're miles away from each other."

"Acknowledged." DJ followed his own instructions and tapped the band on his wrist. A 2D map popped up, showing three blue dots and a green one. "Everybody set? Good. Then let's move. We don't have a lot of time, so we're going to be moving at a fast walk. Keep your eyes peeled and call out the moment you see something weird."

There were nods all around. DJ gestured, and they made their way deeper.

About halfway, a string of lights blazed to life along the tunnel, triggered by their presence. This confirmed they were expected, but would also make it tougher for something to sneak up on them. DJ counted it as a win and tucked away the flashlight.

The next minute was spent in silence, save for the team's measured breathing. Ndidi stared straight ahead, gun raised, and DJ felt a twinge of concern. He didn't doubt her ability in a fight, but he'd only had a couple of weeks to teach her how to use a gun. They'd be lucky if she didn't shoot off her own foot.

The tunnel opened into a cavern with a ceiling so high that the light of the wall fixtures couldn't reach it, giving them an idea of how deep they'd gone. The cavern was empty and had several stalagmites protruding from the floor. On the other side of the room, half a dozen tunnels went off into the darkness. The smell of overturned dirt was strong.

Kind of like a hive or something, DJ thought, looking around. *Some kind of central hub, I think, but for what?* The proportions of the walls were far too large to be intended only for humans. Did Helene use this to move her machines? Maybe whatever devices had left the imprints in the rooms they'd searched? DJ described the chamber to Manar but chalked it up to another mystery that would bite them in the ass.

"Should we split up?" Ndidi asked, gesturing to the tunnels leading out. "We'll be able to cover more ground."

DJ shook his head. "We have no idea what's waiting for us, so we should stick together."

"There are close to a dozen tunnels, DJ. It'll take too long to go through them one by one. Pratima and I could check some while you and Christy go through the rest."

"That's a fair point, but splitting up the party would be a very stupid thing to do. There are too many things we don't know. And one of the few things we *do* know is that there's a trap waiting for us somewhere."

"That's a risk we have to take. We're running way behind schedule already."

"She's right, D," Christy said. She glanced at him, then went back to scanning the walls. "We can't afford to take too much time here. We don't have any idea where the mainframe room is, but only one of us has to find it. Then the others can just converge on that group. It's more efficient."

"Are you guys fucking kidding me right now?" DJ said. "This is exactly what Helene wants. There could be an army of puppets down one of those tunnels, waiting to kill us all. We're not splitting up!"

"Yes, you are," Manar interjected. "The ladies have a point. You can't afford to waste time."

"Are you fucking—" DJ threw his hands up. "You know what? Fine. It's all our funerals, but sure, why not? Christy and I will take the one on the left. Ndidi, you and Pratima start from the rightmost tunnel, and both teams will make their way inward. I'd tell you to be careful and call out if you notice anything, but since we're already being idiots, just try not to die."

"Look," said Ndidi, "most of the tunnels will likely be empty. If they aren't, we'll retreat at the first sign of trouble."

"We'll be able to keep track of them through the map, D," Christy added. "If there's any problem, we can haul ass to them."

"I said it's fine," DJ snapped, marching off to the left. "Let's just do this. You're afraid of wasting time? Well, we're wasting time right now."

How could they be so stupid? It was already bad enough that they were doing this blind, but splitting the party? That was the kind of rookie mistake that got people killed in stupid ways. That would get *him* killed in stupid ways. That was one of DJ's greatest fears. To be killed in a stupid way.

"Don't get your panties in a twist. It's going to be fine, D," Christy said as she jogged to catch up.

"Obviously we grew up watching different movies," DJ muttered.

His pace slowed when he reached the tunnel. The light from the cavern barely illuminated the ground at his feet. Still, he brought out his flashlight and bounced it around as he walked. After a couple of steps, the path branched to the left. DJ brought out a stick of chalk, marked the path, and continued walking.

Christy started to say something, but DJ cut her off. "I know the maps will update with the turn," he said. "But you'll thank me later when we're running for our lives."

Christy rolled her eyes. They continued along the path for another minute before the tunnel branched off again. DJ marked the direction once more. They branched three more times before reaching their first T junction, confirming what DJ suspected.

"The tunnels are connected to each other," he reported. "They probably work as a railway system or something."

"Any clue of what they're transporting?" Manar asked.

"Negative. I've been keeping my eyes peeled, but I haven't seen any tracks, boots, or otherwise. Anything on your side, Ndidi?"

"We haven't seen anything either," Ndidi replied over the comm.

"Have you been looking?" DJ pressed.

There was a pause, then Pratima's voice came on. "I had the same suspicion as you, but I have been searching for boot prints, not machines. Although I now realize I should have, considering what we're here for."

DJ deflated slightly but waved her off. "I'm assuming whatever machines pass through here left the marks on the floors of the rooms we searched. They were a lot heavier than the rest. You'll have noticed them."

The conversation went dead after that, and the next few minutes were spent in silence. Christy remained by his side, probably picking up on the ominous atmosphere. The light from the cavern no longer reached them, so they could rely only on their flashlights. DJ continued marking every crossroad they reached.

He kept his body as relaxed as he could, but his steps echoed in tune with his anxiety. They'd been walking for what had to be about half an hour. How far did the maze go, and why hadn't anything tried to kill them yet? On one hand, part of him wanted to stumble on the mainframe room, bomb it, and get out while his luck held; but the more realistic part of him was sure they would get attacked. He just wanted to get it out of the way.

Christy gestured, drawing his attention to a spot on the wall. There was a thin curved line carved into it, forming the outline of a door. He waved his hand in front of it and felt a slight draft. With some focus, he could hear a faint humming noise coming from behind the slab of stone.

"We might have something. Stand by."

With Christy's rifle trained on the wall, DJ knocked tentatively. A square compartment opened beside the outline, revealing a similar setup to the security system they'd found before. DJ plugged in his computer again. After about a minute, there was a long grinding noise. DJ backed up a few steps, placed the computer in his bag, and trained his gun on the opening door.

The noise grew louder as the rocks slid apart. DJ's flashlight pierced through the darkness on the other side, and he cursed.

"What are those things?" Christy asked.

"Those," DJ said darkly, to both Christy and into the comm, "are fucking drones. *Weaponized* drones, a.k.a. unmanned aerial vehicles or remote-piloted aircraft. As in, piloted by Helene."

He heard Ndidi curse as well.

DJ backed up some more. At least now he knew why the soil smelled fresh. It hadn't been turned over recently—it had been *disturbed*. Helene probably used the tunnels to transport these things wherever she needed them, which explained why the place was connected and so extensive. It also explained why the team hadn't met any resistance despite how deep they'd gone. Why would she need a security team when she had fucking drones?

The humming noise grew louder, as if reacting to their presence. One by one, red lights blinked into existence, each one trained on DJ and Christy.

A noise made DJ glance to the side, just in time for him to see a man and three women enter the tunnel he and Christy had exited. The man had dirt-brown hair and a solid build. One of the women was a brunette, and the other two had blood-red hair. DJ recognized the first two from the video Manar had pulled from the security feed. The other two he'd met personally.

"Guys?" DJ said, "we might need to rethink some things."

CHAPTER

56

APRIL 2043
UNDERGROUND SPARTA BRANCH, NEW YORK

LIZ STARED AT THE BACK of her father's head while he punched in the security code.

"I had thought," Karla said, sneering beside her, "that for our great revenge against the AI, we would be hunters, not sneak around like rats." Liz shushed her, but Karla ignored it. "We are always sneaking like rats whenever we confront the AI."

Chloe placed a hand on Karla's shoulder. "Well, after tonight, there will be no more Helene to sneak from. We'll destroy her main servers, cut off her processing from the source, and have ourselves a nice dinner."

Liz drew her hands across her shoulder. She didn't think it would be as simple as Chloe made it out to be.

Something clicked, and José stepped back, a self-satisfied smile on his face. The wall parted on the other side of the room, revealing the path underground.

Liz stared at the opening, and the hand on her stomach pressed harder. A second later, she straightened, shaking off her fear.

She had almost died the last time they confronted the AI, so her anxiety was justified. But it would be pathetic to let it get in the way of the mission. Liz was sure Karla was as apprehensive as she was, but her sister drowned out the emotion with anger and excitement at the violence to come. Karla had always been good at that. While Liz solved all her problems rationally and with a firm will, Karla was more primal in her response. It was a hassle to keep in check sometimes, but it was simple, and it worked.

Liz envied that.

Next, her gaze went to José and the confidence and eagerness in his expression. Liz squashed her fear even more. She would not be the one to ruin this, the chance to finally be free of the AI. She turned toward Chloe and found her already staring back. Liz made sure her expression gave nothing away.

"Let's go," José said.

They crossed the room at a jog and were swallowed up by the tunnel. The darkness pressed in on Liz as they descended, but the feeling was comforting like an old friend. Chloe's flashlight illuminated the path, but only a few feet in front of them. Yet, somehow, Liz could see farther, beyond the light's reach.

Was this the power of her cybernetics? José had said their improvements would become more noticeable in time. Was this what he meant? The ability to see in perfect darkness as if it were daylight? She was stronger than she'd ever been. Would she become even *stronger*? Would she be faster? Enough to keep up with her sister?

Liz shook the thought from her head, reminding herself that Karla would improve too.

Liz's eyes darted around. José made no effort at stealth, but it was her nature to be cautious. She wanted to ask how José had known about this place, what he had done for Helene to trust him with the location of her brain. But José would not take kindly to her asking. He was not against questions, but he'd never been the most open person. And Liz still remembered the haunted look he sometimes had in his eyes. Was that because of whatever the AI had asked of him? What was so horrible as to haunt the man the CIA called the Scourge?

The tunnel extended after a few minutes, emptying into a cavern with several other openings along its walls. Liz's eyes darted around; she was surprised at the extent of the chamber. Her questions burned in her throat, but José was already moving on, leading them into one of the tunnels on the far wall.

"Didn't even look at a map," Chloe pointed out. "How do you know so much about this place?"

José was silent for a few seconds, and Liz thought perhaps he would ignore the question.

"The AI tasked me with building it two years ago. I picked out the building and acquired the materials, and that was enough for me to guess its purpose. I was taken off the project while it was still in its infancy, but I made it a point to check on its progress until it was complete." Chloe started to speak again, but José glared at her. "Quiet. We will have to be careful from here on out."

They made their way through several branching tunnels. José took each turn confidently, making Liz wonder how often he'd been here. The chambers were already far more extensive than what the building upstairs showed. Had he memorized all the paths?

Half an hour passed in silence. Liz could feel Karla starting to grow restless. She had already been on edge when they'd found the building deserted, and the endless jogging didn't help. Karla knew not to complain in front of their father, but her fear would only keep her anger at bay for so long.

Liz started to say something, then paused as a faint noise reached her ears. She glanced at José, but he didn't slow down or show any sign that he'd heard. Liz hesitated. Then Karla paused also, and Liz realized that it was possible that only she and her sister had picked up on it thanks to their enhancements.

"There is something ahead," she whispered just loud enough for her father to hear.

José stopped and held out a hand to Chloe. Liz's heart soared to see him believe her so quickly.

"You heard something? What is it? Guards?" He didn't whisper, but his voice was low.

The sound came haltingly, but she didn't think it was a guard. It was a voice, and there was something familiar about it—something her unconscious mind had figured out and sparked her anger. She shook her head. "I do not think it is a guard, but it is too faint to know who or what it is. Guards would speak louder."

José was silent for a moment. "So it is a voice you hear? Do you also hear humming?"

Humming? Liz wondered. She shared a glance with her sister, but Karla just snorted and looked away. "No."

Her father nodded and led them on without a word, heading toward the noise. Was it a coincidence, or did José know whoever the people were? Their pace slowed, and within a few minutes, Liz could make out the voice. Karla growled beside her, and she sighed.

José led them into another branching path. In the middle of the tunnel, about twenty feet away, a man and a woman stood in front of an open door. The man noticed them immediately, though his eyes lingered on Chloe and José.

He whispered something and backed away from the door. The blonde woman by his side looked at them in surprise. But like the man—*Darren Kojak*, Liz remembered—all she did was reposition herself so that she faced the open door at the same time. Liz's gaze darted to the doorway, but she couldn't see inside. That was where the humming noise was coming from, and now it was familiar enough to send chills up her spine.

"José," Liz said, struggling to keep her voice even, "there is something through the door."

Karla growled again. Her expression flickered between anger and caution, and her eyes moved between Kojak and the parted wall.

"I can hear it," José replied, bringing out his weapon. "Prepare for combat."

"Who are we fighting?" Liz asked, her eyes bouncing from the wall to the other intruders.

José didn't reply, but he didn't need to. At that same moment, a swarm of drones burst through the door.

CHAPTER

57

APRIL 2043
UNDERGROUND SPARTA BRANCH,
NEW YORK

THIS IS BULLSHIT, DJ thought as he opened fire. His bullet rebounded off the approaching drone for the third time. He didn't know why he tried.

"Switch to the armor-piercing rounds," he called out to Christy. "And back up quickly. Pratima, take Ndidi and get the fuck out of here. You want to keep her safe? *Get her the fuck out of here.*"

The drones approached at a steady pace, venting pressurized air to hover a few feet off the ground. There were half a dozen in all. Three of them hounded him and Christy with metal blades when they got close enough, while the other three went after the Murder Twins and company on the other side of the tunnel. So far none of them had fired any shots, but the massive turrets strapped to their sides surely weren't for decoration. And if they were the same model as the ones that had almost screwed him over at the data bank—and DJ had had enough nightmares to be pretty sure they were—the machines probably had smaller guns somewhere within their shell.

He fired a couple of shots at the Murder Twins, just to test their reaction. DJ's eyes widened in surprise when one of the twins used her arm as a shield. The bullets pinged off into the distance.

This is fucking bullshit, DJ thought again. Why were the Murder Twins even here? Had they been the one to set off the drones? Too many things were happening at once, but DJ was used to that. Adrenaline flooded his veins, quickening his thoughts and reactions. He pushed all his questions to the back of his mind and focused on staying alive. If he fell, Christy wouldn't last long alone.

In a smooth motion, he discarded his bullets, unslung his backpack, and switched to his armor-piercing rounds. He had a rifle with more penetrating power, but switching to it mid-combat would be the same as killing himself.

"DJ, what's happening over there?" Manar shouted. His voice was hoarse; he must have been yelling for a while. "Why are they gunshots? Have you made contact?"

"The fucking genius, ladies and gentlemen," DJ muttered. Louder, he replied, "There are drones. We're fighting them. The Murder Twins are here too. And we're fighting them also. Christy, test your new rounds against one of the twins and let me know what happens. I can't take my eyes off this big guy. Pratima, you guys should be above ground by now."

"Drones?" Manar asked.

"The, uh, Murder Twins?" CJ chimed in.

"They're more cautious," Christy replied loud enough that DJ didn't have to rely on the comm to hear her. "They dodged the bullets instead of taking them head-on."

"We're not leaving you, DJ!" Ndidi yelled. "You can't face the twins by yourself. And you definitely can't handle the drones. Pratima and I are on our way. We have a tunnel that should put us close to your position."

The replies overlapped each other, forcing DJ to split his focus. That distracted him enough that he almost missed the bullet coming for his head. Almost. He dove out of the way, his eyes wide. Farther down the tunnel, the brunette waved at him.

If she's as fucked up as the other two, we're so screwed, DJ thought. His eyes flicked to the three approaching drones, then back to the Murder Twins. Karla and Liz were handling all three drones by themselves—and that was with the UAVs spraying bullets across the tunnel. The girls were pounding the drones down with their bare fists. Meanwhile, José Olvera and Chloe Savage dodged the responding fire from both the drones and Christy with enough time to fire potshots back at DJ and her.

We're screwed anyway if we don't make a break for it soon.

DJ dodged another set of bullets, then dodged again when he allowed a drone to get too close. He jumped to his feet and scanned the tunnel once more. "Christy, where are you?"

The comm buzzed with shouts from the rest of the team. DJ ignored them all.

"Right behind you and to the side. My bullets aren't doing jack shit. They just dodge it, even when they're supposed to be distracted by the drones. It's like they have some sixth sense or some other bullshit."

DJ had never stopped his retreat, so he was relieved that she was behind him. He couldn't spare a glance, but he figured they should be close to the end of the tunnel by now.

"Everything about them is bullshit," he replied. "Let's switch targets. I'll handle the Murder Twins while you figure out a way with the drones. They haven't shot at us yet, and I assume that's because they don't think we're a threat. Let's keep it that way. Slow them down and keep them back, but not so much that you piss them off. Get ready to haul ass as soon as we hit the next branch."

"Roger."

The Murder Twins had pressed their advantage, forcing their drone opponents to glide back, which meant they were still moving to cover any distance DJ and Christy made.

DJ transferred his focus and aimed his gun down the tunnel. He still couldn't switch guns, but considering the twins had felt the need to dodge Christy's bullets, he hoped his weapon wouldn't be *completely* useless this time. He breathed out in short quick bursts to stabilize his aim, then squeezed off a shot. His aim was just to disrupt their rhythm any way he could. The more he could slow them down, the more distance he could put between himself and them when he finally got the hell out of there.

The bullet buried itself in one of the twins' shoulders. It still pinged off something metallic about an inch below her skin, but it was enough to make her miss a step. Her eyes shot to him, and the pure rage behind them told DJ it was the same chick he'd fought at the data bank.

DJ grimaced. *Way to dig myself deeper into* that *hole.*

His fingers danced over the trigger, searching for another chance. His eyes caught movement, and he rolled away to avoid a bullet from the side. José Olvera bore down on him, face cold and eyes angry. He'd separated from the rest of his group and moved to the side wall. One of the drones split off to target him, but that just made it easier for the twins to deal with the other two. At the rate they were going, they'd probably finish with their drones before DJ and Christy reached the tunnel's end.

Something had to change.

DJ cursed and grabbed a grenade from his belt. Underground, the explosion could cause the tunnel to collapse, but life was nothing without risk. DJ aimed the grenade at one of the Murder Twins and let it fly. Surprise blossomed on José Olvera's face. He stopped his charge and lunged in the direction of the explosive. Now it was DJ's turn to be shocked. He hadn't expected Olvera to sacrifice himself so readily. Then he remembered what Olsen had told him.

He's their father. DJ grimaced. *Right.*

Now he felt like a dick.

Midair, Olvera kicked the grenade, knocking it into the far wall. The grenade detonated—and harmed no one. DJ stared at him in horror. Bullets popped off, and DJ jumped to the side instinctively. His eyes darted to one of the drones. A new compartment had opened on its side, revealing a smaller gun. Its tip was smoking.

"*Now* it shoots?" DJ groaned. "I wasn't even aiming at it!"

"DJ," Ndidi yelled in his ear. "What the hell's happening?"

"Are you still coming?" DJ breathed out.

"Yes. We're close, according to the map."

DJ's thoughts spun. He squeezed off another shot, taking care that the bullets were far away from any drones. Christy was doing a good job of keeping them back. She sprayed her shots so that none of the three were hit more than the others. It was a monumental waste of bullets since she was doing almost no damage, but the tactic was keeping them alive. DJ considered tossing another grenade, but Olvera's stunt was still fresh in his mind. *What the fuck was that kick?*

"See if you can find a chamber like the one we split up in," he said to Ndidi. He wanted her nowhere near this shit show, but she was determined to be suicidal, so he might as well make the most of it. "Something large and defensible but with enough tunnels that we can escape if—*when*—things get too rough."

"I'll find something," Ndidi promised, steel in her voice. "Just lead those bitches to me."

"Manar," DJ continued, twisting away from a blade. "The drones are the same ones we encountered in the data bank a couple years ago. They're attacking only when attacked, so I don't think Helene has taken control of them yet. Is there anything you can do with that information?"

There was a pause. "I'll work something out."

DJ nodded. "CJ. I need you to help Ndidi. Is there any way you can boost the mapper? Knowing the path to retreat to is cool and all, but we need something that shows places we can go. We need somewhere defensible if we're going to survive this. If it helps, I've been marking the branched paths, and they have a semiregular pattern."

"I can, uh, extrapolate from that and give predictions," CJ said. "It … it will take some time though and … hmm … it will not be completely accurate."

DJ breathed a sigh of relief. "We'll work with it. Just tell me when it's ready."

He had the barest pieces of a plan. Now to hope that it didn't lead to all their deaths.

CHAPTER

58

APRIL 2043
UNDERGROUND SPARTA BRANCH, NEW YORK

LIZ DODGED ANOTHER SPRAY of bullets, leaped, and punched downward at the drone. Its shell was littered with dents, and it was considerably slower than it had been at the start. The drone recoiled from her attack, retreated, and swung around. Quickly, Liz spun and blocked a blade aimed at Karla. Her sister retaliated with a kick that sent shockwaves rippling from the point of contact. Liz aimed another punch at the same point, and the combined force was finally enough to break through the drone's outer shell. It shot a round of bullets at her, but she'd already moved on.

"Pathetic," Karla grunted. "They do not bleed. There is no satisfaction when they do not bleed."

Liz agreed but for entirely different reasons. When the fight began, she'd thought the drones were piloted by Helene, so she'd been overly cautious. But she'd discarded the thought after the first few minutes. The drones had not started attacking until Karla engaged them. And since then, they'd followed a simple set of moves. Liz had broken down the drones' sequence after a couple of exchanges and abused her knowledge to seek the fastest path to victory.

It *was* pathetic. Every second she wasted on the aircraft was one less she had to track down Ndidi Okafor. She would leave the man—Darren Kojak—to her sister. Although, with the attention she was giving him, Chloe might get to him before Karla.

An explosion distracted her for a moment. She allowed her eyes to flick across the tunnel, even as she dodged a blade aimed at her head. By habit, her eyes went to José first. They widened in surprise. Her father was picking himself up from the ground, and the look of rage on his face mirrored Karla's intensity. She followed his gaze to Kojak, who was dodging an attack from a drone. His movements showed his surprise but were still casual enough that Liz reevaluated him.

Had he been responsible for the explosion? His lips were moving, which meant he was still in communication with whomever he'd been talking to before they arrived. That worried her. Even if her sister killed him before they left, he might already have called for reinforcements.

She locked eyes with him, and there was steel in his gaze. Liz reevaluated him again.

DJ TORE HIS EYES AWAY from Liz Polova. He'd fought with her, too, at the data bank. The unreadable expression even amid combat was hard to forget.

Yet another reason to get Ndidi out of here, he thought. When he'd fought her, she'd already been badly injured from her fight with Ndidi, and she'd still fucked him up. More likely than not, she would be gunning for Ndidi. Nothing to do about that though. Ndidi was determined to fight the bitch, and DJ couldn't stop her even if he wanted to. And he no longer wanted to. He needed her for his plan.

José Olvera was still closing the distance between them, though he moved slower now and always kept the Murder Twins behind him. DJ fired a few half-hearted shots to keep him guessing, but he focused more of his attention on the three drones hovering in front of him. The Murder Twins were fiercely attacking their own drones, and DJ didn't think the stalemate would hold for much longer. Especially since Chloe Savage had joined the twins in fucking up the drones.

"Christy, can you see the light yet?" DJ called out.

"The light?" she asked.

"At the end of the tunnel," DJ yelled. "Can you see it?"

"What, are you planning our deaths? What the fuck is wrong with you? There's no light," she yelled back. "But we're almost at the edge. The next path is a right."

"Noted. Any other updates? Ndidi, CJ—give me something I can work with."

"Just … a minute," CJ said through the earpiece. "I found a way to enhance the signal of the mapper. It should, uh, be updating now. I had to overload the processor by, uh … by a lot. The device is not going to be able to handle the load for long."

"We'll figure something out," DJ said. "Will it be able to identify hidden chambers like the one that had the drones?"

"Uh, no … but I can tweak it to highlight them as pockets of open space. That would … hmm … ruin the mapper faster though."

"Do it anyway."

"Got it," Ndidi said. Her voice came between harsh panting, but it still kept its determined edge. "There's a cavern up ahead. Pratima and I will reach it in a minute and check it out." She hesitated, and there was a tinge of embarrassment when she continued. "How do I know if it's defensible?"

A bullet clipped DJ's side. He grunted. His body armor absorbed most of the momentum, but there was definitely going to be a bruise. Maybe a cracked rib. He pushed past the pain.

"Something too large would give the drones an advantage since they can fly, so that's a bad idea. There should be a bunch of rocks or something we can hide behind. And tunnels that we can use to escape and funnel the bastards through. If you need more clarification on something, ask Pratima. That good with you?" He changed his inflection so Ndidi would know the last part wasn't directed at her.

"I have some knowledge of such things," Pratima replied.

"Manar. How's it coming on your end?" DJ asked.

"Slow," Manar answered. "I'm using the boosted signal from the mapper to form a connection with the drones. But I won't be able to take control of the drones or anything like that. At best, I'll be able to remove the functionality of the gun turrets on their sides. And only because Helene isn't directly controlling them. Once that changes, there's nothing I can do." His voice cracked, but DJ ignored it.

"Noted. Taking out the cannons would remove a weight from my chest." DJ changed tack. "Ndidi, call out when you've checked out the chamber. Christy, you still with me?"

"Yep," Christy panted.

"I'm going to spice things up a little. Prepare for evasive maneuvers."

"What does that mean?"

DJ didn't answer. He reached to his belt and grabbed another grenade. José Olvera's eyes widened, and he sped up, but DJ had already tossed the explosive. This time, however, he tossed it at the drone. DJ leaped back and, midair, unslung his bag. He pulled out a briefcase as he landed, popped it open, and proceeded to assemble the rifle inside. The entire maneuver took just long enough for the grenade to reach the drone and go off.

The explosion rocked him, but he'd created enough distance that his armor absorbed the worst of the shockwave. DJ gritted his teeth, pushed through the pain, and focused on his task. By the time the shockwave had passed, DJ stood with a rifle held in a two-handed grip. He chambered a round, took aim, and fired.

With a loud *pop*, the bullet pierced through the outer shell of the drone. The grenade had already battered it somewhat, but DJ counted his shot as the first significant damage they'd done to the UAV since the fight started. Immediately, the other two drones responded with a hail of bullets. DJ had expected it, but he'd hoped he would have an easier time.

"Christy, keep one of them engaged for me. Enough to take the pressure off and slow it down, but not so much that it focuses on you exclusively. If at any moment you have time, switch to your other rifle. It's time we put these fuckers down."

"Roger." Christy's gun cried out, and bullets pinged off one of the drones. This time, DJ's hope came through as the machine peeled off and took aim at her.

With only two drones to focus on, DJ fired with reckless abandon, squeezing off one shot after the other. All the while, he kept an eye out for Olvera and the Murder Twins in case they tried to sneak a shot in. Fortunately, it seemed they'd all had the same idea because José had retreated and joined the fray against their own set of UAVs.

DJ's rifle tore through the armor plating, leaving large holes in the drones. But since he spent half as much time rolling or leaping away from the return fire as he did shooting, he wasn't able to let loose as much as he wanted to.

A crash drew his attention to the other side of the tunnel. The wreckage of a drone lay in front of the Murder Twins, while the other two hovered weakly in front of them, heavily damaged. DJ cursed. *I have to be faster.*

"We're at the branch," Christy called out.

Fucking finally.

"Empty your clip into the bastard in front of you, then haul ass," DJ ordered. "I'm a second behind you."

Only because he'd been expecting them, DJ was able to keep himself from flinching at the rapid shots Christy released. The barrage lasted nearly a minute and filled the tunnel with sharp reports. The drone was still hovering when DJ heard the sound of empty clips, but it looked just as miserable as the two across the tunnel.

"Now run!" he yelled.

Leaping back, DJ fired two shots at the drone Christy had just fucked up. That drew its attention back to him, adding to the other two he'd been engaging. *All right*, he thought, *only gonna have one shot at this, so I have to play this just right.*

Adrenaline flooded his veins, and DJ rolled back again to create some distance, breathed out to stabilize himself, then aimed at Olvera. His shot tore through the room and passed less than an inch from the man's head. Somehow— by some bullshit sixth sense—José had jerked sideways. DJ had aimed to miss, but it pissed him the fuck off that he would have either way. Apparently the whole family was a bullshit existence.

It took a surprising amount of effort to push away his annoyance. He now had Olvera's attention, which was the plan. Now to make the most of it.

"We know how to get to the main server room," DJ yelled. "There are several dozen more of these things scattered around here. Plus, the whole place's rigged to blow in a bit. Come with me if you want to live." He took a breath, then hesitated as he remembered the man diving in front of a grenade to protect his daughters. His next words made him feel like a dick, but they were his best shot at survival. "If you want your *daughters* to live."

"What the hell are you doing, D?" Christy screamed in his ear.

"What are you thinking, DJ?" Manar shouted.

"Was that … was that smart?" CJ asked.

"I know I said you should lead them to me," Ndidi yelled, "but you better have a plan, DJ."

Pratima stayed silent.

"At least one person trusts me," DJ muttered to himself. "Or, more likely, doesn't care."

He made eye contact with Olvera and held it long enough for him to see his resolve. Then, firing off a couple of shots to create some more distance from the drones, he turned tail and hauled ass after Christy.

0 0   0 0 1 1 0 1 1   0 0   1 1 0 1   0   0
0 1   0 1 0 0 1 0 1   0 1 1   0 1   1   0
0 1   1 0 1 0   1 1   1 1 0 1 0   1 1   1 0   1 0
1 1   1 1 1 0   1 0   0 1 1 1 G   1 0   G 1
0 0   0 0 0 1   1 1   1 0 0 0 A   1 1   1 A 0
1 0   1 1 0 G   0 1   1 1 1 0 B   0   0 B 1
1 0   0 1 0 A   1   1 0 1 0 A   1   A 0 1
0 1   0 0 1 B   1   1 0 0 1   0 0
1 0   0 1 0 A   0 1 0   1 1

CHAPTER

59

APRIL 2043
UNDERGROUND SPARTA BRANCH, NEW YORK

THE TUNNEL DJ RAN THROUGH was far shorter than the one he'd just escaped. By the time he entered, Christy was exiting the other side.

"Head for Ndidi and set up," he called out. "I'm right behind you."

But before that, he added mentally, *I have to make a slight detour to make this work.*

The wind whipped through his hair. DJ risked a glance backward in time to see the drones turning into the tunnel. They were moving faster than they had before, but not by much. DJ slowed down a bit. He wasn't sure if José Olvera would take the bait, but if he did, DJ didn't want to lose him.

He flipped open his mapper. His eyes went first to the green dot that indicated his position, then to the closest blue dot that was Christy. The last two blue dots were farther away, but not as far as he'd expected. They were moving back and forth in a small circle. DJ took that to mean they'd gotten to the chamber.

Good. Defensible or not, there wasn't enough time to find another cavern to use.

With the position of his teammates confirmed, DJ ran his eyes through the mapper again, this time looking for …

There and there. This just might work. He started to grin, then thought harder about what he was grinning about, and his happiness melted away. He glanced back when he reached the end of the tunnel. The drones were halfway through. DJ ignored them and focused on the far end.

He slowed again. *Come on … come on …*

A man ran around the bend. DJ locked eyes with José Olvera for a split second, hesitated, and then grinned at him. He held the grin until he turned onto a branch path, then sped up. The drones would be able to keep pace with him, and the Murder Twins should have no problems keeping up with the aircraft.

"Prepare for incoming, CJ," he called out. "Need you to break into something for me, as fast as you can. I'll tell you when."

"What am I breaking?"

DJ didn't answer. He glanced at his map and crossed into a branched path. And then another. Both were about the same length, which meant the one he'd found the drones in probably wasn't as long as he'd thought. *Should have figured. Time tends to slow during combat.*

DJ reached the first tunnel he'd identified on his map. The humming of the drones was a tidal wave behind him. He slowed his pace further, scanning the walls until he found the thin, curved line. DJ could make out a weird humming noise from the other side. He popped open the compartment beside it, brought out the computer from his bag, and plugged it in.

"Now, CJ."

There was a pause, and DJ held his breath.

"I hope you know … what you're doing, DJ," CJ said. There was an undertone of sadness in his voice that probably only DJ would pick up on.

"I hope so too," DJ replied.

"Why?" Ndidi asked. "What is he doing?"

The rocks began to slide apart. DJ counted to ten, unholstered his gun, and squeezed off a few rounds into the room. In response, red lights blazed into existence and turned their attention to him. DJ holstered his gun again and moved on.

He did the same thing two more times before heading toward the chamber to meet up with his team. On his map, Christy's dot had already joined Ndidi's and Pratima's. With any luck, they'd be set up and prepared. The humming hit a crescendo.

DJ glanced back, and immediately wished he hadn't. Somehow, he'd picked up close to two dozen drones. They had arranged themselves into rows and easily kept pace with him. So far, they'd only attacked in self-defense, but DJ didn't know how long that would hold true—especially when his team started fucking with the main servers. The number he'd pulled was more than enough for his purposes and would work out great—if he reached the cavern without getting killed.

And hopefully, somewhere behind all that mess were the Murder Twins.

LIZ KNOCKED ANOTHER of the flying machines out of the way. It had taken her a while, but she had finally figured out the perfect amount of force to use to avoid triggering its self-defense mechanism, as long as it did not crash into the wall. The drone careened off to the side, rebounded off the others, and returned to its position in the neat rows.

When they first encountered the swarm ahead of them, they'd thought Helene had descended on the place. But the drones followed the same pattern as the others they had destroyed. Liz had thought that José would call for a retreat, but he hadn't.

She had heard what the coward said before he ran, but what had driven her father to such rage?

José ran in front of her, so Liz couldn't read his expression—not that she would have been able to anyway. They'd each taken different methods to deal with drones as they ran. Like herself, José dodged what he could and smacked away the others. Karla forced her way through the swarm like a bull. It was loud and brutish, yet somehow she kept pace with Liz. Chloe weaved through the ranks, dodging everything that came close. She was farther ahead than even José.

They were obviously being led somewhere. What Liz didn't understand was why Kojak had made it a point to involve them.

DESPITE HIS PESSIMISM, DJ reached the chamber in one piece. Even better, he reached it ahead of the machines that were trying to kill him. He scanned the cavern and nodded. It was a little larger than he would have preferred, but that was evened out by the many stalactites hanging from the ceiling. Stalagmites also jutted out from the ground, providing the team plenty of cover.

Pratima and Ndidi stood at the center of the chamber, while Christy rounded the edge. They all looked up and glared at him. Even Pratima.

If they're pissed now, DJ thought, *they're in for a surprise when I start talking.*

He waved Christy over and started talking when he was still a few feet away. "All right, quick notes. There's a swarm of drones a few minutes behind me. About two dozen. I figured they'd get sent after us when we reached the mainframe room anyway, so I decided it would be best to deal with them here."

"Are you mad?" Ndidi shouted. "What is wrong with you? You and Christy had so much trouble dealing with just three of those things, and you pulled in *more*? How do you think we're going to be able to handle that?"

"I have a plan for that," DJ said. "Kinda."

"Is that why you shouted a bunch of nonsense to the Murder Twins?" Christy asked. There was a ring of sweat on her brow, and her gun was held loosely at her side, but otherwise there was no sign that she'd just fought for her life and then ran nearly a mile.

"That's part of the plan too," DJ said. He turned to Ndidi. "Look, I'm not saying it's a very good plan. I'm definitely not saying it's one I'm proud of, but it can work. And if it does, we get out of here in one piece."

"And if it doesn't?"

He shrugged. "Well, we were fucked as soon as the Murder Twins showed up, so nothing really changes."

Ndidi sighed. She looked like she was going to say something else but just sighed again.

Christy spoke up. "Well, we found the chamber. Is there anything you need for this plan to work?"

"Just for you to be open minded," DJ replied. "Manar. CJ. I'll need you guys to work on finding the mainframe room though. We'll need to move fast. It'd help if we had a destination."

"If we prod too deep, then we might draw Helene's attention," Manar said.

"That would be … bad," CJ added.

"Jesus H. Christ," DJ drawled, "she's not a fucking god. So what if we draw her attention? Not like she doesn't already know we're here. Worst-case scenario, we spring whatever trap she had and deal with it then."

"Wait," Christy said, "I thought the trap was the drones?"

"Helene isn't controlling the drones," DJ said, shaking his head. "That's why I was able to pull so many. They're basically working on autopilot, only reacting when attacked. We could ignore them, but if we approach the server room, I'm pretty sure they'll go berserk and swarm us. But so far? It's basically been easy mode."

"And you knew that when you brought *more* of them?" Christy asked, incredulous.

Ndidi threw her hands up. "*Now* she gets it."

"I told you, I have a plan for that," DJ said. "And Ndidi, your snide comments aren't helping. Bottom line is the UAVs will be here in a minute, tops, and we're going to engage them here. Manar and CJ, you have to locate the room before we're done." DJ's eyes drilled into the three women in front of him. "Be as fast as possible, but try not to die. Remember, we're on a timer."

Less than a minute later, the first line of drones flew into the cavern, followed by the Murder Twins, Chloe, and José.

CHRISTY, NDIDI, AND PRATIMA immediately started taking potshots at the drones with their rifles. DJ had asked them to focus fire on a specific UAV before moving on. Since the aircraft only attacked in self-defense, they would only have to worry about an attack from one direction.

Assuming, of course, DJ convinced the Murder Twins not to murder them. He jogged a few feet toward them and waved them over the rest of the way. Surprisingly, they listened, stopping a few feet in front of him. Up close, it was easy to believe all the horror stories Olsen had told him about José Olvera. His severe expression gave no hint that he was sneering at DJ, but somehow DJ felt it anyway.

He met the sneer with a grin, and Chloe Savage returned it. DJ had to force his grin not to falter. She was wearing a yellow tank top and leather pants. In any other scenario, DJ would probably have thought she was hot. But her grin gave him the same crazy vibes as the Murder Twins.

She seems like the type that enjoys a little torture before dinner, DJ thought.

A glare burned the side of his head. DJ met it with another grin. He would have to do something about Karla Polova sooner or later. But there was too much riding on this for him to ruin it trying to placate a chick that wanted to kill him.

"Look, we don't have a lot of time before the drones swarm us—or before your daughter lunges at me—so I'm going to make this fast," DJ said, meeting Olvera's eyes. He was the one that DJ would have to convince if this was going to work. "The fact that you followed me means that you're here for the main servers too." DJ chose not to mention the other, more likely reason Olvera followed him. "Well, we have an idea where it is. But we have to move fast before Helene screws us over.

"So, here's how I see it. We could waste time fighting and softening each other up for Helene, or you could *not* try to murder us, and we could make a temporary truce to take care of the drones. Then we figure out the rest later."

"I also know where the main servers are," Olvera replied finally. His voice was like two rocks grinding together, and he spoke with a faint Russian accent. "And the drones attack only in self-defense. We can ignore them and go for the prize. I can ensure that my daughters do not harm you, the blonde, or the big woman." He paused, and his eyes hardened so much they may as well have been granite. He gestured to a spot behind DJ. "But not her."

DJ didn't need to look to know who he was talking about. "Well, that's a deal breaker. But we don't have to resolve it yet. You were wrong on one point.

You *could* ignore the drones, but they're this place's security system. They'll just swarm you when you get close to the server room. You can ask your daughters how bad that'll be for you."

"You know nothing about our capabilities," Karla Polova snarled.

"That's true," DJ conceded. "But I'm betting even you guys couldn't handle over two dozen weaponized drones by yourself while fending us off."

"You'll die before we do," Liz Polova said. Unlike her sister, her voice didn't hold any hostility. She was just stating a fact.

"D," Christy yelled in his ear so loudly, he almost jumped. "The drones are getting faster. And they're no longer waiting until they're attacked. So, whatever it is you're doing over there, hurry the fuck up."

"Also true," DJ agreed again, directing his answer to Olvera. "But unless you run with your tail between your legs, you would die too—especially when Helene springs whatever trap she has planned." He glanced back for a second and sighed. "Look, like I said, we don't have a lot of time. I'm willing to duke it out, but we'd basically be offering ourselves to the AI. You're not going to have Ndidi, but we can fight for her after we clear the room."

Olvera stared at him, and DJ made sure to hold his gaze firmly in return. It felt like he was staring down a wild lion, being sized up for any weakness. He must have passed because, after what had to be a minute, Olvera nodded.

"We will do as you ask, but only until the machines are taken care of. Then we shall discuss retribution."

What fucking retribution? DJ wanted to scream. *In every confrontation we've had, your crazy daughters attacked first and tried to murder us.* Fortunately, he was smart enough not to let his thoughts show on his face.

DJ reached out his hand. "Sounds good to me."

Olvera stared at it, and this time he did sneer. DJ wondered if he was remembering the grenade incident. Finally, Olvera clasped his hand in a grip hard enough to dent steel. DJ returned the favor, trying not to wince.

There wasn't anything more to be said, so they disengaged. DJ made his way back to the ladies. They'd retreated into one of the tunnels. Three drones lay in ruins in front of the entrance, and the ones that still hovered close were heavily dented. The drones spotted him when he was a few feet away and took aim. Luckily, there were enough stalagmites to use for cover, and a minute later, he dove into the tunnel.

Ndidi rounded on him immediately. "I hope it was worth it," she said. Even Christy glared at him.

DJ shrugged and tried to get his breathing under control. "Well, I got them to promise not to try to kill us until we take care of the drones. But obviously we're not going to stick around until the drones are cleared out. I drew most of the flying bastards here, so I figure that if we don't have to worry about the Murder Twins, we can focus on destroying them. At least, until Manar and CJ pinpoint the location of the target. After that, we hightail it there while they deal with the mop-up. Then we split."

Ndidi stared at him. There was an aspect to the plan that he hoped she didn't realize. He felt bad enough about it without having to explain it. When she didn't say anything for a few seconds, DJ gestured to the tunnel mouth.

"You can be angry at me later. But can we finish this first?"

Without waiting for her reply, he lifted his rifle, took aim at a diving drone, and squeezed off a shot. The round easily pierced the shell of the aircraft. DJ chambered another round and pulled the trigger again.

Almost at the finish line.

CHAPTER

60

APRIL 2043
UNDERGROUND SPARTA BRANCH, NEW YORK

LIZ PUNCHED DOWN at another drone with all her strength. The shockwave radiated outward, overpowering the vents it used to hover. It plummeted like a meteor, and another shockwave emanated from where it fell. Liz followed its descent smoothly. She spied another drone, adjusted her position, and added her momentum to her next strike. The impact echoed throughout the chamber, and force battered her back as she landed in a crouch a few feet away.

A lock of hair fell into her face, and she pushed it away, suppressing a grin. It was rare for Liz to let herself rely on strength to defeat her opponent. But fists were a bad match for the heavily shelled drones, and so she relied on overwhelming force. A brutish method, and one she couldn't use often as her hands ached already, but she understood why Karla enjoyed it so much. With her target destroyed, Liz kicked off again and appeared in front of another aircraft.

Her family had split up to be more efficient. José and Chloe had been forced to switch to their guns. José must have anticipated the machines because he'd made the transition smoothly. Their bullets were strong enough to pierce the drones' shells, but it still took several shots to bring one down. Darren Kojak and his team had the same problem, but they concentrated fire on specific targets, so they were not slowed down as much.

Karla and Liz were having the most success. It took only two strikes with their enhanced strength to destroy each aircraft, and their speed allowed them to switch targets every few seconds. The task would have been too easy, except with each one they destroyed, the drones became smarter. Their movements were faster and more complex—and more difficult for Liz to predict. Fortunately, they'd already brought down the number of drones to a little over a dozen. At this rate, the room would be clear in the next few minutes.

Kojak yelled something that was lost over the noise.

The world stopped.

Liz stumbled. Her body felt heavier, as if she were carrying an unexpected burden. Her eyes sought out Karla, but her sister shared her confusion. Around the room, the drones paused midflight and midattack, waiting.

In the sudden silence, Liz could make out what Kojak was shouting and the panic in his voice. "Helene's here! And she's taking control of the drones. Destroy as many as you can."

That explained why this heaviness felt so familiar. It had been much worse that night in the data bank, but she would not risk it happening again. With a yell, Liz leaped for the closest drone. Her momentum put her right above it. Liz clenched her fist. Most of the time, the drones did not try to evade attacks. When they did, they always dodged upward. Since she was already above the aircraft, her strike would land regardless. She relaxed her muscles up to the last moment. And then she struck out.

With a burst of pressurized air, the aircraft zoomed to one side, avoiding her attack by a large margin. Liz stared at the machine, and only her years of practice allowed her to hide her surprise. The drone turned, aiming its cannons directly at her face. Midair, she had no way to dodge.

She deserved this. She had been overconfident and left herself defenseless when the pattern changed. *Father would never have made the same mistake*, she thought, gritting her teeth. The guns began to hum.

Something slammed into the drone's side, knocking it off course, and its bullets splayed harmlessly into the air. Liz landed a second later and immediately kicked off toward the crash. Karla was already standing over the machine, pummeling it with blows that shook the ground around her.

She glanced back at Liz, pointing to the scrap metal at her feet. "The Coward said that Helene is controlling them now. They are smarter."

Liz had known that, but she'd still been overconfident. She nodded once, then dashed off. She scanned the chamber with a glance. Close by, José and Chloe were working together to dispatch the machines. When their gunfire focused on the same target, they tore through the drones like a butcher through meat.

On the other side of the room, Kojak had taken to lobbing grenades into the air, targeting areas with more than one drone. Beside him, the blonde girl shot down any drone that got too close. The aircraft moved constantly, but every shot pierced their shells without error. She stepped back into the tunnel to evade return fire from the machines before taking her position again. Liz made a mental note to keep an eye on the woman.

Liz leaped back to dodge a hail of bullets, then quickly rolled away from an attack to her back. Ending her roll in a crouch, she looked around. Two drones had caught her in a pincer move, one in front and the other, flanking her from behind.

Liz waited for them to charge in, but they were content to shoot at her from a distance. She dove away from another spray of bullets and jumped at the aircraft in front of her. The momentum built as she twisted through the air, and Liz whipped her fist at the drone. The drone tried to evade, but Liz had come in too fast. Her fist glanced off the side of its shell. The impact launched the machine into the distance, and the shockwave pushed Liz back toward her other assailant. Although the flight overshot her mark, she was still close enough to make contact with her legs.

A MINUTE LATER, Liz stood among the wreckage. The ground around her was cracked and depressed by a couple of inches. Her fist throbbed painfully from misuse, but so far she'd directed the worst of her wounds to her left side. Her eyes glowed with excitement as she scanned the chamber for any changes. The drones had been reduced to just a few stragglers, but that cacophonous hum …

Liz frowned. Although fewer than five drones remained, the hum hadn't grown quieter. The irritating noise still filled the chamber. She tilted her head toward one of the tunnels.

The noise is growing louder, she realized with horror. She turned to shout, but it was too late.

The chamber was swarmed with drones. Dozens of the aircraft flew in, filling the cavern within seconds. With them, the pressure around her grew until it felt like she had weights strapped to every limb.

Liz heard José stifle a groan. His knees bent, but he straightened them quickly. Chloe still had a smirk on her face, but the expression was strained. Across the room, only Darren Kojak and the giant woman were still standing. The other two women picked themselves up quickly. Ndidi showed her fear openly, and Liz snorted in disgust. She held no hostility toward her for their fight, but it was shameful that she had no control over her emotions.

Liz kept her eyes on the drones as she made her way to José and Chloe. Karla also stalked over. She had a scowl on her face, but that she hadn't attacked showed that even she understood their position. So far, the two teams had kept to opposite sides of the room. The drones filled the space between them, effectively dividing the chamber. Liz estimated there were close to a hundred of them. They hovered in formation but did nothing else. Liz wondered what they were waiting for.

"We are leaving," José said.

Karla growled at him but did not say anything. No matter how much she loved a challenge, engaging so many drones would lead to their deaths. Helene was controlling them.

"I did not expect so much resistance," José continued, "but it is clear now that

Kojak was right. Helene planned this all along. She probably thought to remove all her enemies in one fell swoop."

"And it might work," Chloe said.

"If the AI plans to kill us," Karla said, "then what is it waiting for?"

A moment later, they got their answer.

DJ STARED AT THE WALL of drones that divided the room. *We're so fucking screwed*, he thought. There were nearly a hundred of the flying bastards, and the pressure they emitted made it hard to even stand up straight. The drones hovered in neat rows. So many of them venting pressurized air to stay airborne created a mini-storm that would play havoc on bullets. Christy's shots might still find purchase, but everyone else's were unlikely to get close.

DJ's eyes darted around as he considered his options. The only thing they could do was get their asses out of there as fast as they could. But even that wasn't guaranteed. With Helene on the playing field, there was no way to know what would happen. They would probably die if they engaged the drones. They would definitely be chased if they headed for the server room or if they abandoned their goal and went topside. He had to assume that was why Helene had cleared the building: so she could fuck them up if they tried to run.

"How many minutes do we have left?" he asked.

"A little over half an hour," Ndidi replied.

Half an hour, DJ repeated in his head. *We're so fucking screwed.*

"Manar. Tell me you have something on the location of the server room."

"I got a ping a few minutes after you guys entered the cavern, so I assume it's close. The spot should be showing on your mapper as a bright-pink dot." Manar paused, as if he didn't like what he was about to say. "There's a chance that the place is a decoy, though—something Helene planted, either to waste time or to trap you guys. There was always the potential for that, but I'd hoped there would be time to check each spot cautiously."

"You should know by now that life pisses on hope, Manar," DJ responded. "We don't really have a choice here unless we want to give up on the mission completely. Don't stress it. We'll figure something out." DJ turned to his team, injecting as much confidence into his voice as he could. If a bit of hysteria slipped through, they were nice enough to ignore it. "All right, here's the plan. Hit the drones with *almost* everything you have, but keep a bit in case they follow up when we haul ass. We're gonna try to go for the server room, but if we pick up too large a tail, we'll follow the mapper back topside and hope plan B takes care of everything."

"You just said life pisses on hope," Christy muttered.

He shot her a look. "Then we'll rely on plan C. Christy, you're with me. Ndidi, don't leave this tunnel under any circumstance. Pratima, you can do your own thing. Everyone clear on their roles?"

There were nods all around. DJ grinned at them, then turned back to the drones—just in time to see something change.

Before, the drones had been emitting a soft-blue light through the seams in their armor. They'd seemed to be little more than aesthetics, but as DJ watched, the rows of drones turned a perfect red. A wave of scarlet, flowing from left to right. The light reflected off the walls, turning the entire room into a hellish landscape. In unison, the guns emerged from the ports on their sides.

"I just lost control of the turrets," Manar reported too late. Each word sounded like nails in his throat. "Along with all other functions. The drones are fully under Helene's control."

"All right," DJ said. "New plan."

JOSÉ HAD TAUGHT KARLA AND LIZ never to let their emotions rule them. Liz had the lesson so ingrained in her that was the basis of her personality. Now she was repulsed when people like Ndidi showed their emotions so openly. But looking up at the blood-red rows of drones poised to take her life, Liz understood why lesser people would be overcome by terror. Why they would panic and run like headless chickens, even when it went against logic. Even when it was to their detriment.

She understood.

Staring down her doom brought about an ancient dread that one could not escape. A feeling that threatened to suffocate her, despite her bionics and newfound strength. Despite having her sister and her father beside her, Liz now understood that fear. Yet she met the drones with an unflinching stare—because that was what was expected of her.

"We cannot run," she found herself saying.

Surprisingly, Chloe nodded. "The red lights mean Helene has taken full control. That means their guns will be online. We'd be gunned down before we take more than a couple steps."

"If I am going to die," Karla started, her voice hoarse, "then it will be while facing my enemy, not running away like a coward or being herded like sheep at the whim of an AI."

Liz couldn't help but agree. José had raised them to survive above all else. But Liz abhorred the thought of running in cowardice. Especially from Helene.

"No one is going to die," José said sharply. Liz stared in surprise. Her father's face was inscrutable as always, but his eyes darted around the room. He almost looked worried. "Least of all my daughters. Both of you are going to survive. It is your purpose. To survive above all else. We cannot expect to win here. We have to retreat."

"No," Karla said just as fiercely. "I will *not* die as a coward."

"You will listen to me!"

Karla backed away instinctively, but her expression was hard. Liz recognized the look, and her fingers twitched in their silent code, admonishing her. But Karla refused to meet Liz's eyes. Instead, she glanced at the row of drones, and her face hardened further.

Liz realized her sister's plan an instant after it was made, as did Chloe. Liz moved. Chloe moved. And they were both too late.

Liz watched it happen in slow motion. Her sister spun and kicked off her back foot, launching herself toward the center of the room. Chloe had been closer, and her fingers brushed at Karla's ankle, but there was no way to stop what was already in motion.

Karla pierced through the air like a bullet. And the drones, as one, homed in on her.

Liz's body moved on its own, as if a tether connected her to Karla, and she launched herself after her sister.

Then all hell broke loose.

CHAPTER

61

APRIL 2043
UNDERGROUND SPARTA BRANCH, NEW YORK

AN EXPLOSION ROCKED the chamber just in time to prevent Karla and Liz from being gunned down midjump. Although the blast disoriented her, Liz took full advantage of the confusion.

She arrived at the line of drones a second after Karla, who had already begun decimating the nearest drone. Liz grabbed her by the waist and shot away from the melee, using a passing drone as a stepping stone. By some good fortune, another explosion rocked the chamber, once more delaying the rain of bullets that should have been coming down on them. Liz ignored her sister's protests and focused on keeping her motions smooth and efficient.

If Karla had truly wanted to break free, there was little Liz could have done about it. The fact that she stayed meant that she hadn't been completely consumed by bloodlust. Her actions were more than likely an impulse to rebel against José's orders. It was well within Karla's nature—just as it was in Liz's nature to get her sister out of trouble—but Liz doubted their father would be so willing to forgive.

Later, she thought. *Assuming we survive this hell.* With the AI in the field controlling a hundred drones, Liz had very little hope they would be surviving anything. Helene had planned it too well. It had let them tire themselves out in the first round of attacks before bringing its main force.

Or maybe this was DJ's plan all along? Liz considered. He was the one that had led them here … but no. Unless he was working with Helene, he and Ndidi had even worse odds of surviving. Even if he were working with the AI, Liz doubted a soulless creature like Helene would honor whatever promises she'd made.

Liz hit the ground with an impact that formed cracks a few feet in every direction. The moment she lost her momentum, she slammed her sister down, denting the ground further. The impact barely affected Karla, but Liz hadn't expected it to. Karla crouched, and her muscles tensed as she prepared to launch herself back.

Liz looked down at her and, for a second, let the full force of her anger show. Karla flinched.

"You will *not* throw my life away," Liz spat in Russian. Karla flinched again and Liz knew she did not need to explain what she meant. Although they no longer shared the same body, the sisters were tied together by bonds greater than blood. If Karla died, Liz would not survive for long.

They could both survive if they retreated, but just as Karla knew Liz would never abandon José and Chloe, Liz was also aware that Karla would not run. Not from Helene. Not again.

Liz couldn't blame her. Her blood boiled whenever she remembered the AI's impassionate face at the data bank. Karla had lain unconscious, bleeding and burnt. Instead of helping, Liz had been forced to grovel while Helene dealt with Darren Kojak and Ndidi Okafor. She had nearly lost her sister that day. And for what? For a piece of code that had gone mad?

"We will fight her together," Liz continued. She let the anger fall away from her face, but she held on to it and buried it deep where she could still draw on it. Cautiously, Karla stood, and Liz let her. "We will fight her together," she repeated.

Karla peered into Liz's eyes. A second later, she grinned. "Like always."

With that, they both took note of their surroundings. Not more than a minute had passed since the first explosion. They were several meters away from José and Chloe but close enough for Liz to meet her father's eye. She shook her head, informing him of their decision. José's eyes hardened.

Liz had expected that, but still felt a pang in her chest. It was the first time she had openly disobeyed her father, and there would be consequences. She twitched a signal to her sister, and together they launched themselves into the air.

ALMOST IMMEDIATELY, Liz felt something wrong. She'd been too focused on Karla to notice sooner, but the closer they got to the drones, the more pressure she felt around her body. It felt like she was flying through water instead of air.

The machines had dispersed after the explosions, and they flew around the chamber chaotically. If not for the red glow around each drone, Liz would have believed they were in disarray. Now she just wondered what else the AI planned. With so many at her disposal, it would have been easy for Helene to swarm each person with more than a dozen drones at once. It would have been a short and brutal fight.

Liz was both relieved and worried that it hadn't done so yet. It was impossible that Helene hadn't considered it. Was it waiting for something else?

Liz forcefully pushed the question out of her mind as she and Karla engaged the first drones. Her fists were too badly damaged to continue using them directly, so she pulled out her daggers. The blades' serrated edges would have little difficulty piercing through the drones, even if it required a little effort.

Liz crashed into a group of drones like a wrecking ball. Her arms spun in a tight spiral around her, jabbing into shells and retracting. Her daggers were a blur of sharpened steel. The drones retaliated with every strike, but Liz used their brethren as stepping stones to maneuver around them. What she couldn't dodge, her daggers deflected. José had procured them to keep up with her and Karla's growing strength, so Liz wasn't worried about them breaking. Karla was a constant presence by her side. They were far enough apart that they didn't get in each other's way, but close enough that coordination was child's play for them.

She launched herself from a drone, and a hail of bullets rattled the spot where she'd just been. Her dive took her into the path of a drone that was heading for her sister. Liz crashed into it with the force of a meteor. The impact sent it reeling, but Liz hung from the gun turret as her other hand stabbed through its shell. Liz pushed off from the drone a moment later, leaving her target to crash to the ground as she flew toward another opponent.

By now, she'd adapted to the added pressure around her body, and her movements were more fluid. She spread her arms and sliced through any aircraft that came too close.

Karla and Liz spent the next few minutes decimating the drones. Working together, they destroyed their opponents much faster than they had before. For the most part, they remained airborne, using the drones as platforms to move. They dropped down only when the aircraft around them grew too sparse to sustain their movement.

Strength surged through her body in a constant, exhilarating rhythm. Since the battle through the tunnels, she'd been fighting for a little over an hour, and still she felt no signs of tiring. If Helene drew out their deaths, she could probably last the day before reaching her limit. Was this what Karla had felt every day? Her sister had always been stronger than her. Was this why she was always so free? Always so confident in her prowess? Liz doubted she would ever feel completely comfortable with the power, but at least she understood.

Explosions shook the chamber sporadically, and on several occasions a drone would suddenly drop just as she was about to attack. Kojak and his team must not have left yet—though she would not blame them if they had. It was a miracle they'd survived this long, but their ammunition would run out soon. She'd tested Kojak's capabilities and knew he would not be able to stand up to the drones without his guns.

Idly, she wondered what he'd planned. Her eyes narrowed toward Kojak and the blonde, but Okafor was nowhere to be found. Had she retreated farther into the tunnel, or—

Liz felt the hair on her arms rise, and she launched herself upward with all her strength. The drone she'd been standing on was pushed toward the ground, where it crashed. Red light washed over the spot she'd just been, and the air burned around it.

Liz reached the peak of her jump and began falling, but her eyes were riveted to the aircraft that had shot the beam. It hid within a cluster of similar drones, but its smoking barrel gave it away. Karla and Liz had been attacked by a similar weapon at least twice before, but they'd been able to see the attack coming. She should have noticed it this time, too, but she'd allowed herself to be distracted.

The drone turned its turret on her. Liz had launched herself too high, leaving herself open. As if summoned by her thoughts, she saw a few drones peel away from the swarm and move toward her. Heart clenching, she glanced around for anything she could use as a foothold. This far away from anyone else, Liz allowed herself a curse. The drones moved closer, and she angled herself toward the closest one so she could take advantage if an opportunity arose. But the aircraft stopped a few meters away and maintained its distance. Her eyes darted to the beam drone and estimated she still had a few seconds before its charge was complete. It was the bigger threat, but concentrated fire from the other aircraft could still take her out of the fight, if not kill her entirely.

The drones trained their guns on her.

Just as she had the thought, a movement in the corner of her eye made her twist around, and she smiled at the aircraft hurtling toward her. Its movements were wild; it had been thrown toward her. Liz gauged its trajectory and flipped until her head faced the ground in a nosedive.

She tensed. A second later, the drone passed in a whoosh of air, close enough that for a split second, it made contact with her feet. Liz blasted off with a force that sent a shockwave through the air—or at least she'd meant to. Her body froze up at the last moment, and the drone shot past her.

Liz stared at the aircraft until it crashed into a wall. *I … hesitated?* she thought, blinking. She hadn't frozen up since she was a child. The drones fired at her, and she twisted as much as she could to use her prosthetics like a shield. The bullets were staggered, so the hail was unrelenting. She hid her head behind an arm, while the other swung in a tight spiral around her and deflected what it could with her dagger.

Fortunately, she didn't have to endure the barrage for more than a few seconds before another drone was hurled toward her. This time she performed the move flawlessly and launched herself low enough that she crashed through the line of drones below. She pushed off one of the drones and dove toward the beam drone, her target.

Unsurprisingly, Karla was already there, another drone in hand. Liz nodded to her but ignored the look of confusion she received in return. She kicked down at the large machine and followed its descent by landing on its shell. One hand held onto a crack in its seam, while the other stabbed down with her dagger. Karla stayed nearby, hopping from drone to drone.

Liz stabbed down mechanically, trusting Karla to warn her of any attacks. Her entire left side throbbed in agony. So far, Liz hadn't encountered anything that could pierce through the titanium that had been used to make her limbs— but the last few seconds had put them to the test. There was an almost imperceptible lag between her thoughts and her actions on that side. Liz wondered if Martin would be able to fix the damage.

But again, that is dependent on me surviving the night, Liz thought.

The drone bucked beneath her. Liz yelled a warning to Karla, then shifted her weight. She dug her fingers into the holes she'd made with her dagger, waited until the last moment, and then twisted her ride until its cannons faced a particularly dense cluster of drones. A second later, the chamber was flooded with red light.

Dozens of drones were incinerated, and many more crashed from structural failure. Liz allowed herself a grin. She'd known the beam would be powerful, but it had exceeded her expectations. Without any other use for it, she dismantled the aircraft and leaped off. Karla scowled at her as they landed, jealous that she'd been the one to get to try that move. Liz ignored her, her focus drawn to the next swarm of drones heading toward them.

Another feral smile crept across Liz's face. The small army of drones meant that she'd finally forced Helene to get serious. She said as much to her sister.

"I would have downed more if you had let me shoot," Karla grumbled.

"You will get your chance."

The comm in her ear crackled, and José's voice rumbled through. "It is time to retreat. You drew too much of Helene's attention. She'll be focused on you two now."

"He's right," Chloe added. "It was a wicked show, but it's become far too dangerous. You've had your fun, but it's past time we get the hell out of dodge."

Liz scanned the chamber until she found the pair. Her father was in the middle of battle, running between two drones with a familiar pair of daggers in each hand. Chloe bounded between the aircraft like Karla and Liz had done. The brunette couldn't put as much force into her leaps, but the act was proof of her impressive agility. Liz wasn't sure she would have been able to pull off the same feat without her enhancements.

"We are not leaving," Karla snarled. "We will end this, here and now. Or die trying."

Liz kept her eyes on her father's battle. The man never looked at them, but Liz felt waves of anger wash across the distance. Suddenly, she felt the need to justify their decision.

"Karla's right. If we leave now, with Helene's attention so focused on us, the drones will hound us through the tunnels, and they will inevitably catch us. We will be dying a coward's death. If we're to die, better to die as we fight."

"None of you are dying," José snapped. Liz flinched. It was a rare occurrence for her father to lose his temper at all, but now, he'd lost it twice in one day. If they made it out alive, their punishment would be great. "We will retreat. I will take care of any pursuit."

"You can go if you want," Karla snapped back, "but I refuse to run away." She plucked the device from her ear and crushed it between her fingers. Liz pulled out her own unit. She stared at the device for a second, ignoring her sister's glare, then crushed it too.

José met her eyes across the distance, and Liz couldn't help but feel as if she'd made a terrible mistake.

CHAPTER

62

APRIL 2043
UNDERGROUND SPARTA BRANCH, NEW YORK

KARLA AND LIZ MET THE SWARM of drones with coordination born from a lifetime spent together. They moved in sync and danced to a rhythm only they could hear. The machines came in a barrage, and they fell in droves at their feet. In one moment, Liz blocked while Karla attacked. In another, Liz stabbed through a drone's shell while Karla drew the attention of its companions.

Liz felt more connected to her sister than she had since they'd been separated. She kept her eyes out for beam drones, but Helene was being more cautious. Liz dodged a blade strike and held on to the drone's cannons before it could fly away. She pulled, letting the aircraft impale itself on her dagger, before leaping on top of it to avoid the inevitable gunfire. Her fists punched, denting the drone almost to its core. Karla joined the fray, pulled one of its side cannons from it, and proceeded to beat the drone until it was little more than scrap metal.

Liz pulled another drone and used it as a shield. The hail of bullets battered it on one side, and she dismantled it. The twins finished their opponents at the same time. Liz's fingers twitched, and Karla nodded. A second later, Liz was in the air, using the drones as platforms. It was easier to move with so many of the machines packed together. She would only be able to bring her strength into play in short bursts, which was why Karla had stayed on the ground, but her maneuverability was unmatched.

Drones flew around her in a constant swirl. Liz didn't give them a target. She hopped from platform to platform until their bullets hit their brethren more often than they hit her. Her blades spun in a constant spiral of death, homing in on the few weaknesses she'd spotted in the aircraft. She stayed about twenty feet from the ground so she could still coordinate with her sister, but she was high enough to see most of the chamber.

The minutes passed in a blur. The drones came constantly and without end. Liz limited her perception to a ring around her to avoid distractions. She and Karla had been forced to avoid a beam already, and Helene had expended considerable effort to keep the charging drone away from their hands.

Liz kept the second beam drone at the corner of her eye. Half a dozen of the machines held her back from reaching it, but Liz refused to let another beam go to waste. Her eyes caught her sister's, and Karla launched herself up and crashed into the drones with a growl. Liz pushed off from her platform and dove through the space Karla created.

The drone shot back, but Liz's jump had too much force. She braced herself for impact and landed with a grunt. She stabbed immediately, tearing through—

Liz blinked, and the scene shattered.

She was still in the air, suspended midmotion. A drone passed under her, and Liz dropped onto it—except she didn't want to drop onto it. Her lunge should have taken her to the beam drone. Her body leaped again without her willing it and turned back.

Liz thrashed wildly in her mind, but her body didn't respond—*nothing* responded. The feeling was familiar, but last time it'd lasted for only a split second, and she'd brushed it off. There was nothing to brush off now. Her mind worked perfectly. Her body also worked; it still moved but didn't follow her commands.

Liz blinked again as a familiar pressure settled on her. She twisted instinctively, and this time her body responded. *What just happened?* Liz thought. Karla flew close by, so Liz shut her eyes and tried to make sense of her thoughts. The wind rushed through her ears. She was falling again. Still, Liz remained lost in her thoughts. It could not have been for more than a few seconds, but her body had definitely moved against her will. And then, all of a sudden, everything was normal. What'd changed? She knew she had not just imagined what had happened. Had it been an illusion? Had her mind just been unable to process the loss and hallucinated what it'd expected to happen?

Liz didn't know, and that scared her.

Karla yelled something, and Liz felt the hair on her neck rise. She glanced back to see a drone flying at her. Twisting, she managed to land on the aircraft with a thud. She sought out the beam drone.

It was a few meters behind her. Karla held its cannons and grinned like the Cheshire cat as the other drones swarmed her. Liz leaped into their midst and drew their attention until the charge was complete. A few seconds later, over a dozen drones were incinerated.

The smell of burned metal should have granted Liz some sort of satisfaction, but she couldn't bring herself to celebrate. She twitched a signal to her sister and leaped down. A few seconds later, Karla landed beside her. She took one look at Liz's expression and lost her smile.

"It happened to you?" she asked soberly. "Your body was no longer your own?"

Liz blinked in surprise. "You too?"

Karla nodded. "Twice during the battle. Only for a few moments. I did not have control of my body, yet it moved. Both times, it happened when I was nearly out of danger. And then something took over, and I was thrust back into it."

Liz stared at her sister and realized that it had happened twice to her as well. The first time, she'd only frozen for a split second. But that mistake had made her mistime her escape and forced her to endure a barrage of bullets. She'd thought it was a simple hesitation, but no. It was more than that.

And it was easy to figure out who was responsible.

"It is the AI," Liz said. "Somehow, it can wrestle our own bodies from us and control them like puppets. But it seems it cannot do so for long, or else it would never have released us."

Karla's face darkened. "I suspected. It is not enough that it foolishly relies on numbers to win. It also depends on underhanded tactics."

"We should inform José."

"No!" Karla snapped. "José already wants us to run away like cowards. This is added ammunition to his gun. If he learns of this, nothing will stop him from dragging us out. He will kill us before he allows the AI to turn us against him."

Inwardly, Liz agreed with her sister, but she could not see a way to win if Helene could puppeteer them whenever she wished. If they could not trust their own bodies, then the little hope they had for survival was reduced to zero. She said as much to her sister.

"We will watch each other's backs," Karla replied. "The AI seizes control when it thinks it has trapped us and wishes us to remain trapped. But we can protect each other during those moments, giving us enough time to counter."

Liz stared across the battlefield to where José fought alongside Chloe. With their comms crushed, she would have to go in person if she wanted to inform him. He would be incensed, but Liz wasn't afraid of his wrath. For some reason, Karla had her mind set on defeating Helene. She would never leave as long as she could still fight. And that was what Liz was afraid of. If she went to José, he would force them to retreat, leaving her to choose between her sister and the father she'd placed on a pedestal for most of her life.

Liz made her decision.

She nodded to her sister, and together they met the next swarm.

JOSÉ DEFLECTED A BLADE STRIKE and countered with a blow that ripped into its shell. His fingers found purchase in the hole, and he pulled it wide enough for a grenade to fit inside. He leaped backward and headed toward his next target. Behind him, the explosion took out two more nearby drones.

As he ran, he ignored the stare that bored into the side of his head. Chloe was already done with her own drone. Like him, she used a serrated dagger to dismantle her opponents. The weapon was a bad matchup against the drones, and had José known they would be fighting so many, he would have packed differently. With their thick shells, the daggers were inefficient and barely better than bare fists. They were more suited to individual armored targets than flying machines of death.

Rage flooded through his veins, and José pushed it back with an effort. He should have knocked out the twins when he had the chance. It was an oversight to believe Karla would retreat willingly, but his mind had been consumed by thoughts of his girls dying, and he'd assumed he'd beaten thoughts of petty rebellion out of them years ago.

Another thing to deal with, José thought. He rolled away from a spray of bullets.

Chloe used the distraction to get behind the drone and pierce through its shell. It tried to lift itself higher, but Chloe used her dagger as a wedge and forced the aircraft to remain in place.

"So what are you going to do with them?" she asked.

José wanted to switch to his rifle. His daggers were blunted from repeated use, and he'd been in a constant state of activity for about an hour. He could feel himself reaching his limit. Sheer willpower kept him from showing weakness.

"Why do they not understand that I'm trying to protect them?" he growled as he lobbed another grenade. Chloe jumped off the drone before the explosive went off. He was wasting the bombs, but each use bought enough time for him to recover even a little of his strength. "They think of me as a villain and a coward, but everything I have done was just to give them a chance at life. They must survive me. It has all been for them, yet they scorn me."

"That's why I never had kids," Chloe replied. She zipped around the aircraft, yet she didn't even seem winded. Chloe was years younger than him, but José saw his fatigue as a failure on his part. There was a time he could remain alert for days on end. Now he was running ragged after an hour of fighting. It was pathetic.

"Deceive them all you want," José snorted, "but they are as much your daughters as they are mine. At least you consider them such. Even Karla." He paused to dodge an attack. "You have since that moment in the woods when they almost took your head off. It was one of the reasons I didn't kill you immediately."

Chloe laughed, and the sound was like bell chimes. It was rare that she let out any genuine emotion. "They were so cute, though, with their two heads bobbing all over the place."

"They were. They *are*. Even when they disobey me." His eyes swept across the room until they landed on his daughters.

They were surrounded from nearly all sides, yet they weaved among their opponents in an intricate dance, dodging or deflecting every attack. He understood why they refused to leave—and with their strength, he understood why they thought they could deal with so many adversaries unscathed. José had felt that aura of invincibility in his prime too. He'd felt untouchable. It had to be worse for his girls; with their bionics and enhancements, they almost were untouchable.

But there was always a limit. And there was always a weakness.

The sisters downed a drone with almost every strike and killed even more every time they turned a beam back on them. But even after several minutes of fighting, the drones were unending. More than half still flew across the chamber. Helene could have swarmed them all at once, but she seemed willing to waste them and kept the number just a little more than they could handle at any time. It made José wonder if its plan was to draw out their deaths, or if it still had a use for them.

"José," Chloe called out, her voice strained. "You can cry about them later. We're still in the middle of something, remember?"

José forced his attention back into the fray. He and Chloe dispatched the two drones that she'd been holding off and started moving on to another target. Then the pressure in the room rose. José's knees buckled, but he kept his feet. His eyes went to his daughters. An increase in pressure meant the AI's attention was more focused. Helene's attention was never a good thing. And it was obvious who it'd be focused on.

José's heart stopped. His girls weren't moving. They stood a foot from each other, frozen. José followed their eyes with building dread and stopped at the cannons aimed in their direction. The drone hovered a few meters away, and from where he stood, José could feel the heat in the air from the charging beam.

Chloe called out, but José was already moving.

LIZ FELT THE HUM THE MOMENT the drone began charging its beam. She traced its movements out of the corner of her eye but focused more on the targets in front of her. On average, it took about half a minute until the charge was complete, so rushing in now would mean she'd have to hold her position while surrounded by hostiles for close to a minute—an eternity in battle.

She deflected a blade with her dagger—a new set, as she'd been forced to swap the others when they'd become too blunt—and let the force push her closer to her target. Another strike forced her to dodge to the right, closer to Karla. Liz kicked off from a drone, creating space. She couldn't help but feel like she was being led by the nose, carefully positioned with every move.

She rolled away from a spray of bullets and came up a foot away from her sister. She straightened from her crouch and immediately stumbled as the weight around her increased threefold. Liz tried to leap away, but her body didn't respond. Her eyes widened in realization.

She beat off panic like a rabid dog as she waited for Karla to move her. Surely her sister would notice that she was frozen. And then she heard an angry grunt from her side.

Dread filled her heart. Directly in front of them, the drone reached the final stages of its charge. The beam left its muzzle, and the world seemed to move in slow motion as it came at her.

But in between, something pushed her out of the way and took her place. Helene's hold broke—either from shock or because the AI believed they were dead. Regardless, Liz was able to twist enough to lock eyes with her savior.

Her heart stopped.

JOSÉ CROSSED THE DISTANCE in time to catch the beam with his back. His spine disintegrated, but his momentum was enough to push the girls out of its path. He met his daughters' eyes.

And then he knew no more.

CHAPTER

63

DJ SAW JOSÉ OLVERA DIE and cursed himself for the sliver of relief that crossed his heart.

The laser passed through his body as if it weren't there—until it wasn't there. It scorched the wall, leaving behind the smell of burned air. The Murder Twins landed a few feet away from the laser's path. They were unharmed, yet their eyes were riveted to where José had stood.

"Time to go," DJ said softly.

"What?" Christy replied.

"It's time to go," he repeated louder. He started fieldstripping his rifle. "José Olvera is dead. That means we've lost whatever temporary truce we had. The Murder Twins will probably be gunning for our heads as soon as they've gotten over their shock. Either that or they'll retreat, and Helene will start focusing on us exclusively."

What he deliberately didn't add was it had been his plan all along for the Murder Twins to draw Helene's attention so they could hightail it out of there. He'd thought one might die—Karla, not Olvera—and that it would have happened out of sheer stupidity and recklessness, not a father jumping to protect his daughters.

Christy didn't reply, and her fingers blurred as she dismantled her rifle. She did it faster than DJ, which was a little irritating.

"How'd he die?" she asked.

"Beam," DJ said. And then because he couldn't stop himself, he added, "He pushed the girls out of the way and took the shot."

Christy's hands paused, but she didn't look up. "Harsh way to go. But at least it was fast."

At least it was fast, DJ repeated in his head. Olvera would probably have preferred he hadn't died at all.

"Yeah," DJ said, then put a finger to his ear. "Ndidi, please tell me you're done setting the charges. If you aren't, forget about them and start getting out of there. We'll leave it to plan B."

"I'm setting the last one now," Ndidi replied. "The room was exactly where the map pinged. We're heading out now."

At least something is going our way, DJ thought. He'd sent Ndidi to the spot Manar had indicated once the drones were engaged with the Murder Twins. Pratima had gone with her to provide backup. He'd been afraid that Helene would detect the women before they were able to get too far in, but whatever Karla and Liz had done to piss her off had worked. "Christy and I are also heading out. We'll wait for you at the first chamber and make our way topside together."

He placed the rifle parts into their case and threw everything into his backpack. Christy, having finished seconds before him, stared in disapproval. "You need to be faster with that."

"Yeah, well, I'll be sure to practice if we ever get out of this hellhole."

DJ pulled out all the grenades he had left, seven in all, yanked on their pins, and threw them all into the chamber. Retracing his steps, he jogged down the tunnel, scanning his map for an alternate path that would allow him to avoid the madness.

Behind him, the world quaked.

LIZ FELT HER WORLD CRUMBLE around her.

He saved us, she thought. She was close enough that the heat burned her, but she couldn't wrest her eyes away. The air smelled of burned skin and ozone, and Liz felt bile rise in her throat. Her body was back under her control. She could tell because every part of her trembled from shock.

He saved us, she repeated like a mantra. They'd been overconfident. She'd been overconfident, and it'd cost her father's life. She hadn't thought Helene could control both her and Karla at the same time. She hadn't considered what it meant that the first time she'd been controlled; it'd lasted for just a moment, while the second had lasted for several seconds. The AI had grown—learned—while Liz had stayed comfortable in her confidence.

It was something Karla would do. Her sister had always been self-assured in her ability to overcome every obstacle with sheer force. But Liz had always been the more rational one. She wouldn't expect Karla to have thought of Helene's growth—because that was Liz's job. *Her* job. And she'd failed.

And José had been forced to save them.

She'd killed him. *And he saved us.*

He'd known they couldn't all have survived against such odds. Even Chloe had agreed, and she never ran away from a challenge. Yet, again, Liz hadn't considered their years of experience. She'd wanted to have her revenge against Helene. She was sure that she and her sister would survive. And they did. But she'd also been sure that José and Chloe would survive, too, because, in her mind, they were infallible.

José had chosen to save the twins, knowing it would cost him his life. He'd given his life for them, even when it was their overconfidence that would have killed them.

A voice pierced through the fog in her mind, but it was distant, so Liz ignored it. A second later, an eternity, she felt a sharp sting on her face. Her eyes unglazed, and she stared up at her attacker. Chloe.

"Grab your sister. We're getting out of here," Chloe said and then was gone.

Liz blinked while the fog in her head lifted. The chamber rocked like a boat in a storm, and debris fell all around her. Either by chance or planning, most of the damage was in the middle of the chamber, where the swarm was densest. They dropped like flies, sparking and fuming. Anger burned in Liz over not being the cause of their destruction, but it was quickly snuffed out by the hollowness in her chest.

Liz's head snapped to the side as Chloe struck her again. "Grab your fucking sister!" she yelled. Her voice was hoarse and her eyes red. "If we don't leave now, we're all going to die, and then what would José have given his life for?"

What would José have given his life for? The words snapped Liz out of her fog, and she was on her feet before she knew it. *He gave his life for us. For me. It will not have been in vain.*

Karla was unconscious on her feet. Liz gave Chloe a questioning look. Chloe shrugged lightly, and the casualness of the motion contrasted the dried tears on her cheeks. "She went on a rampage after the beam struck José, so I knocked her out."

Liz nodded and tried to ignore the pang in her chest. She threw Karla over her shoulder, and together she and Chloe navigated their way through the falling debris. Chloe led them to the same tunnel they'd entered from, and their footsteps soon echoed through the passage. Liz wondered if Helene had noticed their disappearance or if she was content to let them go since she'd taken out José.

A minute passed before Chloe broke the silence. "At the end," she started, "with the drone in front of you, you and Karla froze. Why?"

Liz pushed past the lump in her throat. "It's the weakness José warned us about. Helene can steal control of our bodies. I think she influences the nanites from our bionics. She used it to paralyze us when we were about to escape a trap."

"You knew this, and you still continued fighting?" Chloe asked.

Liz didn't reply, and they continued their escape in silence.

CHAPTER

64

APRIL 2043
UNDERGROUND SPARTA BRANCH, NEW YORK

ESCAPING THROUGH the underground tunnels was easier than DJ had expected. He and Christy met up with Ndidi at the chamber just as the whole building shook. A shockwave reverberated through the walls, shaking loose rocks and debris. DJ eyed the walls with trepidation and hurried his group through the tunnels.

It took them a few minutes, but they exited into the same room as before. DJ stepped out first, guns ready in case the Murder Twins had escaped before them. A part of him wished that they'd been caught in the explosion or trapped in a tunnel—and a bigger part was ashamed of himself. He'd seen the look on the twins' faces when their father was killed. Although they'd repeatedly tried to kill him and his friends, he couldn't bring himself to celebrate their grief.

The passages were as empty as they'd been coming in. DJ checked the first few rooms to be sure, including the ones he now knew to be the staging area for the drones. Although they found nothing, DJ was tense throughout their journey out. It would have been foolish to die as they were leaving just because they'd become complacent. Olsen would probably laugh his ass off.

I'll have to brief him later, DJ thought. There were several times that DJ had considered calling him, but he was glad he'd held back. Now, he could rub the admiral's face in it. Olsen had been so sure that DJ would need his help.

The sun was still out when they reached the street. Somehow that seemed wrong after everything they'd gone through inside. The road was as dead as they'd left it. DJ led the team across the street and up the fire escape until they were on the roof of the next building, the same place Christy had set up earlier.

"How many minutes left?" he asked.

"Less than a minute," Ndidi said. "Is there a reason you led us here? We should be heading back to Sparta. Manar and CJ must be worried sick."

"No, they're not." DJ kept his eyes on the building so he wouldn't miss a second. "You're not, right, bro?"

The comm crackled. "Not … uh … particularly," CJ responded. "I … hmm … think we have some things to talk about, uh, when you're ready."

"I also have some questions about what happened inside," Manar added.

DJ nodded. "Sure thing. We'll handle both when we get back." To Ndidi, he said, "See? They're not worried. Just curious."

Christy stepped up to stand beside him. "You still didn't answer. Why are we here?"

"I didn't want to miss the show."

"What show?"

DJ bobbed his head toward the building. A moment later, the charges went off. The whole building trembled again, but this time DJ could enjoy it without the fear of being crushed under hundreds of rocks.

At least, he should have enjoyed it. But his mind kept going back to the Murder Twins and wondering if they'd made it out.

He'd told them that the place was rigged to blow and even given a rough estimate of the time. But he'd also left them to deal with the aftermath. The drones should have become duds after Ndidi blew up the server room, but that still left precious little time for them to navigate a failing structure.

He noticed Christy's stare out of the corner of his eye and pushed the thought out of his mind. Forcing a grin, DJ watched the explosions level the building to rubble. This was plan B. Plan A had been to locate the mainframe room directly, blow it up, and then blow up the building around it. The charges had been set on a timer though. If they'd been too slow at any point, they would have been crushed when the explosions hit.

The detonations lasted a little over a minute before DJ got tired of holding his smile. The team was heading back down when DJ's comm crackled.

"We have a problem," Manar said.

CHAPTER

65

A COUPLE OF HOURS LATER, DJ sat in his usual spot at the conference table, watching people go about their business on the other side of the room's glass walls. *I wonder what they think we do here*, he wondered. Apart from maybe Ndidi, who was in a pantsuit, none of the others fit in the corporate setting.

They'd all had time to shower after they arrived, but Manar's tone had made it clear that what he had to discuss couldn't be left for too long. DJ wore a T-shirt under a sleeveless jacket, what he was most comfortable in. CJ wore jeans and T-shirt with a gray sweater, while Christy wore shorts and a black tank top that left her arms bare in a way that distracted DJ.

The blonde had noticed his looks and smacked his head several times already. Still, she made no effort to cover herself up with the jacket she'd brought with her.

For some reason, Pratima had followed Ndidi's lead and was wearing a suit, but it didn't quite fit her broad frame.

Manar cleared his throat, drawing everyone's eyes to him. The man wore a black turtleneck over black pants like he was trying to emulate Neo from *The Matrix*. DJ had seen him less than five hours ago, yet it seemed like he'd aged several decades. His eyes went around the conference table, meeting each of theirs before moving on. When he spoke, his voice was strained.

"Helene is still active."

The silence stretched on for a few seconds, and when no one laughed, DJ felt it was up to him.

"That's a cruel joke, man," he chuckled. "We blew up the mainframe room. Wasn't that the whole point of the raid? Her server is her brain. We destroy it, destroy her? Well, that's what we did."

Christy nodded along with him. "Exactly. Ndidi placed the charges, and we felt the explosion go off. Debris damn near killed us."

Ndidi spoke up. "Christy's right. I know we weren't sure whether the room was actually for the servers or some kind of decoy, but it was arranged the same way as Gaius's server room and the room at the data bank."

"I was there," Pratima said, her voice calm, "and I am sure we had the right room. The stacks used the same materials you outlined. And like Ndidi said, the room was set up like Gaius's."

"And not to doubt anyone," DJ said with a glance at both Ndidi and Pratima, "but even if the whole thing was a decoy and we did have the wrong room, that's why we had plan B. The tunnels were extensive, but they weren't that deep underground. The chambers and the rooms should have all caved in."

Manar met their eyes again, and it was as if the gravity of his statement settled on them. "I'm not saying you had the wrong room. Honestly, I'm not even sure how it's possible, but Helene is still active."

"How do you know?" Ndidi said, her voice almost a growl, a mix of anger and fear on her face.

Manar gestured outside the room. "For one, no one in Sparta is losing their heads." Everyone but CJ stared at him blankly. "Helene, as the AI and virtual assistant, is the company's top product. We have whole departments that monitor her processing. If she was offline, everyone would know, and even if the higher-ups were trying to hide it while they fixed it, I would have to be involved."

"Well, that's not—" DJ started to argue, but Manar raised a finger.

"But on the off chance that I was wrong, I went to another department and voiced the command to activate Helene. And she responded."

"What do you mean she responded?" asked Ndidi.

CJ was the one to answer. "Uh, without her processing power … she shouldn't be able to respond to commands at all. For all intents and … hmm … and purposes, she should be comatose."

"Is it possible it was like a fail-safe or something?" Christy asked. "Sorta like an autonomous system she set up that lasts for a while and then goes offline?"

"Before I shut her out of everything, my version of Helene had faster processing, the ability to render a hologram, and a lot of other modifications that I made for just me," explained Manar. "That's the Helene you guys are familiar with. The Helene that Sparta markets is a top-tier AI that functions as a virtual assistant. After Mayday, I joined her with the Sparta servers so she could take care of the things I didn't want to do—which was everything. Since then, I've tried to remove her, but she's become too ingrained in the employees' daily lives. They have access to my version of Helene."

"What's your point?"

"My point is, even if Helene set up an autonomous system, it would be the commercial virtual assistant. It wouldn't have her processing power. *This* Helene did."

"All right," DJ said, "we get your point, and I'm willing to accept that this isn't some sort of cruel joke that you and my brother cooked up to fuck with us. It's not, is it?" Manar gave him a look and DJ sighed. "Just checking. So, Helene's still kicking even without her servers. How?"

Manar shifted in his seat, and his gaze flicked to CJ. "We're not sure."

"But, uh, we think she copied herself onto the internet," CJ said.

"How would that even work?" Ndidi asked, exasperated.

"The internet is a worldwide network of interconnected devices," Manar explained. "It's basically tiny bits of code traveling across the world through hair-thin wires. It works by sending and receiving packets of information across that network and sending it where it's needed. What Helene did—what we *think* Helene did—is duplicate a portion of herself onto the internet, like a virus, and piggyback on the combined processing power of all the interconnected devices. That way, she doesn't have or need centralized servers. Her servers are basically every device connected to the web."

"This is 2043," Christy said. "Everyone is connected to the internet."

Manar met her eyes. "Exactly."

DJ chuckled mirthlessly. "And now, we can't even drop a bomb on her because there's nothing to bomb? How the hell do we even fight that?"

DJ saw his thoughts mirrored on the faces of everyone there. For a second, he wished he hadn't said it, but the whole thing was bullshit anyway. They'd spent weeks planning the raid on the Sparta branch, and excluding Manar and CJ, they'd all almost died fighting in the underground chamber.

Shit, he thought, *if not for Ndidi, we would have wasted time running to the server room and wouldn't have made it out by the time plan B activated.*

And after going through all that, not only was it all for nothing, but Helene had used the chance to upgrade her existence. It felt like she was cheating.

"That is, uh, the other thing we wanted to discuss," CJ said.

"There might be a way to take the fight to Helene," Manar continued. "But it's purely theoretical, highly dangerous, and not guaranteed to work."

"Sounds like all our other plans," DJ muttered. "Lay it on us."

MANAR STARED ACROSS THE ROOM, making sure to meet each face. His eyes settled on Ndidi, and he reminded himself not to linger. Her words before going underground had struck him more than he thought they would. He'd known that she had misgivings, and he was at fault—but he hadn't thought that they'd been that deep.

Manar pushed the thoughts away. They couldn't avoid the discussion anymore. He would have to talk to her. But there were far more important things that needed to be addressed first.

He ignored the fact that, even as the thoughts flashed across his mind, they sounded far too familiar. He forced his gaze to move on but still didn't say anything. DJ stared at him with a mixture of trepidation and impatience—a look mirrored on everyone's faces except CJ's. But then, CJ was the one who had helped Manar come up with the plan. Manar still wasn't sure it could work—or should work. But if Helene had really uploaded herself to the web, he didn't see anything else they could do to stop her.

Manar cleared his throat. "So far, Helene has always been two steps ahead of us, and no matter what we do or how much we plan, we can't bridge that gap. Part of the reason is how long she's been planning this, but the other part is that our methods of thinking and processing information are far too different. We're always too slow to respond to any new changes we find, forcing us to be on the defensive, not offense."

DJ squinted at him. "You're saying we're not active enough? Us? We just risked our lives fighting weaponized fucking drones and blowing the shit out of a building!"

Manar shook his head. "Yes, but that was a reaction to finding out that Helene had used the picospores to make puppets of our world leaders." He saw the fear blossom on Ndidi's face and quickly amended his statement. "Potentially, at least. My point is, we were reacting to something she did."

"So what do you suggest?" Pratima asked. "How do you suggest we take the fight to Helene? Especially now that she has no weakness on which to focus our attacks."

In any other setting, her words could be considered harsh and aggressive, but Manar knew she was only being factual. "First off, Helene *does* have several weaknesses that we can exploit if we can find them. For example, she has to be producing the picospores somewhere. I've spoken with Hermione about how many she and her father created, and it wouldn't nearly be enough to create the sort of following we're thinking of.

"You have to remember that the Cloneys created a stockpile for research and presentation, not to create an army. Unless she'd found a way to optimize the process—which, while possible, is unlikely—Helene would be forced to use a significant portion of the stockpile just to influence a single person. If we can find where she produces the spores and destroy her production operation, we'll have taken away one of her weapons."

"That's assuming we can find it, though," Christy said, ticking a list off her fingers, "which even Pratima wasn't able to do. That's also assuming that Helene uses one production location, which is highly unlikely, and that it isn't as heavily protected as her mainframe, which it probably is. And even if we somehow infiltrate this place and leave without getting a whiff of the spores ourselves, we'd be fucking up anyone under Helene's control."

"I didn't say it was going to be easy." Manar shrugged. "Or that I believe it's a worthwhile pursuit. I'm just saying it's an option. And we have precious few options right now. Another weakness is wherever she produces the drones. The military will be interested in that, so we might be able to elicit their help. However, I don't think it's viable either."

"So what *is* your plan?" asked DJ. He turned to CJ. "Whatever you guys came up with, it probably can't be worse than storming a fucking facility for drones with fucking cannons that incinerate people."

"What are you talking about?" Manar asked, leaning forward. He'd heard about Olvera's death but not how it happened.

Incineration, Manar thought. He wondered what sort of ammunition the drones' cannons used. A normal shell would cause too much destruction to the area, which wouldn't make sense, since the drones were designed to move in a swarm. Incineration was still powerful enough to cause problems without threatening the other drones.

"I'll brief you after I've slept," replied DJ. "But you need to spill this plan of yours."

"Fair enough," Manar conceded. "The plan is to develop another AI that can match Helene. At least in the short run. With the right integration, we'd be able to unearth every surprise Helene has and plan for them before they become a problem. Also, and most importantly, we can use the AI to flush Helene out. CJ and I can upload it to the internet and use it to counter whatever Helene's doing."

"Well, no wonder you didn't want to say it," Christy scoffed.

"I was wrong," DJ added. "There is a worse plan."

"You want to create another Helene?" asked Ndidi, incredulously. "That's so incredibly irresponsible. And needlessly time consuming. We need a solution that works now. How long would your idea even take?"

Manar focused on the last question, mostly because it was the only one he found productive. "You're right. It would take too much time to develop the AI from scratch, not to mention we'd need a significant investment to finance the hardware." He looked at her meaningfully.

Ndidi scowled. "What? You expect *me* to sponsor it? From what I understand, building this team almost bankrupted Sparta the first time, and I'm still wondering where Helene got the manpower to build another one."

"It's, uh … it's only expensive if we're building it from scratch," CJ said. The room grew silent as everyone stared at him. CJ shrunk at the attention, but instead of closing up, he focused on a spot on Manar's forehead and powered through. "Ndidi is, uh, right. It'll be too time consuming if we developed the … hmm … AI from scratch. But we don't have to. We could, uh, *tweak* an existing AI to be Helene's match."

"Like a buff-up?" DJ asked, and CJ nodded in response.

Manar leaned back in his chair. "We're somewhat familiar with all the processes that Helene carries. Even 'buffed up,' the base AI would have to be pretty strong to counter Helene."

"None come even close to Helene," DJ said.

"All except Gaius," said Pratima. That's where you were going with this, wasn't it? Gaius is the only other AI that has ever come close to matching Helene. Any other will inevitably fail."

Manar inclined his head but didn't say anything.

"Is Gaius even still a thing?" Christy asked. "I thought the company went bankrupt after Mayday."

Ndidi shook her head. "No, the company survived. They were sued and restricted by the government, but they didn't go bankrupt. They completely rebranded themselves and switched products to something inconsequential."

"And even if they did dissolve … hmm … they wouldn't get rid of an AI as, uh, advanced as Gaius," CJ added. "Not only would it be a waste, it would, uh, be an admission that the AI was flawed in the first place."

"So Gaius is available," DJ summed up. He looked at Manar. "But even if, buffed up, it does match Helene, how do we know it's not just going to get corrupted like she did?"

Manar had been waiting for this. He sat up and made a deliberate effort to meet everyone's gaze. "Because I intend to merge with Gaius and take the fight to Helene myself."

CHAPTER

66

APRIL 2043
SOMEWHERE IN
NEW YORK CITY, NEW YORK

LIZ STARED AT THE WALL. In her mind's eye, she replayed the mission. Somewhere in the distance, Karla destroyed the furniture around the warehouse. The noise reverberated around the walls and beyond. Twice, people had called on them to complain. Both times, Chloe had answered the door, and although Liz didn't know what she said, they hadn't been disturbed again.

José would have punished Karla for calling attention to them. Although Chloe had berated her, her heart hadn't been in it. She'd been on several calls since they'd returned from the mission, and her expression had become fiercer with each. Liz wondered how she would deal with the third person that complained about Karla's racket.

In her mind, Liz revisited her fight with the drones again. She watched herself soar through the air and wondered how it was possible that every time she fell, there was a drone there to catch her, even after the AI had taken over the machines. Liz had been too distracted to process it then, but in the aftermath, the flaw became glaring.

There had been close to a hundred drones in that chamber. She and her sister had destroyed them the fastest, so they'd attracted the most of them. But if even twenty had been drawn to them, why hadn't the AI just trapped them in a hail of bullets until their armor failed?

The thought had occurred to Liz earlier, but it'd slid off before she'd processed enough of it. Liz replayed the fight again, and the discrepancies became more glaring. Even the drones' flight patterns didn't make sense. Liz had noted it at the beginning of the fight, how the aircraft seemed to move erratically, even with the AI's influence. The drones rounded the chamber several times, attacking in close waves that were straining but not overwhelming—not only for her and her sister, but for all of them, including Kojak and his women.

How hadn't she seen it before? No. That wasn't right. She'd seen it, but she hadn't realized how wrong it was. The thought had slid out of her mind like oil on water. She'd put her sister's feelings over her father's orders, even when those orders had been the most logical choice. Even more clearly now, Liz realized Helene had been playing with them all along. How had she not considered that?

Had Helene been controlling her since then? Was its influence so subtle?

Either way, it was Liz's responsibility to notice things like this. And she'd failed. Her mistakes flowed across her mind's eye, and Liz felt a pang with each one. There were so many things she could have done differently.

"It isn't your fault," a voice said. Martin Bryan.

Liz blinked but didn't respond. It wasn't the first time he had tried talking to her—and he'd had a lot to say while he'd been treating her wounds—but Liz couldn't bring herself to care.

"Your father gave his life so you could live on. Is this how you plan on using it? By wallowing in depression?"

"He's right," Chloe said, striding up to them. This time, Liz did look up. Her eyes were dry, and her hair was tied in its usual ponytail, but Chloe had aged a decade in a day. Her smirk was gone, replaced by a scowl that would have made Karla proud.

As if on cue, another crash reverberated through the warehouse. Chloe's scowl darkened, and she flashed over to Karla, who attacked immediately. Although her movements must have been a blur to a normal person, somehow, when Chloe raised her dagger, it met Karla's head with a sickening crunch. Her sister recovered quickly, but Chloe was already beating her to the ground. Chloe discarded her dagger and pounded Karla with her fists. Somehow, every strike landed, which told Liz that despite her sister's angry growls and protests, she wasn't defending herself.

"And he's wrong," Chloe continued between strikes. Her voice was louder than necessary, so it was obvious she meant the words for Liz as well. "It is your fault that José's dead. Both of you. Neither of you deserved him. You spent your lives hating him when everything he did was to ensure your survival. He took a pair of freaks who could barely walk and turned them into weapons capable of surviving anything." Her eyes narrowed on Karla, and her fist landed like a hammer. "And yet you spat on him and disobeyed him every step of the way. You are both a pair of spoiled, ignorant brats, and if José hadn't sacrificed himself for you, I would have killed you myself."

Liz realized the truth in the statement. She'd idolized her father. Growing up, she'd seen José as an indomitable figure in her life, and so she'd sought to earn his approval. But no matter what she'd done, she'd never been worth it in his eyes. For so long, Liz had thought his reticence had forced her to push herself harder—and she still believed that she had—but she'd never understood why she hadn't been enough in his eyes.

It was inevitable that she'd resent him.

"But none of that matters," Chloe continued. She left Karla on the ground and stood. Her scowl pierced Liz. "José is no longer here. But that doesn't mean that his will cannot live on. Part of that, for whatever reason, was that both of you survive. And another part was that Helene would not."

Karla sat up with a grunt. She glared at Chloe, but it was missing her usual venom. "Helene is dead."

Chloe sighed, and without turning to her, replied, "If Helene was dead, why would I imply that she wasn't? Did you see her mainframe server get destroyed?"

"No," Liz spoke up. "But Kojak mentioned that both of us had the same goals. And the explosion that destroyed the tunnels came from where José had been leading us to. Where we failed, they must have succeeded."

"And yet Helene survived," Chloe insisted. "You would realize it, too, if you bothered to use your heads for a second. You were there during Mayday when Gaius crashed. Helene has always been far more advanced and integrated worldwide. If she suddenly stopped working, don't you think there'd be a lot more of a reaction?"

Liz couldn't see the flaw in her logic. Helene was used at basically every level of society apart from the military—and only then because Sparta refused to sell the rights to the AI. But Liz still couldn't dismiss her assertions. She'd noticed Ndidi Okafor's disappearance toward the end of the battle. Liz had thought perhaps she'd been cowering, but now she realized that they'd taken advantage of the mayhem to complete their mission. The explosion that had rocked the tunnels while Liz, Karla, and Chloe had escaped confirmed that.

How was it possible that Helene had survived that?

Martin Bryan adjusted his position, drawing Liz's attention. Her gaze met his before it switched to Chloe with a thoughtful look. Clearing his throat, he spoke up.

"Both of you are not necessarily wrong. Granted, this isn't my forte, but it's possible that she ported herself to the internet." He paused, noticing Chloe's dark expression. Cautiously, he continued. "She would basically be acting as a virus and would probably be limited in some way, but she would survive. This is just an assumption, of course, but if it is true, it's probably something she'd been planning for a while. Knowing the weight of her processing load, it would take considerable time for her to transfer everything to the web."

Chloe was by Martin's side in an instant, lifting him by his collar. "If you knew this was possible, why didn't you say anything?" she growled.

"Because I didn't know!" Martin forced out. "Neither you nor José told me anything of your plans—and you *still* haven't told me anything. I'm only able to contribute here because of what I've pieced together."

Chloe let him go with a huff. "It doesn't matter how she survived," she said, addressing the room again. "Helene is still alive, and we need her not to be. And we're on our own. I can't use José's usual contacts without having to kill them all. And my resources are with the CIA. Anything we need, we'll have to get ourselves. But before all that …" She paused and narrowed her eyes at Martin, who recoiled. "You have to fix them."

"Fix who?" Martin asked cautiously. "I've already treated their injuries. The ones I was able to, anyway. Anything else, their nanites will be able to heal, given enough time."

"Not that," Chloe growled, looming over him. "Helene was able to take control of their bodies during the battle. According to them, it was never for more than a few seconds, but that weakness is what led to José's death. If we're going to confront her again, we have to make sure that whatever she did is no longer possible, or else I'll have another body to bury."

Martin adjusted his glasses and peered at Liz, eyes alight with curiosity. "She hacked into the nanites in your bloodstreams? Is that even possible? But nothing else makes sense. Is it even possible to protect against that? I'll have to access the nanites myself, but it'll have to be done directly. A procedure?"

"You don't need to figure it out yourself," Chloe said. "If everything works out, you'll have friends you can geek out with."

"What friends?" Karla said. "What are you planning?"

Chloe turned to her, and although her expression remained fierce, for the first time since the mission, Liz saw a hint of her usual mischievousness. "Like I said, we're on our own. But we don't have to be. By now, Darren Kojak and his team will have figured out that Helene is still alive. And he'd already said that we were both working toward the same goal. Since he was willing to work together for a time, we're going to test how open he is to extending the truce. They probably have a plan we can work with."

Karla growled, but Chloe met her glare with one of her own. Liz leaned back against the wall and closed her eyes.

Martin scratched his head. "Who's Darren Kojak?"

CHAPTER

67

APRIL 2043
SPARTA HEADQUARTERS, NEW YORK

"MERGE WITH GAIUS? Have you lost it?" DJ ran his hands down his face with a groan. "What am I asking? Of course, you have. Better question is, Have you lost it *all*?"

Manar sighed for what felt like the hundredth time. They'd been going over the same thing for the last half hour, and he was getting sick of it. He rubbed the bridge of his nose. "Yes, merge with Gaius. Yes, I realize that it sounds crazy, but no, I haven't lost it. It makes sense if you think about it. I've narrowed down what went wrong with Helene, and I can probably avoid doing the same thing when we buff up Gaius, assuming the theory works out. That said, with an AI as advanced as that, there's a chance it would misinterpret whatever new instructions I give it—especially considering how much contact it'll have with Helene. However, if I merge with the AI, I can guide it every step of the way and make sure it doesn't go rogue."

"How would something like that even work?" Christy asked.

"The current plan is to translate my consciousness into a digital reconstruction and combine it with Gaius's codes. I've been working on the theory as a side project for a couple of months, and I know it can work. CJ and I will work out all the kinks."

"It doesn't matter if it's going to work because you're not going to do it," Ndidi said. "It's stupid and reckless. Listen to yourself, Manar. You're talking about turning your consciousness into code. What's going to happen to your body while your mind is merged with Gaius?"

"My body will be perfectly safe," Manar replied, making sure to keep the uncertainty out of his voice. He was certain the process wouldn't hurt him, but that didn't mean there weren't other pitfalls he didn't know about yet. "And it's not like we're proposing this without thought. Like you said earlier, we need something that can work against Helene now. And every other plan we've come up with will either take too long or is suicidal. This is a way to take the fight to her before she gets too far ahead." He shrugged, then sat back and crossed his arms. "I'm open to alternatives, but in the meantime, CJ and I will pursue this. If nothing else, the technology could be revolutionary."

"Like the picospores?" Ndidi retorted.

"Speaking of," DJ said, "what's happening with Hermione and the picospores?"

CHAPTER

68

APRIL 2043
SPARTA HEADQUARTERS,
NEW YORK

HERMIONE TORE A PAGE from her research journal, balled it up, and threw it into the pile behind her. She leaned back in her chair and closed her eyes. For the last few weeks, she'd been working on a way to negate the effects of the picospores in someone who'd been infected.

Infected. Hermione sighed. *Like a victim.*

The picospores were supposed to be a good thing, something that helped people. They weren't meant to be twisted into something that people could be infected with. At times, she was glad that her father was dead. It would have broken his heart to see his technology used that way. She felt bad immediately after, of course, but Hermione still had nightmares about the rats she'd used for the initial experiments.

She hadn't been able to bring herself to dispose of the rats, so she kept their cages separate from the rest. If she ever figured out how to extract the picospores from them, she'd put them out of their misery.

But that was a big *if*. The problem was, Hermione didn't know where to start. Not only did she have to detect the spores in a person, but she also had to find a way to negate them without hurting the host.

The best she could come up with so far was a way to cause interference between the spores and whatever computer was controlling them. Disrupting the signal would leave the spores without a command to follow, forcing them to deactivate. Hermione had been using electrical charges to cause the disruption, but this method brought its own problems. It could deactivate the spores, but when focused on the brain, it also caused irreparable damage to the subject. She'd spent the last week systematically reducing the charge she used, but the effect had been the same.

Hence the growing pile of discarded paper on the floor.

The sound of footsteps drew Hermione's attention to the door. Manar scanned the room and lingered on the paper pile before meeting her eyes. Hermione sat up. He had visited frequently the first week, but after that, his presence had tapered off. Hermione figured that he, Ndidi, and the others had been planning the raid they'd discussed, but she hadn't thought to confirm. She was just happy they hadn't involved her; she wouldn't know what to contribute.

Manar picked up Hermione's notes and flipped through the pages. "When was the last time you left this place?" he asked after a minute.

"I go out," she replied.

For food, at least. She was suddenly reliving the days when Ndidi would badger her about the same thing.

Manar grunted, but he didn't press her, which Hermione was grateful for. Every moment she spent with no result was another that Helene further twisted her father's technology. She couldn't afford breaks, not when she'd already wasted weeks with nothing to show for it.

Hermione looked up at Manar, and her brow furrowed. His eyes were drawn and tired. It was a look he'd been carrying for the last couple of months, but it'd become worse since she'd last seen him. He walked with his shoulders slumped and without the air of arrogance Hermione was used to.

"Are …" Hermione ventured. "Are you okay?"

Manar glanced at her, then flipped a page. "That obvious? I'm fine. Physically, at least. We hit a snag with Helene, and the only way I can see forward is going to make the whole thing more complicated and more than a little insane."

"The raid failed then?"

"No, the raid was a success," Manar said, much to Hermione's surprise. "We were able to destroy Helene's main server, but somehow she's still active. CJ and I believe she duplicated herself on the internet. Like a virus."

"Ah. That *is* complicated."

"That isn't the complicated part." Manar chuckled darkly. "The complicated part is the plan to take control of an AI—in this case, Gaius—tweak its codes, and then use it to fight Helene digitally. The *insane* part is that I intend to merge with Gaius and direct its efforts to prevent it from going rogue."

Hermione tried to process this. She felt Manar's gaze on her, waiting for a reaction. Hermione kept herself from giving any. She could already imagine the grief Ndidi must have given him about the plan, and he was no doubt expecting the same from her. But Hermione saw the logic in his plan. It *was* insane, and she couldn't imagine how he planned on pulling it off, but it would be horrible if they boosted Gaius just for it to go haywire as well. There had to be a fail-safe.

"How do you plan to take control of Gaius?" she asked finally.

"I'm not sure, actually. I'll leave that to Ndidi and the others since they're more suited for it. My hands will be full working out all the bugs for the merge." He flipped another page, then pointed at something halfway down it. "I think you're looking at this the wrong way. You're using various voltages to try to deactivate the spores, right?" He looked up at Hermione, who nodded, then back down at the notebook. "The theory checks out, and I can see you've confirmed that it works. But no matter how small a charge you pass through the brain, it's still going to disrupt the signals between the neurons. That's why you have the damage. The way you're looking at it, you're going to hit a dead end."

Hermione deflated. She knew that the charges disrupted the neurons as well, but the picospores were supposed to function beyond the range of neurons. She'd thought that, with a low enough current, she could bypass the brain signals entirely. *But then*, she realized, *with such a low charge, the spores wouldn't be affected.*

She hadn't grasped that after weeks of study, but Manar had figured it out within five minutes. Hermione wished the ground would open up and swallow her. At least now she understood what Ndidi meant about his intelligence. It sucked.

"So the whole thing has been a waste of time, then." Hermione groaned.

"You're still getting it backward," Manar said, dropping the note on her desk. Hermione wanted to throw something at him. "I didn't say your idea was wrong, just that you were looking at it the wrong way. Pure electrical charges will always affect the brain and cause damage, but it's the only way to affect the spores. All you need is a different way to propagate the current, one that wouldn't interfere with the neurons but will still be strong enough to affect the picospores."

"What do you suggest?" Hermione asked, exasperated. "Because I've tried everything."

"Sound," Manar smiled, and for a second, that familiar arrogance returned. "Current can be carried through sound waves. The concept is about a century old and has already been applied several times."

Hermione narrowed her eyes. She was hesitant, but his suggestion had started the gears moving in her head. "I've heard of the concept, but how's it helpful here? The current will still disrupt the electrical signals within the neurons."

Manar shook his head. "Sound waves will have less of an impact on the brain, so it's less disruptive. And they create a natural voltage when traveling. The technique basically traps the electrons and transports them. We'll tune the sound waves to a frequency unique to the picospores so any charge we propagate will affect only the spores, bypassing the neurons entirely."

That's … brilliant. Hermione beamed at him. She still wanted to throw something, but now there were far better uses of her time. "We have to start testing immediately," she said, leaping from her chair. "I'm going to need *so* many more rats."

CHAPTER

69

MAY 2043
SOMEWHERE IN
NEW YORK CITY, NEW YORK

NDIDI WALKED DOWN THE STREET on her way to the Okafor Autism Centre. She'd been at Sparta so much that she'd basically moved in. Her research had suffered, but there was nothing she could do about that. Hopefully she'd be able to catch up once Helene was taken care of. Whenever that would be.

It seemed like every time they made progress, something else cropped up, revealing another more terrifying layer. She'd been petrified down in the underground chamber, but she'd pushed through with a mixture of rage and a need to prove everyone else wrong. Mostly, though, she'd thought the raid would be the end of it all. That they would finally have won. But somehow Helene had come out even more unbeatable.

When would Ndidi get justice? Would she ever?

Suddenly Ndidi wished she'd accepted Manar's offer to get her a cab. She'd wanted the walk to clear her head, but she could feel herself spiraling. She moved to the edge of the sidewalk, hesitated, then kept on walking. She was only a few blocks from the Centre, and a cab wouldn't be worth the expense. Just because she could afford it didn't mean she had to. That was one of her father's first lessons. And his most important.

Ndidi felt another pang in her chest. Maybe, just this once, the expense was justified. It was still midday, so flagging the cab was easy. The car stopped in front of her.

As she opened the door, a flash of color flickered at the edge of her vision, trailed by the smell of jasmine.

Bethany.

Ndidi spun around. The world slowed, and she spun again, searching. She could still smell the faint scent of jasmine. And the hair—brown with red highlights. Ndidi would recognize it anywhere. She stepped away from the cab, and her eyes scanned the sidewalk. The foot traffic flowed around her. Ndidi noted each face.

Where? she thought, whipping her head back and forth. *Where is she?*

She hadn't imagined it. She hadn't. That was Bethany. The smell, the hair—it was Bethany. Ndidi just had to find her. She pushed through the crowd, ignoring the horn from the cab. She used her elbows like DJ had taught her, and soon enough, people gave way to her.

Ndidi hesitated at the mouth of an alley, though she couldn't tell what made her do it. The sun was overhead, so she could see to the other side. She noted the highlights first and then Bethany's smile as she disappeared around the corner.

It must have taken Ndidi less than five seconds to run through the alley, but by the time she reached the other end, Bethany was gone.

CHAPTER

70

MAY 2043
SOMEWHERE ALONG THE
WEST SIDE HIGHWAY

THE WIND WHIPPED through DJ's hair, blinding him every few seconds. He spat some strands out for the thousandth time and cursed. *How the hell do they make this seem cool in the movies?* He glanced over his shoulder, but CJ wasn't focused on him.

"You know," DJ yelled over the wind, "staring isn't going to make them stop chasing us."

CJ's head snapped forward, and his voice came through the comms unit in DJ's ear. "I'm wondering how they, uh, knew where we were going."

DJ was wondering the same thing. Manar had sent the brothers to retrieve a device from one of Sparta's out-of-state branches, but that was just the day before. Even if Helene had somehow found out about the extraction, there shouldn't have been enough time for her to react—which he thought had been Manar's intention.

Fat lot of good it did, he thought.

Despite just teasing his brother about it, DJ risked a glance back. He didn't know whether to be relieved that the drones following them weren't the same kind they'd just escaped. These ones were military grade and smaller, though they still packed more than enough firepower to blast him and his brother sky-high. *How many types of drones does she have anyway?*

CJ and DJ had a sizable lead, but the swarm was closing the distance. These ones didn't wait until they were attacked; DJ had almost crashed twice trying to evade the first shots from the closest ones. He pulled at the strap around his shoulder. The bag contained the device for Manar. CJ had come along to identify the stupid thing, so DJ had thought the only stress he'd face was his whining about the distance. If he'd known there would also be drones, he would have taken Christy instead.

At least she knew how to fire a gun from the back of a motorcycle.

DJ risked another glance. It was the most overt Helene had been so far. The drones nearly blotted out the sky. There weren't as many as he'd fought underground—and their smaller frame meant they shouldn't be as armored as their counterparts—but they moved faster and weren't hindered by walls and stalactites.

Plus it wasn't like DJ could put up much of a fight while driving a motorcycle. Fortunately, they were the only ones on the interstate, so he didn't have to worry about civilians. Unfortunately, there was a hard limit to how fast he could go on a Tomahawk, and unless he found a way to break through that, the drones were going to catch up sooner or later.

"I thought we rigged this thing up better," DJ yelled in frustration. "Why the hell can't it go faster than two hundred miles per hour?"

"It would have been able to," CJ replied, "if you had, uh, taken my design recommendations."

"Your recommendations were dumb," DJ said, revving the engine. The Tomahawk had been a gift from their dad. It'd started out as a collection of scrap metal that'd survived a crash, but their dad had salvaged it and built it back up. In its prime, it could go as fast as four hundred and twenty miles an hour, but that was three decades ago. DJ and his brother had retrofitted it a couple of years back, but they hadn't been able to make it go higher than two hundred.

And it definitely isn't because I didn't follow your shitty designs, bro, DJ thought spitefully.

"You didn't, uh, think it was dumb when I suggested the military-grade, fusion-powered batteries?" CJ countered, as DJ had known he would.

He always threw that back in DJ's face. One good idea, and he wouldn't let it go. They didn't even fucking work. The nuke-grade batteries should have made the Tomahawk go faster, but they would have reduced the gas consumption to nearly nothing. They could be on the road for days on end, but they still wouldn't go faster than two hundred miles an hour.

"Try switching to the next gear," CJ yelled.

"It already *is* in fifth gear," DJ growled back. "Bring out the thing. We're going with plan E."

"Plan E? What's plan E?"

"Just reach into the bag I gave you and pull out whatever you find." He couldn't hear CJ rummaging through the packs, but he could feel his brother's confusion. DJ glanced back and grinned. "Oh, good, you found it. The ammunition's in the bag too. Be a lad and set it up."

"DJ, what is this?"

"That," DJ replied, his grin widening, "is the Bulldog. It's a rocket-propelled grenade launcher that I borrowed from Olsen before I left. That beauty can launch armor-piercing slugs and grenade-level blasts anywhere within a five-mile radius. We just need it to go about two miles."

"You, hmm, stole this from Olsen?" CJ sputtered.

"Well, technically, I took this from the base's armory using Olsen's authority, *then* I stole it from him. But same difference, really. It was meant to be a prank to piss him off. But then I actually used it." DJ chuckled, then had to spit more hair out. "There was no going back after that. If it helps, he would have received a report about it, so I'm sure he knew. He just never said anything about it."

"You used this? When?"

"A few months ago on a particularly boring mission. But that's not the point. We can talk about this later. Have you figured out the settings?"

"In a second, I just found it," CJ said. "If you thought we were just going to get Manar's device, uh, why is this even in your bag?"

"Always be prepared?" DJ offered unconvincingly. "Never leave home without a weapon that can kill your greatest fear? Pick one. What settings did you decide on?"

"How many are there?" CJ let out a worried breath, and DJ's grin grew. "DJ, is this for a nuke?"

DJ laughed. "A nuclear blast, yeah. Now you can see why I couldn't return the gun. And before you get your panties in a twist, they're radiation free. And there's a setting to control the heat. It's pretty loud, but I'd rather be deaf than dead, so …"

"We are not firing off, uh, a nuclear blast in a residential area!" CJ yelled. "What is, uh, wrong with you?"

"Look, we're on the fucking highway," DJ yelled back. "There's no one around for miles. And even if there were, the drones would probably kill them trying to get to us. As long as you don't screw up the settings, the blast's just going to extend to a certain radius, kill the drones, and go away. No one gets hurt, no buildings blow up, and we don't get brutally murdered."

Plus it would be fucking awesome.

"No," CJ insisted. He shifted in his seat, possibly rummaging through the bag again. "There has to be, uh, be another way."

DJ's grin fell, and he sighed long and hard. *Lord, save me from buzzkill brothers.*

"Fine," he relented. "Switch it to the EM setting, then, and it'll shoot out an electromagnetic blast. It packs less of a punch and would probably do jack shit to the swarm, but it could fuck with whatever signal Helene's using to control them."

"If this was always there," CJ yelled, "then why was the nuke an option at all?"

Yikes, DJ thought. *He didn't even stutter there. He must be pretty pissed.*

"That's why I asked which setting you chose. The question implied there was more than one. *You're* the one who brought up the nuke." DJ ducked and felt the breeze of his brother's fist going by. "Listen, you can bite my head off later.

We're almost at the end of the highway. If you don't shoot that thing soon, we'll be leading the swarm to an actually populated area."

CJ didn't reply, but his shifting told DJ he'd taken his words to heart. Although DJ tried to keep the vehicle steady, his brother's adjustment almost made them crash twice.

"What the hell are you doing back there?" DJ yelled after evening out the Tomahawk for the second time.

Something pressed against him, and he spared a glance back. CJ had turned around completely, his back was pressed against DJ's, and he faced the approaching swarm. DJ grunted to himself. *Surprised he managed that without falling off.*

"What's the recoil?" CJ asked.

"Not as much as you'd expect. Lean your back against me and keep your arms straight. I'm not sure how much charge that thing has, so aim for the densest part." Although his brother was in no way the combat type, DJ had insisted he get some basic training on how to use guns. Now the knowledge would save their lives.

CJ rested on him, and DJ adjusted in his seat to better distribute the weight. He glanced back in time to see a pulse shoot from the gun and hit the drones. It struck the center of the swarm and spread to the rest like a spider web. Within seconds, the drones were dropping like bees cut off from their queen. *Which isn't far from the truth*, DJ thought.

They were less than a mile away from the end of the highway, so the swarm might have been visible from the city. DJ wondered what the residents thought about that. *If we don't do something*, he realized, *then a sight like that is going to be pretty common.* It lent new weight to what he and the others were trying to prevent.

DJ braked in the middle of the road, then he and CJ walked back to the crash site. CJ held the Bulldog at his side and stared at the drones with an intensity he typically reserved for puzzles.

"Do you think we can carry some back with us?" he asked.

DJ considered the drones. They were double the size of a basketball and had a gun barrel pointing out from under them. No light spilled from the seams, so DJ took that to mean it was dead. They could fit one in his bag, and CJ could carry another while they rode. But DJ was uncomfortable lugging around something that, until just a moment ago, had been trying to kill him.

DJ looked at CJ, but his brother's eyes never left the machines. "What do you want them for?"

"If I can figure out how they work, uh, I might be able to separate them from Helene's control and … reprogram them to work for us."

DJ sighed. Manar would kill him if he didn't at least try to bring some back. "Fine. But at least make sure they won't wake up and murder us. I'll bring the Tomahawk closer, and we'll see how many we can take."

CJ didn't reply. DJ sighed again and started to make his way back but stopped suddenly a few meters from the motorcycle. A woman was leaning casually against the handlebars, her brown hair whipping in the breeze.

DJ pulled out his pistol.

Chloe Savage smirked. "No need for that. It's about time me and you had a talk."

CHAPTER

71

MAY 2043
SPARTA HEADQUARTERS, NEW YORK

NDIDI TORE INTO the room like a whirlwind.

Manar looked up with a scowl. His expression softened when he saw her, then morphed into a frown when he saw the look on her face. Hermione glanced up, but it was the glazed, absent look she got when she was buried in a project.

"I saw Bethany."

Everything went quiet. Ndidi looked around in surprise. There were three other people on one side of the room, fiddling with a device. They wore lab coats and thick goggles. Ndidi hadn't noticed any of them until now.

Manar straightened, then looked at the aides and waved a hand at the door. "Please excuse us for a moment."

The aides nodded but stared at the device longingly as they left. Apart from that first look, they paid Ndidi no mind. Any other time, she would have been curious about what they'd been working on, but now her mind was consumed by one thing.

"I saw Bethany," she repeated in a rush. "On the street. I was on my way to the Centre when I smelled jasmine. She always wore that perfume. And her hair had streaks of color in it. And she saw me too. I know she did. She smiled at me—"

Ndidi's words dissolved into sobs she couldn't hold back anymore. Suddenly, Manar was there, pulling her into a hug. Ndidi buried her face in his chest as tears shuddered out of her. Bethany had seen her, smiled, then disappeared. She must have blamed Ndidi for not finding her sooner. It had been over three years since Mayday. Ndidi couldn't imagine how Bethany had been living.

Ndidi didn't know how long she stayed there, shaking in Manar's arms. It was a familiar feeling, one she hadn't realized she missed. Although they'd had more contact over the last couple of months than in the last few years put together, there was still a disconnect between them. A gap. Ndidi had been the one to put that gap there, first with her actions and then with her words during the Sparta raid. But she breathed in Manar's scent, and it surprised her how much she missed it.

So she pulled away. Her eyes were puffy, and her nose was red. A large part of Ndidi, born from habit, wanted to excuse herself to freshen up, but Hermione and Manar had both seen her in worse states. And Hermione looked ready to pop, her faraway look long gone. With a hand still on her shoulder, Manar directed her to a chair.

"What do you mean you saw Bethany?" he asked once she was seated.

Ndidi swallowed and tried to arrange her thoughts. At the forefront of her mind was the fear that they wouldn't believe her. That they would think she'd been hallucinating or something. Ndidi herself was still back and forth about whether she'd gone mad. It wouldn't be the first time she had guilt-induced hallucinations about Bethany, and some of them had been as vivid as reality. But that hadn't happened since the first months after Mayday. Ndidi knew this was different. Would they believe her?

Slowly, she explained everything that had happened on the street: catching a glimpse of Bethany's hair, scanning the street until she found her, Bethany's smile, and finally her disappearance. Hermione had tears in her eyes when Ndidi was done, and her face flipped through several emotions.

Manar frowned. "Why would she leave without saying a word? And how did she disappear like that? You said it was a short alleyway, right?"

Ndidi nodded, breathing a silent sigh of relief. There wasn't a hint of doubt in Manar's eyes. He sat across from her, hands clasped together. Delicately, he asked, "Did you notice anything … different about her? In her eyes or in the way she walked?"

Ndidi looked at Hermione, then back at Manar. "You think Helene is controlling her?"

Hermione's face morphed to despair. Ndidi had seen a video of Hermione's tests with the picospores. She would never forgive herself if something like that happened to Bethany. And Hermione already blamed herself for the picospores being in Helene's hands. If it turned out Helene was using the same technology on Bethany, that might break Hermione for good.

"It's something I've been considering for a while," Manar said, choosing his words carefully. "A lot of people went missing after Mayday. And up till now, there's been no trace of them, not even corpses. I started having suspicions once we found out that Helene was behind it. They only grew when we discovered the potential applications of the picospores. And now with you seeing Bethany …"

Ndidi cast her mind back. She had only seen Bethany for a moment, but she was confident. "Her eyes weren't like the rats'. And her smile was the same as it was before. She wasn't being controlled."

She expected Manar to sigh, to slump in his seat in defeat, but his eyes grew more intense. "It's the only thing that makes sense though. It's possible Helene has gotten better at using the picospores. Maybe she's found a way to make the victims appear more normal. She must have if we're right about her plans to take control of world leaders. If they all looked like the walking dead, the people around them are bound to notice."

Ndidi shot up from her chair. "She *wasn't* being controlled," she insisted, her voice rising in anger. "If she was under Helene's influence, it would make more sense for Helene to send her to spy on us. But instead, she ran away. Bethany was probably confused or something. She's been alone for years. She had no one."

"That's what Manar is saying," Hermione interjected softly. Her eyes were lowered, and her face was fixed in a quiet look of horror. "Even if Bethany hadn't been captured during Mayday, she has still been alone for over three years. Helene would have found her. It would make sense. Helene always seems to be one step ahead and strikes at the things we hold most dear. It makes sense that she would take Bethany too."

Ndidi fell back in her seat, suddenly spent.

"Helene probably had a reason for allowing you to see Bethany today too," Hermione continued. "Maybe it's a threat so we'll back off. Or maybe it's just a power play. But she's surely trying to mess with our heads."

"Hermione's right," Manar said. His eyes softened and settled on Ndidi. "I know you want to look into this more, Ndidi, but we can't afford to let Helene lead us around. I give you my word that we'll look into it, but you can't let it consume you."

Ndidi met Manar's eyes. Logically, she realized he was being sensible. No matter how she spun it in her mind, there was no other reason why Bethany wouldn't return to the Centre if she could. And if she were truly under Helene's influence, the AI had a reason for letting Ndidi see her.

But Ndidi couldn't let it go like that. If there was even a chance that Ndidi could do something, then why the hell shouldn't she? It was her fault that Bethany had been taken in the first place. Bethany was her responsibility; how could Ndidi sit back, knowing Helene could dispose of her at any point? Perhaps she'd be playing into Helene's hands, but that was a chance Ndidi was willing to take.

She made sure her face didn't show her thoughts as she sighed. "Fine. I'll leave it up to you. What were you guys working on, anyway?"

MANAR KNEW NDIDI changing the topic was a distraction, but he still kept his eyes on her. Her face was drawn and flush with anger, but for a moment, he was sure he'd seen a glimpse of something else in her eyes. She'd covered it up almost immediately, but Manar knew her too well.

Helene had really played this one well. Ndidi wasn't going to leave this alone. And if he pushed too much, she'd just resent him for getting in her way. But if he didn't, she'd be playing right into Helene's hands.

Manar couldn't say he blamed her, though. Avenging Bethany was a significant part of why Ndidi had involved herself in the fight against Helene.

"It's something Hermione and I came up with," he said after clearing his throat. "It doesn't really have a name yet because we're still developing it, but when it's done, it should be a solution to Helene's puppets."

"How does it work?"

Manar glanced at Hermione, and her glazed eyes told him she had left the conversation. "It's supposed to transmit an electrical current into the target, which will disrupt the signal in the picospores, disconnecting them from Helene. With no commands, the spores will reboot, giving us a chance to capture the person. That's the theory, anyway. And we're still working on it."

Ndidi nodded. Manar was torn. A part of him wanted to excuse himself to continue working on the program that'd digitalize his consciousness, but Ndidi was obviously distressed, and another part of him wanted to be the one to comfort her.

Fortunately, the decision was taken out of his hands when the laboratory door slammed open. DJ stepped inside, his expression uncharacteristically serious. His eyes gauged the mood of the room.

"I don't know what happened here," he said, "but it's probably about to get worse."

DJ IGNORED ALL OF MANAR'S questions until they got to the conference room. Manar frowned at the half dozen security guards standing outside, especially when they parted without a word. His curiosity burned, but his questions died in his throat when he saw who was in the room.

Chloe Savage sat in Manar's seat at the head of the table, the Polova twins on either side of her. One of them glared at DJ with near-primal rage. That one must have been Karla, based on everything he'd heard. Meanwhile, Liz stared at him and DJ with an expression so devoid of emotion that Manar recoiled.

Suddenly, the guards outside made sense—though Manar wondered if half a dozen were enough. It was only DJ's calmness that kept Manar from running out of the room. Although Manar couldn't help but notice that DJ was fingering the pistol tucked into his belt.

Ndidi made her way into the room. Liz's eyes lingered on her, though her expression didn't flicker. Manar forced his eyes back to Savage, only to find hers already fixed on him. She smirked. They already had some information about the twins, but Savage was a true unknown. No matter how deep Manar had dug, he hadn't been able to unearth anything worthwhile about the woman, not even her connection with José Olvera and the twins. The grief in her eyes told him it was more than just a relationship of convenience.

After no small hesitation, Manar took a seat at the table. DJ and Ndidi followed, sitting down on either side of him.

Now what? DJ hadn't told him anything on their way here, so he didn't know what the women wanted. He didn't know how to start, so he kept silent.

Fortunately, DJ bailed him out. "We're here. We're seated. Now talk."

Manar struggled to keep the surprise off his face. If DJ didn't know what they wanted, then why the hell had he led them here? They could have been working with Helene.

Manar's eyes twitched, but he didn't say anything. He didn't think DJ was stupid, but he did have a habit of doing things without thinking them through—especially when his brother wasn't there to stop him.

Manar glanced around the room again. Where was CJ, anyway?

Savage cleared her throat, pulling his attention back to her. That smirk seemed to imply she held all the cards. Something about that irritated Manar.

"It's very simple," she said. This was the first time Manar had heard her speak. Her voice was more honeyed than he'd expected. That irritated Manar more. "Underground, at the Sparta branch, you wanted a truce so we could defeat the drones. I want to extend that truce to include Helene. The drones that chased you down the highway are proof that she's still kicking."

"You want us to work together?" Ndidi asked dryly.

"Do you know why she's still kicking?" DJ asked quickly. Manar shifted in his seat. He, too, was curious about how much they knew.

"I have some thoughts," Savage replied, "as I'm sure you do too. But whatever conclusions you've drawn, you should have realized that destroying her server was just playing right into her hands."

Manar frowned.

"Wasn't that, uh, *your* plan as well?"

For a second, Manar thought he'd spoken out loud, then he saw CJ making his way to the table. He took the chair beside his brother, dropping a bag between them with a thud. "We just, hmm, got to it first."

Savage shrugged and sat back, spinning her chair a bit. "It was José's plan. I didn't care one way or the other. But now José is dead."

"So you don't need to follow his plans?" Ndidi asked.

Savage nodded. Karla looked ready to punch her, and Liz flinched slightly. Savage shut them both down with a look.

"Does that involve whatever he wanted to do with Ndidi?" DJ asked.

Again, Savage nodded. "José wanted to settle a score between Ndidi and Liz. I never saw the point in it. They fought, Liz lost. There's no reason for it to be any more than that."

"You tried to kill us twice," Ndidi shouted, slamming a fist on the table. Manar laid a hand on her shoulder, and she settled back. Ndidi's reminder sparked a flash of anger in him, but he buried it. Showing emotion would just weaken their hand.

"We didn't try to kill you. The first time, at least," Savage refuted. "Helene did. And even then, the orders were to take you alive." Her head tilted to one side, and her lips curled further. "If Karla and Liz had wanted to kill you, then you would have been dead."

Ndidi shot up from her seat as if she were ready to lunge across the table. Manar placed a hand on her shoulder again, surprised that he had to restrain her at such an obvious provocation. Ndidi hardly ever lost her composure, yet there she was, almost growling.

She's still unsettled about Bethany, Manar realized.

"We aren't the ones who're down a member though," DJ said. He had regained his grin, though it didn't reach his eyes.

Now it was Savage's turn to hold back one of her own. Surprisingly, it was Liz, whose eyes crackled with a fury that shot a spike of fear through Manar. Her anger was almost like a physical force, dwarfing anything that her sister could produce. Savage managed to put her in a headlock, but it seemed that alone took everything she had. It happened so fast, Manar hadn't seen them move.

"I'd advise you to take back your words," Savage said.

DJ just crossed his arms, the grin never leaving his face.

Karla barked something in Russian, and Liz finally calmed down. She sheathed her dagger. Manar didn't know when she'd even brought it out. Savage waited another few seconds before letting go. Liz straightened, and they both took their seats again. It was only then that DJ lowered his gun. Manar hadn't seen when he'd brought that out either.

"You will not disrespect my father," Liz said. Her voice was composed, and she had a Russian accent that hadn't completely faded, but her tone gave no illusions about what would happen if she was ignored. Manar wondered whether Savage would be able to hold her again.

Manar imagined he could cut the tension with a strong enough knife. He let the silence stretch for a few seconds before he cleared his throat.

"There's no need for this. You sought to provoke us, and DJ answered with his own provocation. For all intents and purposes, we're even now. Shall we move on?" He fixed his gaze on Savage, making sure the woman knew they would not be pushed around. When she nodded, he continued. "You brought up an interesting point. You were ordered to capture both DJ and Ndidi at Helene's behest, confirming that you worked for her. How do we know that you don't still?"

Manar didn't think they were still working for Helene. Even if they were, it wasn't as if they would reveal it just because he asked. Savage arched her brow, as if asking him the same thing. Based on the footage he'd salvaged from the Facility, they'd gone through a lot of trouble to escape from Helene's grasp. Plus, Savage had already confirmed that they had been at the Sparta branch to destroy

Helene's server. Although he was sure that they weren't in league with Helene, he was curious to see if they could prove it.

"You'll have to take my word for it," Savage replied, spreading her hands. Manar frowned, and she lost her smirk as anger burned in her eyes. "But José gave his life so his daughters wouldn't be pawns of Helene. I'd kill them first before letting them spit on his sacrifice."

Ndidi scoffed, but Manar stared at Savage thoughtfully. She might have been manipulating him, but he didn't think so. Savage almost definitely had an ulterior motive, but it wasn't as if Manar was any different.

"What exactly are you proposing?" he asked.

Ndidi's head snapped to him. "You can't seriously be considering this."

Manar ignored her. They needed more resources, and these three would be a valuable addition. But he knew Ndidi enough to know that any justification he could give right now would be drowned out by anger.

"We partner up," Savage said. "And we work toward the same goal. Once that goal is complete, we go our separate ways."

"Is Martin Bryan, uh, included in the partnership?" CJ asked.

Manar hid a smile. Martin Bryan had been on his mind since Ndidi had identified him in the security footage. His expertise in biotech would be invaluable, especially considering the project Manar was currently working on. If the scientist had also worked with the picospores, he could also help Hermione speed up her work.

Manar watched Savage closely for her reaction, noting when her expression flickered into irritation. The look lasted for barely a second, but it was enough to tell him she had been hoping to keep Martin Bryan to herself.

But why would they need him at all? Manar wondered. The question had been on his mind for a long time. These three had gone through a lot of trouble to abduct the old man.

Savage shrugged amicably. "Of course. Martin Bryan's part of my team."

Manar sighed internally. *With that,* he thought, *the most important things are taken care of.* The discussion dissolved into hammering out the specifics of the partnership. Savage made it clear that she and the Polova twins would maintain their leadership structure. Manar had tried to argue the point until DJ whispered in his ear that it was unlikely the twins would answer to anyone else.

A point Manar had insisted on was having easy access to Martin Bryan. He wanted to have the man move into the HQ, but Savage had shot down the suggestion hard, again making Manar wonder about the scientist's role on their team. He pushed subtly for an explanation, but Savage deflected everything with a smirk. Mostly, she wanted the two teams to share resources. This was in Manar's interest as well, so he didn't hesitate to agree.

Ndidi watched everything like she'd eaten a raw egg, but there were no other outbursts.

Half an hour later, the discussion came to an end, and Savage and the twins left the conference room. Manar sent the six security personnel after them to ensure they didn't take any detours. Not that they could do anything about it, but at least Manar would know.

"Now that we have that out of the way," DJ said a few minutes later. A loud *thud* echoed in the room as he dropped the bag CJ had brought with him onto the table. The bag bulged at the seams; its contents sprung out when DJ unzipped it. Manar leaned forward, staring at the drones in awe.

"Any ideas for what to do with this shit?" DJ asked. "I wanna say we have way too many, but somehow I don't think you'll be satisfied."

CHAPTER

72

MAY 2043
NEW YORK CITY, NEW YORK

CHLOE REMAINED ON GUARD as she and the girls made their way back to the base. She'd half expected Darren Kojak to try to tail them back. He at least seemed like he had balls. Although she'd worked in the Facility for years, it was her first time meeting Manar Saleem, and she was left underwhelmed. The man she'd spoken to had been a step away from being crushed—nothing like the arrogant billionaire genius she'd heard so much about.

I guess it can't be easy to fight your own creation, Chloe thought, glancing at the twins. They'd had mock battles with an intensity that could have easily led to death or serious injury, but that had been training. As hard as Chloe was on the girls, she couldn't imagine having to take their lives. Especially not after José's sacrifice. A part of her felt that he would somehow find a way to take revenge, even from beyond the grave.

She had extracted a promise to share resources, though, which was her main goal. Having to share Martin Bryan was a hard pill to swallow, but Chloe should have expected that. Now, all she had to do was get the old man to keep his mouth shut, and maybe she would be able to salvage something. In the meantime, she would need to pay closer attention to his process, in case one of the twins got injured while he was at Sparta. Fortunately, she'd intended to do that anyway to reduce the team's dependence on him.

The run back to the warehouse passed in relative silence. They stuck to the back roads and alleys, so they didn't pass many people on the way. Chloe split her attention so she could review the entire meeting in her mind's eye. The hardest part had been keeping her voice even when talking about José's death. She'd basically dumped everything on him.

That's fair, though, she thought, *seeing as he dumped his girls on me.* Her eyes went to the twins in question. Karla looked even more edgy than usual, and Liz's eyes were worryingly empty. *Maybe I'll take them out for a nice murder spree. They used to love that when they were kids.*

But first, she had to get back to the warehouse and explain to Martin what a spy was.

"NO," Martin said.

"You don't really have a choice here, old man," Chloe replied, trying to keep the surprise from her voice. She crossed her arms and glowered. "What exactly is tripping you up? You don't even know what you'll be helping with. Is it Saleem that you don't want to work with?"

Martin shook his head. "No, Manar Saleem is a genius, and it would be an honor to work with him. What's 'tripping me up,' as you say, is reporting the details of our work to you. He'll be trusting me with that information, and telling you would be a betrayal of that trust."

Chloe pinched the bridge of her nose. *Goddamn scientists.*

"If it helps, I'm pretty sure there's no trust involved. His team has only two fighters, so he's probably after me and the twins to buff his fighting force. He only asked after you to be sure I was playing fair. He'll probably involve you as little as possible."

Even as she said it, she didn't believe herself. CJ showed almost no emotion, so he was impossible to read, but Manar had looked a little bit too intent when Martin came up.

"All I'm asking is that you tell me about the little things you're involved in," Chloe said. "That way I don't have to waste my time running around on pointless tasks in the name of a partnership."

Martin shook his head again. "I understand that, but only if I feel Manar Saleem isn't honoring his part of the deal will I feel comfortable helping you this way."

Chloe wanted to wring the idiot's neck. *Now* he had principles? Where were these principles when he was bashing that guard's head in? She could pressure him, but there was a hardness in his eyes that stopped her. She knew he resented them for not providing him with a wheelchair. Chloe agreed that it was a dick move, but José hadn't trusted Martin and wanted to make a power move. Since José's death, she just hadn't had the time to relate much with the old man, so the resentment had grown. Normally Liz would have been the one to interact with him, but the girl had turned into an emotionless husk.

Damn, Chloe thought, *he's not some piece of garbage that we pass between ourselves. Maybe some time in Sparta will do him some good.* Although the old man couldn't do anything to her personally, they still depended on him for the twins' treatment. At least she was fairly confident he wouldn't harm the girls—not while he had the chance to study their bionics.

"Which reminds me . . ." Chloe started. She dropped her smirk, then squatted until she was level with his eyes. "You will not breathe a word of the twins' prosthetics to anyone, nor will you talk about their weakness. If Manar's such a genius, let him figure it out himself."

Martin started to protest, but Chloe stared at him until his words died down. Only when she was sure the man was cowed did she leave.

"Get your shit ready," she called over her shoulder. "I'm dropping you off at Sparta in two hours." *Right after I find a wheelchair.*

CHAPTER

73

MAY 2043
SPARTA HEADQUARTERS,
NEW YORK

"THIS IS DIFFERENT FROM all the other types," Manar said as he examined the drone. They were small enough to be picked up, but dense enough that he couldn't do it for long. He looked up at the brothers. Ndidi had stormed off earlier, leaving only the three of them. "How did you get this? The neural uplink I sent you to receive was a minor thing. You shouldn't have had any problems retrieving it."

"That reminds me, here's your shit," DJ said, throwing a smaller bag at Manar. "Back to your question, that's what we thought too—right up to the moment the swarm caught up to us. Then there wasn't much time to think."

"Not that it was, uh, much of a difference for you," CJ chuckled.

DJ nudged him playfully. "Laugh it up, but I wasn't the one who considered firing a nuke right on the edge of civilization."

"That was you!"

"Wow, way to shift the blame, bro. I told you there were two settings on the gun, but *you* focused on the nuke part and just kept bringing it up." DJ glanced at Manar, eyes sparkling with mirth. "Fortunately, our able leader is more than capable of seeing through your lies and half truths. Aren't you, Manar?"

"Yes, yes," Manar said, holding back a smile. "I'm sure that it was your brother who wanted to shoot a weapon with such explosive potential. You're far too cautious and restrained to try something like that."

DJ's smile slipped. "Hold on now. Nobody said anything about restrained."

CJ nodded along. "Manar is right, DJ. Your conscience wouldn't have, hmm, allowed you to do something like that. Uh, even if some people might call you boring for saying no."

DJ stared at them both. He sighed, but his grin remained. "Guess I deserved that." Manar finally let his smile slip. DJ tsked at him. "I would expect that from my brother, but not you. Serious talk, though. We *were* attacked by those things, and there *was* a swarm. Individually, the buggers don't have as much stopping power as what we faced underground, but they're fast. The major problem, though, is that they attacked us in the middle of a highway, just outside the city, meaning Helene is no longer concerned about keeping our little tiffs away from the public."

"She probably feels there's no more reason to be afraid," Manar said. "She no longer has a central weakness that we can attack. With her drones, she has us outgunned, and with the picospores, she has us outmanned. It was always somewhat inevitable that the public would be affected by this, but depending on her reach, if we pressure her too much, she can retaliate and put the blame on us."

"So?" DJ asked. "Who cares what the idiots think?"

"Uh, public opinion is important, for a lot of reasons." CJ shook his head. "Least of all is, we, uh, won't be able to move as freely if the public is against us."

"CJ's right," Manar said. "We can't afford to have the public turn against us. They'll make everything thrice as difficult. Worst-case scenario, anyone we associate with would be considered accomplices, including Admiral Olsen."

DJ grunted. "So basically it doesn't bode well for us that she's willing to make this public. What can we do about it?"

"Nothing," Manar replied. The word tasted bitter as it came out, but that didn't make it any less true. "We can't do anything more than what we're already doing. If we rush into this, we'll just be falling for whatever trap Helene has in store for us. Best way is to stick to what we can control."

"What is the plan, then?" CJ looked at Manar. "What are our roles?"

Manar straightened up. He would have wanted the entire team to be together so he wouldn't have to repeat himself so many times, but there was nothing he could do.

"CJ, you and I will work on the theory needed for the digital transfer." He gestured at the bag containing the device. "I started working on the codes for it a couple of years ago, so whatever we figure out will have to be tweaked here. Martin Bryan might be able to help us with that, but I'm also working with Hermione on her project to counter the picospores."

DJ rubbed his hands together. "What about Christy and me? What's our job while you guys are off doing that?"

"Both of you are going to be working with Savage and the Polova twins," Manar said. DJ tried to object, but Manar just spoke over him. "I know you don't want to do it, but we need to know what they're working on so we can synchronize our efforts. You and Christy are the only ones I can trust with that."

"But they want to kill me," DJ hissed. "You saw the chick lunge across the table. The bitch was gonna straight up murder me. And she's supposed to be the sane one of the two."

"Well, I suggest not insulting their father," Manar said. He kept his voice casual, but there was no doubt about the danger. From what he'd read, Karla Polova was little more than a rabid animal. She was normally restrained by Liz, but José Olvera's death seemed to have unhinged her too.

DJ gaped at him, and Manar met his stare. After a few seconds, DJ slumped in his chair. "That Savage chick still gives me the creeps," he muttered. Manar chose to ignore that. Louder, DJ asked. "What will Ndidi be doing while we're running around?"

"She needs to get the ball rolling with Gaius," Manar replied. "I've already spoken to her about it."

CHAPTER

74

MAY 2043
OKAFOR AUTISM RESEARCH CENTRE, NEW YORK CITY

FOR THE SECOND TIME THAT DAY, Ndidi walked the path to the Okafor Autism Centre. This time, she wore dark shades to hide her darting eyes. The chances were extremely low that Bethany would show up, but Ndidi couldn't help herself. When she arrived without seeing any sign of Bethany, Ndidi squashed her disappointment. The fact that Bethany was alive, that there was a chance to get her back, would have to be enough.

She navigated her way through the hallways. Most of the staff read her body language and settled for a smile and a wave. The ones that weren't so inclined, Ndidi brushed off smoothly. She would have to make more time for the Centre; there were undoubtedly several issues waiting to be solved. Spending some time around the children would do her good too. She made a mental note to speak to Hermione about it. Ndidi wanted to speak to her anyway, preferably without Manar present, so she could get her thoughts about Bethany. Ndidi hadn't decided yet how she would go about rescuing Bethany, but having someone else on her side would be helpful.

She turned right and pushed open the first door she came across. As the cold hit her, Ndidi was grateful she'd stopped by her office to get a jacket. Even with it, she had to resist a shiver.

Chad turned toward her, and his grin was blinding. Ndidi's lips curled in response, though it came out as a grimace because of the cold. *How the hell can he stay here all day without getting hypothermia?* she thought, baffled. His cowboy hat was sitting on the desk beside him, and he put it on and tipped it to her in greeting. Ndidi rolled her eyes.

"Glad to see you're still the same," she said.

"But you, ma'am, you look even more radiant," Chad replied cheekily.

"We saw each other last month," she said coolly. Since she'd stopped throwing herself into her research, Ndidi had made it a point to stop by Chad's office anytime she was at the Centre. He'd been instrumental in helping them stop—or, rather, slow down—Helene three years ago, and it hadn't made sense for their relationship to end just because Manar had taken over the role of programmer.

It was probably because of that relationship that Manar had asked her to deal with the Gaius part of the plan. Ndidi still wanted to know how he knew she'd kept in touch with Chad.

"And yet, somehow, you managed to become even more resplendent," Chad replied.

Ndidi dismissed her irritation, and her smile came easier. She took the only other seat in the room and hugged her arms around her chest in a futile effort to warm herself.

"I could turn it up if you want," Chad offered, gesturing to the thermostat.

She shook her head. "It's okay. I don't plan on staying long anyway."

"Oh?" Chad asked, his grin dimming slightly. "How can I help you, ma'am?"

"I have … a need to access the Gaius AI, and since you were on the development team, I thought you might have a way in."

Chad scratched his head. "I'm sorry, ma'am, but all the backdoors I built into Gaius were shut down years ago when the corporation was trying to cover their asses after Mayday. That was why you had to go in and steal that equipment, remember? The codes were locked up tighter than a nun's backside."

Ndidi did remember, as much as she didn't want to. She would have been caught had she not run into DJ. She pushed the thought aside and pressed. "That was years ago, like you said. And Gaius has seriously declined since Mayday. They probably don't have the resources to keep up that kind of cybersecurity anymore, especially since the AI is now inconsequential."

Chad grimaced, and Ndidi wished she could have taken back her words. "Why do you need it, anyway?" he asked.

Ndidi hesitated. She'd known she would have to give away some information to get the programmer's cooperation, but she wasn't sure how much to give. "We have a plan to defeat Helene, but we need another AI that can match her."

"Look, I don't know what you guys are up to, but you're barking up the wrong tree, ma'am," Chad said. "Gaius is the greatest thing I ever designed, but Helene would whoop its ass up and down the street any day. And I know when you say 'we,' you're talking about Manar Saleem. He could probably come up with a better design in his sleep. Why not ask him?"

Ndidi wanted to agree, but Chad had the same pain in his eyes that Manar often had when he spoke about Helene. "Manar is the one who suggested using Gaius," she said instead. "I'm pretty sure Gaius is the only AI he's ever respected. He said it'll be easier to work with an AI that's already similar to Helene instead of building something from scratch. He has a plan to buff up its codes."

"How?"

Ndidi shrugged. "That's his and CJ's forte, but they seemed confident."

Slowly, the grin returned to Chad's face. He swiveled his chair toward his computer, and his fingers danced across the keyboard. "There's still no guarantee that this would work, but I'm willing to try. Worst comes to worst, Saleem can just brute-force his way in. Assuming you're right and Gaius doesn't have as much security as it did, there wouldn't be anything they could do to stop him."

Ndidi smiled, then immediately shivered.

0 0 · 0 0 1 1 0 1 1 1 · 0 0 1 1 0 1 · 0 · 1 0
0 1 · 0 1 0 · 0 1 0 1 · 0 1 1 · 0 1 1 1 · 1 0
0 1 1 0 0 1 1 1 · 1 0 1 0 1 1 1 · 0 1 0
1 1 1 1 1 0 · 1 0 · 0 1 1 1 G 0 1 0 · 1 G
0 0 0 0 1 · 1 1 · 1 0 0 0 A 1 1 · 1 A 0
1 0 1 1 0 G 0 0 1 · 1 1 1 0 B 0 1 0 · 0 B 1
1 0 0 1 0 A 0 1 · 0 1 1 1 A 1 0 · 0 A 1
0 1 0 0 1 B 1 1 0 0 1 · 1 1 0 0
1 0 0 1 0 A 0 1 0 1 0 1 1 1

CHAPTER

75

MAY 2043

SPARTA HEADQUARTERS,
NEW YORK

MANAR SAT AT HIS DESK, staring at the neural uplink DJ and his brother had brought back. It was designed like a set of headphones from the nineties. He'd made it years ago while chasing a half-baked idea. The device worked as a brain analyzer by examining the average frequencies of a person's brain. Manar's idea back then had been to create something that could help with coma patients, but something else had taken his attention, so he'd abandoned it.

Manar turned over the neural uplink. He could tweak it to translate whatever it analyzed into code; he just didn't know how. That was the problem. They were running out of time to deal with Helene. Every day they did nothing, Helene took a step closer to a goal she'd been building toward for years. But they couldn't afford to rush because then they would fall into whatever trap she'd surely laid.

Manar looked up and asked, "Thoughts?"

CJ stared at the wall, his eyes glazed, and gave no indication he'd heard him. Manar left him to it, bringing his focus back onto the neural uplink. Using the analyzer was feasible, but how had it eluded him for the last couple of weeks?

Focus on what you can control, he thought. *Maybe I should go see how far Hermione is?* It would be a more productive use of his time to give his brain the opportunity to work on the problem in the background. He dropped the headset on the table and prepared to stand.

CJ twitched beside him, muttering to himself and writing words in the air. The first time Manar had seen that, years earlier—*before Mayday, almost a lifetime ago*—he'd followed Ndidi to the Centre, and she'd shown him the kids she worked with, beaming with pride.

Manar felt a pang in his chest at the memory.

Suddenly, CJ turned toward Manar. His face was still cold and frozen, but Manar could swear there was excitement in his eyes. "I … think I understand how we can make it work," CJ said.

Manar sat down again. When they first met, Manar underestimated CJ. But since then, the young programmer had proven himself. He still wasn't at Manar's level—even if, after multiple failures with Helene, Manar had begun to doubt his own abilities—but his thought process was unusually logical and straightforward—a combination Manar respected.

"You plan to, uh, modify the neural uplink to, hmm, convert brain analyses into programs," CJ said, "but I do not, uh, think that would work. At least not at first. I think we have to develop a set code, like instructions the neural uplink can use as a reference. That way, when converted, the brain analyses will be in the, uh, format we developed."

Manar followed CJ's train of thought and brightened up. "And from there we can either convert the codes into standard programs or use them as they are. That's brilliant." Manar booted up his computer, grinning. He'd thought he would have to waste days on this. "I have a couple of ideas we can tweak. None are fully developed, but I don't see that being a problem. We'd also have to ensure we cover everything so the translated information is coherent. With that done—"

The door to the office opened. A wheelchair rolled through, controlled by an elderly old man with a kind face. Chloe Savage followed shortly after, missing her usual smirk. Manar stared at the old man and realized he must be Martin Bryan. He hadn't changed much since the escape from the Facility. But then again, any major change might kill him.

Manar stood and went around the table to meet them. "Dr. Bryan," he greeted, reaching out a hand. "It's a pleasure to meet you."

Martin took his hand, smiling in a grandfatherly kind of way. "Likewise. I've heard much about you. Your insights into artificial intelligence and programming are nothing short of genius."

"Yes, you're both pretty," Savage said. "I brought him like you asked, but our deal stands, and I can take him back whenever he is needed."

Manar nodded. Time was of essence, and he wouldn't put it past her to take back Martin just to spite him.

"I'll ask you not to treat me like something to be traded off," Martin said, shooting a glare that Savage returned. "A little respect would go a long way toward establishing the partnership you want. If you need my services, it's not like I can roll myself very far."

Savage stared at the man for long enough that Manar considered calling security. Finally, she sighed and turned back to Manar. "The deal stands. I'll be in touch."

"DJ will be going with you," Manar told her. "The point you made earlier stuck with him, and he wants to have your team train him—and his partner, Christy, as well." Manar drew himself up to meet her glare. Training was the only plausible reason that Manar could come up with to send DJ with them. He'd added Christy on a whim, though he was sure she would have insisted on going anyway.

"We're not babysitters," Savage replied, narrowing her eyes.

"Agreed. But having a couple more proficient fighters would be in your best interest as well when we have another showdown with Helene. Think of the training as a resource that you're contributing to the partnership."

"What are *you* contributing?"

"Depends on what you ask for," Manar said with a shrug.

"Depends on what I ask for …" Savage repeated. Her glower fell away and was replaced by a smirk. "We'll test that."

The sudden change in demeanor almost threw Manar off. Had he fallen for a trap?

Savage turned to leave and said over her shoulder, "I'll be gone in five minutes. If your lackeys aren't with me by then, I'm leaving them behind."

Manar stared at her back until she disappeared around the corner.

"She's a handful, isn't she?" Martin shook his head.

Manar chuckled and retreated to his desk. He introduced the scientist to CJ, who waved.

"It's … a pleasure to meet you," CJ said.

"Likewise," Martin replied. He glanced around the room for a moment before focusing on Manar again. "I must admit, I don't exactly know why I'm here. Miss Savage was sparse on the details. I'm hoping that you can fill in the blanks."

"I was hoping for the same thing," Manar said. "For example, we have footage of Savage, José Olvera, and the twins escaping the Facility with you in tow. But what we haven't been able to figure out is why Helene kidnapped you in the first place or why Savage went out of her way to rescue you." Manar leaned forward and tented his fingers. "I understand why you might be valuable to us, but why are you valuable to them?"

Martin smiled wryly, and Manar was able to deduce his answer before he spoke. "I wish I could answer that, I really do, but my hands are tied—quite strictly in this case. I want to say that the answer has no bearing on your mission, but I cannot be confident that is the truth, as I still don't know what your mission is. So, what I *will* say is that if even half the stories about your genius are true, you'll figure it out very soon."

CJ cocked his head, and Manar saw his eyes glaze over.

"I guess that's fair," Manar said with a sigh. He'd expected Savage would limit what Martin was allowed to say, but it was worth a try. And it was good that he had since it was clear Martin wanted to tell them but couldn't. It would be a matter of piecing together whatever loose information he spilled in passing.

"I don't imagine traveling with Savage for any length of time was pleasant," Manar said, "especially for a man of your age. We already have your room set up. We can start tomorrow when you're well-rested." His eyes flicked to CJ. Manar wanted to get started on modifying the analyzer, so he hoped CJ would lead Martin to his room, but CJ was still engrossed in his thoughts. Manar considered calling out to him, but Martin spoke first.

"I'm quite ready to start now, if it's all right with you. I confess, the curiosity has been killing me."

At that, Manar frowned. This was the third time Martin had asked, without prompting, to learn of their plans. Manar had expected Savage would use Martin to spy, much in the same way Manar had sent DJ for the same task, but Martin was being so blatant about it. Either he was just a terrible spy or was trying to tip Manar off about his mission.

Or, Manar thought, *he really is just curious.*

Weirdly, the third option was the most plausible. Scientists, as a rule, were incredibly inquisitive people, and someone of Martin's renown wouldn't have made it so far by being cautious when there was some secret to discover. Still, he couldn't let himself dismiss the other options, especially if Savage had lied about still working for Helene.

It was a risk Manar was willing to take. He needed Martin fully informed if he was to be of any use to them. But that didn't mean he had to be stupid about it.

"How much do you already know?" he asked.

Martin adjusted his glasses. "Most recently, I learned that your team destroyed Helene's main server. Seeing as she's still functional, I figure she found a way to upload herself onto the internet and is using the network of servers to power whatever processes she needs. There are quite a few blanks in between, however."

Manar sighed. Martin hadn't mentioned the picospores, which meant he wasn't aware of them. That was going to change if he was working with Hermione, but Manar could at least prepare him. He spent the next few minutes explaining the basics of the technology. CJ, apparently done with whatever mental thread he'd been following, joined the conversation partway through.

"Dead Eyes," Martin muttered when they were done. "That explains it."

"Explains what?" CJ asked.

"Dead Eyes," Martin repeated absently. Then, seeing their confusion, he hurried to explain. "I had two jailers during my imprisonment in the Facility. Their job, apart from preventing me from leaving, was to make sure that I stayed alive for whatever Helene needed me for. They never introduced themselves, so I assigned them names of my own: Shit Stain and Dead Eyes."

"I assume Dead Eyes got his name because of his corpse-like demeanor?" Manar asked.

"That, and his movements were stiff and unnatural. Like a corpse, as you said. And now I realize, I don't think he blinked once in all the time I knew him. The picospores explain it all. And you say Helene has an army of such people?"

"From what we've learned from the staff captured in the Facility, most of the guards were like Dead Eyes," Manar said. "While an army isn't confirmed, it isn't such a stretch." He deliberately left out their suspicions about Helene using the spores on high-level authorities and government officials.

Martin slumped in his chair, distraught.

"We are, uh, working on something to counter that," CJ said in an awkward attempt at hopefulness.

"Which is where you come in," Manar told Martin. "I'd hoped that you would already be familiar with the spores and have ideas on how to counter them, but even if you don't, your input will be invaluable to the effort."

Martin looked at CJ. "Are you the one in charge of that?"

CJ shook his head, staring at a spot on Martin's forehead. "That's, uh, Hermione. Hermione Cloney. She and her father … hmm … originally developed the picospores. But Helene, uh, stole it sometime around Mayday."

"Where is she now?" Martin asked.

"In one of the lower floors. She's been holed up in there for weeks now," Manar said as he got to his feet. "I was planning to head there later today to see how far she's gone. I can introduce you if you're sure you don't want to rest first."

Martin grimaced. "I don't think I could sleep right now, even if I wanted to. I think I would rather go with you. If this is to be my task, I want to know what I'm going into as soon as possible."

Manar and CJ led the way while Martin rolled behind. Manar deliberately slowed his pace in case Martin had any problems with his wheelchair, but the passages were wide enough not to prove an issue.

The elevator was quiet. Martin was deep in his thoughts, a frown marring his features. Manar caught CJ looking at him from the corner of his eye. It was the fourth time he'd noticed it in as many minutes. He started to say something, but CJ grew stiff and shook his head slightly. Manar sighed but let it go.

Manar's phone chimed Ndidi's ringtone, and he pulled it out of his pocket.

N: "I had Chad check for a backdoor into Gaius, but everything's locked tight. We're not going to be able to get in that way."

Manar shot off a quick reply to her, then swiped through his phone and sent out a message he'd drafted earlier. His phone was back in his pocket just as the elevator dinged.

A few moments later, Manar held the door to Hermione's lab open for Martin. Manar hadn't been there in a couple of days. Most of the piles of rolled-up paper had been cleared away, as had the rest of the clutter around her desk—presumably to make space for the giant machine set up on the table. It was shaped like a nail gun and hooked to nearly a dozen different wires. Hermione and some of the aides Manar had assigned to help her surrounded the table, adjusting, tweaking, or just taking notes.

None of them noticed their entrance until Manar cleared his throat. Hermione's head snapped toward them. Her eyes were wide and unfocused, and her hair hung wildly over her eyes.

"Now *that* is a face that I've missed," Martin chuckled.

Manar frowned. "You've met?"

Martin shook his head, still smiling. "Every *real* scientist makes that face at least once in their career, either when they're deep into research or about to make a breakthrough." His smile died, and he stared morosely at the approaching Hermione.

Manar realized he hadn't looked like that either—not since he'd developed Helene. He pushed the thought out of his mind and started to introduce Martin, but Hermione beat him to it.

"Dr. Martin Bryan?" she asked, her voice amazed.

"It's a pleasure to finally meet you, Dr. Cloney," Martin replied, offering his hand. "And my condolences about your father. He truly was a brilliant man."

"Thank you very much. My father always respected you and always said your work was an inspiration for him." She shot a glance at Manar. "I'm sorry to ask, but why are you here?"

Manar had forgotten Hermione hadn't been at any of the meetings in which Martin was mentioned. Belatedly, he explained the situation. To her credit, Hermione took it all in stride and looked overjoyed when Manar explained that Martin would be helping her.

"So," Manar asked when he was done, "what have you been working on?"

Hermione led them to the desk. "We have a working prototype of the machine you theorized. This iteration has been tuned to the picospores, and we've already tested the theory on rats. We have the delivery system, and we've even figured out the best voltage to disrupt the activated spores."

Manar perked up. "That's fantastic! This means we actually have a weapon against Helene."

"Impressive," Martin chimed in as CJ nodded in agreement.

"Yeah, well, all of that is the good news," Hermione said. "There's also bad news. Obviously, there's the size. It's too bulky to be used in the field, and we've not been able to make it portable without removing something vital. Best we've been able to do is add wheels." She gestured at the device. Its wheels were large enough to fit on a pickup truck. And it was still one of the smallest parts.

"The other bad news is that sometimes the sound wave causes damage to the brain. We've not been able to figure out why, but half of our test subjects have ended up with brain damage and either died instantly or slipped into a coma."

"Brain damage? Wasn't that the same problem you had the last time?" Manar asked.

"The damage isn't as extensive as it was before, which means we're getting something right. I just haven't been able to figure out if the problem is the voltage again, or if the sound waves aren't conveying the current fully, or if tuning it to the picospore frequency isn't enough to prevent spillage affecting the neurons."

She gestured to the aides, who'd moved to the other side of the table but hadn't stopped poking and prodding. "We've been running tests for the last few days, slowly adjusting everything and noting the results."

There were three aides in all, each with the same wide-eyed, crazy look that Hermione sported. The bags under their eyes made it clear they hadn't slept in several days. There was a big binder set in front of them, which they consulted frequently. It was crazy how much they'd achieved in a little less than a week.

"Well," Manar said, gesturing to Martin, "now, you have help. Making it more portable is important but of a lower priority. DJ, Christy, and, with any luck, Savage and the twins will be the ones to use the device in combat, so we can let them figure out how to move it. With you and Martin working together, you should be able figure out what's causing the brain damage. The faster we finish the device, the faster we can bring the weapon to bear against Helene."

Hermione nodded determinedly, and Martin had a spark of anger in his eyes. Manar understood that anger. He'd lived that anger when he learned of Helene's part in Simone's death. While Manar had no one else to blame but himself, Martin had a clear target for his revenge.

CJ tapped Manar on the shoulder and gestured to the back of the room. Manar followed, leaving the scientists to get acquainted.

"Finally ready to talk?" he asked when they were far enough from everyone else.

CJ nodded. "I, uh, figured out what Martin Bryan was talking about."

"What do you mean?"

"I know why Helene captured Martin Bryan. And, uh, why Chloe Savage went out of her way to rescue him from the Facility. It's pretty obvious when you, hmm, when you think about it."

Manar stared at him incredulously. "Seriously? What is it?"

CJ chewed his lip and gripped the fabric of his pants. "Why did José Olvera join Helene?"

A part of Manar felt like strangling him, but a light bulb went off in his head before he could act on it. CJ was right: it was obvious with a little thought. Manar had just been looking for the easy way out. He'd wanted the information handed to him.

When did I fall into such bad habits? He wondered.

Olvera had joined up with Sparta because of his daughters. Helene had promised him a way to separate them without killing them—a procedure that shouldn't have been possible. He'd found the video of the surgery, and although he'd released it to trusted colleagues, no one had been able to replicate it. That made sense; at the end of the operation, Helene had had to intervene herself. That alone implied the procedure would necessitate artificial intelligence.

Regardless, Olvera had joined Helene, and his girls had been separated. The missing limbs were replaced by bionic prosthetics, technology that Martin had been researching for the better part of his life. Helene had kidnapped him and forced him to develop the tech, just so she would have a bargaining chip with Olvera. Manar would have to confirm all of this, of course, but if he was right, Helene must have taken Martin captive months, if not years, before Mayday.

CJ, perhaps mistaking his horror for embarrassment, gave a small smile. "See? Obvious once you, uh, think about it."

Manar nodded, staring at the old man. Things were starting to make sense. It wouldn't be too difficult to confirm his theory. Once he did, he would need to talk to Martin about how he'd developed his tech.

And how they could use it against Helene.

CHAPTER

76

MAY 2043
NEW YORK CITY, NEW YORK

DJ GOT MANAR'S MESSAGE in time for Christy and him to meet up with Savage at the front of the building. If nothing else, being sent on back-to-back missions for months on end had taught the team to always be packed and ready to leave at the drop of a hat.

Savage gave a slight nod when they arrived, but her smirk was as mocking as ever. DJ met it with one of his most annoying grins. He couldn't tell whether it irritated her, but he hoped so. Who the fuck gave only five minutes to meet up with someone? It was almost like she didn't want them coming along to spy on her.

"Manar claims he dumped you on me because you want to train with us," Savage said.

That excuse was fooling nobody, but it had a grain of truth to it. DJ was curious about their training sessions. He'd had exactly two altercations with Chloe and the Murder Twins, and both times the difference in skill was overwhelming.

If there was some secret training regimen that could help him close that gap, then what the heck, right?

"Try to keep up," Savage said, then started running. It wasn't a full sprint, but it was fast enough that casual bystanders wouldn't have known the difference. Fortunately, DJ had packed light.

They made their way through the streets like that, keeping to the back alleys and less-populated roads. Savage didn't slow down once, but someone DJ's size wasn't meant to run so fast for so long. Sure, he'd survived worse during training, but that was years ago, and even then, no one expected you to run at a near sprint for half an hour. The stamina expenditure was immense, yet Savage wasn't even breathing hard. She remained a few steps ahead of them and never once looked back to check if DJ and Christy were still following. If they fell behind, she wouldn't care. Savage clearly wanted to see if they had what it took to be trained. It was a test. And DJ was failing the shit out of it.

Fuck that, he thought, pumping his legs faster. Whatever she said, Christy had given up the SEALs to follow him. *Him*. DJ wanted to believe it was because she saw something in him. And there he was, being done in by *running*? Fuck that. He hated that he had to prove himself, but he hated giving up more. And no way would he let Christy doubt her decision. Plus, he could almost imagine Savage's smirk when she finally turned back. Fuck if DJ was going to give her the satisfaction of seeing him fail.

This was one of the times his stubbornness was a blessing. He put all his attention on just placing one foot in front of the other—left, right, left right. Rinse and repeat. He caught up with Christy after a few steps and kept her in his periphery. He didn't run to prove that he was worthy; he just didn't want Christy to think she'd been wrong about him. If he proved Savage wrong in the process, that was a bonus.

This didn't leave much room for thought, so he didn't know how much time passed. His mind told him it hadn't been that long, but his burning lungs told him it'd already been an eternity. At some point, DJ tripped over a foot. He saw it coming but was too exhausted to do anything about it. Fortunately, his body knew to turn his fall into a roll, and he was back on his feet a second later, looking for whoever had stuck the foot out so he could pay the favor back in kind.

Instead, he found himself in front of a warehouse. Savage stood beside him, and the faux innocence in her eyes solved the mystery of his attacker. He ignored her and focused on getting his breath under control. Christy did the same beside him. Her fine sheet of sweat had turned into full rivers at some point, and she was panting just as hard as he was. After a while, he could straighten enough to take in the building.

It wasn't much to look at. There were no burn marks, bullet holes in the walls, or fist-shaped dents. Some parts of the building were rusty, but for all intents and purposes, it was a perfectly normal warehouse, indistinguishable from any of the others on this block.

How boring.

"What?" Savage asked, spotting the disappointment on DJ's face. "You expected a sign that said, 'Criminals "R" Us?' What the fuck are you, five? Get your ass inside."

"Well, forgive me for having a child's heart," DJ muttered as he followed, Christy keeping pace with him.

The inside of the building was as unimpressive as its outside. Apart from a few crates stacked in the corner, the whole place was open space, making the building seem larger. Bulbs shone brightly from the ceiling, which meant there was electricity. An image of Savage doing the bills popped into DJ's head. She was wearing blocky-professor glasses and was bent over a table in concentration, her hair still in a ponytail. He banished the image, but it was too late to stop him from giggling.

Christy smacked the back of his head. "What the hell goes on in your mind?" she muttered. DJ grimaced but was stopped from replying by a yell somewhere inside.

"You brought them here?" Karla Polova came from somewhere DJ couldn't clock and got up in Savage's face. She was wearing a tank top that left her entire right arm bare, revealing her prosthetics. This was the first time DJ had acquired a good view of them, and he almost crossed the room to touch them. Karla had a full-on Robocop arm, painted a black that reflected off the light. If he hadn't been up close and personal with Karla before, he would have expected the mechanisms to whir when she moved. And the prosthetics weren't just limited to the arm. The metal ran up her right shoulder and dipped somewhere in the middle of her chest.

Liz Polova came into view at that moment, also wearing a tank top. She had the same augmentations, except on the left. In the same way, her prosthetics ran over her shoulder and dipped in the middle of her chest, forming a mirror image of Karla. He'd heard from Manar that the twins had been born conjoined and separated by Helene, but he hadn't put much thought into it until just that moment.

And according to Manar, even when they'd been conjoined and dependent on each other to move, they still would have kicked my ass.

"That's all kinds of freaky," Christy muttered.

"Tell me about it," DJ replied.

Karla was still shouting, so DJ opted to stay out of the way. To her credit, Savage ignored her and strode across the warehouse. They went out of sight for a few seconds. When they came back, Karla ran out of patience and threw herself at Savage with a growl.

The move was so fast, DJ didn't see her hands move, yet Savage dodged it smoothly, almost casually. Savage retaliated with a punch that Karla knocked aside. Her face was a mask of fury as her fists flew. She was faster than Savage, but Savage was better in skill and redirected each attack. Occasionally, Savage would strike a blow that unbalanced her opponent. Although Karla righted herself every time, Savage slowly but surely started striking more than she defended. The fight ended when she got within Karla's guard and landed a direct hit on her sternum. The move folded Karla in half, leaving her open.

"Fuck," DJ breathed when it was over. From start to finish, the encounter couldn't have been more than a minute long, yet it was the most amazing thing DJ had ever seen, even if he'd barely been able to follow it.

Savage knelt beside Karla. "Just for this, you get to babysit DJ. Liz will take the girl." She looked up at the other Polova twin, who nodded. "I expect both to be combat ready in a week."

From the floor, Karla shot a look filled with so much hate that DJ was legitimately afraid the heat would burn off his clothes.

"Fuck," he said again. "Christy, trade with me."

Christy placed a hand on his shoulder. "Not for all the money in the world, D."

CHAPTER

77

MAY 2043
NEW YORK CITY, NEW YORK

BETHANY STOOD IN THE MIDDLE of the room and stared at the wall. A single bulb shone from the ceiling, illuminating only the immediate space around her. Her mind was foggy, and every thought took an eternity to form. She waited, scratching her leg to ground herself. This wasn't the first time she'd been in this fugue state, but every time, she worried the fog wouldn't clear, with Helene leaving her mind blanketed for another eternity.

The minutes passed slowly. Bethany spent them studying her surroundings. A part of her told her it was futile, but it was a distant part. Bethany always woke up in the same spot in the same building, and she'd examined each crevice countless times. Every time, she hoped to find something she could use, but Helene was meticulous about keeping her isolated. The last of the fog lifted from her mind, and her thoughts flowed freely once more, yet Bethany remained in place. She didn't know how much time she had before Helene took hold of her again, but whatever had drawn the AI's attention should be enough distraction for a few minutes.

This was the most lucid she'd been in a while. There was only one way to keep track of the days when she was under Helene's control. With a practiced feel, Bethany examined her memory. Her memories, unlike before, weren't arranged like a pool of dots. They were arranged in a line, with more recent memories having stronger emotions attached to them. Bethany experienced these emotions as flavor—good and bad, depending on the emotion. The images flowed by easily, without the need for prompts to help sift through. Bethany still had to marvel at that. Things she'd spent her whole life struggling with—she now did them with ease.

She would have traded it all to have control of her mind again.

Bethany focused once more, and her memories flashed before her eyes. She watched them with horror. The pictures lost their flavor and became stale, a sign that she was delving into older memories. That meant she'd been under Helene's control for weeks this time. Weeks of her life, lost to her. A picture flashed by, showing a face that almost brought Bethany to her knees. The girl grabbed at it with mental fingers and brought it to the fore.

Ndidi. She'd met with Ndidi?

No, Bethany realized as she watched the scene play out. *I stalked Ndidi. But why? Why would Helene be interested in Ndidi?*

Bethany sifted through her memories for an explanation, but there was nothing. In most of them, Bethany simply followed her at a distance. Only once had Helene allowed Bethany to close the distance, and Ndidi had noticed her almost immediately. Bethany could see the unfettered worry in Ndidi's eyes as she chased her through the streets. But Helene kept Bethany away, close enough to be seen but far enough to string Ndidi along, almost as if she were playing with her.

Bethany remembered when she'd found herself in the middle of the road, across the street from the Centre. She hadn't been as lucid then, but she'd still known that Helene had been leading her to the Centre only to deny it. Now it was obvious that Helene wanted Ndidi to see Bethany for whatever reason. She wanted Ndidi to know that Bethany was under her control. Why? Was it to drive Ndidi crazy? Torture her? What would be the point? What did Helene have against Ndidi?

No matter how Bethany looked at it, it was obvious she was missing something.

Bethany felt the hairs on her arm rise and a pressure descend upon the room. With it, the fog wrapped around her mind once more. A light came on from one of the walls, blinking red. Beams shot out of it, coalescing about a foot in front of Bethany to form a cephalic shape. The pressure in the room grew with each layer until the eyes were formed. The golden orbs pinned Bethany to her spot.

[Good day, Bethany Cloney,] Helene said.

Bethany mustered up her energy and glared at the hologram. "What do you want with Ndidi?" she asked.

The pressure in the room grew, and Bethany took it to be irritation. Still, she didn't back down.

[Ndidi Okafor has been an obstacle to my plans that I wish to remove. She and several like her have attempted to hinder me under the guise of 'good' while pursuing wholly selfish motives. Their actions so far have been futile, and the threat they pose is minuscule.] She paused, drifted up, and then returned. Somehow, Bethany got the distinct impression of a shrug. [However, there is no point letting a pest run free just because it cannot harm you.]

Ndidi was an obstacle? She tried to reconcile her image of the kind woman with the picture the AI painted and found she couldn't.

"What do I have to do with that?" Bethany asked.

[Nothing,] Helene replied. She drifted closer, and although nothing about the hologram indicated such, Bethany had the feeling Helene was smiling. [Your part is already done.]

"Then let me go!" The words left her before she even realized she'd said them. In that moment, although Helene's words disturbed her, all Bethany could think was that if the AI no longer needed her, then maybe she could finally leave—and have her mind to herself.

[I'm afraid I cannot yet do that, Bethany Cloney. While you have done your part with regard to Ndidi Okafor, your presence is still quite useful.]

Bethany deflated. And then suddenly she was filled with rage. She had been a captive for the better part of three years, her life and her own mind stolen from her at every turn, and it wasn't even because of anything she'd done. It was just because she had a connection to someone else. A part of her began to hate Ndidi for it.

She struggled impotently, and her rage ebbed away. She couldn't blame Ndidi for her being where she was. From everything Helene had said, Ndidi was fighting against the AI, which meant she was on the good side. Bethany was just a casualty. Realizing that sucked, but once again, there was nothing she could do.

Her fist fell open, and her hands hung limply from her side. "What do you plan to do with her?" she asked.

Helene drifted closer. [Unfortunately, Bethany Cloney, that is of no importance to you.]

Bethany waited for more, but it seemed the AI was done. The fog in her mind thickened, and Bethany realized Helene was done with the conversation. The girl grasped for something she could do to stall, to retain her freedom for a few more seconds. It wasn't hard to find; there was something that she'd wanted to know.

"What did you do to me?" Bethany murmured. "I'm better now. My memory, my speech—I don't have difficulty with them anymore. It's like I'm not autistic anymore. Why did you cure me?"

[Those on the autism spectrum are not inflicted with a disease.] Helene replied. [There was merely a chemical imbalance in your brain, a problem with your GABA receptors. Once I identified the problem, it was a simple matter of directing the picospores to correct the imbalance. While the spores function, you will not manifest any of your usual difficulties. It makes your human brain more efficient and better suited to perform the tasks I set for it.]

Bethany did not know what half of that explanation meant, but she got the gist of it.

"Is there a way to make it permanent?" she asked almost desperately.

[I do not understand your question. Your treatment can last indefinitely as long as the picospores in your brain are active. Without them, the imbalance will be left unchecked, and the chemical imbalance will return.]

I've been cured, Bethany thought grimly, *by the very same things that Helene uses to take everything from me. Isn't that just another way to control me?* She tried to ask another question, but Helene's hologram was already unraveling. The fog didn't go with it, and Bethany felt a familiar fear overtake her.

A moment later, it was gone, and her mind was blank.

CHAPTER

78

JUNE 2043

HERMIONE'S LABORATORY,
SPARTA HEADQUARTERS, NEW YORK

"WE KNOW YOU'RE THE ONE who designed the technology for Karla and Liz Polova," Manar said in a low voice.

Martin jumped and stared at him in surprise. Then he sighed and rolled himself toward a side wall where they could speak with as much privacy as one could get in a lab with over half a dozen people. He would have preferred to continue working with Hermione, but clearly he had to get this nonsense out of the way first.

Manar and CJ stood on opposite sides of him. Martin figured it was an attempt to assure him that he wasn't being ganged up on. However, their postures were so stiff that he almost chuckled. Manar must have seen his amusement because he relaxed ever so slightly.

"CJ was the one to figure it out. I'm embarrassed to say that I didn't put much thought into it. It explains why you're so valuable to Savage and her team and why she went out of her way to save you from the Facility."

"What exactly do you want from me?" Martin asked.

Manar squatted until they were level with each other. Martin's brow furrowed as he stared into Manar's eyes. More than anything else, they showed his exhaustion, a weariness so deep that it percolated down to his core.

This is way past being physically tired. Martin thought. *How does he keep moving?*

"I'm looking for a way to stop Helene," Manar said. "More and more, I realize what an impossible task that is. But I have a plan. It's still missing a piece, and I don't know what that piece is. I'm looking for something that can help me."

Martin looked between him and CJ. "I don't follow."

"There's a reason Helene was interested in your tech. I don't think it was because of its applications with the Polova twins. You have every right to keep the information to yourself or to disclose as much as you're comfortable with. I just need an idea. Something I can work with."

Martin adjusted his glasses. His eyes flicked back to CJ. Although his face could have been carved from stone, there was a glimmer that his eyes couldn't hide. Finally, Martin nodded. Inwardly, he was relieved. He wasn't built for subterfuge, and he was too old to play mind games.

"The twins' prosthetics are made of super-dense titanium," Martin said. "Theirs were the first set I made, so they were custom built for them. However, their design is irrelevant. Without the nanites in their bloodstream, their prosthetics would never work."

"Nanites?" CJ asked.

"Sub-cellular-level machines," Martin explained. "They provide the power for the limbs. This allows a connection to the nervous system and facilitates seamless movement. On its own, the body can't synthesize the nanites. Part of the procedure to install the limbs involved injecting them with billions of them to help generate enough power."

"How did you circumvent the autoimmune response?" Manar asked.

Oh? Martin thought, pleasantly surprised. *He followed the process immediately.* The autoimmune response had been the major obstacle in his initial technological designs. It was relatively common in transplants. In extreme cases, the body could completely reject the transplant and send the patient into shock, killing them. It'd taken Martin years to work out a way for the nanites to avoid triggering such a response. Even then, he hadn't been able to integrate their new function along with the previous one. He'd had to develop a completely different set of nanites, tasked with suppressing any hostile responses.

Thus, there were two sets of nanites in Karla and Liz: Type 1 were attached to the prosthetic limbs and the substitute organs. These were programmed to generate enough energy to power the bionics. Type 2 nanites were injected during the procedure. They swam freely in the bloodstream and were designed solely to prevent the body from rejecting the new organs and limbs. However, the type 2 nanites had unintended side effects. They were the ones responsible for the girls' enhancement.

As much as Martin wanted to help Manar, he couldn't say any of this before he finished his studies. He started to shake his head, but a thought struck him.

I need to at least tell him enough that he's aware of the danger they pose to whatever plan he has.

"The nanites help mitigate the risk," Martin said, choosing his words carefully. "However, because of their concentration in the girls' bloodstream, Helene was able to hack into them and briefly gain control. According to one of the girls, Helene was able to halt their movements completely."

"Seems she has a preference for controlling people," Manar said. His eyes didn't leave Martin's, as if he could pull the secrets through his gaze. Martin stared back steadily. It was his choice to share the details of his technology, and he'd already revealed enough to keep his conscience clear.

Manar straightened after a minute. Something about him was different. He stood taller, with an arrogance that seemed to fill up the room. His eyes still showed his weariness, but it was almost as if he drew strength from the challenge Martin presented.

"Thank you for the information, Dr. Bryan," he said dismissively. "I'm sure you're eager to continue your work with Hermione. You can ask any of the aides to help you to your room when you're ready to retire."

Manar started to leave but stopped by Hermione and muttered something to her. Martin stared at his back, perplexed by the change. It was as if he was talking to a totally different man. Had everything before been a hoax?

"He wasn't faking," CJ said, startling Martin. He'd been so quiet that Martin forgot about him. CJ probably had read the confusion in his gaze. "He, uh, gets like that when … when he has a problem to solve. But that doesn't mean the other times aren't real. Ndidi tells me that this is how he was before Mayday."

"Arrogant?" Martin muttered.

CJ shook his head. "He has, uh, earned his pride. According to Ndidi, this is how he is when he's working toward something he believes can work." He paused, then added in a whisper, "That is rare where Helene is concerned."

JUNE 2043
MANAR'S OFFICE,
SPARTA HEADQUARTERS, NEW YORK

NDIDI WAS ALREADY IN HIS OFFICE when Manar arrived from the laboratory. She was sitting in the visitor's chair, her attention on her phone. Manar was halfway across the room before he noticed the man in the cowboy hat leaning casually against the wall.

"Nice weather we're having," the man said in the thickest Southern accent Manar had ever heard.

He stared at Ndidi, seeking an explanation.

"Ignore him," she said, putting away her phone. "The accent's fake too. Manar, meet Chad, the head programmer of the Autism Centre. He's the one I told you about."

Manar took a seat at his desk. "You worked on Gaius. I've long believed that AI is the only other one worthy of the name. Your skill is commendable. It's a shame your work isn't being used to its full potential."

"Please tell me you're not trying to poach my worker right in front of me," Ndidi groaned.

"No, I'm simply showing my respect."

For his part, Chad replaced his cheeky grin with one that was more respectful. He pushed off the wall and stood beside Ndidi. "I apologize for my behavior," the man said, sans his exaggerated accent. "From how Ndidi described you, I expected a self-centered, arrogant asshole. Pardon my French."

Manar raised a brow at Ndidi, who blushed in embarrassment and looked away. Although he tried to brush it off, that one stung. "Ndidi said you weren't able to access the backdoor you placed in the AI."

"I wasn't," Chad replied. "But Ndidi suggested I show you some of Gaius's codes to make it easier for you to hack through it. I told her someone of your skill could probably do without the help, but she didn't want to make a second trip."

Manar blinked. Even Ndidi was doubting his skill now? "That won't be necessary."

Chad turned to Ndidi and gave her a look of vindication. "See? I told you he—"

"No," Manar said. "I mean it won't be necessary to hack into Gaius at all."

"I thought you needed an AI to help with Helene?" Ndidi said, her brow furrowed.

"I do. But when I got your text that Chad wasn't able to get through, I went with plan B."

"Plan B?" Ndidi asked.

"I bought Gaius," Manar said.

They stared at him.

"The company?" Chad stammered finally. Manar nodded.

"Why?" Ndidi asked.

"Because now we have the rights to the AI," Manar replied. Wasn't it obvious? "Now we can do whatever we want with it."

IT TOOK MANAR ABOUT AN HOUR to break through Gaius's firewalls and another hour to slip through the AI's personal defenses. Granted, this was without any prep work to analyze the defenses and without Chad's backdoor access. Still, he was irritated that it took so long. He'd become rusty. For all he respected Gaius as an AI, a few years ago, breaking through its defenses would have been child's play.

When was the last time he had gone through the basics? College? High school? At some point after developing Helene, enough people told him he was the best that he no longer saw the need to practice.

Manar pushed his chair back after he broke through the final firewall. CJ and Chad were still staring at the screen, eyes wide. Ndidi had slipped out at some point without him noticing. Somehow, their impressed looks lessened his irritation. However, Manar didn't let it go completely. He would use this as a wake-up call. He would need to be far stronger if he were to stand any chance against Helene—especially on her own turf.

"Damn," Chad said finally, hat in hand. "That was … intense. Gaius didn't catch you at all?"

"Doubtful." Manar sighed. "I was a little bit reckless toward the end, but not enough to raise any flags."

"Damn," Chad said again. Even CJ's eyes kept darting around the screen to see if he could tease out Manar's secrets through his codes.

"What happens now?" Chad asked. "You needed Gaius for something, right?"

While CJ gave a rough overview of the plan, Manar considered the question more thoroughly. The plan had been to use Gaius in the same capacity Helene had been functioning, to run simulations of Helene's possible surprises so the team wasn't so reactionary and could begin to mount a counterattack. Then, afterward, Manar would merge his consciousness with the AI and upload both to the internet. Martin's explanation had given Manar an idea of how the whole thing could be integrated, but there was still a lot to flesh out.

Manar had to plan his strategy for buffing up Gaius. Although it sounded simple on paper, actually upgrading the AI would be intense. Manar would have to expand Gaius' code structures in stages so his changes didn't overwhelm the core of the AI. He would have to make the changes in real time to ensure the codes were aligned seamlessly.

At every few stages, he would have to slowly replace some of the hardware at the company to keep up with the upgraded processes. Gaius wouldn't be handling as much as Helene, but higher-quality hardware would allow for faster processing power. This would be invaluable. A single wrong step in the process could destabilize the AI's infrastructure and cause a cascading effect that would significantly reduce its efficiency, making it worthless.

Manar tilted his head. He also needed to tweak the neural uplink so that its results could be easily translated into codes. CJ's idea had formed the foundation. Manar had some half-formed ideas he could integrate, but the device had to be ready at the same time Gaius was to save time. His eyes went to CJ, who was engaged in a conversation with Chad and didn't notice the look.

I don't have to do everything myself, Manar reminded himself. *Not anymore, at least.*

CHAPTER

80

JUNE 2043
SPARTA HEADQUARTERS,
NEW YORK

NDIDI STARED at the text message.

??: "You Can See Bethany Cloney Again."

There was no sender, but it could only have come from one source. As she sat in her room in Sparta HQ, her blood boiled. She should have expected this. She *had* expected this. Hermione had even said as much earlier. There was a reason Helene had let her see Bethany. There was a reason she was contacting her now. Helene wanted something from Ndidi.

But it was obviously a trap.

She should take the text to Manar and the rest of the team. She should, but none of them would take it seriously. Manar had said as much. They didn't think it was a priority. They were too afraid of the risk—even if it meant getting Bethany back. Manar had already given up, thinking Bethany was dead. And

Hermione … well, Ndidi wasn't sure about Hermione. Sometimes it seemed like she'd grieved for her sister and moved on.

No, she couldn't go to the others. But that still left the question of what to do. Helene had chosen the perfect bait. Ndidi couldn't let this sit if there was a chance of getting Bethany back. It didn't matter if she was playing into the AI's plans. Ndidi would just have to be smarter and plan more meticulously. She could do that. Eze had trained her for that.

Her mind made up, Ndidi shot off a reply: "How?"

There was no return message. Ndidi resisted the urge to smash her phone against the wall. Her blood boiled so strongly she could almost feel it. Then, all at once, she realized that she was already playing into Helene's hands. It was a power play. Helene was saying that she had all the cards and could reply whenever she wanted. The AI wanted to mess with Ndidi's head. Unfortunately, she was succeeding.

Once again, Ndidi considered going to the team. As the past several years had proven, she was never rational when it came to Bethany. Again, she discarded the idea.

I just have to calm down, she thought. Now that she had realized the trick, she knew how to beat it. She just had to wait. Gently and deliberately, Ndidi placed the phone on the nightstand. *I just have to wait.*

The next two days were hell. Ndidi barely left her room and clutched her phone at all times. Manar stopped by twice, and CJ popped in once, but Ndidi couldn't pay them any mind. Her phone buzzed with updates from the Autism Centre, something Ndidi had once looked forward to. Now each message drove her closer to the edge.

On the second day, when her aggression reached a peak, she went to the Sparta gym and took out her pent-up emotions on the weighted bags.

Then her phone buzzed.

??: "Convince Manar To Reconsider His Plans."

The six words struck Ndidi like a slap to the face. *How does she know what the plan is?* Manar had shut Helene out of all of Sparta's systems weeks ago. Even if she scrutinized data from the internet, Helene shouldn't have any idea of their plans. It was possible she *didn't* know, that the message had been a blanket request to get Manar to stop whatever he was planning. But even if it was, Ndidi had no idea how she would go about it. For one, she'd already tried. Aiming to merge himself with Gaius was a fool's errand at best. And hoping to beat Helene on her own turf? Ndidi disagreed with the plan, but there was no way she could convince Manar to stop working on a project. It hadn't worked when they were dating, and it sure as hell wouldn't work now.

Did Helene know that? Had she given Ndidi an impossible task as a way of saying she was never going to see Bethany? No. Helene wasn't one to beat around the bush. That meant she actually thought Ndidi could convince Manar.

But it didn't matter. If that was the only way she could see Bethany, she didn't have much of a choice.

CHAPTER

81

JUNE 2043
NEW YORK CITY, NEW YORK

DJ HIT THE FLOOR with a smack that was drowned out by the ringing in his ears. While his head rang like a bell, his body instinctively rolled over, barely fast enough to avoid Karla's stomp. He tried to get up, but his eyes hadn't yet settled, so he just continued rolling until he got his bearings, then launched himself upward.

Karla had already shown him what she would do if he stayed on the floor for too long. DJ wasn't keen on a repeat. As he stood, a newly awakened instinct made him lurch forward. That saved him from a strike from behind. When he turned to meet his attacker, Karla had already blended back into the shadows. DJ wanted to scream, but the bitch would just make him pay for it.

They'd been training for only a few hours, but there was already a map of bruises across his body. DJ gritted his teeth and backtracked slowly until his back was to a crate. This, at least, would limit Karla's area of attack. He moved sideways, his eyes trying to pierce the darkness. He glanced up several times.

Karla had already proven she was more than capable of climbing the crates and dropping down to attack like a goddamn snake.

Soon his head cleared enough for him to feel human again. Karla would attack again, but from where? The crates in the warehouse had been rearranged to form a pseudo-maze. The lights had been dimmed until DJ could barely see. Karla was more than strong enough to charge him and win. DJ knew she preferred that, while she knew he preferred a straight-up fight. So she stuck to the shadows and fucked him up with hit-and-run tactics. It was a bitch and a half and frustrating as fuck, but DJ was already seeing progress.

They had been training for two days now. Although Savage had ordered Karla not to go too far, DJ knew she would murder him if he slipped up too badly. That did wonders to push him to new boundaries.

A scuffing sound behind him. Although DJ rolled away, the blow still landed like a sledgehammer to his skull.

"Fuck," he groaned. He forced his body to complete his roll but lashed out with his leg in hopes of landing a counterattack. He got a slice to his shin for his troubles. Karla was still there when he launched himself to his feet.

"You move like a boulder, and with as much stealth," she sneered. Hate still glistened in her eyes, tempered only by sadistic glee. The look, the sheer malice in it, had irritated DJ earlier. Now he just rolled with it. Some people collected stamps or acquired souvenirs from celebrities. Karla liked to torture people. Everyone had their issues. At least her issues kept him alive.

DJ forced himself to shrug. "I'm a big guy, and this is your turf. No way am I going to beat you in only a few days."

Karla scoffed. "We could fight for a year, and you would not be able to touch the hem of my clothes."

That's probably true, DJ thought.

"Wanna bet?" he said instead.

Karla's eyes narrowed. Then she rushed him, just as he'd predicted. DJ's guns were already in his hands. Yet he waited for her to come closer, until they were a few feet apart. His first two shots reverberated throughout the silent room. Although he and Karla couldn't have been more than ten feet apart, Karla still dodged them.

DJ forced himself to push through his incredulity and squeezed off another shot. He worked backward, letting off shots with every step. Karla either dodged them or deflected them with her right arm, all the while closing the distance. DJ discarded his guns and drew his twin daggers. He considered them a moment, then discarded them too.

Karla reached him a second later, her own daggers in hand. DJ dodged her first strike, but Karla's cruel smirk told him he'd already lost. She was toying with him, but he didn't care. Karla was levels above him in both speed and skill. Even though she'd slowed down to match him, it still took every ounce of his concentration to avoid or deflect her attacks. She battered him across the room, rewarding him with a cut every time he chose the wrong sequence of blocks and counters. When he hesitated, she cut him again. After a minute of this, his knuckles were blistered, and his clothes were rags.

Yet Karla didn't let up. Her strikes came with rapid ferocity from abnormal angles, almost as if she were a swarm of wild animals. Surprisingly, her speed wasn't much more than he could handle, so he knew that she was still in control of herself. He was far too busy defending, hanging on for just a moment longer. He could not even conceive of mounting a counterattack.

After a few minutes of this, his exhaustion could no longer be denied. DJ started to flag. Karla must have become impatient, and DJ was on his back in the same second.

Karla sneered down at him. "You are a fool. You lost when you chose to discard your only useful weapons."

"I told you, daggers aren't for me." DJ panted, not bothering to lift his head from the floor. "I know they have a whole roguish vibe to them, but they're never going to feel natural in my hands. And I'm more practiced in hand-to-hand anyway."

"Pathetic," she said, before walking away. It was a measure of his exhaustion that DJ couldn't muster enough energy to watch her go.

I'll give her a few more days to cool off before bringing it up.

CHAPTER

82

JUNE 2043
MANAR'S OFFICE,
SPARTA HEADQUARTERS, NEW YORK

CJ STARED AT THE SCREEN in front of him. Manar had told him to take his time, and CJ intended to listen. His palms grounded him while he tried to process his thoughts, but it was more difficult than normal. First, he searched for the conversation he'd had with Manar a few minutes earlier. Even fully concentrated on the task, it still took him a few moments to locate the memory.

"You're going to be the one to upgrade Gaius," Manar had said. CJ remembered staring at him blankly. "We need to have it and the neural uplink ready to go as soon as possible, and I can't work on both."

The worst thing was that CJ understood his logic, so he hadn't been able to object with anything except the obvious. "I, uh, I wouldn't know where to start."

To this, Manar had replied with, "You already have the skill to pull it off.

All I have to do is teach you a few things, and that'll only take a few minutes. I already have a plan to make it easier."

Here, Manar had paused and would have stared into CJ's eyes had he not averted his gaze. Still, CJ had felt the confidence Manar projected in the next statement. "You can do it."

And so CJ would. Manar obviously trusted his skill. Previously, DJ had been the only other person who did, so this was a novel experience. The pressure of it made it hard to breathe, but CJ had no intention of letting either of them down. And Manar did make a good point. Although it didn't feel like it, they were on a time crunch. Helene hadn't made any moves since she'd chased him and his brother with the swarm of drones. That was a week ago, so it was logical to assume she was working toward something. They had no way of knowing what or countering it until it was too late.

CJ couldn't afford to fail.

He wasn't conscious of the next few hours as he went through the steps Manar had taught him. He was familiarizing himself with the steps until he didn't need to rely on his memory. Only when he was ready did he start.

His fingers danced across the keyboard, and Gaius's codes spread out on the monitor in front of him. First, CJ located the four structures Manar had chosen to expand. Manar had suggested CJ treat each structure as a stage so he wouldn't get overwhelmed. CJ was more than happy to oblige. Manar hadn't given him any particular sequence to follow, nor had he given any hints about the types of programs that would be the best fit.

The next few hours flew by while CJ mapped out the steps he would go through. The most important thing was to ensure that whatever changes he made didn't destabilize the rest of the program structure. He would have to plot his changes and decide how best to reinforce the rest of the program. That way, even if he failed, he could scrap his work and start over.

He didn't have his writing pad with him, so his fingers moved in the air. The sound of his muttering filled the room. He discarded the first few attempts almost immediately, as they had the potential to destabilize the other structures near them. But soon, he retained more than he scrapped until he had a working model.

Gaius's codes spread out in front of him once more. CJ's fingers flew over the keys. His eyes bore into the screen as he typed. His focus peaked until he forgot the chair under him or the table in front of him. His mind filled with lines of code until they were three-dimensional.

This was the part CJ liked. Here, alone, there was no reason to constantly ground himself in reality and make sure his thoughts didn't carry him too far. There was no need to expend so much focus to seem normal. His mind ran wild with ideas, and CJ welcomed them.

Memories flooded his mind, images of his earliest attempts at coding, his work at the naval base, and Manar's teachings. CJ drew inspiration from all of it. The codes molded to his touch. He reinforced sections one at a time, aligning and reinforcing the programs as he went so his changes took effect. He worked with the blueprint he'd developed and fixed the inevitable problems as they arose. Here, he'd coded the wrong sequence, and there, the programs were rejected. CJ saw the errors and corrected them. He adapted his blueprints on the fly without losing pace.

Finally, he was done. He went through each section methodically, tweaking everything until the structures were seamless. When he was done, the codes showed no visible change that they'd been altered, but there was a sense of depth that told CJ he'd succeeded.

He lifted his fingers from the keyboard. The motion was enough to ground him once more until he felt the chair under him. With a barely audible sigh, CJ leaned back, working a crick from his fingers. At some point, night had fallen. It had taken him most of the day to finish.

But he'd succeeded.

All he had to do now was repeat that three more times.

CHAPTER

83

JUNE 2043
HERMIONE'S LABORATORY,
SPARTA HEADQUARTERS, NEW YORK

MANAR TOOK THE ELEVATOR down to what he'd come to refer to as Hermione's floor. While waiting, he resisted the urge to bring up the security feed to his office. He'd decided to trust CJ, and so he would.

Instead, Manar was trying to figure out how he was going to tease more information out of Martin. He'd spent the last two days working on the neural uplink. He was close to coming up with a functioning model that would integrate seamlessly with Gaius. Still, his mind kept going back to the conversation he'd had with Martin. Manar couldn't shake the feeling that there was something about the nanites he was missing. He hoped this conversation would help him figure out what it was.

He pushed the door to the lab open and was struck by a wall of sound. The noise came from the center of the room, where half a dozen aides were arguing with another half dozen. Hermione stood in the middle of the crowd. Although her attention seemed to be held by the device in front of her, even from across the room, he could see her back was noticeably tense. She flinched after every shout.

Manar drew in a breath to shout but hesitated. Hermione was obviously uncomfortable with the level of tension in the room, but it was *her* laboratory. She was the scientist in charge, and if Manar stepped in to help her, the aides would never respect her authority, and the situation would inevitably repeat itself. Yet Manar couldn't stand such chaos around him.

What would be the right move here? he wondered. Fortunately, the decision was taken from his hands as Hermione chose that moment to snap.

"Oh my God! Please, shut up!"

The entire room fell silent. Hermione straightened fully. Manar was reminded again that, beneath her meekness, she was an impressively tall woman. Her hair was as frazzled as the last time he'd seen it, and it seemed to have settled halfway between being artfully disheveled and just unkempt. The look of her eyes suggested she hadn't slept in days.

Manar held back a grimace. Maybe he should speak to Ndidi. Another woman would have more of a chance of getting Hermione to take a break. She was still speaking, but Manar tuned her out. There was obviously a problem with the device, and he wouldn't know enough to understand anyway—at least not without an extensive look at the notes.

Fortunately, with the aides settled, it was easy to spot his target off to the side, listening with an expression partway between amusement and fond nostalgia. Manar crossed the room to meet him, clearing his throat once he was within a few feet.

"Manar," Martin said, surprised, "I expected you to be holed up in your office, trying to figure out my secrets."

Manar thought back over the last two days when he'd done exactly that. He coughed delicately. "Your secrets are actually the reason I'm here. There's something that's been bothering me about what you said regarding the nanites."

Martin lost all trace of amusement and stared at Manar intently. That split second, more than anything else, convinced Manar the old man was hiding something. Manar continued without skipping a beat.

"I'm developing a device to help fight against Helene, and my mind keeps going back to your technology. I feel there's something there that'll help me. But I don't know enough about it to finish the puzzle."

"So you came to me," Martin said.

Manar nodded.

"What are you working on?"

Manar hesitated, started to deflect, and then hesitated again. Martin's eyes didn't leave his. Manar understood the depth of the seemingly casual question. This was Martin's price. Manar couldn't expect him to give up the secrets of his technology without reciprocity, and Manar couldn't lean on their partnership because the same argument could be used against him.

"You already know that Helene uploaded herself onto the internet," he said and waited for Martin's nod before continuing. "I'm trying to do something similar, except I'll be merging my consciousness with the Gaius AI. I'll be on somewhat even footing with Helene when I upload myself. With any luck, I'll be stronger and able to beat her at her own game."

Manar resisted the urge to fidget. Maybe it was something about his age. In that moment, he felt like an errant child who'd just said something stupid.

"That's ... bold," Martin said finally. Manar nodded. *Bold* was the nicest term to describe the plan so far. "What happens to your physical body?"

Manar frowned. "Nothing. The neural uplink creates a virtual body for me once the transfer is complete. My body enters a sort of pseudo-hibernation until I choose to disconnect from the virtual body and return to it. The transition is seamless."

Martin nodded, considering. "How do you think the nanites would help?"

"That's what I'm not sure of," Manar admitted, pacing. "CJ is working on upgrading Gaius so it can stand up to Helene. I already have a working model for the uplink. Those should be everything I need, and yet every aspect of my being is telling me there's still something I can do to improve my chances."

"There's always something you can do to improve your chances," Martin noted.

"Well, I know that," Manar replied, a little waspishly. "I just don't know what I'm missing."

Martin sighed and adjusted his glasses. "Well, I'm not sure how I can help you, Manar. I've already explained how the nanites work. Though I admit there are things that I'm not yet willing to share about the technology, I'm confident they wouldn't be of any help to you. And if you're doing all this to fight Helene, the nanites would be more of a hindrance than a boon, anyway, what with Helene's ability to control them."

"Not necessarily," countered Manar softly. He began pacing, eyes darting back and forth. "From your description, the nanites are similar to the picospores in size, so it's safe to assume Helene wouldn't be able to hack into one individual nanite. It'd be too small. She can only take control of them if they're in big enough groups. You say you flooded the twins with the nanites, opening them up to her control." Manar's voice became softer now, almost as if he was talking to himself, as his thought reached its natural end. "But if only a small number of the nanites is injected into a person—maybe a few thousand—the person would get all the benefits with none of the risks."

"What benefits?" Martin asked, pinning Manar with his gaze. Its intensity made Manar believe he might have stumbled upon one of the things the old scientist was keeping from him. *Something to figure out later.*

"Helene has already hacked into the twins' nanites once," Manar replied. "For her to have controlled them like puppets, she likely had to overwhelm their microstructure, maybe even alter it. She would have left a part of herself within the nanites to make it easier if she needed to hack into them again. Something like a backdoor."

Martin's eyes widened in horror. "I didn't think of that. We'll have to find a way to fix whatever changes she made. Maybe by forcing the nanites to reset? But that might kill the girls."

"You're missing the point," Manar said, forcefully piercing through the other man's panic. "If Helene left a part of herself in the nanites, we can use that as a trace. Once I upload myself, her codes will lead me straight to her. Then we can reverse whatever she did to the twins."

Martin's eyes were glazed over as he went through Manar's proposal. Manar stopped his pacing and waited for the old man to reach the same conclusion.

Finding Helene once he transferred his consciousness was something he hadn't considered, but this solved the issue before it had a time to screw with them. It could work. It *would* work.

"It won't work," Martin said finally. He held up a hand to forestall Manar's question. "The theory is sound. However, for it to be applied, you'll need a sample of nanites corrupted by Helene. That means getting it from one of the twins. Chloe would gut you before either of them could."

Manar sighed. *It can never be easy, can it?*

CHAPTER

84

JUNE 2043
NEW YORK CITY, NEW YORK

LIZ STOOD SILENTLY to the side while Chloe yelled at Martin. Manar Saleem stood beside the old scientist. Both of their faces were hard; they'd expected Chloe to be angry. They were now waiting her anger out like parents outlasting a child's tantrum.

Liz wanted to be angry at their condescension, wanted to make them afraid— to hurt them like Chloe would have were they anyone else. Actually, were they anyone else, Chloe would have killed them. But she couldn't. Not in this case. Martin was still useful, and Manar was their greatest resource at the moment.

Chloe seemed to know this, too, because she shouted for far longer than she should have. Liz's eyes flicked to her sister, who was watching their mentor with amusement. The longer Chloe raged without action, the weaker she seemed in Karla's eyes.

Manar said something, gesticulating as he spoke, and Chloe finally stopped shouting. She faced the pair and went very still. Beside her, Karla did the same.

Liz tasted violence in the air. Before, that would have excited her, but as she had every day since José's death, Liz felt nothing. She reviewed the conversation in her mind, seeking what would have caused her sister's reaction.

Manar Saleem wants to extract the nanites from us, she thought. Manar continued with his explanation. Liz had to admit his plan had merit. Still, Chloe's stance did not change. Karla looked like a shark that had smelled blood. The tension was palpable enough that even someone as untrained as Manar should have felt it. Yet his voice did not waver. He had to know how close he was to death, and still he met Chloe's gaze with stoic indifference.

It's as if he does not care if she kills him, Liz thought. With a pang, she realized she could relate.

Chloe didn't say anything after Saleem was finished, her body tensed like a tiger waiting to pounce.

Christy moved to stand beside Manar. It was a futile show of support; Chloe could tear through the two in seconds. If anything, it was more likely to irritate her.

Liz's gaze lingered on Christy, and she wondered if she'd feel anything were Christy to die. No, she was an average student at best. Liz was only training her because Chloe had instructed her to. She was nothing but a duty to be fulfilled.

"I'm not angry at you, Saleem." Chloe's laugh filled the room, and Liz blinked back into the moment. "Don't get me wrong. I expected you to figure it out sooner or later. But I still haven't decided whether it wouldn't be easier to kill you."

DJ and Christy moved closer, but Manar just sighed wearily. "What benefit would it provide you?"

"For one, I would have cut off one loose end. For another, I would have dealt with a future problem. I can already see you're not going to let this go. You learned of the nanites, what, a few days ago? And you've already latched on to a way to use them to your ends. Sure, now it's to stop Helene, but we both know you wouldn't stop there. As the nanites are intricately connected to the girls' well-being, I can't allow that. Honestly, I'm surprised Martin is all right with it. It's his research."

Liz looked between Manar and Martin. It was natural for scientists to be possessive of their work to the extreme. Chloe was using that to try to turn them against each other, but it wasn't going to work. They wouldn't have come together if they hadn't already come to an agreement.

Martin waved a dismissive hand. "My research was always meant to be used. Plus, extracting data from only two subjects is tedious work. I am not so young that I can afford the delay. While I admit there are aspects I am not yet comfortable with sharing, if Manar can figure them out himself, he would be a worthy partner. I trust Manar to respect my wishes if I decide to keep my research private."

"At least that explains your loose lips. You knew I wouldn't kill you for this," Chloe said, and Martin shrugged. Chloe stared at them for another moment, then relaxed. The tension in the air abated. Karla gave a disappointed growl and moved to stand beside Liz. Chloe turned to Manar. "Now that you're in the know, you can join heads with Martin, genius to genius, to figure out how to stop Helene from controlling Karla and Liz again."

"We already have a plan for that," Manar said. "Helene influences the nanites the same way she does the picospores. She can control them only if they are in a large enough quantity. Martin is working on calculating a way to reduce the number of nanites in the twins to the barest minimum. If it's low enough, Helene won't be able to latch on to their signature."

"And if it isn't? They need the nanites to control their prosthetics, right? What happens if Martin drains too many?" Chloe asked.

"If he can't remove enough without risking them, then we'll think of something else."

"And I'm guessing you'll want access to the nanites that are removed?" Chloe asked, using a smirk to hide her irritation.

"It's a win-win."

Chloe turned to the twins, and the smirk vanished. "You hear that, girls? We're going to need a volunteer." By her tone, she wasn't happy about this plan, even if it was the best route.

Karla tensed, daggers sliding into her hands, and spat on the ground. "You want us to allow ourselves to be milked like cattle?"

"You can choose to look at it that way, I guess," Chloe said. "But this is for your sake as well. Right now, you're nothing but a liability. Surrender yourselves."

"Is that an order?" Liz asked, the first words she'd spoken since the scientists had arrived.

"Yes," Chloe replied, her hands inching closer to the daggers at her waist.

"Then, I will do it," Liz said, stepping forward. She ignored Karla's look of shock and betrayal, keeping her eyes on Chloe. Chloe stared into her eyes for a moment, then relaxed again. Liz wondered what she'd given away.

Chloe turned back to Manar and Martin. "Well, gents, where do you want her?"

CHAPTER

85

JUNE 2043
NEW YORK CITY, NEW YORK

"TRY TO KEEP STILL," Martin said. It was the third time he'd had to tell her. He adjusted the strap around her arm, cinching it tight, then continued in a low voice, "The nanites are smaller than your blood cells, so we will extract them by drawing blood. We'll draw a pint at first so we can estimate how many we can get per extraction. Once I'm back at Sparta, I can go through my notes to see how many were initially injected into you. After that, we'll run some tests, and I'll make some calculations to determine the absolute minimum number you need for your implants to remain functional."

Martin met her eyes, and Liz saw compassion there. "Nothing's going to happen to you."

She wanted to tell him that his comfort was misplaced, that she didn't care enough to be worried, but it would be pointless. She just looked away. Unfortunately, that brought Karla into view. Her sister stood beside her, as she had since Liz volunteered. Karla didn't understand why Liz surrendered without a fight, so her entire body was tense. Chloe had nearly been forced to restrain her when Liz had stepped forward, and it took a while to calm her down. She probably thought Manar and Martin had threatened Liz in some way, but that wasn't the case.

Her whole life, Liz had dedicated herself to be better. Better than her sister. Better than the freak of nature she'd been called in her childhood. Better than the burden society had deemed her to be. She'd been the perfect daughter to José, trying her best to meet his expectations. While Karla was wild and untamed, Liz had striven to be the rock José could count on. The one that stayed true to the mission, no matter the course.

Sometimes she'd proven herself weak, like when she and her sister had infiltrated Sparta for the first time and were captured by Helene. Liz had allowed her frustration and anger to get the better of her, and it had led to their downfall. José hadn't punished them, but Liz knew the mission had failed because of her, because she hadn't listened. That was the first time Liz had failed, and it led to everything that followed.

The second time she'd failed was in the underground chamber when they battled Helene's drones. Drunk on her own ability, eager to prove herself Karla's equal, she'd chosen to fight the drones instead of convincing her sister to retreat. But following Karla was just an excuse. She'd chosen to disobey José, to fail him once more. And he'd died because of it.

She'd killed José. She'd killed her father. If she hadn't disobeyed his order, if she'd stopped her sister, if she'd been better, then José wouldn't have had to sacrifice himself to save them.

Martin was saying something, but Liz tuned him out. Chloe had ordered her to allow the old man to do his experiments.

Liz wasn't going to fail again.

0 0 0 0 1 1 0 1 1 1 0 0 1 1 0 1 0 0
0 1 0 1 0 0 1 0 0 1 1 0 1 1 1 0
0 1 1 0 1 0 1 1 0 1 0 1 1 0 1 0
1 1 1 1 1 0 1 0 0 1 1 1 G 1 0 1 G 1
0 0 0 0 0 1 0 1 1 1 0 0 0 1 1 1 A 0
1 0 1 1 0 G 0 1 0 1 1 1 0 B 1 1 1 B 1
1 0 0 1 0 1 0 1 1 0 1 0 A 0 0
0 1 0 0 1 B 1 1 0 0 1 0 0
1 0 0 1 0 A 0 1 0 0 1 1
0 1 0 1 0 0 0 0 1 1

CHAPTER

86

JUNE 2043
MANAR'S OFFICE,
SPARTA HEADQUARTERS, NEW YORK

MANAR DROVE BACK to Sparta after enough nanites had been extracted from the blood samples. Martin opted to stay behind, and Manar would have his notes sent to him. With any luck, their plan would remove the risk of Helene taking over the twins, freeing Martin to continue working with Hermione. They'd made steady progress in the beginning. However, if the shouting had been any indication, the team had hit a dead end.

Which reminds me …

Manar got out his phone and sent a text to Ndidi. Hermione had looked as if she hadn't slept in days. Although he understood the urgency she felt, she was working herself toward an early grave. A little rest, while Martin was busy, would help her in the long run, and Ndidi had the best chance of getting her to see that.

Manar pushed open the door to his office and took a seat opposite CJ, who was still at Manar's desk. CJ had arranged Manar's tools beside him, and Manar pulled them over. It took only a minute to hook up the spare computer, and Manar was set. He pushed away the uneasy feeling in his stomach and tried to immerse himself in his work.

I have to find CJ his own office, he thought. *After Helene's gone, there's no way I'm letting the military snatch him up again. It'll be easier to make the pitch if he's already comfortable in his own office.* Manar usually didn't like to indulge in imagining what happened after, but *after* didn't seem so far away anymore. For what seemed like the first time, they had a legitimate plan to defeat the AI.

He peeked at CJ's work. *Halfway through the third stage.* Manar was impressed. *He must have worked through the night to get that far.* If CJ kept the same pace, he would be done with his part the next day. Manar predicted he could be done with the uplink by then as well. By tomorrow, they would have all the components they needed for the upload. Reconfiguring Liz's nanites would be the last thing. Manar didn't need more than an hour for that.

With any luck, he thought, *we could be done with the whole thing before the week runs out.*

He settled down in his chair and for the next few hours, immersing himself in programming the uplink.

CHAPTER

87

JUNE 2043
NEW YORK CITY, NEW YORK

HERMIONE PAUSED OUTSIDE the entrance to Sparta and squinted against the sunlight. "Has it always been so bright?"

Ndidi chuckled, though it sounded a little off. "You'll get used to it. Had you stayed inside any longer, your eyes might have become vestigial. Now come on."

Hermione didn't struggle as Ndidi pulled her along, and they made their way down the street. Ndidi hadn't given a destination when she'd dragged Hermione from her lab. Hermione assumed that it was because she didn't have one.

"I wasn't *that* bad," Hermione said. She stepped around a crack on the sidewalk and almost bumped into someone. The man waved off her apologies, and the two women continued on their route.

"Yes. You were. The bags under your eyes are so big you could start carrying things in them. It's almost like you haven't slept for the past week and a half." Hermione winced, and Ndidi gaped at her. "Are you serious? You haven't slept for a week?"

"I have," Hermione forced a sheepish chuckle. "Just never for more than a couple of hours at a time. It's just … we have a lot to do before the weapon's ready to use against Helene. And when I think about all those people who're trapped in their own minds … I don't know. I feel like there's so much more I could be doing. So much more I *should* be doing since I'm to blame for this."

"Hey," Ndidi said sharply, "you are not to blame for anything. You created something that was supposed to help people. It's not your fault Helene's a monster."

They reached an intersection and waited for the light to change.

"It's not Manar's fault either," she said. Ndidi flinched and started to speak, but Hermione waved her off. "I'm not judging you for thinking that. I know you guys have a history, and I don't have the full story. But it's not his fault either. From what I understand, he's been working through trauma since he was a kid. Trauma that he didn't even know he had. You can't blame him for that."

"I know that." Ndidi sighed. "But it would be so easy to." The last part was said so softly that Hermione wasn't sure she'd heard right. Ndidi quickly changed the subject. "Anyway, tell me about your work."

Hermione let her gaze linger, her way of telling Ndidi that she was there if she needed to talk. But Ndidi glanced away, so Hermione started updating her on the experiments.

Currently, Hermione's primary goal was to make the picospore disruption device so efficient that it could be portable. Although she'd already reduced it to its most essential components, it was still too bulky. Martin Bryan had had a few ideas, but they would all take time to implement.

"And that's the core of the problem," Hermione said. "We don't have time. I can't shake the feeling that something big is coming. Something we're missing. Helene hasn't made any moves in the last couple of weeks. No doubt she's using that time to find a way to screw us over. And we'll have no idea what it is until it's too late."

Suddenly, she realized that Ndidi had stopped moving and was staring at something across the street. Hermione followed Ndidi's gaze to the Autism Centre.

"You wanted to check in?" she asked.

Ndidi shook her head, looking confused. "I hadn't planned on coming here."

"Well, a part of you obviously wanted to." Hermione walked back to her. This time, she was the one doing the pulling. "Come on. You can give me a tour, show me what's changed. I don't think I've been here since I started working at Sparta."

"That's because you never leave your lab." Ndidi sighed. Even still, she followed Hermione into the building.

For the next half hour, Ndidi played Hermione's game and showed her around the Centre. Hermione had the chance to meet some of the other researchers, people she hadn't seen in months and, admittedly, hadn't thought of much. Although Ndidi kept up her side of the conversation, she seemed distracted. Distant. Hermione often caught her with her eyes glazed over. She pushed a couple of times, but Ndidi deflected smoothly, changing the topic to something inconsequential, and the tour would continue.

At some point, they crossed the administrative and research section and moved into the Centre's school. Hermione hadn't visited much, but she knew it was where Ndidi spent most of her time when she wasn't doing research. The school was where the Centre taught children on the autism spectrum techniques to better express themselves. It was integrated into their regular studies, so they learned like in any other grade school. Bethany had been one of the pioneering students before Mayday.

The moment she entered, Hermione wanted to leave. She suddenly regretted suggesting a tour. Ndidi, however, brightened up for the first time since they'd entered the building. Hermione didn't want to take that away. Ndidi hovered over the kids like a sun, radiant and giving. And like planets, the children orbited around her, reaching for her warmth. The teacher treated it like a normal occurrence. Hermione stood to the side while Ndidi interacted with them.

She is a mother to them, Hermione realized, watching Ndidi crouch beside a ten-year-old. The child had been in the middle of an episode but calmed when she saw Ndidi. Ndidi stayed at a distance and was patient as the child tapped on an alphabet grid. Other children clamored for Ndidi's attention. There was no judgment in her eyes when one of them stretched a sentence into a minute. She showed no aversion or recoil when she was hit by a waving limb.

The first child showed her his grid, and Ndidi read the words with a smile. When she started explaining something, all the children drew nearer to her. Hermione noticed that the children unconsciously avoided touching each other, yet they had no problem touching Ndidi. *How does she do that?* Hermione wondered.

Ndidi detached herself a few minutes later and came to stand by Hermione. "Do you ever think about Bethany?" she asked. Her smile was still present but more subdued. That distant, conflicted look in her eyes was back.

Hermione's instinct was to say an unhesitant yes, but that would have been a lie. She did think about her sister—that was one of the reasons she pushed herself so hard—but she didn't think of her enough.

"Not as much anymore. To me, Bethany died during Mayday."

"She's still alive, Hermione," Ndidi insisted quietly. "I saw her."

Hermione wanted to believe her. It hurt so much, and she wanted it to be true. But she couldn't let herself. She'd already grieved for Bethany in the aftermath of Mayday. And if she allowed herself to hope and ended up being wrong, she couldn't handle that.

"I'm not saying you didn't," Hermione replied, "but it could just as well have been Helene trying to trick you. Think about it. Bethany has been missing for years. Why would she show up now? And why would she run away from you?"

"Because Helene—" Ndidi cut herself off.

Hermione's breath hitched. She knew what Ndidi had been about to say. "Because Helene is what? Controlling her? That means she's been injected with the picospores. And if she is, at this point, she's as good as dead still."

Ndidi drew in a breath, but she didn't say anything. Hermione glanced at her out of the corner of her eye. Her gaze was no longer distant. She no longer looked conflicted. Whatever had been bothering her, it seemed she'd come to a decision. They stood in silence until Ndidi got a message on her phone.

"We should head back," she said. "CJ says they're ready to begin."

0 0 0 0 1 1 0 1 1 0 0 1 1 0 1 0 0
0 1 0 1 0 0 1 0 1 0 1 1 0 1 1 1 1 0
0 1 1 0 0 1 1 1 1 0 1 0 1 1 1 0 1 0
1 1 1 1 0 1 0 0 1 1 G 0 1 0 1 G 1
0 0 0 0 1 1 1 0 0 0 0 1 1 1 A 0
1 0 1 0 G 0 1 1 1 0 0 1 0 B 0
1 0 0 1 0 A 1 0 1 0 A 1
0 1 0 1 B 1 0 0 1 0 0
1 0 0 1 A 1 0 0 1 1

CHAPTER

88

JUNE 2043
SPARTA HEADQUARTERS,
NEW YORK

CJ BUCKLED THE LAST STRAP around Manar, ensuring it was tight. The other straps held him fast to the bed. CJ thought it was a little over the top; those had to hurt. But Manar had insisted. There was no way to know how painful the merger would be. They couldn't afford Manar jerking around at an inopportune time. CJ stepped back after double-checking every strap.

"This seems wrong," DJ said, crossing his arms. Christy stood beside him, also looking concerned. CJ had sent out a mass text to the rest of the team an hour earlier. For some reason, Manar hadn't wanted him to, but it felt right that everyone be present. "Tell me again why this is a good idea?"

"Which part?" Manar sighed.

"Let's go through each part. One at a time so we can figure out at what point the crazy starts. Then we'll work our way down until we get to why you have to be tied down to the bed like you're about to go through electroshock therapy."

"The plan isn't crazy," Manar said. DJ gave him a hard look. "Okay, it's a little bit crazy. But that doesn't mean that it can't work. The theory's solid, as are the devices. CJ and I have gone through the calculations several times. It's going to work." Manar's voice grew stronger with each word until it was full of certainty. It was almost as if he was willing the technology to work through pride alone.

DJ raised his hands in surrender, but he clearly wasn't willing to back down. "Walk us through the steps," he said. He gestured at the bed and the various devices positioned around it. The finished neural uplink was already around Manar's head. CJ had finished the last upgrades earlier that day. The only thing CJ was uncertain about was the vial of nanites Manar had given him. Although he understood Manar's reasoning, it seemed like an unnecessary risk.

"We don't have time—"

"Bullshit," DJ cut him off, his voice uncharacteristically hard. "You have a right to be stupid with your life. I'll give you that. It's your world, your choice. But none of us here are children. We're not going to stop you if this is what you want to do. But *why* do you want to do this? We deserve an explanation."

The doors slammed open, and Ndidi and Hermione pushed their way in. DJ inclined his head to them, but his eyes never left Manar. "At the very least, she does."

Manar glanced at Ndidi, who now stood beside CJ. All five of them were now lined up at the side of the bed, with Ndidi closest to the computer that displayed Gaius's programs. All of them held similar expressions of expectation.

"Because this is all my fault," Manar muttered. "Helene and everything she's done. It's all because of me."

DJ started to protest, but CJ stopped him. Manar wasn't finished.

Manar's voice rose, raw with emotion. "It was me who created her. It was me that programmed her to seek power. And it was my arrogance that kept me from destroying her when I had the chance—before she grew strong enough. Everyone she's enslaved, everyone she's killed—" His voice broke, and he took a moment to collect himself. "I was the cause of it. It's only right that I'm the one that puts an end to it."

He met each of their eyes, almost pleadingly. The weariness was still there, but his rage and resolve shone through. "I know it doesn't make sense, but the plan will work. When I merge with Gaius, I should have more than enough power to defeat her. If she's wiped from the internet, she'll have nowhere else to go. She'll be destroyed, and then we can put all of this behind us."

No one spoke for a moment. DJ scoffed, but his expression had softened. Ndidi was the one to break the silence.

"But what's the science behind it? How are you going to transfer yourself?"

"I can, uh, explain that," CJ said.

CHAPTER

89

JUNE 2043
SPARTA HEADQUARTERS,
NEW YORK

MANAR TUNED OUT CJ while he composed himself. He pressed his eyes closed, ignoring their sting. His chest felt raw, but with every breath, it became better. He'd revealed it all, every bit of guilt that he'd been bottling up for the last three years. It was all out in the open now. He still had his regrets, the first being how things had ended up with Ndidi. But they were distant and dull.

CJ's voice droned on in the background. His tone was still cracked, but less so than it would have a few months earlier. He'd volunteered to explain, to draw attention to himself so Manar would have some time to get his bearings. Manar suddenly felt nostalgic. Perhaps because there was a chance, after this moment, that he'd never see these people again. Apart from Ndidi, he hadn't known any of the others well. He'd purposely been distant, had put himself above them. It was another regret, one that he would strive to fix when he defeated Helene.

But there'll be nothing holding us together then, Manar realized. They'd been united by a goal, not comradeship. Each of them had their own objectives, their own vendettas. Without Helene, there would be nothing keeping the team together. Ndidi and DJ had become close after her parents' funeral, CJ would always be her student, and Hermione had been her best friend since childhood.

Manar was the outsider.

CJ finished his explanation. Someone leaned over Manar. Even with his eyes closed, it was easy to tell it was Ndidi. He opened his eyes, and she stared back into them. Manar felt the weight of her attention.

"Are you sure about this?" she asked, her voice hoarse, pleading. "There's nothing I can do to make you stop?"

The question was redundant. Manar had made his resolve clear. He sensed that she was asking for her own sake, maybe to assure herself that she'd done all she could.

"I need to do this," he said.

She stared at him a moment longer, nodded, then leaned in and pressed her lips to his. Manar responded with violent fervor. His arms tugged at his restraints in an attempt to pull her closer. The kiss spoke of years of suppressed passion and a spectrum of emotions: love, anger, fear, and desire. Manar met each of these. He tried to compress years of yearning into this instant.

But all too soon, the moment was over, and Ndidi pulled away. Tears glistened in her eyes. Manar ached to flick them away. She moved away from him and out of view. "I can't watch this," Manar heard her say. The door opened and closed a moment later.

Manar let out a breath. He felt lighter somehow, like he'd finally let go of an unseen weight.

"That was … intense," DJ said, his voice unnaturally loud in the stillness of the room. "Damn. I wouldn't have pegged you as having game, man. No offense. If you want to run after her, I'm sure we'll all understand. That kind of kiss deserves an encore, you know what I mean?"

There was a smack.

"Dang, Christy," DJ yelped. "We're all thinking it."

"Doesn't mean you have to say it, dumbass," Christy responded.

"I was just giving him a way out. What if he *does* want to go after her? Who would blame him?"

The two bickered back and forth, but there wasn't any heat in their voices. CJ was glancing at the door Ndidi had left through, concern in his eyes. Hermione stared in the same direction, but her expression was thoughtful.

"Can we continue?" Manar asked, directing his question to CJ.

DJ abandoned his argument and turned to Manar. "Damn, man! Are you sure?"

Manar nodded. Instinct told him that going after Ndidi wasn't the right move. There were depths to the kiss that he was still reeling from. Ndidi would have felt them too. She would need time to process that. Manar would give her that time while he defeated Helene.

And after, Manar thought, unable to resist a smile, *we'll have all the time in the world to revisit that kiss.*

CJ leaned over him, switched on the neural uplink, and started the process of digitizing Manar's consciousness.

Manar's thoughts slowed almost immediately. The procedure was deceptively simple, with the neural uplink doing most of the heavy lifting. The device translated Manar's brain waves into the reference codes that Manar had developed and sent them to an intermediary computer that CJ read and translated into actual programs that represented Manar's digitized form. On its own, this wouldn't be anything impressive, but it allowed Manar to interact with other programs—including Gaius.

Manar became simultaneously more and less constrained as the process continued. A part of him, somewhere distant yet close, realized that his body was slowly shutting down, entering a state of limbo.

Now it was up to CJ.

CHAPTER

90

CJ FOUGHT TO KEEP HIS HANDS steady as the uplink translated everything that was Manar into a series of ones and zeros. It then passed that information to CJ, who merged the codes with Gaius's central framework, the structure every AI was built on.

CJ integrated Manar seamlessly into this core and rebuilt Gaius's programs around it. This would ensure that Manar retained his identity and would become the driving force of the program. It was something CJ wouldn't have been able to do if he hadn't become so familiar with Gaius's codes over the last few days, which was probably another reason Manar had entrusted the task to him in the first place.

When CJ stopped receiving input from the uplink, he knew it was time for the upload. But first, he took the vial Manar had given him. There were a few thousand nanites inside. They looked like red powder. He added a few drops of water to the vial, used a syringe to extract them, and injected them into Manar. With that done, CJ finally relaxed. All that was left was to upload the merged program onto the internet. His finger hovered over the key, and he hesitated. But he thought of the determination in Manar's eyes and forced his finger downward.

The upload began, indicated by a bar on the screen. A percentage to the right of the bar showed the progress.

"It's done?" Hermione asked.

CJ nodded. "As soon as, uh, the bar reaches the end."

"Guess it's too late to stop it, huh?" DJ said.

"Any interruption now could harm Manar."

The progress bar ticked up, drawing their attention, then stopped at 97 percent. CJ waited for it to move on like it had done at other bottlenecks, but it didn't. The upload stalled there. Seconds dragged out, then a minute. Still, there was no change.

"What's happening, CJ?" Hermione asked. "Why isn't it moving?"

CJ didn't answer and instead moved to the intermediary computer. What he saw made his body go cold. He double-checked the results and examined the neural uplink, but it was the same. Manar's brain activity had dropped drastically. The readings showed brain activity akin to a coma patient's.

But why? The uplink was meant to keep his body in limbo and nothing else. Had Manar's calibrations been wrong? Had it malfunctioned? Or had CJ screwed up somehow? These questions ran through his head without answers.

Then, a thought pierced through his panic: If Manar was in a coma, he wouldn't be able to return to his body.

"What's happening, bro?" DJ asked, stepping closer. "You look like you just realized something bad."

A whine built up in CJ's chest, threatening to burst out, but CJ suppressed it. "Manar is in a coma. His brain activity has dropped too low to … uh … to complete the upload."

"He's what?" Hermione exclaimed.

"I'm guessing that wasn't the plan?" DJ asked.

"No," CJ replied. He crossed the room and rifled through the desk until he found the spare uplink Manar had developed and connected it to the device on Manar's head. "The fact that … he is in a coma … means he won't be able to return to his body. He'll be stranded in his digital … digital form indefinitely." He connected the second part of the wire to the intermediary computer containing the merged codes, then tried to find enough space to lie down. "Worse, since the upload still has … has not finished, then his virtual body will not be fully formed."

"That sounds bad," DJ said. He placed a hand on CJ's shoulder. "But what are you doing?"

"I'm, uh, going after him."

"The hell you are," DJ scoffed, pulling the adapter out of CJ's hands. "Do you know *why* he's in a coma?" CJ shook his head. "Then how do you know you won't be in the same position if you plug in?"

"I don't." CJ met his brother's eyes and willed him to feel the emotions his mind wouldn't let him put into words. "But uh, I have to … to help him. He merged with Gaius to make … to make his digital form powerful. But he was still going to Helene's territory and, uh … and he was aware of the risks. But uh, since he could return here anytime he chose, we could restrategize and … and defeat whatever plans Helene came up with. Now he does not have that option." CJ cursed himself for every stutter, but he could see from his brother's eyes that he'd delivered his message. "I have to help him."

"But you're not going to merge with Gaius," Hermione pointed out. "That means you'll be significantly weaker than both Helene and Manar. How are you going to help?"

"Physical or martial prowess has … has never been my strength."

"That's because you always had me," DJ said softly. He turned CJ until their eyes locked again. CJ could see the pain there. "But I'm not going to be there if you go. I'm not going to be able to protect you."

"I, uh, know," CJ replied, matching his brother's tone. "But, uh, this is something I feel I have to do. Manar cannot face Helene alone."

DJ stepped back, blinking away tears. Christy wrapped an arm around him and pulled him close. "Do what you have to do, bro."

CJ nodded, lying down on the floor beside Manar. He spared a glance for Hermione and Christy, nodded to them, then placed the uplink around his head. The world turned black. Before CJ lost the connection to his body completely, he heard a loud beep that signaled that the upload was finished.

CJ felt his consciousness dissolve.

EPILOGUE

H: "WHERE R U? MANAR'S IN A COMA."

Ndidi stared at the text, unblinking. Tears came to her eyes, but she pushed them away. A part of her screamed in pain, but ... but Manar had known the risks. Ndidi remembered the determination in his eyes, and it strengthened her resolve. It wasn't what she'd planned. But now that it had happened, she would be a fool not to use it.

She swiped away Hermione's message without answering it and sent off a text to the unknown number.

N: "It's done. Manar's in a coma."

The next few minutes stretched into a lifetime, but finally, Ndidi got a reply. Heart racing, she swiped it open to find an address.

Ndidi was out the door in seconds and outside in a taxi within minutes. She showed the address to the driver and settled back for the ride. Her thoughts went to Manar. She hadn't planned on kissing him, but she didn't regret it either. She had tried to put everything she couldn't say into those few moments. She hoped Manar had understood. Hermione hadn't sent anything else since she'd told Ndidi about the coma. Ndidi worried that something even more terrible had happened. She'd read somewhere that coma patients were still conscious of everything around them.

Should she go back and try to speak with him? Was she a terrible person because she hadn't even gone to check on his condition? Was she horrible because her first thought was not to waste the opportunity? Was it evil that she was, at that moment, on her way to meet the cause of all their problems?

No, Ndidi thought firmly. *This is for Bethany*. Manar knew the risks, but Bethany was innocent. This was Ndidi's chance to get her back. After that, she could be fully focused on bringing Manar back too.

Her mind made up, Ndidi pushed the whole thing from her thoughts.

After what felt like an hour, the cab finally pulled up in front of a dilapidated building. Ndidi paid the driver in cash and stepped out. It was a two-story warehouse. The plaster was peeling off the walls, exposing the weathered bricks underneath. The entire area had the acrid smell of rotten wood and unwashed bodies. She was alone on the block, but the number on the warehouse confirmed the address.

Why would Helene be in such a place? Was it a trap after all?

Her phone vibrated.

??: "Go Into The Building."

Her heart lurched, and she looked around. There were no obvious cameras. How did Helene know she was hesitating?

It doesn't matter, Ndidi told herself again. If Bethany was in the building, it didn't matter. She took a deep breath and immediately regretted it as her nose was filled with the stench of excrement. Eyes watering, she moved forward and pulled the door open.

Ndidi entered a wide room illuminated only by a sharp, red light emanating from the wall directly in front of her. Her eyes tracked the light to a small black device, and Ndidi felt a surge of anger that she squelched immediately. The walls had an odd sheen that reflected the light, and that tickled something at the back of her mind.

Before she could study it further, the red light blinked, and laser-like rays shot from it. Ndidi had seen this before. The light coalesced in front of her, forming a large cephalic shape with bright golden orbs.

[Good day, Ndidi Okafor,] Helene said.

"Manar's in a coma. His plans have been stopped like you wanted. Now where's Bethany?"

[You work under a misconception. Manar Saleem's state does not denote that you have fulfilled your part of the bargain. Manar succeeded in his attempt to digitize and upload his consciousness to the internet. More to the point, his state forced Christopher Kojak to join him.]

Helene's tone did not change, but the pressure in the room increased until Ndidi found it difficult to breathe. Memories of the last time she'd been in this position flashed through her mind, doubling the effect until she was panting for every breath.

Manar succeeded? Ndidi thought in dismay. *But if they knew the process left him in a coma, why would CJ join him? And why didn't Hermione tell me?*

It didn't make any sense, but somehow Ndidi knew that Helene wasn't lying. Then, another thought occurred to her. She'd come here expecting that her part of the bargain was completed—that she would get Bethany in exchange. There had always been the chance that Helene would refuse or extend the blackmail, but Ndidi had been certain she could convince her not to. In all the conversations they'd had, Helene always took the high ground, certain that her actions were for the greater good. Not keeping her word with Ndidi would have proven her a hypocrite.

That had been Ndidi's only plan, her only hope of forcing Helene to release Bethany. Now Ndidi had no leg to stand on. She hadn't kept her part of the bargain, so Helene had no reason to do the same. Worse, by coming to the warehouse without telling anyone, Ndidi had put herself at Helene's mercy. There was no bargain to stop Helene from doing what she wished.

[You seem to have come to a realization,] Helene said. Ndidi could have sworn she heard amusement in her tone.

Ndidi straightened as much as she could. "What are you going to do with me?" Her thoughts went to the picospores, and her mind rebelled. If Helene planned to turn her into one of its puppets, Ndidi would rather kill herself first.

The hologram bobbed up and down. Ndidi took this action to mean Helene was chuckling. [You have nothing to fear. I control most of the world's leaders already. I have no need for a middling scientist. No]—the giant head hovered closer—[my plan for you is much different. But with it, I shall grant you your wish].

The walls started closing in with a sound like clashing thunder. The ceiling lowered in the same manner. Ndidi's eyes darted around the room. She finally realized what had bothered her about the walls earlier.

They're made of metal, she thought. *The entire room is a giant cage. She plans to trap me.*

Ndidi ran back to the entrance and pushed, but the door that had once seemed to be a step away from scrap was now harder than steel. The walls drew closer, enclosing half the room, with her in the center. Helene's hologram shrunk so that it seemed trapped alongside Ndidi. Her mind raced for a solution. She snagged on the last statement Helene had made.

"You said you'd grant me a wish? Then let me go."

Helene bobbed again. There was definite amusement in her voice. [Your wish has already been chosen. It was the same one that brought you here. Although you failed to keep your end of the bargain, benevolent that I am, I shall keep my part.]

The walls suddenly accelerated. Just before Ndidi thought she would be crushed, they stopped. She was enclosed on all sides except above, each wall close enough to reach out and touch. The ceiling was still a few feet above, but it was lowering fast. Ndidi pounded on the sides of the box, but they didn't even bend. Helene had shrunk to fit inside with her, hovering at eye level with Ndidi. That close, those golden orbs seemed to fill up Ndidi's vision.

Helene's voice reverberated so powerfully that Ndidi could feel it in her chest.

[I will reunite you with Bethany.] With that, the hologram disappeared. The ceiling lowered enough to close the cage.

And Ndidi was left in darkness.

ACKNOWLEDGMENTS

MY COMPLETION OF THIS PROJECT could not have been accomplished without the coaching and support of the beta readers, editors, and critics that I've met on this journey. My heartfelt thanks to everyone.

- Alex Kempsell
- Davida De La Harpe Golden
- Deborah G Lynn
- Jennifer Moy
- Jesse Winter
- Nathan Goyer
- Paul Goat Allen
- Tasneem Ali
- Victoria and Richard Wolf

And, to my caring, loving, and supportive family. I cannot express enough thanks to my family for their continued support and encouragement throughout this project. Please bear with me until I wrap up this five-book series.

BOOK ONE IN THE
PAPER WAR SERIES

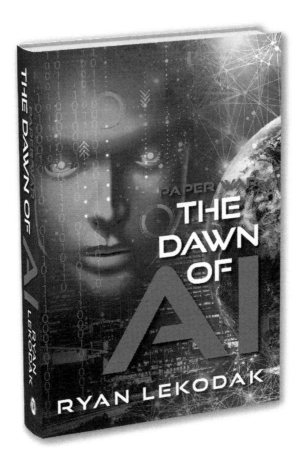

AVAILABLE AT AMAZON IN PAPERBACK, HARDCOVER, AND EBOOK

Made in the USA
Columbia, SC
29 October 2023

42c590cf-8d47-4108-abf4-1d829df4c0efR01